LOOK DOWN IN MERCY

'O God, our refuge, and our strength,
look down in mercy on Thy people who
cry to Thee . . .'

                    Prayers after Low Mass.

LOOK DOWN
IN MERCY

by

Walter Baxter

London 1953

READERS UNION
WILLIAM HEINEMANN

TO

EVE DISHER

*This RU edition was produced in 1953
for sale to its members only by Readers Union Ltd at
38 William IV Street, London WC2, and at Letchworth
Garden City, Hertfordshire. Full particulars of member-
ship may be obtained from either of these addresses.*

*This edition has been re-set in 11 pt. Fournier, printed
and bound at the Aldine Press, Letchworth, Hertfordshire. The book was first published by William
Heinemann Ltd.*

PART
ONE

I

ANSON stood under the shower with his head thrown back and let the cool water splash on his hot face. Goodwin was standing under the next shower, soaping his body with one hand and rinsing it off with the other. Both of them carried the marks of several years' service in India, brown forearms and knees and the tan of their faces extending to an ill-defined V on the chest; the rest, the exhausted dead white of constant sweating.

But there the resemblance between them ceased. At twenty-two Anson was a few years younger than Goodwin and his hair was curly, light brown, and his skin was fresh. He had high cheek-bones and an almost straight nose; his mouth was generous. His features were not outstanding, but the expression of his eyes and his youthfulness gave him charm and an impression of sincerity that was completely lacking in Goodwin, whose hair was dark and straight, and who seemed to have lost all the attributes of youth. His skin was coarse and the lines across his forehead and from the nose to the corner of his expressionless mouth were already ineradicable. He lathered his hands and turned to Anson.

'Catch.' With his eyes half shut he lobbed the soap in the direction of the next shower; it fell on the concrete floor and slid into the guttering. Anson picked it out, taking no notice of the grey ropy slime that grew like a water-weed from the concrete. Goodwin finished washing his face and neck, blew his nose into his fingers, and rinsed his hands under the shower. He dried himself on a scruffy towel and started for the door.

Anson leisurely turned off his own shower and then Goodwin's. The taps were stiff with age and verdigris and their constant drip had pitted the concrete. The sound of the barracks came slowly after the noise of the water, a waltz sung with conventional pathos, mingled with the tinkle of the dripping showers and the clash of pails from the cook-house as breakfast was dished up; from above a kite-hawk whistled musically as it circled the barrack area.

He left the showers without bothering to dry himself. It was only seven o'clock, but the freshness of the morning had long disappeared in the sweat and boredom of half an hour's P.T. There would be a little time of cool grace while his body dried, and then the sweat and heat would return with his clothes.

He reached the lofty wooden barrack-room and crossed the veranda. It was a strange room, cleaned and tidied every day by

3

thirty men, inspected every morning by four people all of whom tried to find fault, and yet there was an impalpable atmosphere of chaos and a very palpable one of sour sweat and urine. Above his head the punkahs swished their weighted fringes, pushing the limp air this way and that, their gentle squeaking and creaking filling the room with an hypnotic background that was always ready to step forward and dominate. But no amount of airing, nor hot dry winds blowing steadily all day through the open doors and windows, could dissipate the strangely animal smell.

Anson stood in the gap between his own bed and Goodwin's and looked vacantly at his clothes.

'Come on, kid, for Christ's sake hurry up.' Goodwin spoke without anger, almost without thinking. It was always 'for Christ's sake hurry up, get a move on, stop mooning about'. It was often unnecessary, but it helped fill a corner of the void caused by the barren years of being a private soldier, of having no home, no work, no responsibility, and hating the strange lands and incomprehensible people. By a gradual and unsuspected process Anson's vagueness had become a mutual comfort. He started to dress quickly, suddenly realizing that he was hungry, and they walked in silence to the dining-hall. The sun was high enough to strike in broad swathes through the tangle of low buildings and tamarind-trees. It was already hot and the wind was beginning to build itself up in warm little eddies. A pariah-dog scuttled behind the cook-house, emaciated in spite of the prodigality of waste left by the men, functionless except as a scavenger and sustainer of its parasites.

'What are we on this morning?' Anson asked.

'Dunno. Didn't look at the detail. Some balls, I suppose.'

They joined the last of the queue being ladled out pints of tea. Anson nearly asked the man in front of him the same question and then stopped. Whatever they were due to do would be as familiar to him as the monotonous plains around Sialpur and the pale-blue foot-hills of the Himalayas in the distance.

2

By ten o'clock in the morning the garrison hospital was in a state of siege against the sun, its windows and doors shaded and shuttered, its walls and verandas throwing back a white blaze of heat. Coming in from the glare of the sun it certainly felt a few degrees more cool, but it was still far too hot to be comfortable, and by the middle of the afternoon the sun's assault would have subdued everything. The quiet talk and the tintinnabulation of medicine bottles would have ceased and their place taken by the sound of the wind in the palms and trees of the hospital compound, and the thin noises of the patients as they dozed uneasily on their hard damp pillows.

In the dispensary a young Anglo-Indian was mixing medicines with infinite care, humming softly to himself. Although he was absorbed in his work he allowed his mind, deep down, to think of Helen, who might at any moment come into the dispensary or whom he might meet in the wards or corridors of the hospital. He had never been in love before, and whatever sexual experience had come his way had been truly adolescent, quick to have and quicker to despise, either himself or his partner. Now all that was not only gone but genuinely forgotten, put out of mind because it seemed too grotesque to remember.

It never occurred to him to try to persuade Helen to become his mistress, it would have cut across the whole pattern of his up-bringing. That section of the Eurasian community from which he came guarded the morals of their sons and thereby the virginity of their daughters with a cold ferocity, intent only on improving their daughters' chances of making a good marriage, by which they meant primarily to a European or at least to a comparatively fair, reasonably well-employed Eurasian. He had never met any English girls because they would have considered it an insult to have been introduced to a Eurasian of his class, nor had he mixed with Indian girls, the parents on both sides would have forbidden it, and his own parents had conditioned him to find all Indian women un-attractive. But now, at last, he had fallen in love with someone from his own class and he had a reasonable position. He could probably marry in a few years, and he was very happy.

There was a slight tap on the door and she came in, cool and beautiful. He stood up hurriedly and felt himself blush and the sweat start on the pale palms of his hands.

'Good morning, Miss Dean.'

'Good morning, Mr Johns.' When they were not on duty they called each other Helen and Robert, but they were very young, and that was the way they had been trained to address each other at the hospital. She handed him a prescription.

'Please make this up for me, it's for the sergeant in the private ward. He is a very sick man, I think; Dr Rowland is very worried.'

'Yes, of course I will. I'll do it at once and bring it to you, shall I?'

'Well, yes,' she smiled at him, thinking that he was very good-looking, not at all dark, and a good boy too, the doctors were pleased with his work. She turned to go and to keep her for another moment he stammered out:

'Are you looking forward to the dance this evening?'

She turned and took a step towards him. 'Yes, it will be lovely, but I hope the soldiers behave themselves; they get so drunk at dances and . . . troublesome.'

'Yes, I know,' he said eagerly, delighted that she should criticize the English. 'They behave like animals, some of them. I mean when they get drunk,' he added hastily, thinking that he might have gone too far. 'But you will be with me so there will be nothing to worry about.' In his eagerness the curious Welsh accent and the stressed sibilants of the Eurasians were more pronounced than usual. He wanted to add that he would kill anyone who insulted her, but the words, fortunately, would not form on his tongue, transmuting themselves into another painful blush.

At once she was nervous. 'Oh, but you mustn't be silly and get offended with them or there will be a scene and I'm sure they don't mean it. And I think Dr Rowland will be there and Dr Gidden.'

'Please don't worry, please! Of course I wouldn't make a scene.' She smiled with relief. 'I'll see you later, don't forget the medicine.' The door closed behind her and he stood still, listening to her footsteps fade away. Jealousy and resentment against the British seethed in his mind. Of course I dare not make a scene and have some drunken sweaty pig, not fit to be allowed inside a brothel, call me a nigger or a blacky-white in front of her. And if I knock him down have about three of his friends set on me and beat me up! His hands were trembling with rage, his eyes bright and bitter with his self-imposed humiliation. God! he thought, how I loathe the English. Loathe them, loathe them!

3

Kent picked up two letters from his wife that had been lying on his dressing-table for some days and walked slowly downstairs. There was an hour and a half before dinner in which to write. He hated writing letters but one had to do it, and of course one wanted to do it. He was sure that it was only because he had always been a lazy correspondent that he found all letters difficult, either to his mother and father or Celia.

He crossed the little ante-room of the mess, dingy with wicker furniture, thin crumpled cushions, and a table of dog-eared magazines, and went on to the veranda. There was no fan out here, but it was impossible to write letters under a fan, one required at least two pairs of hands to keep the paper still. In any case he preferred the veranda, from which he could see almost the whole of the barrack area. Beyond the barracks and the plain, towards the north, the hills rose irregularly, washed with a blue haze.

He settled down at a table and his bearer brought a tray of whisky, soda, and ice and left it next to him. He poured himself out two fingers of whisky, filled the glass to the brim with soda and ice, and took a long drink. Then he glanced quickly through the two letters, merely letting his eyes flicker over the sheets, and began to write.

'DARLING CELIA,

'Both your last letters, one dated the 28th Feb. and the other the 5th of March, have arrived safely although they've taken months to get here. You really are sweet to write such long letters so often, I can't possibly write like that, not even to you, so you can imagine how short my letters are to other people. However this time I really will manage a long one. I'm sure Dad and Mum are furious with me for not having written for such ages, I do want to write awfully badly to them but I just never seem to get the time.'

He paused a moment and drank. The quality of the light was beginning to change, the wind had almost died away, and the setting sun lay more thickly golden over the trees and buildings than it did in the morning when the dust from the city and the plain had settled during the still nights.

'You don't say very much about the bombing, my sweet. I suppose you are trying to avoid adding to the white man's burden, but nothing you could say or not say would make me worry more than I do. And I feel so phoney too, living out here in the lap of luxury, literally thousands of miles away from the nearest shot being fired in anger and with nothing more dangerous to cope with than being poisoned by the mess cook. But it's no good grumbling, I suppose, there's nothing I can do about it and, as you can imagine, the Army could scarcely care less about my personal problems.

'I think I told you in my last letter that I've just been given command of a company and am doing a few months' detachment duty in Sialpur. Running a company is fascinating but hell of a worry in many ways. We are very short of officers so I'm here by

7

myself, it means a lot of extra duties like going round meals and inspecting barracks every two minutes, which normally one's platoon commanders would do, but I don't mind. In some ways I prefer being by myself. I've a particularly good company sergeant-major, a man called Tarrant. He's so much like a sergeant-major that it's almost a caricature, but we get on well together, and I think he likes me. One might have to put up with some appalling second-lieutenant who would want more supervising than the rest of the company put together.'

He laid down his pen and poured out another drink. He knew what he wanted to say but it was too embarrassing, too difficult to express, compounded as it was of so many reasons, some only half understood. The fact was that he would be jealous of another officer, who might come between himself and the men, he wanted his company to be devoted to himself only, to feel that if they were in trouble of any sort they would come to him for help or advice. And being in charge of over a hundred men gave him a novel and delicious sense of importance; having another officer in the company could only diminish that feeling. It would also probably disrupt the balance of power that he had tacitly achieved with Tarrant, whereby he surrendered to Tarrant the day-to-day minor discipline and office work of the company, leaving himself free to pursue his own theories concerning the training and handling of the men.

He shifted uneasily in his chair and looked across the hills; the lowest slopes were indigo, the colour shaded to a suggestion of saffron that imperceptibly faded from the highest points even while he watched. A bat flew purposefully in a straight line across his gaze and he picked up his pen:

'There's an All Ranks dance in the town tonight. I don't want to go in the slightest, even if I liked dancing (Poor darling!—how you suffered!) there wouldn't be anyone there for me to dance with. There're never any English women at these small dances here, and I'm not supposed to dance with the blacky-whites. Their one aim and object seems to be to marry a white; we can't stop the men marrying whatever shade of colour they like best, but it's discouraged as much as possible and officers are meant to set an example. It's no hardship for me, I assure you, they scare me stiff. But anyway I have to go and watch, and stand the N.C.O.s a few drinks. It's useful; you hear a lot of stuff you wouldn't hear otherwise, about the men, of course.'

He took a long drink and looked at his watch. It was a quarter-past seven, and he decided to have one more drink before dinner and finish the letter. He realized that he had been a hypocrite about the dance but he didn't care. There was no compulsion for him to go, he went because he liked standing at the sergeants' bar, watching the men dancing, encouraging the senior N.C.O.s to tell him every possible bit of scandal about the dancers, not for the sake of the scandal but because in some obscure way he felt that it might enable him to understand them better. At least it was true that he never danced with the Eurasians, they embarrassed him and he found it difficult to think of anything to say to them.

He started again hurriedly:

'I must close now, they've just started putting dinner on the table. I think of you all the time, my darling, and long and long to see you again. And until I do I promise you I shan't even want to be unfaithful! Good night, my dearest, take great care of yourself; with all my love, Tony.'

He was relieved that the sentiments came so spontaneously. He had not seen his wife for two years and imperceptibly he found himself thinking less and less often of her, and less intensely. Secretly he was worried by this, and would have liked to discuss it with someone, but whenever he was drunk enough to broach such a personal question the problem would have disappeared and been replaced by maudlin reminiscences.

He sighed deeply and put down his pen, stretching himself. His bearer appeared and stood silently by the doorway into the ante-room.

'Dinner in ten minutes, Ahmed, I'm going to have another drink and look at a paper. Bring the bottle and some more ice.'

'Yes, Sahib,' he answered quietly. Kent slumped into a long wicker arm-chair and lazily pulled a newspaper off the table. It was very pleasant to be able to put back dinner just like that; before he could check it the thought came to him that that sort of behaviour would not have drawn a round of applause from Celia.

4

At six o'clock that evening the wet canteen was opened, and ten minutes later Anson walked in carrying a mug of tea. He sat down next to Goodwin at their usual table; he had nearly finished his first pint of beer and was gazing out of the wire-covered window.

'Not bad grub tonight,' Anson said as he sat down. 'Cold meat sandwiches, onions, and beetroot. I've put two of the sandwiches under your pillow.'

'Ta, kid. What about dominoes?' He spoke rather quickly, his habit of not eating supper on Saturday night had been the cause of many arguments between them, and now that his persistence had finally worn Anson into silence he tried to avoid the subject. He told himself that in any case there was nothing to talk about, it was simply that he liked to get drunk on Saturday night and it was quite hard enough doing that on canteen beer without having a bellyful of grub mopping it up as well. He knew that Anson didn't mind him getting drunk, it was what happened afterwards that was the cause of all their arguments, but as he had pointed out to him there was no need to stay around and get into trouble as well.

As they slowly shuffled the dominoes on the table, with the indifference of those who have played some simple game far too many times, Goodwin wondered why he always got into trouble when he drank too much. He tried to comfort himself with the thought that most people had trouble when they were drunk, but it was a poor consolation because he dimly realized that his drunken quarrels and unpredictable violence were only safety-valves to drain off the strangely attractive nightmares that tumbled about his mind. He thought that in some way they were created by drink and only existed on Saturday nights; that seemed to make the whole thing all right somehow. In any case he no longer worried about it, now he almost enjoyed it; it was exciting and secret, like trespassing in someone's garden, creeping about in the shrubbery and peering through the leaves at the house, letting the windows stare back at you, wondering if you could be seen.

Sometimes when he was half drunk he would try to persuade Anson to come with him to a brothel, but he knew that Anson disliked going, and usually by the time they had finished arguing and had walked some distance from the barrack area, going a long way round to avoid the regimental police, the mood had passed, and he would want to drink instead. Sometimes, when there was a moon, he would slip away from the barrack area, roaming aimlessly round the outskirts of Sialpur, stumbling among the shrines and ruined tombs, creeping through the hedges and tiptoeing through gardens, barked at by dogs and occasionally shouted at by servants. Once he nearly stepped on a cobra and kicked at it savagely as it shot away. When he was tired out he would lean against a tree or a wall and his head would begin to spin, his mouth fill with saliva and then the rush of vomit, his mouth gaping fantastically as it gushed out. When it was finished he would go to a clear space and look for the minaret that rose just beyond the barrack area, whiter by moonlight than by day, and, pale-faced and sweaty, let it guide him home.

But mostly he would sit in the canteen swallowing pint after pint of heavy beer, served in the thickest and ugliest of glasses, sour and warm. As his mind clouded he would sit silent and glowering, laying down the chipped dominoes carefully and slowly, waiting for something to happen on which he could pick, someone to knock against their table or tread on his foot as he elbowed his way through the crowd round the serving-hatch. But his chances of picking a quarrel had grown steadily less. He had learnt to leave certain people alone, and the weaker ones now avoided him.

They finished the first game and leisurely started to play again. There was no fan in the troops' canteen, and their faces shone with sweat; as the time passed the canteen filled up and the atmosphere grew stifling with the acrid tang of sweat and smoke. Most of the men were going to the dance in the town; their trousers stiff with starch and impeccably creased, they walked unbendingly to avoid crumpling them. Their faces were bright and smooth from the razor; their hair plastered with water, fantastically finger-waved. They shouted to one another, cigarettes jerking in their mouths, and they clustered round the serving-hatch, with great good-humour heaping the old Indian (who had worked in the canteen for years) with every possible insult connected with his religion or family. Unsmiling, unperturbed, he rinsed the empty glasses in a bowl of swipes and refilled them from the barrel. No trick to avoid payment ever succeeded with him; he had a curious air of serenity and courage. 'You black bastard,' they would say, 'you son of a pig'; and to make sure, in case he was a Hindu and not a Moslem, 'how's that cow of a wife of yours? Gimme another pint and chalk it up.' Into the swipes and under the barrel, his thin hand held out for the money, the beer safely out of reach. 'You miserable old fool, I hope your wife gives you a dose', then they would pay without rancour, and equally unthinkingly, unresentfully, he would thank them.

By eight-thirty most of the men who were going to the dance had left and the smoke was beginning to clear a little. Goodwin had been drinking steadily and as the canteen emptied and the noise died away he began to get restless. Anson looked at him anxiously and at the same time felt a flush of irritation; he was tired and the heat and noise had frayed the edges of his usual placidity. When he had first started going with Goodwin he thought that he would either be able to stop him getting drunk or at least control him when he was, and he used to do everything he could to persuade him to go to bed, to have something to eat, to stop the quarrels before violence became inevitable. To begin with, he thought that Goodwin behaved as he did because he was lonely and disliked, and he was sorry for him; now he realized that it was his nature. The knowledge only came slowly, and as it came, so Anson's affection for him began to die. But it took a long time. He had been in India for four years, he was starved of affection, and most of the time Goodwin was a pleasant enough companion and they had been happy together. But over the last months he had become aware of a change in Goodwin, as though a shadow had fallen on him, and he seemed more and more unable to throw off the moods of depression that followed on his bouts and that Anson thought were caused by them.

Their dominoes became more and more desultory and Anson suddenly looked up. 'Come on, Dicky, let's chuck it and do something else, eh?' Goodwin looked up quickly, surprised and on the defensive.

'Why, I'm all right, what's wrong with this?'

'Nothing. But I'm browned off tonight. Why don't we go to the dance, we haven't been to one for months now, we needn't stay too long if it's lousy.'

There was no definite plan in Anson's mind, but the dance was about a mile and a half away, it would take them three-quarters of an hour to get ready and walk that far, maybe longer, and if they went back to the barrack-room Goodwin might eat some food. He should be reasonably sober by the time they arrived, and then one could only hope for the best. He was almost bound to get into some sort of trouble tonight, it might as well happen at the dance as here, and there was a vague idea in the back of his mind that perhaps the music and the crowds might make Goodwin feel relaxed. In any case it would be better than sitting here for the rest of the evening, utterly bored, waiting for something unpleasant to happen.

'That's O.K. by me,' Goodwin answered. He sat with his head propped on his left hand, idly tapping a domino on the table. He understood that Anson was planning to keep him sober and expected that when they had nearly reached the dance hall he would suggest they went to the pictures instead. 'If that's what you'd like to do we'll do it.' The beer and the heat made him feel slightly unreal. He had no intention whatever of going to the pictures, he wanted to get drunk and he would. It was a good idea going to the dance. Maybe he would get a woman, no, a young girl, dressed in white, a little gold cross resting on the ivory skin below her throat.

Slender, small-breasted. His throat felt hard. He got up from the table and smoothed his hair with his hands as he started for the door.

'Hey! Hang on a minute while I finish my beer!'

'Sorry.' He smiled vaguely, standing by the side of the table while Anson gulped down the last few mouthfuls. It tasted vilely and he twisted his mouth with disgust.

'God! Talk about cat's piss and pepper!' He stood up and they walked out of the canteen. The moon, almost full, was low in the sky, the shadows that it threw were blurred. Without speaking they walked to their barrack-room; there was only one light burning, at the far end of the room where the rifles stood in locked ranks. There should have been an orderly on duty guarding the whole room but Anson could see no one. He made no comment, it was nothing to do with him. They changed their shirts and trousers and put on the regulation side caps. It was too difficult to shave in the unlighted showers; they combed their hair carefully with the fixed look of people who have no mirror on which to concentrate and Anson dabbed at his wavy hair with his fingers.

Still in silence they left the barracks and joined the white dusty road that curved away and led into the town. It was rough and irregularly lined on either side by tall thick tamarinds, flamboyants, and gnarled palms. The moon shone almost directly in their faces and Anson kept to the middle of the road where he could see the small holes, but Goodwin walked by the edge where the dust muffled his footsteps and the shadows of the branches lay thick.

5

By ten-thirty Kent was nearly drunk and having difficulty in hiding it. He had spent most of the evening in the bar set aside for officers and sergeants, watching the men dancing with their women and with each other, gossiping on and on about the company with the persistence and inanity of a man in love. But for the last quarter of an hour they had been joined by the two doctors from the garrison hospital and he had been forced to talk about things in which he had no interest. He had not wanted to dance, but now he thought it was a good idea, it would sober him, and by the time he came back maybe the doctors would have gone and he could resume his talk with Tarrant. He waited until the band started to play and stood up.

'It's time I did my duty and had a dance. Got any nice nurses here, Doc? I really do mean nice too. Married man and all that, you know. Mustn't let the wife down.' He smiled inanely but rather charmingly. He knew that he was being pompous and ridiculous, but the words seemed almost to have been spoken without his own volition and he had smiled, hoping they would be taken as a joke.

'Sure thing,' Rowland answered, 'charming girl sitting very near us. A nurse, first-class kid, a touch of the tar-brush, *ça va sans dire*, or she wouldn't work in the hospital, scandalously bad pay.'

They left the bar. Two sergeants were standing in the doorway, and deferentially, with the gravity of the half drunk, made way for Kent and the doctor. It pleased both of them, they looked at each other and smiled, as much as to say 'Good chaps, soldiers, don't take liberties'. They worked their way a few yards down the hall, and suddenly the doctor saw Helen; she was on the point of standing up, and Robert was waiting, his mouth and eyes smiling, his arms moving towards her.

'Miss Dean! Hang on a sec!' Rowland shouted jovially over the heads of some troops, 'I want to introduce you!'

She looked round, surprised and embarrassed, but as soon as she saw who it was she was pleased and immediately dropped her arms and half turned her back on Robert, smiling at Rowland as he came towards her.

'Miss Dean, this is Captain Kent. He's stationed here.'

She saw a tall, broad-shouldered man standing in front of her. He was smiling, and his teeth were white and regular, his hair and skin were fair rather than dark, his features even.

'How do you do, Miss Dean?' He smiled more affably than he felt. I suppose she's quite pretty, he thought, but black as the ace of spades. Her skin was flawless, the colour of dark honey. 'May I have this dance?' He stepped closer to her and stumbled slightly, catching her arm to steady himself.

'Thank you very much, Captain, I would like to.' She spoke seriously as though she had had plenty of time to consider his request, and then stepped on to the floor. She looked over her shoulder at Robert with a smile that contained no apology. Neither Kent nor the doctor had really been conscious that he was standing there, nor did Robert think their behaviour at all unusual; he sat down again, his face expressionless, waiting tormentedly for the dance to end.

Helen was nervous and danced limply, her hand resting damply in his, her body unresponsive. He was smiling to himself over her head and shoulders, very conscious of the fact that he was attracting a good deal of surreptitious attention. He had almost forgotten her existence until she looked up and spoke to him.

'I'm sorry, Miss—er . . . what did you say?'

'I asked how long you are going to be in Sialpur.'

'I'm not very sure; why, do you want me to stay?' He looked at her intently and when she blushed he laughed. 'I'm sorry, I was only joking, I think I shall be here for another two months or so.'

She started talking more easily to him now, but the conventionalities that followed one another did not reflect her thoughts. It had been so unexpected, she wondered if he had been watching her for some time, and had had rather too much to drink in order to pluck up courage to be introduced to her. She had to admit that it was not very likely; soldiers were not usually shy in asking girls like her to dance—not that she was like a good many of the girls here, some were very dark indeed, and obviously hadn't been brought up as well as she had. But still, he was an officer, a captain, perhaps they behaved differently. She had no means of knowing, she had only joined the hospital a few months before, and her experience of the British was confined to a few middle-aged doctors under whom she had worked. Occasionally she had danced with soldiers, but to her they were quite unreal, she found their accents difficult to understand, and compared to the courtesy with which men of her own class treated her they were abominably crude.

They were dancing the last encore and Kent was feeling better. He held a handkerchief in one hand and kept wiping the sweat from his face. She knew that the dance would be over in a few minutes and she stopped talking in order to see if he would ask her to reserve another dance for him later on, or even suggest that he might see her again. It wasn't really so improbable, she thought. He's so young he probably isn't married, and there aren't any English girls in Sialpur, he might easily want to see me again.

But Kent was bored and only wanted to return to the bar. Fundamentally he found her unattractive, her voice, her thin body, and her colouring. Pretty, perhaps, but nothing else. The music stopped and he clapped effusively, knowing from past experience that no amount of applause would induce the band to play a fourth encore.

'Thank you very much indeed, I did enjoy it.' He smiled at her and she thought that he was quite sincere.

'So did I, very much.' She led the way back to her chair and Robert stood up. There were some troops standing near them watching, and before she sat down Kent took her hand and pressed it.

'I shall see you again,' he said, 'and once more thank you very much.'

She murmured an inaudible reply and sat down. By the time she had settled herself and glanced up he had almost reached the bar. Neither she nor Robert spoke for some little time; as far as Robert was concerned he could think of nothing to say.

While they played 'God Save the King' the parade ground crept back into the dance hall, even the women stood quite still, neither looking into their hand-bags nor patting their hair into position. Then it was over and the band immediately started to pack up their instruments with an air of relief. The dancers slowly made their way to the main exit and spread out in a confusion of departure as the rickshas and gharries edged among the crowd and the women prepared to defend their dresses against the dirt and uncertainties of the journey home.

Robert and Helen came out of the hall and she stopped near Tarrant, who had come to the wide veranda so that his presence might act as a deterrent to any drunken brawling. He looked at her idly and then realized that it was the girl Kent had danced with and smiled at her. She started to arrange her cloak carefully, she looked at the still considerable crowd of people and shrugged her shoulders. Robert knew that she would wait for a few minutes, he was almost certain that she was waiting for Kent to come on to the veranda, but there was enough doubt in his mind to make the idea bearable. He wanted to go and bring a gharry to the door and take her away, but he was frightened to leave her, and all he could do was to help her on with her cloak and make futile little movements of departure.

'Do wait a minute or two, Robert, Dr Rowland will be out soon and I expect he will give us a lift to the hospital, it's not out of his way,' and a half-felt pity for him lent warmth and meaning to her smile. She knew that he was in love with her, but however kind and good she might be it was not possible to feel his pain, and even if she had considered becoming engaged to him she could not have resisted the latent opportunities of an association with someone in as exalted a position as she considered Kent to be. She would have felt ashamed if she had not tried; she would have been acting against the whole conventions of her class, a betrayal that would have included not only her family, but also in some way Robert himself.

And apart from that, she found Kent physically attractive, the antithesis of the men that she had known all her life. She thought

16

that he could not possibly be more than twenty-five or six, and his regular features were given character by an expression that was almost one of sadness in his eyes, violet-shadowed. She had noticed his hands particularly, long-fingered and beautifully shaped, the hairs on the back of the fingers golden. And then she heard his voice and Rowland's answering guffaw, and as they came through the door on to the veranda she turned and faced them smiling, one hand unconsciously smoothing her dress.

'Ah! Miss Dean! Waiting for the milling throng to disperse?' The doctor would have brought out his favourite cliché about the brutal and licentious soldiery but he thought that Kent might not find it altogether tactful.

'Yes, Doctor, although I don't really want to go home yet, it's been such a lovely evening.' Perhaps Kent might ask them back to his mess.

'When you get to my age you won't feel like that, my dear!' Rowland patted her on the shoulder and laughed heartily; he had just accepted Kent's invitation to go back to the mess, and he looked forward to several more hours of drink and gossip; he had no intention of having her restraining presence. In any case she was with Johns, so the question of Kent asking her back could hardly arise. 'I would run you to the hospital but I've promised to take Captain Kent back.'

'Good night,' Kent smiled at her; he tried to remember her name but it had gone again. 'Sergeant-major, send one of the police for a gharry, will you?' He turned to Rowland: 'Can we give the sergeant-major a lift home, Doc?'

'Sure, sure! Delighted!'

'I won't come just yet, sir, if you don't mind. I'll just see this place clear first and lock up. Good night, sir.' He turned away and sent one of the police standing next to him for a gharry.

'Well, good night again,' Kent said to Helen, and walked down the veranda steps with Rowland.

'Good night, Captain,' Helen answered, not sure whether that was the proper way to address him. If they had been alone for a brief moment she would have asked him to come and see her at the hospital, but with Rowland there it had been impossible. She was helped into the gharry by a most attentive military policeman and Robert climbed in and sat down as far away from her as he could. He was so preoccupied with his own jealous misery that he did not notice the soldier ostentatiously turn his back as soon as Helen had sat down. She glanced at him as the gharry jolted and swayed along the road. She felt depressed and lonely; it was too

17

bad of Robert to sit there so sulkily, by the look on his face anyone would think that she had misbehaved herself at the dance.

Most of the crowd had gone, but there were still small groups of twos and threes standing back in the shadows of the trees and knotted clumps of bougainvillæa, the indecisive ones, pulled between tiredness and desire or desire and fear. Rowland unlocked his car and turned on the lights, then he reached over to unlock Kent's door. The lights shone through a tangle of thin bushes and behind them Kent saw two figures, one of them half kneeling and being supported by the other.

'Wait a minute, Doc, leave the lights on.' He went round the bushes and walked up to the men; in front of the kneeling man on the bare earth was a mess of beery vomit.

'Is he all right?' Kent asked.

'Yes, sir,' Anson answered quickly, 'he's perfectly all right now, I'm just going to take him back to barracks.'

Kent looked unwillingly down, trying to avoid noticing any details in the puddle's composition. 'You're a bloody fool to drink if you can't hold it, what the hell's the sense of wasting money?'

Goodwin looked slowly up at Kent. His face was scarlet and lined from the strain of his retching, and the moonlight glistened in his wet eyes and on his sweaty forehead. Coarse-looking bastard, Kent thought, but the man with him looks a decent sort.

'What are your names?'

'Mine's Anson, sir, and that's Goodwin.'

'Are you muckers?' He used the word that means more than mere friends; he sometimes wondered exactly what it did cover.

'Yes, sir.'

'Well, get him back to the barracks as soon as you can, and be quick away from here or the sergeant-major'll whip him.' He turned and went back to the car.

'O.K., Doc, one of the men has had too much beer and his buddy's helping him home.' The car moved down the drive and Kent saw Anson pull Goodwin to his feet and then they were hidden. 'They're damn' good blokes, you know, Doc, a few of them might get drunk at a dance but don't we all? In spite of what some of the senior N.C.O.s say I'm sure there's no real vice in them, and they're fantastically loyal to each other.'

But Rowland was not interested in the friendships of soldiers. It was not often that he managed to spend an evening away from his wife and indulge in a long talk about the sexual behaviour of women in general and Eastern women in particular; it was the only

18

incontinence he was permitted, and tonight he intended to be very unfaithful. 'Do you think,' he asked with the air of a man putting forward a serious proposition, 'you ought to have a regimental brothel?'

6

As soon as the lights of the car had swept away from them Anson put his arm round Goodwin and steered him towards the drive. Goodwin let himself be led until the dazzle of the lights had left his eyes and then jerked himself roughly away.

'Take your arm away, I'm all right. If you and that bleeding officer think I'm drunk you're wrong. And stop mauling me about, for Christ's sake, I don't like it. I want a woman.'

Anson felt a dull rage start in his stomach, he wanted to turn and hit him in the face, but he knew that he couldn't, and in spite of his anger he understood that it would only make things worse. They walked out of the drive and turned along the tree-lined road that led towards the barracks. But that was no comfort to Anson; he knew that Goodwin only took that way in case any of the military police were watching. The barracks were a long way off and whatever Goodwin had in mind did not concern the barracks. And suddenly he felt utterly tired and sick of himself and of Goodwin. It's no good, he thought, it's no good, I'm going to chuck it, he can do what he damn' well likes. I've tried for months to help, it's useless. A small street crossed their road at right angles, running towards the outskirts of Sialpur and towards the hills that lay like dim clouds on the horizon. Mean little bungalows lay back from this street, hiding behind tangles of white and pink camellias and hibiscus. A few of them were brothels of a haphazard kind, the women would earn a living of a sort working in the bazaars or washing clothes, but were always ready to supplement their negligible earnings by something as quick and meaningless to them as prostitution.

Goodwin stopped in the shadow. He wanted to prowl round the bungalows and let his presence be known, scratching with his nail on a shutter, gently tapping on a wooden wall. The smell of fear would seep out of the house as palpably as the stale reek of sweat and betel-nut rose from their grimy beds, and even as that smell excited him so did the knowledge of their fear; the slither of their feet as they shuffled to each other's rooms and whispered in terror, the creak of the floor-boards, the furtive sound of a key turning, a shuttered window being pushed open an inch so that they could peer into the misty chaos of a garden. As his blood thickened in sympathy with theirs he would feel an overpowering eroticism, he would go and knock urgently on their door and when it was cautiously opened and they stood looking at him . . . nothing. As the door opened everything seemed to drain out of him, drink and desire and excitement, and usually he would stumble away with a muttered apology. But sometimes the girl, bold with relief at finding only a customer, would be insistent and he would go inside, embarrassed and ill at ease. He would sit on a chair smoking a cigarette while she undid his trousers and tried to arouse him. He would permit it for a few moments and then roughly push her hand away and walk out.

One of the few times he could remember being satisfied in a brothel was on almost the only occasion when Anson came inside the house and waited near the cubicle for him to finish. Alone he had gone back twice to the same girl, but it had never been the same. And then, standing in the shadow under the tree, with Anson poised irresolutely half in and half out of the moonlight, he realized that he wanted Anson to come again into a brothel with him and wait, not outside the cubicle this time but inside, standing inside, watching.

'Kid!' He moved quickly as he spoke and caught hold of his arm. 'Come on, be a sport, come with me to the brothel down here where those two sisters are. Come on!' He shook his arm gently, his voice urgent.

'Are you all right in the head?' Anson spoke contemptuously. 'You know bloody well I don't go into knocking-shops, I've told you often enough. But don't think I'm trying to stop you, go right ahead.' That'll shake him, he thought, but Goodwin hardly heard him, he was far too intent on putting his plan into operation.

'Look, be a pal, do come. I tell you what, I'll be a sport; you come, you needn't have a woman, you can watch me!' He spoke with an air of astonishment as though he had just thought of a brilliant solution to their differences. There was a silence between them. The moon had entered a narrow belt of transparent cloud, the shadow of the trees had lost its sharpness. The silence stretched on, the leaves of the tree rustled, and an owl cried a long way off. Anson knew what he wanted to say but it was too bitter, too complicated, too inadequate.

'O.K., you're coming,' Goodwin said and pulled his arm, half turning to go down the road.

20

'I'm not coming,' Anson answered quietly. He wrenched his arm away and started to walk down the road.

'O.K., kid, give me a cigarette before you go.' He stopped and pulled out a packet. Goodwin walked slowly up to him, and as he took a cigarette with his left hand hit him as hard as he could in the mouth with his right fist. As he fell he kicked him savagely in the thigh. He turned and ran down the street exultantly, laughing to himself. When he had gone some distance he stopped behind a tree and peered back. He saw Anson had picked himself up and was limping out of sight. He put his head in his arms and tried to be sick again, leaning against the tree, but all he could do was to retch a few times, and he rested there breathing heavily until he felt a little more calm. He could not make up his mind what to do next; he did consider going back to the barracks and apologizing, but of all the alternatives in his mind that seemed to him to be the most difficult and least rewarding thing he could do. The idea repelled him to such an extent that he found it impossible not to think about, he kept on imagining himself mumbling words of repentance by the side of Anson's bed.

At last he pushed himself away from the tree and felt through his pockets for some money. Apart from a few small coins he had nothing, and then the idea started to flounder around in his mind of stealing some money. He thought of the canteen but decided immediately against it, it had been tried so often and no one ever seemed to succeed. Apart from the fact that one of the Indian servants always slept by the side of the heavy old-fashioned safe, over the years there had been such an accumulation of bolts and bars as to make the canteen almost impregnable. He thought of breaking into a house or shop, and then he remembered the jewel bazaar in the Aranyaka Temple, and immediately he started walking towards it. He had no clear plan in his mind nor did he try to work one out; it was sufficient satisfaction merely to have the intention. He had not been inside the temple for a long time but he knew that it was always open at night, and that running at right angles from the main building was a long arcade used by the sellers of semi-precious stones and jade that came by caravan from Tibet and Burma.

The temple was on the outskirts of the city, and his way lay along obscure roads. Apart from a few figures cocoon-like in threadbare blankets by the side of the road he saw no one. There was a large open space in front of the temple, banyan-trees and palms fringed it on all sides. He stood in the shadows some yards away from the black high-arched doorway; his head was aching and the silent archway repelled and attracted him. Almost like a sleep-walker he stepped into the moonlight and crossed the empty space through the archway. As soon as the darkness had engulfed him he stopped and swept his hands in front of his face as though he was brushing away a cobweb, then he knelt and took off his shoes and pushed them inside his shirt, not caring what filth he might have stepped in. When he stood up again the blackness seemed a little less opaque, he could see that there was some obstruction in front of him. He moved a few paces to the right, and now at the far end of the temple he could see a huge seated Buddha and little points of light burning near the feet. He was aware of a strange smell, like incense, but richer, a mingling of overblown tuberoses and frangipanni, wood smoke and cooking.

With vague memories of a church at home he thought that there might be an offertory box near the Buddha and he started to walk carefully round the colonnade that led to the foot of the Buddha and supported the mass of the conical roof. Half-way round he passed another open archway on his right that he believed led to the jewel bazaar. A few beggars slept at the foot of the columns, the tiny noises of their sleep filled the temple with a sound so indeterminate as to be silence.

He reached the last column before the Buddha and stopped. There were a number of small glass lamps with burning wicks floating in oil and a medley of vases of flowers put indiscriminately down near the base, tall tuberoses, a child's fistful of marigolds, a spray of golden orchids laid across the very feet, its stem stuck in a small blob of wet moss. The lights from the lamps carried his eyes up to the face of the Buddha forty feet above him, and the light gleamed on the gilded face, leaving the black stone of the body in total shadow. It was enigmatically calm, heavy lidded, half smiling, perhaps the smile was a trick of the light. He stood still for a long time looking at the face, and when he moved again he could not remember why he had come; there was a reason, Anson! No, not Anson . . . money, that was it! He looked again for something that might have been used as an offertory box but there was nothing. There wouldn't be, he thought contemptuously, not with these heathens.

He turned back and went through the archway that led to the jewel bazaar, walking under a corrugated iron canopy across a stone-flagged courtyard into another colonnade. It was much lighter here, the colonnade gave on to the courtyard he had just crossed and moonlight struck in. Opposite him was the jewel bazaar and across the entrance were drawn two iron grilles locked in the centre and reaching up as high as the roof. That's that, he thought, just my luck. But really he was pleased, he was tired and now there was nothing for him to do but go back. Tomorrow, he told himself, he would come again and have a good look round. The tension and confusion in his mind seemed to relax and begin to clear; he lit a cigarette and inhaled deeply. As he turned to go, out of the corner of his eye he saw the outline of a sleeping figure by the far end of the iron grilles, wrapped from head to foot in a blanket, half hidden in the shadows.

Christ, it's the watchman! he thought; he'll have the keys of the gate and maybe the keys of some of the stalls: By God, this is good! His whole body suddenly seemed to come alive, his lips parted, and his mouth felt dry. He took his shoes out of his shirt and laid them soundlessly on the ground and then tiptoed towards the sleeper with a curiously eager step. It was not easy to tell which was the head or foot, but something seemed to have taken possession of his actions, he knew without hesitation which was the head, where exactly would be the place to put his thumbs. He reached the body and straddled it gracefully, at the same time his fingers dug viciously into the throat and his fingers pushed the blanket tight around the neck and then locked together. He smiled gently at the terrible paroxysms of the body as it writhed in the blanket and twisted in terror and agony, trying to break away from this unseen, unimaginable horror. There was no sound except the muffled thumps of legs flaying wildly, but he hardly noticed. The thin writhing body between his open legs, the sense of power, moon-light, a golden face, if only Anson was watching; he felt a slowly swelling pressure of desire that took its tempo from the twisting body against which he now pressed his own, exquisite pleasure that made him whimper; in that split second between the unbearable pleasure breaking and the flood of relief he dug inwards and upwards with his thumbs and felt the neck snap.

He took his hands slowly away and turned his head towards the courtyard. It was still and empty. He was breathing heavily and stayed squatting on the thin body for a moment or two before he got clumsily to his feet. He felt utterly exhausted, all his intentions were forgotten in the face of his achievement, he would not have used the keys if they had been lying at his feet. He wanted to get away in case he was found out, that was all, for what was under the blanket he was quite indifferent. He did wonder what sort of a man it was, but the idea of pulling back the blanket and looking did not form in his mind. He went quickly back to his shoes and picked them up; as he stood up he saw the cigarette that he had dropped. It had gone out on the cold stone and he pinched the burnt end and put it behind his ear. He passed through the courtyard and the temple, the smell that a little time ago had seemed attractive was now repellent and he wondered if his socks were fouled by betel-juice and phlegm from the stone floor. He knelt in the shadow by the main door and put on his shoes. As he stepped into the moon-light he remembered Anson had said something about sandwiches, and he hoped that they were still under his pillow. He felt very happy and uncomplicated, but at the same time excited. He wanted inquiries to be made in the barracks; if it was treated as just another bazaar murder it would make it all seem rather pointless, somehow.

7

Kent lay on his back and watched the sunlight that streamed through the port-hole swing up and down with the small motion of the ship. He felt drowsy and at peace, the noise of the engines seemed to press his body gently into the bunk, and he slept again.

When he awoke Anson had come into the cabin and put a large enamelled mug of tea by the side of the bunk. Now he had picked up Kent's boots and leather belt and had almost reached the door. Kent sat up and brushed his hair back with his hands.

' 'Morning, Anson.'

' 'Morning, sir.' He hesitated by the door, wondering if Kent had any particular orders for him.

'Where are you going with that stuff?'

'I was going to clean them outside in the passage, sir. Did you want me for anything else first?'

'No, nothing that matters. You needn't go away, do them in here.' Without saying anything Anson crossed the cabin and put the boots and belt on the broad ledge beneath the port-hole. He took his cleaning kit out of his haversack and began to polish the boots while Kent sipped the sweet tea absent-mindedly and watched him.

'I don't think you'll have a lot more leather polishing to do, Anson, not where we're going anyway.'

'You mean Burma, sir.' It was a statement.

'I can't think why everyone's so damn' sure we're going to Burma,' Kent protested. 'It might be Hong Kong or Malaya or anywhere for that matter.' He had known almost from the start of the move, a month ago, that the battalion was going to Burma, and it had irritated him that the elaborate security measures insisted on

24

by Brigade had all been futile. Within a matter of a few days every-one in the detachment, and the shopkeepers in Sialpur itself, seemed to know their destination. The pleasure he would have derived from the knowledge that only a few other officers in the battalion beside himself knew of the move died almost as soon as it was born.

The note of irritation in Kent's voice reached Anson and he said nothing. It was a matter of indifference where they went; to him the battalion's move had come as an incredible piece of good luck; without it Kent would have gone on employing Ahmed as his bearer and Anson's break with Goodwin would have been infinitely more difficult. He felt no anger against Goodwin now, in fact his anger had never been more deep than a purely physical reaction. But it was as though the treachery of the violence, held against the background of the preceding months, had destroyed all Anson's sentiments for and against Goodwin, leaving him utterly indifferent. Not only were those feelings gone, when he awoke the next morning, the remembrance of them was wiped away as well.

But all that day and from then on Goodwin seemed determined to behave as though nothing was changed between them. There was no remorse in his mind and very little fear of detection, yet at the same time, without understanding why, he felt more strongly than ever the need for affection. Anson was the only one from whom he could obtain it, and he felt that he had a right to obtain it from Anson, who in some obscure way he looked on as his accomplice. He knew at once that Anson had withdrawn from him and he resented it bitterly because he could not believe that the reasons were sufficient; an invitation to a brothel and a drunken punch in the face, to him it was as commonplace as breathing. He apologized for being drunk, and swore that he could remember nothing after Kent had spoken to them; as far as he was concerned that should have been the end of the matter.

For Anson it had become an unendurable exasperation, always having Goodwin fall in next to him on parade, sit next to him at meals, and follow him into the canteen. And so he had gone to Tarrant and asked for some special employment or a transfer to another company, and Tarrant had looked at him coldly and told him to go away. But some weeks later, in the middle of the upheaval of the move, Tarrant had sent for him and said that he was detailed as Kent's batman. He had been very grateful, and thought that per-haps Tarrant was not as inhuman as people made out. He hoped that Kent had chosen him personally, it would have made his employment the more secure, but that same evening Kent had sent for him to come to the mess, and after their interview Anson knew that Tarrant alone had been responsible for his choice.

'Are you certain you want this job, Anson?' He was standing with his hands above his head and his stomach pulled in while the bearer went round his body slowly rolling on the long silk cummerbund that was a part of his white mess kit.

'Yes, sir, quite sure!' He spoke eagerly, anxious in case Kent had someone else in mind and would use any hesitation as an excuse to put him off.

'That's good. When the sergeant-major mentioned your name I told him to make it clear that it was voluntary. But he's been so busy he might have forgotten and more or less detailed you. I want you to understand that you needn't take it on in the first place and can go when you like in the second.'

'Thanks, sir, I don't exactly know what I'll have to do, but I'll soon pick it up.' And Kent had said something pleasant and he had left, with a last glimpse of Ahmed producing an enormous safety-pin out of his mouth and carefully fastening the cummerbund in the small of Kent's back.

Kent finished his tea and lit a cigarette. It was very pleasant lying in bed, listening to the unfamiliar noises of the ship and to realize that the responsibilities of the preceding month, that had weighed so heavily on him, were now over. And in truth it had been difficult, his detachment was some eighty miles away from battalion head-quarters, and he had been responsible for the unravelling of the mass of instruction and counter-instruction that poured into the detachment.

Without Tarrant's help it would have been impossible, it was only due to his experience and the hours of work he put in that none of the possible administrative disasters had happened. It had seemed as though Tarrant was seized by a frenzy for work. Even in the sweaty heat of those September days, with the monsoon still trailing its warm blankets of rain over Sialpur, he had found the time and energy to do his own work and then go to the garrison hospital and help Rowland with the move of the medical unit which was part of the brigade. And even on the slow train to Calcutta he had not deserted them. Whenever they stopped in some siding for their meals he would see that the nurses were given their food first, and he would go to their carriage at the rear of the train to make sure that they were comfortable.

Sometimes on these halts Kent would see Helen standing by the side of the train looking in his direction; when their eyes met she would smile and make a small movement with her hand. He would smile back vaguely and then turn away and speak to one of the men.

He dropped his cigarette end into the dregs of his tea and lit another. Remembering Helen standing by the side of the train recalled Celia to his mind with a sense of guilt. He had only written once in the last month, a hurried scrawl in which he had hinted vaguely at his move, and stressed how busy he was, and that she must excuse him if his letters were irregular for a little time. Now that he was on board he told himself that he would write again, deliberately forgetting the hours he had spent in the train doing nothing but gaze out at the slow monotony of the plains. He tried to conjure up Celia's face, but it was curiously difficult. Of course he *knew* exactly what she looked like, he had only to open his wallet to see, the difficulty lay in projecting her face from his imagination. And another curious thing, and one that he found increasingly disturbing, was that the sight of her photograph or her handwriting no longer stirred him physically. Since he had been away from her he had fantasied to himself so often, so inevitably, the first night they had slept together, or some Sunday afternoon in May when they had gone to deep woods and lain together on an old raincoat under a miracle of beech leaves; the only sound the noise of a small rain that fell steadily from a windless sky, a blackbird singing a long way off and the little noises as they gently moved their bodies together.

And now those fantasies no longer moved him, and for several months he had been completely sexless, except now and then for some fantastically improbable dream that he preferred to forget as soon as possible. He told himself that when he saw her again everything would come right, that it was understandable and at least he was not like a lot of other people, who seemed obsessed by the thought of sex. He decided that perhaps he was not making sufficient effort to help himself, that he ought to write more often.

Anson finished his cleaning and unpacked a clean pair of shorts and a shirt from the valise. Kent climbed slowly out of bed and went to the wash-basin. Before he had finished lathering his face there was a knock on the door and Tarrant came in, saluting as though he was on the parade ground.

''Morning, Sergeant-major.' Kent smiled at him through the mirror. 'Everything all right?'

'Yes, fine, thank you, sir. Will you be coming round breakfasts with me?'

'Yes, of course. I'll be ready in a few minutes, sit down. Anson, you'd better give my revolver an oil up before the sea air rots it.

Do it here, I shall want it in a minute.' He finished lathering and picked up his razor. 'Thank God we're back with the battalion for a bit, this last month was a nightmare, or at least it would have been without you. The orderly room can do our administration from now on.'

'Oh, I don't know, sir, it wasn't too bad at Sialpur. I liked it; it makes a break getting away from the battalion.' His tone was genuinely regretful. 'Besides, there was quite a sporty crowd of civilians there, look how drunk they all got our last night in Sialpur. That police officer could hardly walk to his car.'

'Which one?—there were two of them.'

'The pleasant one that came and saw us about the murder in the Araṇyaka Temple.'

'I remember. Wasn't that absolutely typical of the civilian attitude towards the troops—anything they can't solve, blame it on the Army. I suppose they weren't getting anywhere and probably paid some wretched Indian to say that he saw a soldier in the temple. Can you imagine any of our men going there in the middle of the night?'

'Not in the temple, I agree, but the body was by that jewel arcade, which is rather different.'

'But they said that the soldier was seen watching the Buddha and that I can't believe, not at one in the morning. Even if the woman had been raped I don't see why the Army should always be suspected, rape isn't exclusively military. But she hadn't been touched, in that way.'

'Maybe because she had leprosy.'

'I asked the superintendent about that, but he said you couldn't have told from her face unless you were a doctor, she only had a few sores on her legs. And don't forget that we offered to have an identity parade but he said it wouldn't be any use because the witness swore it was too dark to see his face. The whole thing was a nonsense, we were only dragged in as a face-save for the police.'

He put down his razor and rinsed his face, suddenly remembering with pleasure the peacefulness of their first few months in Sialpur, the lazy set routine of the parades, the long hours of siesta in the baking afternoons, the evenings spent drinking and talking at the club or the sergeants' mess. Already those days were taking on a golden glow. 'Do you remember the dance that same night? It was a good evening, Rowland came back to the mess with me and I got paralytic on Scotch while he talked about women.' Something rose in his mind. 'Hey, Anson, that's the first time I think I spoke to you, apart from parades. Weren't you being a good Samaritan and taking someone back who was drunk?'

28

Anson turned and looked at Kent. 'Yes, sir.'

'Did you have any trouble getting him back? I meant to ask you the next day but I forgot.'

'Oh no, sir.' His face was expressionless, he looked steadily at Kent and then turned back and finished wiping surplus oil off the revolver.

You're lying, Tarrant said to himself. I bet you had a fight or something with that surly bastard Goodwin, and that's why you came to me a few days later and asked for a job. For a moment he did connect Goodwin with the murder but he dismissed the thought, it would have been unlike Goodwin not to have interfered with the girl, and in any case it was over and done with now. He stood up and looked out of the port-hole at the dazzlingly blue water sweeping by, watching, without interest, a few flying-fish suddenly break the surface and flutter shimmeringly away from the ship.

'All set, Sergeant-major?' Kent was standing by the open cabin door and together they started to make their way down to the hot human reek of the troop-decks.

8

Apart from the battalion and Rowland's unit there were several other parties of Brigade troops on board, including a draft of six nursing sisters, and inevitably someone arranged a dance the last night on board.

Kent and Rowland were sitting in the bar before lunch discussing the war and had just agreed that Japan was far too involved in China to commit herself anywhere else when they were joined by several officers from the battalion.

'Hiya, Doc, hiya, Tony. Mind if we join you, or are you in secret medical conference?'

Kent smiled at the speaker. He liked Maguire, who was light-hearted and kind, running his company with an ease and apparent indifference that Kent partly disapproved of and partly envied.

'Hullo, Tom, come and sit down.' He moved his chair to widen the circle.

Maguire turned to Rowland. 'We thought of having a bit of a dance this evening, Doc, you wouldn't mind if we asked your nurses?'

'Good lord, no, as long as I come too, and see they don't get led astray. I don't want to have any unauthorized increases in the strength of my unit, you know,' and they all laughed.

'No, Doc, we'll be very careful. Of course you'll come, Tony?'

'I'll come but I shan't dance, I'll prop the bar.'

'Come off it!' Maguire said. 'You married men are all the same, pretending you're not interested. It's we bachelors who're the ones to be trusted, what we've never had we never want.'

'Of course you'll dance,' Rowland said. 'Dean would never forgive you, I think she's rather sweet on you.' And at once Maguire and the other officers were in full cry.

'How long's it been going on, Doc?'

'Dirty dog! As soon as he's safely away from the battalion . . .'

'Is that the very attractive *café au lait* one?'

And Kent tried to protest his innocence, but at the same time he was pleased that she was thought attractive, and that he should be suspected, however jokingly, of having an affair. Though all of them knew he had a wife in England they seemed to expect him to be unfaithful whenever an opportunity arose. He hated the mere idea of being considered different or priggish, and when they talked about women, which was very often, he tried to convey the impression that his silence did not necessarily mean his innocence. He despised himself for this but perversely went on doing it.

By the time they had had a few gins and the party broke up for lunch it was taken for granted by all of them that Kent had a prior claim on Helen and would be her particular escort at the dance.

At six o'clock that evening Kent left his cabin to attend a C.O.'s conference about the disembarkation at Rangoon, and Anson sat down on the bunk to darn a pair of socks. He heard the cabin door open and stood up quickly, expecting that Kent had forgotten something. Goodwin came into the cabin and shut the door carefully.

'Hullo, kid.'

'Kent'll be back here shortly, he hasn't changed yet.'

'That's O.K. I just thought I'd see if you were going to play Tombola as it's the last night.'

'I've got too much to do. I've Kent's kit to pack and my own.' It was a lie, the packing was finished.

'Come for a little while, anyway.'

'I've told you I can't.'

'O.K.' He turned to leave but his need for Anson's companionship was too strong. If Anson knew what had happened in the temple Goodwin would have put down his behaviour to a fear of being implicated, but he couldn't know. He decided to make a last attempt to restore their friendship.

'Look, kid, I've said I'm sorry about that night, but you know how drunk I was. I suppose I lost my temper because you ratted on me and wouldn't come along to see I was all right. For all you know I might have landed slap in the dirt that night.' There was such a ring of sincerity in his voice that almost without thinking Anson said:

'You didn't go anywhere near the Aranyaka Temple, did you?'

'Are you barmy?' His voice was perfectly under control but he felt stunned with terror. So Anson did know, he must have followed. Quite unconsciously his eyes flickered over the open port-hole. 'Why should I go there, why should anyone go there?' He had to go on talking to let his mind recover. 'What a funny place to look for a woman in the middle of the night, or any time for that matter. Why should I go there?'

'No reason at all except I know you hadn't any money and were drunk enough to think that bazaar place might be open.' He remembered Tarrant's remark.

'But I don't get you. I went to a brothel as I said I would. Why should you ask at all about the bloody temple?' He was afraid that Kent might return at any minute and his anxiety to find out as much as possible before they were interrupted forced him to press with questions that he knew were better left unasked.

'Oh, nothing, it doesn't matter. But someone was murdered.'

'Where? Who?'

'How the hell should I know who she was?'

'She! Do you mean a woman?' Relief flooded through him. It was all some stupid mistake.

'Yes, a girl. She had leprosy.'

'Are you sure it was the same night after that dance?'

'I'm positive. I heard Kent and Tarrant talking about it this morning, the police came and saw them in Sialpur. It was a young girl with leprosy, a beggar or something, anyway she had no home, poor brat. She was sleeping right next to the gates of that arcade, and she was throttled and her neck broken.'

'Christ Almighty!' But it wasn't possible, it had been a man.

'Are you looking for me, Goodwin?' Kent stood in the doorway and Goodwin thought that his voice sounded cold. He wondered how much he had heard, whether he had been listening outside the cabin.

'No, sir, I was just talking to Anson, I'm sorry, sir.' He saluted clumsily and left the cabin quickly; his thoughts were so chaotic as he hurried down to his troop-deck that all he could do was mumble

31

meaningless obscenities to himself. He felt that he would never be clean again and he knew, beyond any possibility of dispute, that he would rot away with leprosy. As soon as he reached his hammock he searched feverishly for his soap and towel and still without conscious thought hurried into the showers.

9

Helen leaned into the cabin mirror and inexpertly began to use her lipstick. It was already after half-past eight and Kent might be expected to arrive at any minute. Before he came she must tidy the cabin and there was still that bottle of eau-de-Cologne to be found.

When he had come to her table after lunch the surprise and pleasure of his invitation made her blush painfully. It seemed to her to be such unexpected good fortune that she could still scarcely believe that it was true, and the long afternoon had drifted by with a dream-like quality that made it impossible for her to think clearly. After their first meeting she had waited for him to visit the hospital and seek her out, or send her a note suggesting that she might come to tea at the mess. But as the days passed and nothing happened she told herself bitterly that she had been a fool to expect him to have anything to do with a Eurasian, and she had tried, unsuccessfully, to put him out of her mind.

But when the orders came that Rowland's unit was to be put on a war footing and accompany the brigade to Burma her hopes revived a little. Under the new establishment she would have the status of an officer and she felt that this at least narrowed the gulf between their social positions. In the face of his continued indifference (an indifference that even she felt was studied), it was a poor consolation, but it served to keep alive the emotion she felt for Kent and at the same time raised a barrier between herself and Robert, who had emerged from the change-over with only the rank of sergeant. Poor Robert! she thought. It was a shame, but there was nothing she could do about it; she was sure that he resented her new position, although she had to admit that so far he had not shown any outward signs whatsoever. As she thought about Robert she suddenly realized how at peace she was when they were alone or working together and to her horror found herself wishing that the British did not exist. That was disloyal, and she bundled the thought out of her mind.

She had just finished tidying the cabin when there was a knock on the door. She hastily shut a drawer and called: 'Come in,' facing the door with a nervous smile.

'Hullo there, how are you?' He came into the room and she saw that he was carrying a bottle of gin about three-quarters full. 'I thought perhaps you would like a drink before we go up, have you got any glasses?'

'I'll look, I don't think so, only the tooth mug.' She went to the basin and picked it up hesitatingly, wondering what she ought to do.

'That's O.K., we'll share it.' He smiled at her, taking the glass and pouring out some gin carefully, trying to gauge how much more he ought to drink to keep his present mood of confident gaiety. She took a sip and the unexpected flavour of the gin surprised her into a grimace of dislike. 'Don't you like it?' he asked.

'Well, not very much, I don't usually drink gin, Captain.'

'You mustn't call me that, it's not . . . usual.' He spoke almost sharply, thankful that there was no one to hear what he considered to be her *gaucherie*, imagining the surreptitious smiles and nudges of the other officers if they had heard, and Maguire sidling up to him later on and asking if she saluted before getting into bed. 'You must call me Tony, and I must call you . . . what? You never told me your Christian name.' He spoke as though it was her fault.

'Helen . . . Tony.'

He took the drink from her and swallowed it; the evening looked as though it would be more difficult than he had thought.

'Let's go on up, shall we? I'll leave the gin here, if you don't mind.' He would have to see her back to cabin later on, he could pick it up then.

The dance had already started when they joined their table. They danced together for a little time and then the other officers partnered Helen in turn while Kent sat out, talking shop and drinking. But all the time he was conscious of the role he was expected to play and he assumed a possessive air, standing up with elaborate politeness whenever she returned to the table, insisting on her sitting next to him and becoming more and more demonstrative, calling her 'darling' in a voice just loud enough to be heard by Maguire, who sat next to him. Their chairs were pressed together and they held damp hands resting on Kent's knee. She had drunk far more than she ever had before, it was still very little, but enough to blur her mind and make her feel physically weak. She genuinely believed that Kent was falling in love with her; she knew

* B

that she was in love with him. By the end of the evening Kent was almost drunk and had forgotten that he was only playing a part.

No one had put on a new record for some time, and people began to say good night. He looked at his watch and saw that it was one o'clock.

'I think we ought to call it a day, I've got to be up at six, darling.'

She looked at him adoringly, the thought that the word 'darling' might be meaningless never occurred to her. She pressed his hand gently: 'Whenever you say.'

There were only one or two people at their table now and she said good night to them shyly. Arm-in-arm they went slowly back to her cabin. As the door shut behind them he thought that it would be better to have one drink and then leave. But he was too drunk to reason clearly, the whole mood of the evening still too close to him and he brushed his reluctance aside angrily, one should not think like that. He quickly took her in his arms and kissed her mouth, and she clung to him, kissing fiercely with closed lips. That's uncomfortable and stupid he told himself, and doesn't fool anyone, and he pushed his tongue until her lips suddenly parted. He rubbed his mouth on hers and he could feel her body respond and her breath quicken, and his own body stirred although his mind drew back a little.

'Let's sit down and have a drink, my sweet.' He poured out a very large gin and splashed water into the glass and they sat close to each other on the bunk. 'Drink up,' he smiled at her and gave her the glass. 'Go on, knock it back, it's good for you.' She drank about a third but could not manage any more and he took it away and drained it. For a moment she felt sick, but she kept still and it passed. He put his arm round her shoulders and gently pushed her down until she lay on the bunk and he was lying next to her. He kissed her again with his open mouth, wet with gin, and when he thought that she was responding sufficiently well without warning slid his hand down the front of her dress and cupped her naked breast in his hand.

Half drunk and thinking herself in love she was defenceless. Had Robert done such a thing she would have been beside herself with outraged modesty, even if they had been formally engaged. But it was impossible for her to judge Kent's action, she was afraid that if she tried to disapprove it would only underline her difference from other women that he knew. And even while confusion bubbled in her mind she could feel his fingers press and fondle her nipple and

34

her senses melted into pleasure past anything she had ever imagined, her whole body seemed to be waiting for his touch.

So you like it, Kent thought, and suddenly he was disgusted with himself and then angry and vicious against Helen. He took his hand away and got up from the bed, and she opened dazed eyes.

'The light,' he whispered. He crossed the room and turned out the light and came slowly back. His outstretched arms touched the bedside table and he felt for the bottle of gin. He took a big mouthful, letting the saliva break it down before he swallowed.

She was frightened now and protested, trying to hold his hands away from her body and whispering: 'No, Tony, my dearest, please no.' But he went on, kissing her with a semblance of passion until her struggles ceased. He thought her gasps of pain were pleasure, too drunk and too indifferent to wonder whether she was a virgin.

After a few moments he got up. She lay absolutely still, and he wondered if she had drunk too much. He bent over her: 'Are you all right, Helen?'

'Yes.' He bent over again and kissed her perfunctorily, he felt very tired and his head was aching.

'Darling, I must go, let me put the light on.'

'No, Tony, please!' It was the only thing he could have said to rouse her out of her lethargy. She felt so ill that she knew it must be reflected in her face, her hair disarranged and lipstick smeared round her mouth. 'You go, Tony darling, I'll wait here a minute or two. Shall I see you before we get off the boat?'

'Yes, of course you will. Or anyway, some time tomorrow.' He tried to keep his impatience out of his voice, but every moment he stayed in her cabin increased his longing to be back in his own bed, alone.

'Good.' She was too exhausted to think, all she wanted was for him to go so that she could lie in the darkness.

'Good night, Helen, and thank you for a lovely evening.'

'Good night, Tony, my dear.' She waited until the last thread of the sound of his footsteps had gone, then she got up and crossed the cabin unsteadily and turned on the light. It dazzled her and she looked uncomprehendingly at the smeared patch of blood on the pale blue bed cover. Tears filled her dark-rimmed eyes and ran down her face as she leant against the wall. She cried almost silently for a long time, but not because she regretted what had happened; that was still to come. Now she cried because she knew that her white evening frock must be stained with blood, and it was the only one she had brought from Sialpur.

PART
TWO

I

Kent and the battalion commander sat on the top of a small hill waiting for the other company commanders to arrive. They were shadowed by a clump of low trees, and there was a soft breeze to temper the sun. The hill they sat on was the most dominant feature in the wide valley; to the south and north the land stretched away into haze, to the east and west rose the hills, those to the east clear-cut, only a few miles away, pagoda-topped, those to the west blurred by distance. The plain was split from north to south by an avenue of leafy trees, hiding the straight track that was raised a little above the level of the plain. Nothing moved on the road or in the plain, the sun poured from a pale-blue sky, and the leaves above them rustled gently. To Kent it seemed exquisite in its peacefulness, although the Japanese could not be more than thirty miles away. He turned to the C.O.

'Do you know, sir, I'd really rather like to live here.' His voice was faintly apologetic, and the C.O. smiled.

'Would you, Tony? So would I. But further south for me; I'm told that there're small hills coming down to the sea, with wonderful beaches and swimming. But neither choice is practicable, from May to October they would be uninhabitable. No, Tony, it's no good, I'm afraid in the end one's Shangri Las always boil down to Suburbia or Cheltenham, it's what they're there for. In any case you're married.'

'Yes, I know,' he answered quietly, thinking to himself how odd it sounded. There had been so much to do in the preceding weeks, so much hurrying from one part of the country to another, that he had scarcely thought about Celia, whole days went by together until a chance remark would recall her momentarily. And she had receded even further from his mind after he had been woken early one morning by Anson with the news that they were at war. He smiled as he remembered his surprise that Anson could have waited with his news until he had made Kent's early cup of tea. The days that followed until now had been so strange, watching unbelievingly the Japanese draw closer and closer, fascinated and secretly appalled by the apparent ease with which great ships were sunk and fortresses fell. Then they reached Burma, and it was still the same story; already they had taken the southern strip that ran towards Malaya, and only two days ago Kent had been in the railway station at Pegu and seen the remnants of the troops that had swum the wide Sittang river. Apathetic men with exhausted faces armed only with revolvers and dressed in a medley of uniform or Burmese clothes. From their confused accounts of what had happened he had not been able to form any clear picture, but while they talked of atrocities and road blocks and fifth column he had felt their fear.

And he could still feel it, sitting on the hill looking in the direction from which the Japanese would come, but only very faintly and with contempt for himself that he should have paid attention to the talk of defeated troops. He told himself that it was only natural to feel some fear when in a day or so death might come, horribly. All that mattered was not to show your fear, not to let it influence your actions, not to let your mind dwell on what might happen. And with a conscious effort he turned his thoughts to Celia.

He wondered again if the episode with Helen had deepened the gulf that on his part lay between them, but how could it when even that meant no more than a feeling that bordered on disgust? He still remembered vividly the shock when he had undressed in his cabin and how frantically he had washed himself, as though he would never be clean. There had been no feeling of remorse or gratitude, he despised her that she should have been so easy, should have wanted him so badly that she allowed him to have her. He had been thankful not to see her again. The battalion had left Rangoon the same day that they disembarked and Rowland's unit was attached to another formation. After a few days he had written a brief note saying how sorry he was not to have been able to say good-bye, and how much he appreciated their friendship. Then he forgot her, except to glance with indifference through the letters she wrote.

He could hear a group of people climbing the hill and he stood up, opening his map case and taking out a note-book. The three company commanders arrived and saluted the C.O., talking cheerfully together for a few minutes.

'Well, let's to business,' the C.O. said, and they stopped talking and sat in a half-circle around him. 'I've brought you all here so we can look at the country and talk about other matters at the same time. First of all I'll give you the gist of the latest Sitrep from Brigade. Information about the enemy is pretty vague. They're known to have crossed the Sittang in force in spite of the bridge being blown and last night there was a rumour that they were in Pegu, about thirty miles from here. There are also rumours that some of their advance parties are closer than that. There is no concrete evidence yet which direction their main thrust will take, but it's almost certain it will be for Rangoon. At the same time we can expect strong thrusts up the two main valleys, on either side of this one, that lead to Northern Burma. One talks about valleys but of course they're enormously wide, even this tinpot thing we're in is twenty miles across. Our own forces have had to split, one division blocking the Toungoo valley, on our left as we face south, and the other falling back to cover Rangoon. If reinforcements don't come in time Rangoon will have to be evacuated and the division will then hold the Irrawaddy valley. Our own role is to stop the Japanese coming up this small central valley and crossing the hills behind either of the two divisions. To do that there's a brigade consisting of ourselves, one Indian battalion, one Gurkha battalion, a battery of twenty-five-pounders and a few armoured cars.' He paused and spread out his map on the ground.

'From now on the only way we can tell what troops we have against us will be by constant patrolling. Immediately you get back you will send out standing patrols at least six miles in front of your company positions and no patrol is to come back until it has been relieved by another patrol. Take down the map references now.' He read them out slowly and then went on: 'While I'm talking about patrols I want to make one thing quite clear. As you know, officers seem to be in as short supply out East as everything else and we're particularly badly off. I've been promised first priority by Brigade but at the minute the situation could hardly be worse. Maguire and Kent for instance have no other officers in their companies, Brampton and Rogers only one each. I do not want officers to go on minor patrols and until we build up our strength I do not want you company commanders taking unnecessary risks. Are there any questions so far?'

There was a low murmur of no.

'About our own domestic affairs. First of all A Company. We've only been here thirty-six hours and already I noticed this morning that the men are making what I can only describe as a semi-permanent camp of bamboo shelters and heaven knows what. It must stop. I never preach discomfort for discomfort's sake but from now on they must accept slit trenches and nothing else. C Company. All the latrines in the battalion are unpretty but yours are vile. Fill them in and start again. I didn't have time to look at your company, Kent, or Brampton's, but I don't expect they're perfect. I can no longer spare the time to supervise all these details, don't let me have to mention them again. Now it's your turn. Are there any points in administration that have gone wrong,' he smiled wryly, 'or should I say gone right?'

The conference wandered off through the usual maze of domestic detail; boot repairs, the use or abandonment of mosquito nets during actual fighting, the issue of latrine paper, chlorinating tablets for water, a speedier distribution of mail. Finally the C.O. stood up. 'That's enough for one morning. Get back and get those patrols out, otherwise most of the problems will only be of academic interest.'

They saluted and started quickly down the hill, trying to behave as unconcernedly as if they were leaving the usual weekly C.O.'s conference. They reached their jeeps and separated. Kent was very silent driving the few miles to the little town of Paganle round whose outskirts the battalion was in position. He was watching the sunlight piercing the canopy of leaves above him as they moved in the wind. He had never noticed it before, it seemed fantastically beautiful.

2

At the end of an hour and a half Corporal Bonar's patrol had almost reached the base of the ridge, but the track that had started off so well, just as it was shown on the map, had now deteriorated into a rock-strewn riband, the terrain on either side broken and confused, thick with bamboo and scrub. To their left they caught occasional glimpses of the ridge, steep and matted with jungle, but to their right they could see nothing except the tangle of under-growth. Bonar kept looking at his map, trying to find the reference he had been given, but it no longer made any sense to him. He was worried in case another track had branched off unnoticed; he thought it extremely unlikely but once the doubt was in his mind it would not be dismissed. He was afraid that if there had been another track the relief patrol might go that way; it would put him in a difficult position, Tarrant had given him strict instructions not to return until he was relieved. He felt aggrieved that Tarrant should have sent him on the first patrol and put Venner in the section as well: they hated each other with a meaningless hatred. If they had to use their rifles, which he was sure they would not, he would be careful not to let Venner get behind him. He tried to forget him and looked again at his map, turning it vaguely in his hands as though by doing so he hoped the country would suddenly fall into position. Then he looked at his watch and decided to halt at the first likely place they came to between three o'clock and a quarter past. By that time they would have covered six miles and that would have to do.

The track continued to climb and the eight men were sweating The warm wind that now blew steadily from the south only reached the track fitfully, the sweat dripped from their faces on to their shirts and ran from beneath the brims of their bush hats. They had not halted for the usual ten minutes' rest at the end of the hour's march, and now when they stumbled their profanities were no longer meaningless.

Only Goodwin had been too preoccupied to swear or notice the heat. One of the straps supporting his pack was chafing his shoulder. Or was it the start of a sore? Ever since the evening on board ship when Anson had told him about the girl, the slightest spot on his body had made him wonder whether it was the beginning of leprosy. He knew nothing about the disease and was too frightened to ask in case it might connect him with the murder, but he had a hazy idea that people became covered in white sores and then whole limbs rotted and fell off. But he had no idea what the first symptoms would be. As the weeks went by and his spots and pustules came and went in their usual cycle his fears began to subside, but they could still be conjured back by any unusual irritation such as he now felt.

He often wondered what he would do if a white sore suddenly appeared; on the whole he thought that he would report sick as soon as he was certain it was leprosy. He could always say that he had bumped into a leper in one of the bazaars. In any case they never hanged white people out here. Or did they? That was something else he dared not ask. He twisted his hands behind his back and tried to feel the place. It was probably only the pack strap but as soon as he could he would have another wash.

They toiled up a steep slope and suddenly came to a clearing about thirty yards in diameter. Immediately on their left was a dilapidated resting-hut with a raised bamboo floor and a tattered-looking roof supported by four poles. The track crossed the clearing and disappeared into a slanting gorge. As though this was the place he had been looking for, Bonar left the track and led the section into the hut. He took off his equipment and lay full length on the springy floor, using his pack as a pillow, and the rest of the section followed suit. To begin with, the hard packs and the uneven floor seemed comfortable, and the breeze dried their sweat-soaked clothes and cooled their damp hair. Goodwin lay a little removed from the rest of the section; now that his pack was off he was no longer conscious of the skin on his shoulder. He smoked a cigarette as though he was hungry, and listened idly to the small sounds of the wind. Something puzzled him, there was an undertone that came fitfully across the clearing, like water falling. He listened more carefully; it was water, and now he could wash. He turned to Bonar.

'Corporal, I can hear a stream just the other side, can I have a look?'

'If you like. But don't be long, this is meant to be a patrol.'

'O.K., Corp.' He got up and put on his equipment.

'Can I go too, Corporal Bonar?' Venner stood up; perhaps it was deep enough to bathe in. Bonar wanted to refuse and would have done to anyone other than Venner, but thought it best to agree.

The two men walked across the clearing and followed the track as it plunged down the slope. Now the noise of the water blotted out every sound except the scrape and clatter of their nailed boots and Goodwin instinctively began to feel uneasy at the loss of one of his senses, like a dog that cannot bear to have its eyes covered. But his uneasiness had very little to do with the possibility of meeting the Japanese. That was something no one in the section expected to have happen, it was as improbable as walking into the jungle and meeting a tiger.

They reached the bottom of the gorge and the stream ran tetchily between the big stepping-stones that carried the track to the other side and away up the far slope. On their left was a deep pool and into it fell a sheet of water. There were trees growing by the stream, their smooth trunks ran to the sun and broke in branches of dark-green leaves. Yellow butterflies criss-crossed the pool and rested on the stepping-stones with open wings.

A large flat rock some yards to their left on the other side of the pool was an obvious choice from which to bathe and Venner crossed the stream and made his way there. The excessive noise of the water still repelled Goodwin and he walked back a little way and undressed behind a large boulder, folding his clothes neatly and putting them under a bush that had burst from beneath the rock. He took a cake of soap from his haversack and walked gingerly into the water, floundering about in the deep part of the pool. Then he climbed on to Venner's rock and lathered himself thoroughly.

'Not bad, eh?' Venner shouted from the water, lying on his back and threshing his legs, laughing with pleasure at having been hot and sweaty and now feeling fresh and cool. Goodwin slipped into the water again; Venner's cheerfulness made him feel more easy, he forgot his dislike of the noise. After he had rinsed himself he went back to his clothes and dressed slowly; it took him a long time to brush off the damp dirt picked up by his feet, but at last he was ready and scrambled up from behind the rock. Normally he would

44

never have considered waiting for anyone except Anson, but Venner had been so pleasantly friendly that despite himself he felt warm towards him, and decided to cross over and offer him a cigarette. He looked to see whether he was dressed. Venner was sitting on the rock naked, his arms around his knees and a cigarette in his mouth. Two yards behind him stood a big man; his uniform seemed very untidy. He took a delicate step forward with his left foot and something flashed behind his head and swept down in an arc from right to left. Venner's head hit his left knee, bounced on the rock, and fell into the pool. A fountain of blood shot into the air and drenched his naked body as it toppled slowly over. The big man seemed to laugh as he picked up Venner's shirt and wiped his sword. He turned and waved, two or three men stepped from their hiding-places and went quickly towards him.

Goodwin dropped swiftly behind the rock and then ran doubled up towards the clearing. His boots slipped and clattered on the stones, and the flesh of his buttocks and back crawled as he waited for a burst of rifle-fire to come tearing through the undergrowth. Christ Almighty, his mind kept repeating as the nails of his boots tore at the track; Christ, what a marvellous escape!

He reached the clearing and ran across it. Not daring to shout he waved his arms grotesquely at the section still lounging in the rest-hut; they did not understand, but one or two stood up. When he was still a few yards away he gasped at Bonar:

'Quick, Corp. Japs just behind me, get back,' and everyone scrambled up looking shocked and dazed, running into the scrub a few yards behind them, utterly indifferent to the thorns and branches that lashed their knees and faces. They threw themselves down, squirming their bodies into the roughness of the ground, watching the far gap with blank faces and wide eyes. Goodwin lay next to Bonar and panted out his story.

'Did they see you?' Bonar asked before he had finished.

Goodwin tried to think clearly, but his mind was too chaotic. He suddenly remembered the extraordinary way Venner's head had bounced on the rock and he wanted to roar with laughter. He made a tremendous effort to control himself, and his brain cleared.

'They couldn't have done or they would have had me when I stood up, and the water makes such a noise they couldn't have heard me running.'

There was a pause. A twig snapped under someone's weight and Bonar looked angrily round. The only other sound was the soft wind and the distant falling water.

'Do you think they'll come this way?' Bonar whispered.

'Yes, Corp, they're bound to, there isn't anywhere else they could go, except back.' Something kept nagging at his mind, puzzling him. 'They must have been Japs, of course, but the man with the sword was big, he must have been over six foot. I thought all Japs were little blokes.'

Bonar shifted uneasily. It seemed uncanny to him that the man should be so big and use a sword. Until now he had been contemptuous of the Japanese, small, buck-toothed and bespectacled; this was very different. 'But the other blokes were smaller?' he asked.

'Yes.' It was only a crumb of comfort, but better than nothing at all. Bonar started to work out in his mind what he would do himself if he were the Japanese and decided that they would continue along the track. He realized that they could move through the jungle, but he thought that it was so thick that he could not possibly be surprised by them. He told himself that the only surprise likely to be dealt out would be by those lying in wait.

He expected that the first thing to happen would be the appearance of a scout on the other side of the clearing. Then he would wave the scout behind to come on, and when the second scout arrived the first would double across the clearing and peer down the track. After the second scout had doubled across the section would appear. He would wait until they were half-way across and then he would open up with everything he had, leaving the scouts to be dealt with later. Then it occurred to him that there might be more than one section, and he decided to send a message back to the company by Goodwin. There was a double advantage in doing this; it was not only correct according to the Manual of Military Training but also it might mean his earlier relief.

He turned to Goodwin. 'Go back now and report to the company commander. Tell him your story and say we don't know how many Japs there are but we're waiting for them here. Say we've laid an ambush for them. And be quick getting there.'

Goodwin wriggled back through the undergrowth. It was impossible not to make a noise, and by the time he had gone far enough back to reach the track without any possibility of being seen, Bonar was sweating with excitement, and he found it difficult to stop his voice from shaking as he gave his orders in a hoarse whisper.

3

Down by the pool Venner's body lay on its side with the legs drawn up as though he was sleeping in the sun. Blood still oozed very slowly from the stump of the neck and lay in a congealing puddle on the rock. His head had sunk to the bottom, but in a few days it would rise again. The officer lay on his stomach on the top of the high bank from which the water fell, waiting for the man he had sent in advance through the jungle to come back and tell him what lay beyond the steep slope. The officer was a professional soldier and had killed many people during his short life, mostly Chinese civilians; this was his first European, and he was pleased that he had done it with his sword and that his men had watched him. It had been like a game, creeping up behind him. Perhaps there would be some more troops near at hand lounging about in the way of troops who thought they were secure.

He saw his man come swiftly down the far slope, jumping neatly in his canvas shoes across the stepping-stones. He waited until he had reached the top of the bank and had bowed to him. There was a clearing at the top of the slope, he said, and on the far side was an open hut. The track continued across the clearing. There were no troops there, but he had heard sounds coming from the far side, like men moving in the undergrowth. It was difficult to be sure, the wind was in the wrong direction, and the noises were very faint.

The officer was surprised, they should have been lounging about in the hut. He realized at once that someone must have seen them. It was clear to him that this was the outermost defence of the small town shown on his map; now the enemy would send a message back and another patrol would come out, either to reinforce or relieve them.

Earlier that day he had climbed the ridge from the southern end, and had seen the paddy-fields stretching below him and the straight line of the road. Through his binoculars he had picked out the big white pagoda in the centre of the town. He had been too far away to see more, but the town had formed a dark patch on the light plain and he knew what it was. All day, as the track twisted and dipped until it reached this point, he had judged accurately how far they had travelled and how much further they should go. His instructions were to by-pass the town at dawn tomorrow, and set up a road block at the first suitable place some distance along the road.

Now he could kill two birds with one stone; he would lay an ambush and at the same time be closer to the town, shortening the distance he would have to travel in the darkness tomorrow morning. He would get between this patrol and the main body by following the stream far enough down until he could strike through the scrub and march parallel with the track without being heard from the clearing. Further on he would rejoin the track and lay the ambush, not for any troops going to the clearing, but only coming back. There were twenty men with him; he and the machine-gunner would hold the track and the rest of the men could be strung out in the jungle on either side to try and stop survivors getting back to the town.

He called softly to his men, and when they had crawled round him he explained what he intended to do. They were very tired and very hungry, but it never occurred to any of them to feel resentment at these further demands; that would have been sacrilege.

4

When Kent heard the swish of the falling bombs he fell on the ground, angry with himself because out of bravado, and in spite of the C.O.'s warning, he had not crouched with the rest of the men in a slit trench. The noise of the bombs was very different from what he had imagined, and then they crashed into the town behind him, and he felt the thud of the explosions kick through the ground against his body.

When the noise died away he got to his feet and searched the clear sky for the planes. He found them at last, very high in the sky, wheeling back to the south-east. The men were talking excitedly and beginning to jump out of the slit trenches; he shouted to them to get back in again and wait for the All Clear. Tarrant came strutting over to him, his face beaming with pleasure.

'If it's all like that I shan't grumble, sir. I counted eighteen planes, did you make it that or were there more?'

'About eighteen, I think,' Kent answered, although it had not occurred to him to count them.

'Well, whatever happens now no one can say we never heard a shot fired in anger. I wonder if they'll give us another doing over or whether that's our lot for today.'

Kent did not answer. He was looking in the direction of the town, and watching the cloud of dust drifting away above the trees

48

under which the company position lay. A thick column of oil-smoke was already flattening out and drifting with the dust, and there were one or two thin grey columns rising swiftly and carrying with them black cinders and sparks.

The All Clear whistles started blowing in the distance, and the men jumped out of the trenches, and some of them made for the edge of the trees to catch a last glimpse of the planes. Tarrant walked away from Kent and shouted roughly at them to get back and carry on with their digging.

Kent turned away and walked slowly back to his bivouac. It was also company headquarters and he could sit on his bed-roll and read with the comforting feeling that he was at his command post should he suddenly be required. Just as he reached it he saw Anson coming from the direction of the cook-house carrying a mug of tea. He walked carefully, his eyes fixed on the rim of the mug, like a somnambulist. Kent watched his progress, smiling to himself, and when he was still some yards away called out to him:

'Be careful, Anson, it would be a tragedy if you spilt a drop of the precious stuff!' Anson smiled without looking up.

'I'll believe you don't like cook-house tea the day you refuse it, sir.'

Kent took the mug from him. 'Why am I having tea now? It's only four o'clock. Did you think I'd need a nice strong cup of tea after the nasty bombing? You really are an old woman.' But he was pleased. His tour of duty at Sialpur followed by the breaking up of a communal officer's mess since Japan had declared war had deprived him of a great deal of companionship, and although he liked Tarrant and had been happy with him in Sialpur, absorbed by the company's affairs, there was very little warmth in his affection. Slowly he had become more and more attached to Anson, who was associated in his mind with the few relaxing moments of his uncomfortable existence, who brought him his morning tea, his hurried and unsavoury meals made palatable by hunger, mended and washed his clothes, and made his bed at night. That, and the many little things he did over and above his bare duties. He always carried spare pencils and paper, extra cigarettes and food filched from the cook-house that he said had been given him; his haversack was a cornucopia of trivialities that might be wanted at some time or another. Above all he was pleasant and gentle and when they were alone together Kent sometimes felt that he had put aside the slowly accumulating burden of his responsibilities. Unsuspected by him these moments of relaxation were becoming a necessity.

49

Kent started to speak about the bombing when he saw Tarrant hurrying towards him.

'You're wanted at battalion H.Q., sir, I've just met the runner. The C.O. says you're to report at once.' He looked at Kent enquiringly, wondering if he had any idea as to why he was wanted.

'I'll take Anson with me, and if we're to hold up Bonar's relief I'll send him back with a message straight away. Get your equipment on, Anson, and wait for me outside battalion headquarters.'

He set off quickly, cutting through the maze of right-angled lanes, and the gardens of areca palms and mangoes that seemed to form the outskirts of all the towns and larger villages. The fires in the town were spreading rapidly, and he could hear the crackle of flames and every now and then the deeper boom as drums of kerosene or petrol exploded. Headquarters had been set up in a mean little bungalow; although they had only been in the town two days it was already bursting with paper. He walked into the C.O.'s office and saluted.

'I've got a job for you, Tony, and not much time to explain it in. Brigade have just been ordered to start withdrawing up the valley. Evidently a strong force of Japs have slipped by our people in the Toungoo valley and are already past us on the other side of the range—not only past us but there's an extremely reliable report suggesting that they might be about to cross into our valley. You can imagine the flap Brigade's in! If it's true it means the Japs are doing the exact opposite of what they were expected to do. There's also a party of Japs about two hundred strong reported on the road south of us, about twenty-five miles away. One of the Burmese police brought the information in; he said they were resting in some jungle just outside his village, so his estimate of numbers might be very wrong either way. My guess is that they'll get near here to-night and attack the town at first light tomorrow, by which time we shall be in our new position, but in case they get hold of any transport we're to leave a company here to block the road till we get dug in.' He looked closely at Kent's expressionless face. 'That's you. I suggest you have one platoon covering the south road and another platoon responsible for that track coming from the east. The third platoon and yourself in reserve in the town. You're to withdraw at first light and march to rejoin the battalion here, make a note of the map reference. It's about twenty-five miles away, and it's impossible to leave you transport except one three-tonner for your heavy stuff and any casualties. If you're fighting by first light you must break it off and get clear of the town, otherwise the Japs might get across the road behind you in strength.' Before he could go on Tarrant came quickly into the room.

'Excuse me, sir, but we've just had a report from our standing patrol. They've encountered the Japs strength unknown about six miles away. Private Venner's been killed, no casualties to the enemy.'

The C.O. reached for a pad. 'Where is it on the map?'

'Point 096045, sir.'

'I've held the relief patrol back until I'd seen you, sir,' Kent said.

'Good. It's quite simple. Send the relief patrol out to take up a position about three miles in front of you, and give them a couple of extra men to go on and bring the forward patrol back. If the Japs press at that point give way until you can take them on as a company. Are you quite clear on the other stuff, Tony?'

'Quite clear, sir. What time is the battalion moving out?'

'Some are going now, the main body as soon as you report you're in position.'

'Right, sir.' He saluted and went out with Tarrant. Outside the bungalow Goodwin was talking earnestly to Anson. Kent started walking quickly back to the company, telling Tarrant what they were to do. All the time he talked he was curious to know how Venner had died, and yet at the same time he wanted to delay the knowledge.

5

A little before eight o'clock that night Kent sat on his bed-roll and started to unlace his boots. A hurricane lamp gave a feeble light and Anson knelt on one knee waiting to coat the boots with dubbin. Kent had set up his H.Q. in the square brick-floored courtyard that surrounded the big pagoda; he chose it because it was the easiest point in the town for runners from the two platoons to find and because he thought that the Japanese were unlikely to shell it unless they were certain of his presence. A low wall enclosed the court-yard, and the reserve platoon were spread round the four sides. The courtyard was surrounded by trees; they shadowed the area thickly from the glare of the fires, but the pagoda rose out of the shadows and the spire seemed to move in changing shades of yellow and orange. The centre of the town had been completely gutted, but flames still came from the heaps of glowing ashes, and it seemed as though subterranean fire had crept in all directions of the rest of the town; a house would suddenly blossom yellowly on the southern outskirts and be answered in a short time to the north.

Kent pulled off a boot and absent-mindedly thrust his hand into its damp warmth. God I'm tired! he thought; and from the south-east came a long faint burst of automatic fire. He sat quite still and listened, trying to determine which side were firing. It seemed to go on too long for a tommy-gun; if it was a Bren, then the men were not firing it in bursts as they had been trained to do. Without thinking he pulled on his boot again. His fingers shook a little as he laced it up and made him afraid that he might show his fear. The firing started again, another long uninterrupted burst, and he leant over and turned the lamp down until only a blue flicker showed. He could hear the men moving furtively in the darkness, the scrape of equipment being pulled over the bricks, the tap of a rifle-butt; suddenly in the town a building collapsed slowly and a column of sparks and fire swept upwards. The firing broke out again, spasmodically this time, rifle-fire. He got to his feet and strapped on his belt and revolver.

'Get your bed-roll, Anson, and put it at the foot of mine, then wait here and try and get some sleep. I'm going to have a word with the sergeant-major.'

'Hadn't I better come in case you want a runner?'

'If I go anywhere I'll collect you. But get some sleep now, you've got a hell of a day in front of you tomorrow.' Kent left him and went to the far side of the square; Tarrant was sitting up in his blanket.

'What do you make of it?' Kent asked.

'It must be those Japs Bonar bumped today, it sounds as if they've hit Robins's patrol.'

'It sounds further away than that. Bonar should have started on his way back at least an hour ago, maybe they've caught up with him.'

'There's nothing we can do about it, it's no good rushing out every time there's any firing and if it's anything really serious we shall know soon enough.' Tarrant spoke with conviction. 'Besides we must get some rest tonight; twenty-five miles in the heat is enough for one day, and we're bound to have to dig in when we arrive. If we start taking patrols out now we shall get everyone worked up and jumpy and they'll be dead beat before they start tomorrow.'

'Yes, you're right,' Kent answered, 'we'll wait till we get a

52

message back and then see. I'll go and rest.' He smiled in the darkness. 'I won't say good night, that'd be asking for trouble.' He went back and sat on his bed. The glare of the fires had died down and he was aware of the moonlight and that Anson had thrown back his blanket and was about to get up.

'Stay where you are, I'm going to bed now but I won't bother to take my boots off.' He lay on his back looking up at the sky; the smoke from the town was much thinner and he could pick out the stars, pale in the moonlight. There was no more firing, but he lay for a long time waiting for it to begin again, straining his ears. Gradually his mind wandered as other sounds came to him and he fell asleep.

It seemed to him that he slept for a long time, dreaming that he was in bed with Celia, and impotent. He caressed her body with his lips, but it was no use, she was twining her soft legs round his, fumbling at him with her fingers. For God's sake! she was saying, for God's sake!

He was awake and bitterly cold. There was a noise of movement in the courtyard, and as he sat up he heard a terrible cry, not frightened or loud but full of agony. 'Oh God! God! Do something!' There was no anger or impatience in the voice, only entreaty to be spared unbearable pain. Then he heard footsteps coming slowly across the courtyard and somebody called out loudly: 'Where shall we put them?'

Kent lay back. I'll count ten, he told himself, and then I'll go. Perhaps they've recovered Venner's body and I shall have to look at his head. He saw Anson moving and without thinking he got up at once.

'Come with me and bring the hurricane lamp.' He walked towards the dark group of men clustered at the base of the pagoda. Some were kneeling on the ground and others were bending forward. Kent wondered how many casualties there were, trying to estimate the floor-space of the three-tonner. He reached the group and they made way for him. There were three men lying on blankets on the ground, the one nearest him lay on his back with his eyes closed, his shirt and shorts blotched with patches of black blood; then Anson arrived with the lamp and the black gleamed tackily red, and Kent looked quickly away, with a feeling of shame.

'Are there any more?' he asked quietly. 'Where's Corporal Bonar?'

'I'm here, sir.' He edged his way towards Kent. 'Clifton's been killed, and Crumb, Myler and Rasby wounded. Crumb's hurt bad, Smith and me had to carry him in between us.' He held out his hands, they were covered with blood. 'Myler was hit through the arm and Rasby through the mouth.'

'Through the mouth? Then why . . .' He did not know how to go on.

'Sideways, sir. It looks rather a mess.'

Tarrant arrived and stood next to Kent. 'Where's the medical orderly, Dobson?' he asked. 'One of you get him over here at the double and tell Sergeant Peters to detail two men to help him. Someone stay here until Dobson arrives, the rest of you get back to your sections.' The group broke up and Kent turned to Tarrant.

'I think we had better have a word with Bonar and get his story first; come over to my bed.' He turned away, glad to have a reason for not staying, and Bonar started pouring out his story before they reached the bed, as though by telling it to Kent he could then immediately begin to forget.

'We got your message to come back, sir, soon after it was dark.' Before he could go on Kent interrupted.

'Wait. What about the two men who brought the message, where are they?'

'. . . I don't know, sir. They fell in behind my men. They've probably rejoined Corporal Robins, they came from him.'

'Why the hell don't you know, Corporal?' Tarrant broke in; 'you're responsible for those two men; too busy saving your own hide, I suppose.' He spoke scornfully, and Kent was angry and embarrassed, those things should not be said even if they were true.

'Leave that for a minute, there's more important stuff first; what time did you start back?'

'It was after six-thirty, sir. We must have been going for nearly an hour, Clifton was in front. Suddenly they opened up on us at almost point-blank range just where the track was running between high banks. I . . . I . . . it's difficult to say exactly what happened after that, the noise was terrific and the bullets seemed . . .' He swallowed and then went on. 'We took cover in the jungle on the left of the track because the bank was less steep that side. Then I heard Crumb groaning on the track so Smith and I crawled down and dragged him in. When we got him half-way up the bank he made a lot of noise and they opened up on us again. But it was too dark for them to see anything, and while the firing went on we made our way back a bit and then struck down the hill on to the plain and made our way back here. That's how it was, sir.'

Bonar was silent, looking at the ground. He remembered every detail, stumbling along in the dark thinking all the time what

54

reason he should give for not having sent someone down to the pool to see if the Japs were still there, and then suddenly the machine-gun opening up; it felt as though it was point-blank, but it must have been twenty yards away. They had stood paralysed while Clifton seemed to turn half round and then they were all bolting up the bank with a stream of bullets and ricochets flying all round them. Crumb had nearly reached the top of the bank when he was hit. The rest had lain together a few yards away, and he had heard the two men from Robins's section floundering and crashing through the dry scrub and jungle behind them. And the Japs must have heard it because they opened up again, firing blindly into the the jungle. He had said 'Come on!' and under cover of the noise they had started to crawl away and Crumb had started calling much too loudly for them to help him, not to leave him, that he couldn't move. The Japs would have been on to them in a few moments with all that noise so he had caught hold of Smith and they had gone back to him, shaking and sweating. They must have hurt him pulling him by the arms, he had shrieked once as they dragged him over the rough ground and then luckily fainted. The Japanese started firing again, single rounds now, and he thought he heard some of them moving slowly through the scrub towards them. Smith had heard it too. They had picked Crumb up between them and ran as fast as it was possible in the darkness, falling heavily once or twice, but Crumb was still unconscious so it hadn't mattered. But he had recovered a little when they reached the platoon covering the road from the south and they had rested. He would be all right once he was back in hospital, he was lucky to be alive.

And now all Bonar wanted to do was to crawl into bed and sleep, but Kent and Tarrant went on asking endless questions until he wanted to tell them to go and find out for themselves what it was like. But at last it was over and Tarrant told him to fall out. He walked over to where Dobson was still busy dressing wounds; he saw Smith leaning against the pagoda watching Dobson curiously as he bandaged Crumb's thigh. To Bonar it seemed to be enormously swollen, the flesh raw and distorted.

'How are they?' he asked.

'Dunno. He's only done Crumb so far. He's been hit in the guts as well as the leg.'

'That's his lot, then,' Bonar said. He thought to himself that it had been a waste of time dragging him in. 'Let's go and doss down somewhere, if we hang about here we shall only be given a job to do.'

Smith straightened himself. 'O.K. I'll get a blanket and you find the rest of the section.' Bonar saw nothing strange in being told what to do by a private soldier, he had never felt very much like an N.C.O., and at this moment he would have been more than happy to hand in his stripes.

6

Kent and Anson left the courtyard and started down the road to visit the platoons. Tarrant had argued fiercely against Kent's going, saying again and again that it was not the company commander's job. But Kent had been adamant, he believed that the Japanese were getting into position to attack the town before daylight and he wanted to satisfy himself that both platoons were prepared and knew exactly what to do if they were attacked. He also wanted to reassure himself that there would be no hitch when the time came for them to withdraw past the pagoda, for their withdrawal would be his own signal to leave. The presence of the casualties and his own isolation made him acutely aware of his responsibilities.

The moon was still high as they walked in the muffling dust by the side of the road. Tendrils of smoke had drifted all through the town, and the cool air was heavy with the smell of burning, burnt cloth, burnt spices, burnt flesh. The smell was not unpleasant, but Kent held his breath as he walked through the patches of smoke, picking his way through the tangled coils of telephone wire and smashed branches of trees that littered the road.

They crossed the market-place, which was a smouldering ruin. The corrugated-iron roofs of the stalls lay blackened on the piles of charred goods which every now and then would burst into a weak flame and then peter out. The first platoon area was a quarter of a mile away, along a straight stretch of heavily shadowed road and as they started down it a thick tongue of flame suddenly licked above some palm-trees from a house just to the rear of the platoon's position and stained the road with its light. It made him uneasy, it was the only fire of any size now burning in the town and he wondered if it had been started by fifth column to mark the platoon. The thick shadows through which he moved and the orange patch that came steadily nearer suddenly seemed hostile, and he was glad that Anson was walking unconcernedly by his side. When they had almost reached the burning wooden house he turned to Anson.

'Drop back some yards till we get past this light,' he whispered, 'and keep a sharp look-out for anyone moving near the house. Don't wait if you see anything, fire, carry your tommy-gun at the ready.' He walked on alone, quickening his step as the light grew brighter, glancing left and right as he tried to interpret the flickering shadows, and suddenly he was in the shelter of a thick hedge of lantana, waiting for Anson to join him. They stood closely together for a few moments until Kent's eyes readjusted themselves to the dark moonlight, and in the darkness, their shoulders touching, Kent felt his nerves relax.

They reached the platoon and found the sergeant watching the plain from the edge of some trees, lying on the ground behind a natural ridge of earth. Kent lay next to him, and Anson stood behind a tree and waited. He could hear some men talking very softly amongst themselves and then one of them tiptoed to him.

'What's on, kid? Why's the C.O. come round?' There was a note in his voice that puzzled Anson for a moment and then he understood that the man was afraid, asking not out of curiosity but compulsion, and without thinking he laughed lightly.

'What are you feeling windy about, seen any bogies?'

'What the hell do you mean, "windy"? What's windy about asking a simple question? I don't want to know, the blokes over there asked me to find out. It's easy for you to laugh, stuck on your bed-roll all day long.'

'Go away, you're making me tired.' He turned his back and heard the man walk back and the whispering start again.

Half an hour later they had visited the second platoon and were walking back to the pagoda through the narrow straight lanes. Another fire had started, and Kent stopped to watch the flames streaming above the trees. Now that he had visited both platoons and neither had reported anything unusual his anxiety began to lessen. Just as he was about to start walking again he heard something move behind him. He turned his head sharply and peered down the road, then he caught hold of Anson's arm and signalled him to get down. They lay down carefully by the side of the road behind a tall clump of grass.

'People coming up the road; when I say shoot, shoot,' he breathed into his ear. Anson slid his tommy-gun forward and nodded his head slightly. Now he could hear faint sounds coming towards him but the haze of smoke and shadow made it impossible to see anything. He felt Kent edge himself nearer, the sound of his breathing was close to his ear, mingling with the sounds that drew nearer. He felt confused and for the first time excited, his mouth dried and his throat seemed paralysed; very gently he lifted the tommy-gun, pressing the butt into his shoulder. And then the sounds stopped and a man's voice spoke softly from the haze, a low quick murmur of unintelligible sound. There was a pause, Kent peered through the grass not daring to move his head, his heart beating slowly and with tremendous violence. He could see nothing except a spider's nest that bent some blades of grass together; the sound started again and suddenly two figures appeared in the moonlight about ten yards away, barefooted and dressed in Burmese clothes. Out of the corner of his eye Kent saw the muzzle of the gun waver and begin to drop. 'Fire!' he whispered quickly and one of the men raised his head and looked in their direction, but they still came on. 'Fire, damn you, Anson!' Kent managed to choke out, raving at him in his mind, tugging his revolver out of the holster and then the ear-splitting noise of the tommy-gun started and the two men sank untidily into the road, their bodies jerking sideways. The gun stopped and Anson swiftly clipped on another magazine.

He looked curiously at the two crumpled figures in the road, blaming himself for not having fired as soon as Kent had told him, remembering the choking anger in his voice. He turned his head to explain why he had not fired, but before he could speak Kent shushed him, and they lay for several minutes straining their ears for any further sounds. There was nothing except the faint noise of the fire and their own breathing, and then Kent turned and looked at Anson.

'In future for Christ's sake do what you're told, this isn't a bloody duck hunt. Maybe they're only ordinary Burmese but for all you know they might be Japs or fifth column, why should they be out at midnight at a time like this? Anyway, that's beside the point, when I tell you to do anything you do it or you're no good to me.'

He was surprised to hear himself speak so severely to Anson. As he got slowly to his feet he told himself that it had been a bad day, the bombing, patrols being ambushed, the responsibility of being left as rear-guard; and what he had said about the two Burmese was perfectly true, at least it could be true. And yet he was not entirely happy about the incident, he wondered if there might have been any other motive in his mind just as he gave the order to fire: a curiosity, a sense of power.

'I'm sorry, sir.' He looked away from Kent embarrassed by what he had to say but compelled to try and explain. 'I haven't . . . er . . . this is the first time and it seemed queer firing at Burmese people. Of course they might be Japs or fifth column,' he added quickly, 'but you know, dressed like that . . .' he tailed off lamely.

'That's all right,' Kent whispered, 'I understand how you must have felt.' They looked at each other and smiled and then walked to the bodies. They had been riddled with bullets, the grimy shirts and loongyis were soaked in blood. Kent bent down and tugged at the knot that secured the loongyi around the waist; it came undone easily, and he moved round to the feet and pulled off the almost ankle-length piece of cloth. The man was wearing nothing else except his shirt, there was no knife or gun strapped to his waist or thigh. He took out his revolver and prodded the upper part of the man's body but he carried nothing except a paper packet of bazaar cigarettes in the breast pocket of his shirt.

In the meantime Anson had stripped and searched the second body but it was as innocent as the first. Kent stood for a few seconds looking at the bare bodies; the bullets had torn large holes in the flesh and had smashed in the sides of their chests. He felt a cold repugnance at what he saw, but not the feeling of nausea that mutilated living flesh gave him, and the dark brown skin toned down the redness of the blood. Kent turned away. 'Ah well,' he said, 'they were probably looters.'

7

As soon as Anson shook his shoulder Kent was wide awake. He was very cold, and moved his head slowly from side to side to ease the stiffness in his neck. More than anything else he wanted a pint of scaldingly sweet tea but that was impossible, he had forbidden the two forward platoons to make tea, and the ban therefore extended to the whole company. The blanket he had wrapped round himself so carefully had worked loose during the night and he wondered if his bare legs had been bitten by mosquitoes. He lay quite still and felt warmth gradually come back, waiting for Anson to finish rummaging in his haversack for his shaving kit. The moon had set and the tiny yellow flame of the hurricane lamp held Kent in a bubble of light beyond which he could see nothing.

At last Anson was ready and Kent sat up and started to shave. As usual the water was like ice to his face, and in spite of the new blade the bristles felt as though they were being dragged out of his chin.

'What's the time?' he asked, not bothering to look at his own watch as he felt down the side of his face for any missed patches.

'Just on five, sir.'

'Nip over and tell the sergeant-major to have everyone standing-to as soon as possible, I'll finish dressing by myself, I've only got to put on my puttees.' He finished shaving and put out the lamp, feeling a little guilty that he had had it on at all. While he knelt to roll the short puttees round the tops of his boots he listened to the muffled sounds of men reluctantly getting up and then his body jerked as one of the wounded men shrieked. He turned quickly in their direction and called out softly: 'Hold it, Crumb, I'll be with you right away, try not to make a noise.' Poor devil, he thought, however many blankets he's had couldn't stop the feel of these bricks, and no proper dressing and no dope. He put on the last puttee as quickly as possible and started to walk towards the three men, dreading another cry almost as much for its intrinsic horror as the anxiety he felt that it might betray their position. The whole courtyard seemed full of noise as the men leant against the low brick wall staring blankly into the darkness of the trees, and suddenly a rifle fired.

He turned and ran towards the sound, and as he reached the wall two or three other men fired into the blackness. He heard Tarrant call his name in a casual voice, and ducking behind the wall he answered. They stood together trying to see into the black tangle in front of them. There was absolute stillness, and the man next to Kent fired.

'Shut up, you bastard, or I'll kick your teeth in,' Tarrant hissed. He turned to Kent. 'Quick, sir, go round that way and warn everyone that if they fire and can't produce a dead Jap you'll have them court-martialled; they'll all start blazing away in a minute and then the other platoons'll start.'

Don't fire until you're certain. Don't fire. Don't fire until you're certain. They slowly made their way round opposite sides of the square and it seemed to Kent that the tension drained away, and when another cry came from the wounded men he waited quietly for Tarrant to join him on the far side of the square.

'Come and look at Crumb with me, we must shut him up some-how. And where the hell's Dobson, hasn't he got anything to dope him with?'

'He's only got aspirin, and he told me he couldn't get Crumb to take anything last night. He can't give him water because of his stomach.'

They reached the casualties, and Tarrant filtered the light from his torch through his fingers and shone the beam on Crumb's face. His eyes were wide open and his jaw sagged; blood had run out of his mouth and clotted on his chin and throat, the blanket was stickily smeared.

60

'But he's dead!' Tarrant exclaimed, and was answered by another scream that made Kent's forehead damp with sweat. Myler tried to struggle into a sitting position, his face grey with pain.

'It's Rasby. It's his jaw. Do something to stop him.' Tarrant walked quickly round and Kent followed. He shone the torch in Rasby's face, the bandages had fallen off, and before Kent could look away he saw that his lower jaw was smashed out of place, his mouth forced open by the swelling, white pieces of bone showing where the bottom teeth should have been. Tarrant knelt by his side and turned to Kent.

'Hold this a moment, sir.' He kept the light shining on Rasby's face while he passed the torch back to Kent. Now he had to look while Tarrant gently slid his arm behind his shoulders and lifted him into a sitting position. Immediately blood and slime oozed from his mouth, and he started struggling with his arms while strange noises came from his throat. Dobson joined them, and he and Tarrant propped Rasby against the base of the pagoda. Now that Dobson had arrived Rasby was quieter, dimly remembering through his agony that Dobson was a medical orderly and expecting that he would stop the pain.

'We can't do any more here, Tarrant,' Kent said. 'Dobson, you stay here and as soon as it's light enough boil a little water and do what you can for these two. Make Myler some tea, but don't go making gallons and giving it to your buddies.' He turned to Myler. 'How's your arm? Is it very painful?'

'Yes, sir, it's started throbbing, and it's very swollen.'

'Well, it won't be long now before you're both in the lorry and on your way back to the battalion and by midday at the latest you'll be well on your way back to a proper hospital.' He looked at Rasby again. 'Try and stick it for a little longer, it'll only make it worse if you get worked up.'

He nudged Tarrant with the torch, wondering if he would leave it with Dobson, but Tarrant put it quickly away in his haversack. Kent led the way to the far side of the pagoda and leant against it. A long way off he heard a cock crow and suddenly he was a child again, warm and half asleep in his bed at home, watching the first light gently move in the flowered curtains. He felt a longing for the remembered peace and security and then violently wrenched his mind away.

'What shall we do with Crumb, have him for breakfast?'

'I'll stick to bully if you don't mind,' Tarrant answered, 'I know his medical history. We shall have to bury him, that's all there is to it.'

'But there's not time, it's too risky in the dark, and as soon as it's light we're away. Why don't we pop him in the lorry with the other two, and send four men to act as escort? They can go six miles up the road and then halt; by the time they've made tea for everyone and dug a grave we shall be there, we've got to breakfast somewhere.'

'That'll do nicely,' Tarrant answered. 'I'll start loading the lorry as soon as we stand down.' They looked towards the east; the sky seemed to hold a suggestion of light in its darkness and again a cock crowed. High up in one of the bordering trees some leaves rustled. Kent shivered suddenly and drew in his breath.

'Cold, sir?'

Kent laughed without amusement. 'No, not cold, someone just walked over Crumb's grave.'

8

From the south the leading groups of Japanese came swiftly through the grey light towards the town. The advance scouts marched as quickly as the troops behind, scarcely bothering to watch the sides of the roads for ambushes, knowing that a properly laid ambush would be impossible to detect however hard they strained their eyes. It was easy for them to go forward so quickly and impassively, for them the issue was simple. They could either go forward and perhaps die gloriously, with the absolute certainty of eternal bliss, or not go forward and be even more certain of a swift death and utter disgrace. There were a few to whom the gift of faith in heaven had not been granted and there were some who feared the pain of dying, but they would be ground on the mill-stone of their own comrades if they allowed those sentiments to show, and with a certainty that made the life of a leading scout seem full of promise.

When it was light enough to see a few yards the Japanese officer got to his feet. He felt numbed with cold and his body ached with tiredness; it was so usual a condition that he no longer thought about it. Soon the vile fishy taste in his mouth would go and he would feel hungry, perhaps they would come across some water once they moved.

He told his senior N.C.O. to bring the men up to the track immediately, in the meantime he walked towards the dark patch on the dusty track that he knew was the English soldier; perhaps there were some more lying dead in the jungle. He drew his revolver from force of habit; he was convinced that there was no one hiding in the jungle, he had listened contemptuously to the cries for help and the noise they had made as they crashed down the slope; if his own men behaved like that he thought that he would commit suicide.

With his foot he rolled Clifton's stiff body over and searched it, transferring everything of possible interest to his haversack. Then he went on. He found more blood-stains and left the track and pushed his way into the jungle.

When he came back the men had fallen in on the track and bowed as he reached them. He gave his instructions in a low voice and they listened stolidly. When he finished he walked to the head of the line of men and began to pick his way through the jungle towards the ridge.

The group that he led were not picked men nor did they receive any special pay, although their tasks were much more dangerous than those that usually fell to the ordinary Japanese infantry. But even so these groups were envied by the others, it was not only more honourable, but also part of their role was to spread fear by committing atrocities and letting their handiwork be found by the other side. It was exciting and amusing to watch your enemies die bizarrely, and at the same time shocking and horrifying to listen to them begging for mercy on their knees, begging for the incomparable disaster of being taken prisoners.

As far as the Japanese were concerned such men deserved to die, it was blasphemy to call them men, they were lower than dogs or swine.

9

Both the forward platoon sergeants were called by their sentries while it was still dark, and they crept round their positions waking the men, most of them sunk in the exhausted sleep that comes to those who lie awake until the early hours of the morning. But when they remembered the firing in the night and thought of the march in front of them they forgot their tiredness and the atmosphere was one of relief that the period of waiting was almost over.

The men dressed in a matter of minutes, the majority had only taken off their equipment and slept in their clothes. When they were ready they sat in pairs huddled together with blankets over their shoulders trying to get warm. There was no attempt made to take up firing positions and wait for a possible attack, it hardly seemed worth while as they were going to leave so soon, and the sentries would give them plenty of warning if anything should happen. But there was very little talking and only those men furthest away from the platoon sergeants smoked under cover of their blankets or broke wind as loudly as they could.

As soon as the sky in the east was beginning to pale, but while the night was still absolute under the trees, the sentries were called in and the men stood up and collected together in their sections. For a short time there was a confusion of folding blankets and heavy equipment being shrugged on; someone started whispering loudly that he had lost his bayonet and the men near him half-heartedly shuffled their feet over the ground until it was found. The section commanders made a swift check in the dark and when everyone was accounted for the platoon moved slowly away from its position in single file until they reached the road, then the pace quickened and the last section had to run to catch up, their boots clattering on the metalled surface and their packs thumping up and down on their shoulders.

Sergeant Peters arrived first on the road that ran by the pagoda. The lorry was already being loaded with the company's office equipment and heavy stores, cases of biscuits and bully beef and cook-house paraphernalia. There were some opened bully beef cases by the side of the lorry. Tarrant called to Peters to load his blankets and draw two tins of bully beef per man.

Kent walked over to Tarrant. 'Do you think we can get everything on and the casualties as well?'

'I think so, sir; it'll be a tight squeeze but we'll manage somehow. Crumb will be the difficulty.'

Yes, Kent thought, I suppose he will be, and once the two wounded are settled the fatigue party will grumble and pretend there's no room for Crumb's body. Until one of them is told to get out and march, then space will appear miraculously.

'Do the best you can,' he said, turning away, 'they'll only have to put up with it for a few minutes, but Crumb's body goes on that lorry even if none of the fatigue men do. Here's the other platoon now, I'll keep them down the road till you're ready for them.'

After he had halted them he came back to the lorry. The light was growing rapidly, trees and the low-built houses seemed to materialize out of nothing; ghostly half-guessed-at forms were sketching in their own outlines, those in the distance still unrelieved in shades of black but near at hand there was already a wash

64

of palest colour under the grey. Kent was impatient to get away, as the darkness went it took with it his feeling of security. He knew it was the most dangerous time of all for them, disorganized and betrayed by the inevitable noises of departure, and he stood near Tarrant and kept looking at his watch, urging the loading party to be quick. It was difficult lifting Rasby on to the back of the lorry but he had drifted into a delirious land of his own, where he forgot to scream, and they had managed to push Crumb's blanket-covered body along the side of the lorry with his head touching the tail-board and his legs buried beneath a pile of cooking utensils.

Tarrant had put Dobson in charge of the party and he and the driver stood next to Kent while he spread his map on the bonnet of the lorry. The driver was trying to make up his mind whether to tell the truth and admit that he could not read a map or say nothing and rely on Dobson to find the way, but Kent had already decided to give him instructions that were foolproof.

'You needn't look at the map, driver. Six miles from here there's a small stream that crosses the road. There's a rest-bungalow this side of the bridge on the left and big clumps of bamboo and scrub on both sides of the road and stream. Pull up under cover as near the bungalow as possible. Dobson, you find a suitable spot in the garden and bury Crumb, you won't have time to dig a proper grave, but see it's a fair depth and put a little cross up with his name on it. Before you start see the other two men are getting on with the tea, they can use the bungalow cook-house. Sit next to the driver and take the mileage so that he knows when he's done six miles.' He glanced at his watch. 'It's nearly a quarter to six now, we shall be there by eight o'clock. Any questions?' Both men shook their heads; for a moment the driver was tempted to ask Kent if he could go straight on to the battalion with the wounded as soon as the fatigue party had been dropped, but he suddenly realized that if he did he would miss his tea and he decided to say nothing.

Kent watched the two men climb into the lorry. The self-starter ground on for some time, but the engine seemed lifeless, he could see the driver's hand fiddling with the dashboard and he felt a surge of panic and anger. As he started to move forward the engine came to life, the driver turned his head and smiled at him and he smiled back, trying to hide his anxiety, still shaken by the possibility of what might have happened. He watched it move away and then gather speed, the three men standing up in the back smiled self-consciously in the direction of the company, and one of them waved his hand.

In the front of the lorry the driver turned to Dobson: 'That made him jump, if the old cow hadn't started when she did I'd have had an earful. All these officers are the same, anything go wrong and the nearest bloke cops it.' But he only spoke in order to hear himself talk, and Dobson was looking out of the window at the charred remains of the bazaar and did not bother to answer. Now that it was light he could see smoke still rising from many different parts of the town, dead-looking piles of ash and debris had dribbles of smoke coming from them, waiting for the morning breeze to fan them into life again and carry their seeds of fire. The lorry went slowly along the road trying to avoid the tangles of wire and the occasional shallow bomb craters. A dead bullock lay on its side by the edge of the road; as far as one could see, it was unmarked except for the trickles of blood on its muzzle that the crows had caused by pecking out the eyes. When they were almost clear of the town they passed a large brick-built house that lay back from the road and was almost hidden by trees. Dobson turned his head as they went by; it was an unusually large house for a small town and the bricks lent it a strangely foreign air. He saw two men dart from behind some shrubs and run to the back of the house. He opened his mouth to tell the driver and then stopped; he settled back on the seat and started to watch the milometer.

By the time they reached the rest-house the sun had risen above the top of the ridge; its warmth was pleasant after the remembrance of the long cold night on the hard ground. The lorry was parked under a low-spreading flamboyant opposite the front of the bunga-low and they gathered at the back of the lorry and lit cigarettes before off-loading the tea dixies and carrying Crumb to the back of the deserted garden. One of them offered Myler a lighted cigarette and put it in his mouth. Nobody spoke to Rasby, who lay inert on a pile of blankets, his bandages already grimy from the dust sucked into the back of the lorry.

After the noise of the engine it seemed very quiet; one could just hear the stream ripple beyond a screen of bamboos and areca palms, and every now and then the engine gave out a metallic ting as it cooled. There was one very tall clump of bamboos growing near the water, and the wind was able to move the tops of their plumes. They finished their cigarettes, and Dobson lowered the flap of the lorry; he nodded to one of the men and together they pulled Crumb's body out and carried it behind the rest-house. There was a small patch of earth near the end of the garden where the Burmese caretaker grew potatoes, and they laid the body by the side, and went back for the pick and shovel.

The cook-house was joined to the main building by a covered

strip of concrete. The whole place was padlocked and deserted, the caretaker had left the night before as soon as the sight of the retreating soldiers had confirmed the bazaar rumours current for almost a week that the Japanese would soon arrive. It would have been better if he had not padlocked the cook-house, it was very strong, and finally the two cooks burst the door from its hinges.

In the course of half an hour the back of the work was broken. The cooks had made tea for themselves and taken some to the two diggers; now they stood watching them as they shovelled out the hard lumps of earth, sweat running down their faces. The driver had managed to unscrew the padlock on the front door and wandered about the gloomy rooms lit by chinks of mote-flecked sun that slipped through the shutters. The place was bare except for a few rickety pieces of furniture, but he found a tattered copy of *Blackwood's* dated July 1926; he dragged an arm-chair to the veranda and sat drinking his tea and reading odd paragraphs that caught his eyes, his lips forming the words.

He heard a slight noise and casually looked across to his lorry, thinking that one of the wounded men might have dropped something, but the lorry was broadside on and he could see nothing. He went on reading and then something moved into his line of vision. He looked up quickly and only a few yards away were three men in uniform coming towards him, a young man in front carrying a thin revolver. He knew at once that they were Japanese, and he got up slowly, glad that he had left his rifle in the front of the lorry because he thought that as he was unarmed they would not shoot him. He was dazed by the shock, and all he could feel was bitterness, not against the Japanese but against his own people for allowing this to happen, allowing a lorry-load of dead and wounded to go unescorted and be captured.

The officer stood on the bottom step of the veranda and said something to him. The driver shook his head: 'No speak Jap,' he said very quietly as though they were in a conspiracy together. They stood for a few seconds looking at each other, and then the officer beckoned him to walk forward. He came down the steps and they prodded him gently in the back and made signs that he should go in front of them. They walked round the bungalow and past the cook-house towards the group of men at the grave, the two soldiers on either side and the officer a few paces behind. Dobson stared at them uncomprehendingly, wondering for a moment if he was doing wrong by digging in the rest-house garden, thinking that maybe they were civil police.

'What's up?' he called out.

'I . . . I don't know,' the driver answered, 'they're Japs.' There was a moment of frozen silence and then some dry earth pattered into the grave and one of the cooks turned quickly and started to run towards the trees that hid the river. He ran clumsily in a straight line and everyone watched him. It seemed to take a very long time to reach the edge of the trees and then there was a shot and he pitched forward and rolled against the slender trunk of one of the palms. The officer spoke harshly and waved his revolver in the direction of the lorry. They were too dazed to resist, their rifles which lay close at hand were as useless to them as twigs, movement towards them meant death and to die was unthinkable. Burns had died because he had run, they would not run and would live.

They started towards the lorry. While it was still hidden behind the bungalow they heard screams, and when they turned the corner they could see a little group of men prodding at a body on the ground. They came nearer and saw that Rasby's bandages had been torn off and his smashed jaw was being whipped at and prodded with little sticks; one man had pushed a long piece of bamboo into his mouth and was gouging at the back of his throat with the broken end while Rasby moved his head from side to side carefully, screaming when he could. The officer shouted to them and they stopped at once, shuffling back a few paces and watching the body move on the ground. The officer spoke again and one of the soldiers caught hold of the driver's shirt, ripping it down the front and dragging it off him. He rolled the shirt lengthways, and while someone held Rasby's arms he twisted it twice round the gaping mouth and jerked the knot as tightly as he could.

Some of the Japanese climbed into the lorry and threw everything out, others started tearing blankets into strips and gagged and bound the uninjured prisoners. Myler's and Rasby's clothes were torn off, and they were tied to the flamboyant tree under which the lorry stood. No one resisted, they were outnumbered and unarmed, and they did not believe they would be killed. When all the baggage was thrown out of the lorry Dobson was sure that this party of Japanese knew nothing of the company marching towards them and intended driving them back to the town as prisoners. He thought it was much more likely that they would be shot by their own side than killed by the Japanese, who would have no time to waste on prisoners once they met the company. He couldn't understand why the two men should be stripped and tied to the tree so securely; it was dreadful but it wasn't happening to him.

Everything had now been thrown out and quickly examined, the tins of bully beef seemed to attract them more than anything else

68

and their haversacks were bulging with them. He was seized roughly by two men and made to hop over to the lorry and then pushed in with the others. They lay on the floor waiting for the tail-board to be put up, but instead all the baggage started to be thrown in again, blankets first and then the heavier articles. They tried to escape from the soft suffocation of the blankets but they were only partially successful; the four of them managed to roll together to one side of the lorry but they were smothered in blankets and heavy cases lay across them in confusion. They could hear the Japanese laughing and whispering outside and unscrewing the spare two-gallon tins of petrol. The driver was the first to interpret the sounds, but he did not understand that they were going to be burnt alive until one of the Japanese climbed into the lorry and poured petrol on the pile of luggage until it soaked into the blankets. The sudden knowledge seemed to separate his mind from his body, and he started jerking and heaving to escape from the stifling horror of the blankets, and the sounds that came from his throat and filtered through the gag infected the others and they too began to writhe in terror, strange sounds pouring from their blanket-stuffed mouths. There was a muffled explosion and they heaved their bodies this way and that, the flames reached down quickly, but to them the interval was timeless. The blankets blazed on their bodies and as the fire scorched them they made a last effort to burst loose and the driver stood upright in an oven of fire, blinded by the flames, his arms and body blazing like a torch. He managed to turn towards the open back and tried to step forward, he toppled across the burning cases and fell to the ground. His head lay in a puddle of fire. It was the last thing Myler saw before the petrol tank exploded and enveloped the whole flamboyant tree in flame.

10

Kent was marching behind the leading platoon when he saw the column of oil-smoke billow into the blue sky. He gave the signal to halt and sent Anson back to fetch Tarrant. The men sat in the shade of the trees with the quietness of those who realize that something has gone wrong with their plans, but who must wait for a decision to be made for them. Tarrant walked up the road from the rear of the column and joined Kent, who stood watching the spreading smoke. The bungalow and compound were hidden from sight by a line of small trees, but they could pick out the course of the stream below the compound and there was no doubt in Kent's mind that the lorry had in fact arrived at the bungalow some time ago and had only just started to burn.

He spoke quietly. 'I suppose it is just possible that one of our own men has set the cook-house on fire with a can of petrol, but I don't believe it myself. I think the Japs have got there.'

'Have you heard any firing?'

'No, but we're still almost a mile and a half away, and the wind's in the wrong direction. Firing or no firing I'm not walking straight into that. I remember this place when we came down, the rest-house is just where the smoke is, the road runs right by it, and there's a narrow bridge over the stream. There's a bit of a village on the other side, you can see the ground sloping slightly uphill where those trees are, it's an ideal place for an ambush. We've no transport now and what the hell shall we do if we have many casualties? Even if we had stretchers it's a bit too much carrying wounded men twenty miles during the hottest part of the day, and if that place is held in any strength we're bound to have quite a lot of casualties.' All the time he spoke he wondered if he was talking as the company commander or as an individual. He realized that he was afraid to cross the bridge and walk through the village, but then he told himself that if he was ordered to do so of course he would, it was only having to make the decision himself that was difficult. He turned to Tarrant.

'We'd better try and get through. We've got to find out about the men in the lorry, and I can't turn up in front of the C.O. and say that I thought there was an ambush and didn't like to go on. I shall take Sergeant Peters's platoon across the paddy-fields here and do a wide sweep to the river, then I shall come upstream to the bungalow. Wait till you see that we both have the same distance to cover and then bring the rest of the company down the road; if the Japs are in the rest-house compound don't wait for me, attack it as soon as possible.   It's easier for you because you've got a certain amount of cover along the road, but I shall be in full view from the moment I leave here. We'll join up at the rest-house and decide what to do then.'

Tarrant started to protest, offering to take the platoon across the paddy-fields himself, but Kent refused; if he had not been afraid he would have done as Tarrant suggested. He explained his plan of action to the platoon and led them down the bank of the road and over the paddy-fields, making a wide circle until they reached the stream half a mile below the compound.

Two sections lay down preparing to give covering fire to the third, which advanced at walking pace in extended line for a hundred yards and then lay down while the next section did the same. It was Kent's intention to get the whole platoon to within fifty and a hundred yards and then rush the bordering hedge while the third section raked its length with fire. He walked with the centre section, his eyes fixed on the hedge; the only sign of life was the column of smoke, which was no longer black with oil.

The sun shone in their faces, and he felt the sweat gathering under the band of his hat and then run hotly down the left side of his face. It seemed a long time before they came within striking distance of the hedge.

The section on his right ran swiftly to their flank and threw themselves on the ground while Kent and the other two sections advanced slowly. His mouth was dry, and he wanted to urinate and then the Bren gun on his flank started to fire, and both the sections began to run forward. He could see dust and dirt kicking from the hedge and hear the high-pitched whine of the ricochets; a second Bren broke in and then scattered rifle-fire; it stopped and they were throwing themselves through the dusty broken line of the hedge falling carelessly on to the hard ground, panting for breath. The garden was empty, there was the mound of newly dug earth and Crumb's blanketed body and nothing else. The third section came running up, and at the same time he saw that Tarrant had arrived with the rest of the company and they were taking up positions in and behind the long hedge that ran the length of the compound.

He stood up and told Sergeant Peters to post two sections along the bank of the stream and ordered the section he was with to follow him. They reached the back of the bungalow and burst open the door. There was a passage lit by the open door in front of them and he and Anson walked slowly towards it, the rest of the men pushing open the doors and peering into the empty rooms on either side. It seemed easier for Kent to walk on tiptoe. They reached the open door and looked cautiously round the space in front of the veranda; there was a charred body on the ground and two more slumped against the foot of the blackened tree, the lorry was almost burnt out, but thick smoke still came from the piled-up baggage. They left the veranda and walked across to the lorry. Kent tried to identify the body on the ground, but what had been the face was black and swollen and bore no resemblance to a human being. The two figures under the tree were more easily recognized although their naked bodies were swollen with huge blisters and black patches. The strips of blanket binding their feet to the tree had not burned completely away, and he suddenly realized that the circles of less discoloured flesh round their waists and chests had been caused by being tied to the tree. He smelt the sickeningly appetizing smell of cooked flesh and drew back sharply, white with nausea, the tips of his fingers shaking as he pictured how these men had died. He looked up and saw Tarrant watching him closely and he tried to smile.

'I suppose the rest of them are keeping warm inside,' Tarrant said lightly, successfully hiding his own qualms, thinking that the men were dead and that there was no point in going as white as a sheet about it. 'I'll get some men and have a look.'

'Wait a minute,' Kent said quickly, 'before you start I'm going to take another platoon and push on through the village. If it's O.K. I'll fire three shots and you bring the rest on at the double, we must get clear of here as soon as possible. Which platoon's nearest the road?'

'Sergeant Cording's.'

'All right. Get the rest of the company spread round the compound in case I have to come back at the double and be ready to come to me as soon as you hear the signal.' He turned quickly away; something about the smoke rising from the lorry sickened him, and all the time he was speaking he had breathed through his mouth in case the smell of flesh had come to him again. He walked back to the hedge that ran at right-angles to the road and pushed his way through, holding back a bough until Anson had joined him. A man lying in the hedge looked up at them and Kent saw that it was Goodwin.

'Where's Sergeant Cording?' he asked.

'Down there I think,' Goodwin answered. He saw Anson and dropped his eyes.

'Down there you think,' Kent mimicked quietly, and then raised his voice angrily: 'Think what?'

'Sir.' Goodwin spoke sullenly to the ground.

'Get up when you talk to an officer, damn you.' Kent spoke viciously, a rage that he did not understand seethed in his mind and as Goodwin scrambled awkwardly to his feet it was as much as he could do not to kick him savagely in the side. It was on the tip of his tongue to tell Goodwin that he would be sent through the village with the leading section, but he knew that would be impossible for him to do, and some of the men were watching them. 'If I have any more trouble from you, you'll find yourself doing one or two things you won't like,' he said, and abruptly turned away towards the end of the hedge where it joined the road, and lay down beside Cording.

72

From here he could see the narrow bridge fifty yards in front of them, and beyond that the road sloped gently up between thick trees and a few scattered huts surrounded by irregular hedges of cactus. At the top of the rise the road dipped out of sight, running on through flat country. It seemed very near, the gap at the top. He sent for the section commanders and told them what he wanted.

'We'll go in bounds to the bridge and when the first section sees the second one leave here they're to go at the double to the centre of the village, when the third one leaves the first will go to the top of the slope. I shall be with the second section. Don't muck about now and tell everyone a long story, get moving at once and tell them what's happened when it's all over.'

In a few minutes the first section had collected behind Kent. He watched them push through the hedge and begin running down the road and he noticed that Goodwin was amongst them. There was no embankment here until the road almost reached the stream, it was bordered on either side by scrub and trees, and Kent suddenly cursed himself as he realized that it would have been possible to reach the bridge behind the cover of the thick shrubs. But it was too late now and perhaps it wouldn't matter. The section reached the bridge and flung itself down, taking what cover they could behind the wooden sides. The next section was ready and Kent got to his feet, then they were running down the road and a machine-gun was firing from the village mingled with some small explosions. The bullets smacked into the bridge and came whipping past them, and Kent saw the leading section scrambling towards the cover by the side of the road, and then his own section swerved away and plunged into the shrubbery next to the lorry. At the same moment there was a splitting roar that seemed to come from the ground on which they lay flattened. Someone threw himself down and pressed against his side, one arm across his shoulders.

'Are you all right, sir, you weren't hit?' Anson's face was red and streaked with sweat. Before Kent could answer the machine-gun started again, and they lay on their faces flat in the dust and pushed together as closely as possible, while the bullets swept through the tangle of branches above them and twigs pattered on their backs. Before the gun stopped firing there was another splitting explosion and they could hear bigger branches falling. Kent opened his eyes and tried to get to his feet but his body felt as though it was rooted to the earth, which was no longer hard and rough, but soft and desirable as his own bed is to a sick man. He looked at the ground and could see each individual grain of dust, they were of exquisite beauty, glittering and many-coloured. The soft hair on Anson's

73

cheek was powdered with it and there was a broad smear of dust, wet and black with sweat, that divided his lips from the gold of his skin.

'We can't stay here, I must do something,' Kent whispered, 'come with me.' He wriggled through the shrubs, making his way towards the last thickets before the bridge. There were a lot of men lying on their faces in the bushes, and his mind began to work again; he whispered to some of them to make their way to the edge of the cover and the road and to watch the bridge. When he reached the end he found a shallow rain gulch formed a natural trench. In it was the leading section commander with four or five of his men watching the far bank of the stream and the village through the last screen of leaves. He crawled next to the section commander and some of the men looked at him hopefully, as though now that he was with them everything would be all right.

'Any casualties?'

'Two men slightly wounded, sir. And Goodwin, he's still on the road.'

'Is he dead?'

'No, sir, his leg's hurt pretty badly, I think.'

'Why hasn't someone brought him in?'

'I have asked for volunteers, sir.' He spoke in an expressionless whisper and then said nothing; the men next to Kent seemed absorbed in watching the far side of the stream and one of them edged his body further from the protection of the gully, craning his neck as though to get a better view. Kent flushed angrily and turned to the two nearest men to order them to go and bring him in. And suddenly he remembered the jewelled dust, the warm earth, the weight of Anson's arm as it pressed him down while the twigs fell. And he said nothing, asking himself why should they volunteer to risk dying for a man they possibly hated. His thoughts were confused but he understood how these men felt about such a thing. If they were ordered to go they would, but there was no inner compulsion to make them do it for its own sake, all they understood was that it was infinitely desirable to be alive, that the mere act of living was a sufficient justification, the only true reality. To live, to move, to have their being, that, he thought, was the only worthwhile thing; why therefore should he expect them to volunteer? And then he knew that he himself would have to go and fetch Goodwin in, because if he did not people would say that he had been afraid, that he had failed as a company commander. He might not succeed in the attempt, that was not important, the attempt had to be made.

74

He slid back into the gully and started to crawl to the end. He thought contemptuously that the real truth was quite simple, he was too cowardly to give orders and so frightened of the possible consequences that he had to do everything himself. And now he would probably be too clumsy to do whatever had to be done properly and the outcome would be his own death. As he wriggled uncomfortably along on his stomach it occurred to him that possibly Goodwin was dead; he hoped fervently that he was and decided that if there was even a faint chance of being able to say so, and that it was useless to risk further lives, he would.

The gully ended abruptly, and he found he had reached the last of the cover and was looking down a short steep slope which flattened out across bare ground for five yards and then climbed steeply again up a twelve-foot embankment to the road. He could see Goodwin lying behind the near end of the bridge, his body stretched straight out. As far as he could judge, the whole distance between himself and Goodwin was exposed to the machine-gun in the village. He called his name softly and Goodwin turned his head inch by inch towards the sound. Kent glanced round to see if anyone was looking; Anson was already next to him, and two men further back were watching with avid interest. He signalled angrily to them to watch their front.

'Don't go, sir, he's a chum of mine, I'd like to go,' Anson was whispering in his ear, and Kent's head dropped forward as relief swept through him. He tried to control a long sigh but it was impossible. He turned his head and looked at Anson, his eyes soft with gratitude. They looked at each other for what seemed a long time; the dust still glittered on Anson's cheek, the sweaty streak of dirt, a dried spot of blood on his chin, the pulse in his throat, all were beautiful, and suddenly, without knowing why, Kent was calm and happy. He smiled and put up his hand and rubbed the smeared dirt on Anson's face with his finger. He could feel the roughness of the beard on his finger-tip.

'No,' he whispered, shaking his head, 'not you.' The words were spoken without thinking, and immediately he was embarrassed. He went on quickly: 'I want a batman, not a corpse, besides I know you loathe the man.'

'But don't you go, sir, don't bother with him, he's not worth it, no one will know.' He edged nearer to Kent. 'Look, sir.' And he moved the muzzle of his tommy-gun.

It flashed through Kent's mind to pretend either that he did not understand or that he was shocked, but it was too much trouble to do either. In the last twelve hours violence and death had become

75

commonplace, and although he knew that it would be wrong for Anson to pretend that he had seen something on the other side of the river in line with Goodwin's body, and to fire low and kill him, he was not shocked. Under the immediate circumstances it seemed quite logical. But in his heart he could not agree to such a thing, and his whispered 'No' as soon as Anson moved the muzzle was compounded of many things; he felt repugnance at committing a cruel act, he was afraid of being found out, and his pride rebelled at putting himself so completely into his servant's hands. It never occurred to him that he had done so even by saying 'No.'

'I'm going now, when I come back be ready to pull me in.' He squatted on the edge of the gully and then leapt through the screen of leaves. He stumbled as he landed at the bottom of the slope and his rush across the flat carried him to the top of the far bank without a check. He flung himself down next to Goodwin and pushed his body over so that they lay face to face behind the bridge end. A bullet smacked into the woodwork very close to them, but there was no automatic fire.

'Listen, Goodwin, I'm going to roll on my face. Get on my back and lock your arms round my neck. Don't choke me, that's all.'

'I can't move, my leg's hurt bad.'

'Sod your legs, I don't care if they're both off, get on my back or stay here.' He rolled over on his face and another bullet struck the road a few inches away, and a splinter of stone cut Kent's cheek. He looked upstream; not more than two hundred yards away he could see men wading across from the far bank and he felt his stomach contract.

'Come on, for Christ's sake, the Japs are crossing the stream, they'll be here on the road any minute now!' He felt Goodwin throw himself on to his back and put his arms round his neck. He raised his chest from the ground and took the strain on his arms, he could feel them shaking with fear and the sweat streamed from his body as he imagined the Japanese appearing through the cover on the other side of the road. 'Hold tight now, I'm going.' He dragged one leg up under his body and straightened up. Something stung high up in his right arm and he heard shots. He went down the bank as quickly as he dared, but Goodwin's body made him top-heavy and he was terrified of falling. He lumbered quickly across the flat and his impetus nearly carried him to the top. He fell forward on the bank just below the gully and tried to scrabble up with his hands and knees. Anson leant far out and caught Goodwin by the arm and dragged him in. Before he could turn

Kent had thrown himself on top of them. He scrambled to his feet and wanted to roar with laughter for pride and relief.

'Hey, you two. Pick Goodwin up and go as quickly as possible to the far end of the compound and wait there. Corporal, take your section down the stream-side and collect everyone you can at the bottom. Stay under cover and lie down, the Japs are crossing the stream and they'll either get right round us or else rush the road. I'll go round the other way and collect everyone else, we're getting out of here as soon as possible.'

He went back through the bushes whispering to everyone he passed to make their way to the end of the compound immediately; when he reached the spot where he had left Cording he found Tarrant there.

'We're moving from here at once, bring everyone down to the bottom, I'm going there now to pick a route over the paddy-fields. Be very quick.'

'Right, sir. That was nice work of yours, I watched it from here.' As Kent turned away he nodded absent-mindedly as though he had almost forgotten the whole incident or in any case it was of no importance. He ran back to the rest-house in case any of the wounded had sheltered inside, but the place was empty. As they reached the cook-house Anson touched his shoulder.

'There's a lot of blood on your sleeve, sir, right sleeve.'

'It must be Goodwin's,' Kent answered and then remembered the sting in his arm and looked down. His sleeve was bright with blood and when he touched the place with his hand it was swollen and began to ache. 'It's not,' he said, 'I have been hit, I remember something stinging as I stood up.' He leant against the cook-house and tried to pull the shirt off his shoulder. 'We'll leave it for now, it can't be anything serious, my arm seems all right. Once we're clear of here you can have a look at it.'

'And your cheek's cut as well,' Anson said, 'but not much, I noticed that before.' They hurried on to the ledge at the end of the compound and as they went Kent wiped the blood from his sleeve on to the front of his shirt and shorts.

Two platoons were already lying down behind the hedge when he pushed his way through. He stood facing the direction from which they had first attacked; the paddy-fields stretched away in front of him without cover of any sort. To his right on the other side of the stream there were only a few scattered palms by the bank. He decided to go straight across the fields as quickly as possible, keeping the garden and bungalow as a screen between himself and the Japanese. Once they were out of effective range

77

they could cross the stream and either make their way back to the main road or keep to the open fields. He told the nearest platoon to follow him, and set off at a quick pace, constantly looking back expecting to see the enemy bursting through the hedge and listening for the small cough of discharge from the mortars. The last section left the hedge, and he went more quickly; he knew that he should have left at least one section to hold the hedge until the remainder were out of range but he had forgotten.

When they had covered half a mile he began to feel almost safe, but Goodwin's presence was a constant worry. He was being helped by two men, his arms round their shoulders and using his good leg to hop with, but they could not keep up and Kent was forced to slow the pace so that they should not be left too far behind. There was still no sign of the Japanese, and now the bungalow and compound were beginning to waver and be eaten up by the shimmer of heat rising from the fields.

His arm was aching below the shoulder and he changed direction and headed for the stream. When they came near he made his way along it until they reached a spot where the banks shelved and the waters broadened out, and here the rear platoon formed a perimeter while the remainder waded across. He knew that the men resented the delay caused by ordering them to take off their boots and socks but he didn't care, knowing that if this was not done most of them would be crippled after two hours' marching. He went gingerly across the stream feeling the soft mud squelching between his toes and the roughness of little shells and pebbles; the water came half way up his thighs and ran with surprising swiftness. It was too muddy to see the bottom and he was glad when he reached the other side and had not floundered into a pot-hole or cut his foot on a broken shell. As the men climbed the bank he made them spread out in a wide semicircle while they put on their socks and boots and the last platoon crossed. Tarrant sat next to him while Anson helped him off with his shirt. The bullet had torn a long narrow groove in his skin divided in the centre by an unbroken ridge of flesh; he was disappointed that it was so superficial.

'It's hardly worth using a field dressing,' he said casually as Anson tied one on, 'still I suppose I might as well try and keep it clean, I'd hate to leave you all and go back to hospital with a poisoned arm.' He smiled at Tarrant.

'That would be terrible, wouldn't it?' he answered. 'If you give me a call when it gets dark I'll come over and rub some dirt in it for you. Then you can kick me hard on the ankle and we'll both have a month in dock.'

'Shall I wash this sleeve in the stream for you, sir?' Anson asked, holding out the shirt, on which the blood was already drying.

'No, don't bother, you'll only make it worse, besides I like it like that, you don't get a nice easy wound every day.' He finished winding on his puttees and turned to Tarrant. 'You realize that we've lost all our equipment, spare food, blankets, picks, shovels, everything.' For some reason the thought was not displeasing. 'We'd better get on at once and keep off the road for a little while, as long as the going's easy I think we're better off in the open until we're well clear of this area. And Tarrant, before we get back to the battalion I shall want a complete list of all our casualties.'

'What about food, sir? It's getting on for twelve and we've had nothing yet, not even a cup of tea.'

'We can't start picnicking here, can we? They'll have to wait until we find a village or some cover and then we can eat. It's lucky we've lost all the tea and dixies or they would have started drumming it up here. It won't hurt them to go a few more hours, and I don't think we're going to have many stragglers somehow. Make Cording's platoon responsible for Goodwin for the first hour and then they can hand him over to Brewster; as soon as we can we'll rig up a stretcher. Bring up the rear and I'll go in front.'

Towards the end of the third hour there was still no sign of cover or a village, and he decided to halt in the open and let the men eat and rest for half an hour. They were exhausted and sat down in silent groups and began to open tins of bully with their bayonets. Kent lay on his back with his hat over his face; the ground had been rougher than he expected and his body ached with tiredness. The bandage on his arm was cutting into his flesh but he was too tired to care. Whenever he closed his lips they stuck together and the inside of his mouth was hot and slimy. He moved a little and unstrapped his water-bottle, weighing its fullness in his hand; his longing for water stopped being a torment and turned almost to pleasure as he imagined the feel of the water soaking into his mouth and trickling down his throat. Near at hand he could hear the stoppers being pulled out of the men's bottles, and by the hollow sound of some of them he knew that they had been drinking without permission.

He heard Anson scraping the inside of a tin with a fork and sat up. Once he had had a mouthful of water and started eating he realized that he was ravenously hungry. They shared the same mess-tin and he finished his half first. Some of the men were going a short distance away and squatting down to defecate; he also wanted to, but he had never been able to cultivate the necessary indifference to being watched.

He lay down again and tried to doze but the heat of the sun made him restless, and flies seemed to have materialized out of nowhere and settled persistently on his bare legs and arms. He stood up and let Anson help him on with his equipment and walked over to Tarrant.

'I'm going to head back to the road now; before we start get the men to fall in round here, I want to have a word with them.'

Kent waited until they formed a half-circle round him; he stood with his right arm thrust into his shirt, partly to take the weight off his arm. As soon as they were silent he began to speak.

'I know you're all tired but the longer we hang about the worse it will be for us. I reckon that we've still four hours to do, more if we stick to the paddy-fields, so we will work our way across to the road again and keep going as fast as we can. We left the rest-house a long time ago and we've hurried, I don't think the Japs can have caught up with us even if they went straight along the road. It's my opinion that there weren't many there and I think there's a good chance that we won't run into any more between here and the battalion, but we must hurry. I know it's tough on the people helping Goodwin but that's not his fault; consider yourselves lucky it's not you. From now on there'll be no more halts until I say and no more drinking. You'll lead, Sergeant Cording, then Sergeant Brewster and Sergeant Peters. Lead on now.'

The half-circle of men started to unravel itself into a long single file, and Kent walked beside Cording until they could distinguish the line of trees bordering the straight road and then he dropped back to the head of the second platoon. The time passed quickly until they reached the road; there was an air of tension about the column as soon as they felt the trees close in above their heads after the expanse of the paddy-fields, but as they marched on and nothing happened fatigue came swiftly back, and the minutes stretched themselves into quarter hours and they in turn seemed endless.

They halted among a small cluster of deserted huts when the sun was low and broke off a bamboo door to make a rough stretcher for Goodwin, and then Kent started again before their feet began to ache intolerably and the raw circles of blisters set. Just before dark he passed back a message that there was only a mile and a half to go, and he sent Tarrant on ahead to find out where they were to spend the night. They passed the battalion's outlying sections, and a few of Kent's company called out to them: 'Get ready, chums, they're just behind us,' but the majority were silent, and when they reached the centre of the battalion position and Tarrant told them to halt they lay down by the side of the road too exhausted even to smoke.

'I've sent a message to the M.O. about our casualties,' Tarrant said as soon as he found Kent, 'he's sending a truck down straight away.'

'Thanks,' Kent answered, 'but personally I must see the C.O. first and tell him what's happened. Have you got our list of casualties?'

'Yes, sir, it's a total of nine dead, two missing from Robins's section, and four wounded including yourself.' He handed over the list. 'I've also seen the Q.M. and he's sending a hot meal down to us and a few spare blankets. When they've eaten there's a place a little further back where we're to sleep, it's rather overgrown but that can't be helped.'

'I'm afraid I shall have to leave you to do all this, I don't know how long I shall be with the C.O., and I shall go straight on to the M.O. afterwards. Where's Anson?'

'Here, sir.' He got up stiffly from the ground and Tarrant walked away to look for Goodwin.

'How are you feeling?' Kent asked. 'Strong enough to come with me to battalion H.Q.? I'd like to let you rest but I must take someone with me. I'll try and get some grub for you once we get there.'

'No, I'm all right, sir,' he protested, 'I'd rather wait till you have food.' They walked in silence up the road, trying not to limp. Kent found the C.O., who had set up his headquarters behind a screen of shrubs; as he saluted his arm hurt and he winced.

'Tony! I was beginning to get worried about you. I knew something must have happened to the lorry when it didn't arrive and Brigade were going to send some armoured cars to look for it. Have a drink and some food and tell me what's happened.'

'Thank you, sir. Could my orderly have something as well?'

'Yes, of course. Macky, take Captain Kent's orderly to the cookhouse and then bring some food back here.' He turned again to Kent. 'What have you done to your arm?'

'It's just a scratch, sir, I got wounded slightly.'

'I hope to God it's not bad enough for you to be sent back?'

'I don't think so, sir, I'll go to the M.O. as soon as I leave here.'

'Mind you do.' He poured Kent a stiff whisky from what was his last bottle and added some water. 'Now tell me what happened.'

Half an hour later Kent sat on the back of a lorry while the M.O. swabbed and prodded his arm. It was hurting a great deal and he was cold and very tired.

'It's not too bad,' the M.O. said, 'it's only a slight flesh wound. What I prescribe is a comfortable bed here for the night with something to make you sleep, and in the morning I expect you'll be all right. You'd better keep your orderly here in case there's any trouble in the night, and you have to go back to your company. I'll send someone down to Tarrant and let him know.' He turned to one of the stretcher-bearers: 'Have a couple of stretchers made up as beds in the back of this lorry and when Captain Kent is in bed let me know.'

The man climbed into the back of the lorry and hung a hurricane lamp from the roof. It was dark now, and a few fireflies were dancing erratically round the edge of the clearing to the intermittent rasp of crickets, and the moon was beginning to strike down through the tops of the taller trees. Occasionally they could hear men moving on the road or pushing through the undergrowth. Anson knelt in front of Kent and started to take off his boots.

'No, don't,' Kent said. He pulled his legs up and leant against the side of the lorry to take off his boots and socks; his feet were red and swollen, tacky with two days' grime. There was a flask-shaped canvas water-bottle hanging near him, its outside gleaming with moisture that seeped through and cooled as it evaporated. He took it down and poured the water slowly over his feet with one hand and rubbed the dirt from between his toes with the other. Then he picked up his shirt and dried his feet. He sat for a moment trying to make up his mind whether to wash any more, but he was too tired. He pushed himself backwards with his hands, keeping his feet clear of the dirty floor until he could sit on one of the stretchers; then he took off the rest of his clothes and laid them under the first blanket where the warmth of his body could dry them.

The rough blankets against his bare skin were deliciously soft. The stretcher was too narrow for him to do other than lie on his back and he lay still, looking up at the light with his fingers touching across the hair on his chest, waiting for Anson to finish washing and the M.O. to come back. He thought of the day just past, it seemed infinitely remote, like a half-forgotten dream; he tried to recall what the dead had looked like, prodding at his mind to see if fear was there.

The M.O. came back and gave him a small white pill. He swallowed it and then Anson turned out the lamp and Kent could hear the stretcher creak as he sat down. He listened to the flame of the lamp die with a series of tiny pops. He lay in the darkness with his eyes open, watching sleep drifting into his mind and thinking about the Japanese and the burnt bodies that were probably still lying in the moonlight in front of the bungalow. He remembered the smell of burnt flesh and the feel of the earth as he laid his face against it; he knew that he had been afraid but he could not recall what that feeling was like.

Nor did he remember until shortly before the dawn. Anson was shaking him gently but strongly, and in the distance a machine-gun was firing long bursts and men were talking in low voices outside the lorry. Then he remembered perfectly, it was as though he had never forgotten.

I I

Helen lay on the cool tiled floor of the veranda as she heard the first bomb explode somewhere in the town. She lay with her face turned towards the wall and her eyes open. The split and rumble of the exploding bombs rushed towards the hospital and then the noise stopped and she could hear the sound of the planes dying away.

She stood up and walked to the veranda steps mechanically brushing dust off her white uniform. Standing in the drive in front of the hospital she looked into the sky for the planes but they were already out of sight. The sun glittered on the broad shallow lake in front of her, and a steady warm wind blew in her face and rippled the surface of the water. Columns of dust and smoke were rising over the town, but the only sound she could hear was the wind as it moved through the scattered trees. A wire-meshed door squeaked open behind her and then snapped to, and Robert hurried down the steps.

'Why are you not in the shelter, Helen?' He caught hold of her arm and tried to shake it angrily; she looked at him and smiled.

'Don't be silly, Robert, I didn't have time.' She turned back and walked up the steps again. 'I wonder if there are many casualties; they didn't drop very many, did they? We had better go and find Dr Rowland, I think. I wonder if the planes will come back?'

'I think that you hope they will,' Robert accused her, holding open one of the screens so that she could enter the ward.

'You are wicked to say things like that, of course I don't!' But even so, she thought, it had been quite exciting and it was the first time she had seen any enemy planes.

They passed through a ward that was full of Indian troops sick

83

with malaria or dysentery; they lay on blankets under their beds and as she walked by some of them asked her where the bombs had fallen and whether they could get back into bed. She answered them in Urdu, making, as she had always been taught to do, deliberate mistakes in grammar and pronunciation to show her unfamiliarity with any tongue other than English, telling them to stay where they were until they heard the All Clear. Though they knew that she was a Eurasian they spoke respectfully to her, not only because she was kind and they liked her, but also because the slightest liberty of address would unleash on them a torrent of abuse at which their friends would laugh and repeat back to them as soon as she had left the ward. Although she would not even admit it to herself she was fond of the Indian patients and found nursing them satisfying and easy. She never felt the slightest embarrassment at having to bath them or perform the most intimate services for them. Their bodies, beautiful with youth, left her completely unmoved, the thought of sexuality with any of them never entered her head.

Although she had given the matter very little conscious thought, in some ways she preferred looking after these Indian troops to the British other ranks in the next ward, who did embarrass her. They regarded her as young and pretty and because she was a Eurasian they treated her with far more familiarity than they would have done most English nurses, thinking that she would not understand their innuendoes and not caring very much if she did. They would make a tremendous fuss at having to expose themselves, demand screens round their beds, ask for male orderlies to attend them, and having drawn as much attention to their modesty as possible finally give in. Her upbringing made it difficult to treat these men with firmness, it was her first experience of having to look after large numbers of comparatively young Europeans at the same time and she did not understand them, believing everything they said. A week before, she had complained to Rowland about one of the patients. He was a private soldier, bigly built with dark curly hair, good-looking. He was always laughing and joking with her, thanking her with sincerity whenever she did some little service for him. One night when she had been on duty and was walking through the wards he had called out to her softly as she passed the foot of his bed. The mosquito nets were all down and the room was divided by them into square white cubicles; his bed was nearest the wall, and she had gone to him and asked him what he wanted. He sat up in bed with a groan.

'Oh, Sister, my stomach feels awful, sort of swollen.' He untucked the mosquito net and caught hold of her hand. His skin was

84

hot and dry, and she thought that he had a temperature. Without thinking she allowed him to pull her hand under the tumbled bed-clothes and ran her finger-tips over his muscled stomach through the line of hair below his navel and suddenly he was stroking his genitals with her hand. She had stood still by the side of the bed, horrified but excited, and for a brief moment he had thought that she would put out her torch and lie down on the bed beside him; as he moved his body to make room she snatched her hand away and walked out of the ward.

In the morning she had reported the matter to Rowland, who listened sympathetically, but did nothing to punish the man except to have him sent further back to another hospital. He left her with the feeling that she had been partly to blame for not having taken an orderly round with her, and now when she went on night duty Robert usually accompanied her. She had been very shocked for a short time, not only because she considered it was a gross thing to have happened to her but also because she could not forget that for a fraction of time she had felt desire. She had gone back to her own room and cried bitterly as she remembered the unearthly combination of pleasure and pain that she had experienced with Kent.

And as she and Robert walked through the wards to Rowland's office she thought of Kent again, glad that the town had been bombed so that she could write and tell him. It seemed to bring them closer together and perhaps when he realized that she might · have been killed he would answer her letter and tell her to be careful and that he would come to her as soon as he possibly could. But she smiled at herself for the conceit; however irregular the mails might be, however busy he was or lazy as a letter writer, if he had been at all in love with her she would have heard from him at some time during the last two months. But though she realized all that, she still made excuses in her mind for his silence.

She did not regret having given herself to him so easily; she had been on the brink of love and, looking back, as she often did, she realized that she had not been to blame, at least not in her own eyes, although she knew that Kent might look on her as little better than a whore.

She had been desperately unhappy after the night of the dance, so unhappy that in some ways she was glad that he had left; at least she could now pretend to herself that if he had stayed everything would have been very different, and it gave her sufficient excuse for writing often to him and making believe that they were in love with each other. It was only recently, in the face of his continued silence, that she began to admit to herself that it wasn't true and that Kent must think her persistence merely a measure of her morals.

Before they reached Rowland's office they could hear him booming away at everyone in earshot. They found him walking quickly about his room, throwing bandages and wads of cotton-wool at his desk from various cupboards in his room. The air-raid had made him feel immensely cheerful, and he talked away, mostly to himself, because he liked the sound.

'Ah, Sister and Sergeant Johns! Just the people I want. Pop those bandages and things on my desk into that bag, Sister, and come with me in the jeep. Sergeant, you go and hurry the ambulance along and follow us down to the bazaar, we're going to do a little rescue work. Warn the other drivers to stand by in case there's a lot of casualties.'

'Yes, sir.' Robert saluted in the self-conscious way of people who always remained civilians at heart and hurried out of the office. He would always feel uneasy with Rowland; he thought that it was due to their difference of race, and that secretly Rowland despised him; but in fact Rowland scarcely ever thought about his male staff at all, and was always surprised when some incident occurred to give them an individuality of their own. It had given him a reputation for kindness that bordered on other-worldliness. When there was some breach of discipline among his Eurasian orderlies that necessitated a punishment he would look at them with a puzzled air before passing sentence. 'I don't know what to make of it,' he would say with a reproachful look on his face, 'it never entered my head that you would do such a thing, that you *could* do such a thing.' And he was quite genuinely puzzled and hurt by their little offences; it was disloyal to him.

'Are you ready, Sister?' He stood by the desk patting his pockets to make sure that he had matches and cigarettes. 'Have you packed some splints?'

'Yes, Doctor,' she answered, closing the bag with a snap and starting towards the door. He hurried in front of her carrying a khaki-coloured bag. They reached the jeep and he drove busily past the wards, looking up into the sky with a puzzled frown on his face as though he was not quite sure whether he could hear the sound of planes behind the noise of his own engine.

They drove quickly by the side of the glittering lake, and Helen turned a little away from Rowland and tried to feel unhappy and sentimental, but it was not very easy. As the days had gone by she found it more and more difficult to remember what Kent had looked like. She knew that he was tall and had fair hair, but she

86

could not remember the colour of his eyes nor the shape of his mouth. She was often irritated to find that when she tried to conjure up Kent's face she only saw Robert's features. She knew that she was more than merely fond of Robert, and that he was in love with her, but there was no conflict in her mind as to which of the two she would marry if she had the choice. And she realized that she would prefer to marry almost any Englishman than Robert. She knew that it was wrong, and very unjust to Robert, but she could not help it, and she thought to herself that Robert after all was a man and men did not suffer like women, for instance they did not cry as easily as women, except sometimes when their mothers died. They made a lot of fuss when they were ill, but that was only male vanity wanting a little attention. And although Robert was in love with her at the minute he would soon forget all about it and settle down happily with someone else. Many girls, she reflected virtuously, would keep Robert as a second string and encourage him while Tony was away; she on the contrary had discouraged him, and once when it had been impossible to stop him asking her to marry him she had said immediately that she was not in love with him. It was true that when he asked if she was in love with Kent she had denied it vehemently, but that was a permissible lie, it was nothing to do with him.

The road swung away from the lake, and the scattered hovels grew in numbers and size until they were in the main street of the town; she looked back and saw that the ambulance had caught up with them. The street was crowded with people, and already there were a few bullock-carts standing outside some of the shops being loaded with the pathetically valuable stocks and machinery, lengths of cheap cloth, and foot-driven sewing-machines. The people stood about in groups and talked excitedly, but there was no laughter; they were constantly looking up to the sky and when the groups broke up everyone would hurry away and the women called angrily to their children.

Rowland drove slowly along the street until they came to the square in the middle of the town where the weekly markets were held. A few bombs had made shallow saucers in the ground and the white stucco buildings were pocked with fragments. He stopped by one of the craters and looked at it with disgust.

'Call that a crater! A hand grenade could have done better than that, still I suppose it's all that's necessary to start these stinking places burning.' The columns of smoke were swirling into the sky, and they could hear the sharp explosions of bamboo and the shrill cries of women. A group of Indian supply troops appeared on

87

the other side of the square pulling a bullock-cart. They saw the ambulance standing near the jeep and came towards it.

Rowland called to Robert: 'Pull into the shade and get them to lay the wounded on the ground until I can sort them out', then he drove the jeep into the shade against the front of a shop.

A small crowd was already collecting, and when the bullock-cart had been pulled into the shade the onlookers began to close in and peer at the casualties. Rowland had to push his way through the people in order to reach the cart. There were three men and a woman with a child lying beside her. The child and one of the men were dead, the remainder lay still with closed eyes and Rowland began his examination immediately. Most of the wounds were below the level of the chest, and he remembered the shallow craters. He wanted to give the survivors an injection of morphia but supplies were very limited. He decided to drug the woman as quickly as possible to stop her hysterics when she was put in the ambulance, and the child was left in the square.

While he prepared the hypodermic he glanced up at one of the Indian soldiers.

'Are there a lot of casualties?'

'I don't know, Sahib, the police officer sahib is down in the bazaar arranging everything.'

'Go back now and ask him from the doctor sahib how many more wounded there are likely to be.' He spoke in bad Urdu and nearly added that he would leave the bodies in the square for the civil authorities to dispose of, but he thought that perhaps the woman might understand and he said nothing. As he bent over the woman again the crowd craned forward and Helen turned on them angrily, ordering them away. Impassively, unresentfully they went slowly back for a few yards and then squatted down again on their heels, their out-stretched arms resting on their knees.

Two of the hospital orderlies brought stretchers from the ambulance and laid them down by the side of the cart. Rowland spoke to them quietly, pointing to the two men, and they lifted them very gently on to the stretchers. They made no sound when they were moved, but as the orderlies touched them they opened their eyes and looked into the sky, filled with sadness that this disaster should have happened to them, wondering when their families would find them.

The orderlies laid the dead man in the shadows and covered him with a blanket. One of them looked enquiringly at Rowland and then at the woman. He waited a few moments for the drug to take effect and then nodded; they took the child and laid it under the same blanket as the man. Then they carried the woman to the ambulance and put the men in after her.

'Take this lot to the hospital and then come straight back, Sergeant, and you had better bring another ambulance with you.' Already there were groups of people coming towards them from the direction of the fires, bringing more casualties. They worked on steadily until the two ambulances returned, and just before they were both filled a car drove into the square and pulled up near Rowland.

'Morning, Doc, how goes it?' Rowland turned round and smiled at the man getting out of the car.

'Ah! Grant, there you are. Did you get my message about casualties?'

'Yes, I'm sorry I couldn't let you know earlier but I had to go round all the different spots trying to get an estimate. There shouldn't be more than about twenty-five that will concern you, I should think you've probably got them all here already. Thanks very much for coming down and giving us a hand.'

'Think nothing of it, my dear chap, only too delighted to be of some assistance. Are there many killed?'

'We've counted twenty so far, I don't think there will be many more.' He looked at the blanketed figure. 'If you have any more die on you leave them here in the square, I shall be sending some police round collecting all the bodies once we've got the fires under control. And you might also leave the blanket there, will you, it'll stop the crows and dogs having a go. I'll send a peon back with it to the hospital tomorrow. I must push on now if you'll excuse me.'

'Yes, of course, I've got a lot to get on with myself. Come up tonight and have a drink with us or some food.'

Grant hesitated a moment, weighing the bother of having to shave and change against the advantages of a few stiff Scotches and an hour's gossip. 'Thank you, Doc, I'd like to but dinner's impossible, I'm afraid; could I come for an hour at about six-thirty?'

'Yes, rather, that will suit us magnificently.'

Grant got back into his car feeling very pleased with himself. Now he could look forward to an evening alone in his own bungalow; his wife had left for the north only a few days before and his solitude was still a delightful novelty.

It was nearly midday before the last casualty had been sent back to the hospital and the shade in the square had shrunk until it was only a narrow strip on the southern side. Flies were settling on the patches of blood and one or two dogs had been attracted by the smell and stood just out of range of the stones that the orderlies had thrown at them when they first came sniffing round. The busy life of the town had not returned, the relatives of the wounded had left the square and were walking to the hospital, and the onlookers had at last become bored and wandered away. Today no one sat in the shade with a few limp vegetables or exhausted chickens to sell, and the children had disappeared. Helen tried to tell herself that it was hardly surprising, it was the first time they had been bombed, and of course everyone was frightened. They were probably staying near their homes in case sparks from the fires settled on their bamboo houses or else they were digging the shelters they had been told to do months ago and had not done, but she was unable to rid herself of a feeling of depression. It was as though in the course of a few brief seconds the town had died and would never come to life again.

They drove back to the hospital slowly; they were both tired from constantly bending low over the wounded and in the sheltered square the sun had struck at them fiercely. Helen was thirsty, and the unaccustomed cigarette Rowland had given her was bitter and strange in her mouth. She looked at the lake and longed to be able to take off her clothes and lie in the cool waters, but that of course was impossible; only the poorest of the Burmese and Indians bathed in public.

They turned into the hospital drive and drew up outside Rowland's office and he raced the engine, switching it off as it reached a crescendo.

'Quite a morning, Sister.' He stretched his arms above his head and yawned; as he bent his head back and closed his eyes the sun was hot on his face. He was very satisfied with life. Now he would go round the wards and see that everything was in order and then there would be time for one, possibly two, large pink gins before lunch. 'I've asked Grant to come up for a drink before dinner this evening, perhaps you would like to come along too. I'm sure he would rather look at a pretty girl like you than talk to me. I'll ask Welsh to come as well.'

'Thank you very much, I'd like to.' As always she was surprised and pleased by such an invitation, and as she walked to her own quarters before going round the wards her depression left her.

Back in the town most of the fires had been put out and the work of digging a communal grave was far advanced. Some of the dead were Hindus and the relatives had wanted to burn the bodies, but the arrangements and ceremonies would have taken too long and

90

the day was uncomfortably hot. Grant had ordered that everyone should be buried by sundown and was surprised by the lack of opposition on the part of the Indians; men who the day before would have rioted rather than allow their relatives to endure the uneasy horrors of a communal grave now stood in front of him with downcast eyes, and having satisfied their consciences by asking, agreed to whatever arrangements he ordered.

And when he sent them away they went back to their homes and started to pack their belongings and prepare to leave, without any clear idea as to why and with only a vague notion of going toward India. It was a phenomenon that was taking place all over the country; a few bombs would fall and immediately there would begin an exodus of Indians. People who had lived all their lives in the same town, and their fathers before them, would decide independently of any advice outside their family circle to leave at once for India. It was said that they were afraid of the bombing, afraid of the Burmese or Japanese, but it was none of these things. A sixth sense warned them that the country as they knew it was dying, and that if they stayed they would die as well.

In the evening when Grant drove out to the hospital there were already a few family groups walking slowly by the side of bullock-carts piled high with luggage, luggage that in the weeks to come was to kill its possessors by the score. He stopped the car and asked two of the groups where they were going and the men answered evasively, not because they were ashamed of leaving or were frightened that they would be turned back, but because they themselves scarcely knew; they were going towards India and more they were unable to say. He told them vehemently that they were mad to go, that there was nothing to be frightened of, and they agreed and said that they would only go to the next town where they had relatives and would return in a few days. But that was only courtesy as both they and Grant well knew, and when he drove on he was disturbed and restless.

He reached the hospital and a peon took him to Rowland's quarters. Stopping on the road had made him late; the two men had finished their first drink and Helen had arrived. Rowland introduced him effusively, and when they had settled down in their wicker-chairs he put his feet on the veranda rail to show Grant that there was a war on and formality a thing of the past.

'Did you hear the six o'clock news?' he asked.

'No, I didn't; was there anything startling?'

'Oh no, a bit of bombing on London, but nothing very much. They mentioned Burma right at the end, as usual, something about our patrols being active and casualties on both sides, so we can expect some more patients in a day or two. God! Was I furious when they dumped us here! You know we were all set to go with that brigade and then at the last minute they discovered that there weren't enough ambulances or the right equipment or something like that, the usual sort of mess-up. I wonder how long some of these people would last in civvy street if they ran things there in the same way as they do in the Army.' He took a deep drink and was pleased at having made one of his favourite little speeches to such an appropriate person. Poor chap, he thought to himself. It wasn't his fault, of course, that he was a civilian, someone had to carry on with policing, although young Corry had managed to get himself released. He paused while Welsh spoke to Helen and then turned to Grant again.

'How's young Corry getting on, do you ever hear from him?'

'Oh yes, he's doing fine. He's attached to the Frontier Force and goes round the various villages near the Siamese border picking up information. The trouble is that there's too much information. He only has to appear and they all rush at him with stories, hoping to get a few cigarettes or money. And if he mentions anything he's heard from the next village it's always flatly denied.'

Helen broke in, leaning forward in her chair and speaking seriously: 'But surely it's very difficult to get any information in the jungle. Any number of men could hide without being found out or giving themselves away, it's almost uninhabited.'

'No,' he said, 'all the mountainous country round Burma is surprisingly thickly populated, and the jungle is infinitely various. When people talk about jungle they usually picture a tangle of creepers and vines hanging in festoons from enormous trees set almost trunk to trunk and the ground a swamp. Through this the white man is supposed to stagger, clutching wildly at creepers to prevent himself from being swallowed alive and letting go with a half-stifled cry of horror when the creeper turns into a snake. It's not like that at all. There are some deep valleys in the hills where the jungle is certainly very thick, but they're exceptional. Generally speaking, jungle is hilly and there are a lot of trees and under-growth but it's not impenetrable, and any flat country in the hills is invariably cultivated. The whole of the area that Corry is covering is dotted with villages wherever there's a constant supply of water and it's flat enough to cultivate, and all these villages are connected by at least one track. If your area of cultivation is ten square miles your village becomes a town of several thousand people, like

Kengtung. If it's only half a square mile you'll have an enchanting little village of a hundred.'

'But aren't these tracks impassable except for human beings?' Welsh asked. 'I mean they're useless for troops to move on because they couldn't use any transport.'

'Yes, that's true up to a point, but the tracks are mostly excellent, your transport gets foxed by things like fords which are passable for mules or bullock-carts but not cars, or else by a short sharp piece of hill only passable for men or mules. Most of the bits in between would be quite all right for motor-bikes and probably jeeps. What I'm really getting at is that it would be impossible for even a small body of men to stick to the ordinary village tracks and keep their presence hidden. If they kept off the tracks and had enough food they could still get through, but their rate of progress would be much slower and less sure. It's difficult to keep direction in the jungle even with a compass, and apart from the minor inconvenience of the undergrowth the ground is rough and difficult and the hills steep. The man-made tracks have already picked the eyes out of all the easier routes. However, the Japs don't seem to be coming that way; now that Malay's gone they can come from the south where the belt of hills is much thinner and less high. And they're through that now.'

'I don't think that matters,' Rowland said, 'I think we've done that on purpose so we can deal with them on the plains. After all we seem to have plenty of troops.'

There was a pause and a slight feeling of unease. The whole of the progress of their war had been a series of disasters, Pearl Harbour and Hong Kong and now Singapore. It all seemed fantastically improbable and indecently quick.

'I'm sure it will be all right,' Helen said, thinking of Kent, 'after all we've got wonderful troops and now Malay's gone they're sure to reinforce us straight away.'

'I hear there's a whole new division landed at Rangoon,' Welsh said, 'and there's talk of an armoured division as well.'

The conversation became the inevitable review of the whole war and its possible repercussions on Burma until Grant looked at his watch. 'I must run along now. Thanks a lot for a most enjoyable drink; you must all come to me next week. We'll fix a day tomorrow; I shall have to come up here to find out about the casualties.'

They watched him walk away from the veranda and made polite and meaningless conversation until he was out of hearing in case he should think they were going to discuss him behind his back.

Grant knew that they were, but he cared neither one way nor the other. He felt sad and at the same time excited. As he drove by the side of the lake he decided not to go back to his bungalow; there was a small club on the outskirts of the town and he drove towards it, looking forward to the drink that was waiting for him, hoping that the club would be empty. He wanted to steep himself in the familiar shabbiness of tattered magazines and dusty punkahs, and the bamboo chairs that always seemed to have one leg shorter than the others. He started to drive more quickly, as though he was late for an appointment.

Helen finished her ten o'clock round and left the ward with regret. After dinner she had felt tired and lay down on her bed and slept for almost an hour; now she was wide awake and stood irresolutely on the veranda trying to decide whether to go to the mess and borrow some papers or go to the dispensary and take a sleeping-powder. She heard someone coming towards her from the far end of the long veranda and she recognized Robert's step. She smiled to herself, knowing in advance that he would pretend to be surprised to see her, ready at once with some excuse to explain his presence if she looked at him with the cold accusing stare of the pursued caught by the pursuer.

But tonight she was pleased to see him, she was bored, and at the same time the drinks she had had before dinner still gave her a feeling of restlessness. She waited until he was near enough to see her face in the darkness and then smiled at him.

'Hullo, Robert, what are you doing up so late?'

'Is it late? I didn't know, I have been writing letters.' He glanced down, wondering why it was that he told more lies to the person he was most fond of than to anyone else, and half expecting her to take him up and ask him to whom he had written. 'One of the other sisters ought to have done your round tonight,' he put in quickly, 'you must be worn out after this morning. Did you manage to have a rest before dinner?'

'Don't be silly, of course not. Besides I had to go and have drinks with Dr Rowland, he had some people in. Well, not people exactly, but Dr Welsh and Mr Grant were there; he's the head of the police for the district,' she added nonchalantly.

'Was he a nice man?' Robert asked, making an effort to keep any trace of jealousy out of his voice.

'Oh yes, charming. We got on awfully well together, like old friends.' Her feeling of well-being made her relent: 'He's married, his wife's in Maymyo. Not because she's frightened of the bombing,

94

of course, but he's away from home so much nowadays that she is staying with friends.' She had no idea at all why Mrs Grant should be in Maymyo, but she didn't look on her statement as being untrue. Ever since she had been brought in closer contact with the English she had endowed all those who were even remotely polite to her with all the virtues, and the endowment was prodigal enough to embrace their relatives and friends.

'Oh, I see,' Robert answered, both the Grants being swept to oblivion by the wave of relief at hearing that he was married. Helen seemed to be in a very good mood; he decided to take a chance.

'Shall we go for a very, very short walk, just down to the lake and back? It's a lovely night, and it's really quite cool.' He stopped, sweating, telling himself not to argue with her if she said that she would rather not come; that she would refuse simply because he wanted her to so badly.

Helen looked over her shoulder towards the lake. It gleamed through the scattered clumps of oleanders and the bright moon splintered itself on the almost motionless palm fronds by the edge of the lake; it was beautiful and the silence invited her.

'Yes, all right,' she said, 'but we mustn't be too long, just there and back, it might make me sleepy.' As they went down the steps the moon shone on her white uniform and she felt as though she had stepped into a patch of limelight on a dark stage. She stopped and drew back into the shadows.

'Robert, run and get my cloak, please, it's hanging outside the ante-room of the mess.' He went quickly away in case she should change her mind. She stood in the shadow looking at the night and the lake, telling herself how beautiful it was and how much she was in love with Kent. She tried to imagine where he was and what he was doing, and she closed her eyes and kept repeating to herself I love you, I love you. She wished her eyes would fill with tears, not so as to overflow because Robert might notice, but enough to make the palms swim in the moonlight. When Robert came hurrying back she slipped the cloak over her shoulders and pulled the hood almost over her head. She walked quickly until they were partly hidden from the sprawling hospital by the first clumps of bushes and then more slowly, watching the uneven ground with its patches of withered grass. She would have liked to have taken Robert's arm but she was afraid that he might misunderstand her and start talking about his love. Besides, it would have spoilt the effect of her cloak, which billowed softly around her.

The lake was little more than a hundred yards away, and when they reached the edge they stood silently looking across the water and up at the almost full moon. Towards the centre of the lake a cat's-paw of wind made an irregular patch of light, and nearer at hand a fish broke the surface noiselessly and the silver ripples spread towards them. A little to their right was a clump of squat palm-trees that threw its shadow to the edge of the water and Robert touched her arm through her cloak and they moved slowly towards it. They stood together in the shadows and Robert leant his body as near her as he dared, waiting nervously for her to edge away, but she stood still.

It was better to stand in the shadows, she thought, they were less likely to be seen from the hospital. She started to think about Kent and then she noticed that the side of Robert's body was touching hers; she felt his arm move and suddenly she was intensely curious to know about his body. Here, under the dark palms.

'What are you thinking about, Helen?' He spoke very softly, gazing into her face, and she raised her head and looked steadily into his eyes.

'Nothing, why?' Her voice was faintly husky, and he thought that she was unhappy.

'What's the matter, you look sad. Are you home-sick?'

'No. Yes, of course I am.' As she looked at his familiar face, at the dark eyes and skin and straight black hair, she felt desire dwindling away from her, leaving her bewildered and resentful as though he had persuaded her against her will. She could not imagine how a few minutes ago she had felt like . . . like that, it was disgusting and it was all Robert's fault. She turned abruptly.

'Come on, Robert, I'm getting cold and it's very late. Dr Rowland would be furious if he knew, let's get back.'

'All right, Helen.' He caught up with her and they walked silently back, skirting the hospital. When they were still some distance from her quarters she stopped him, not bothering to soften her action.

'Good night, Robert.'

'Good night, Helen, sleep well.' He wanted to say many other things but he sensed her antagonism without understanding its causes. He felt utterly flat and despondent as he turned away to go to his own bunk, but his very misery drove him to scrape up some crumbs of comfort from the wreckage of the evening. To begin with she had been kind and pleasant, agreeing to come for a walk; perhaps if he hadn't been a foul beast pushing his body up against hers they might still be down by the lake. What a fool he was! He knew that she hated anything like that, and quite rightly too. Tomorrow he would apologize, just say: 'I'm sorry about last night', nothing more, not even if she begged him to explain. In her heart of hearts she would know what he meant. It was a lucky thing for him that she was so good, he need never be jealous, not really jealous.

By the time he fell asleep he had made almost a loaf out of his crumbs.

12

Kent lay on his back with his eyes shut, trying to imagine that he was asleep, and only dreaming that Anson was shaking him awake, but all the time a chill was spreading in his mind, he was like a man awaking from a drunken sleep who looks vacantly at the grey fingers of light moving his curtains, he begins to push the jig-saw fragments of his memory with the tip of his finger and slowly, with a growing sense of disaster, the pattern takes shape, a drunken public quarrel, an uncontrollable flood of tears, the betrayal of a great confidence. And he closes his eyes again with a groan of despair.

He tried to turn away, and the movement of his arm broke the newly formed scab, and the pain made him open his eyes. He turned his face towards Anson, but it was black inside the truck, and he could see nothing; outside men were whispering, and then a machine-gun started firing and was taken up by others until the noise ran in a wide half-circle round their front.

'What's the matter, what's happening?' His whisper was still thick with sleep.

'It's the Japs, sir. The sergeant-major's sent a runner back wanting to know if you're fit enough to come to the company, he's waiting outside.' Kent lay still on the stretcher, dully resenting the fact that he always had to make the decisions himself, wishing that someone would send him an order, you *will* go to the company or you *will* stay in the ambulance.

'Tell him to wait a few minutes while I get dressed, and come back and give me a hand.'

'Yes, of course, sir.'

He lay back waiting for Anson to return. His mouth felt bitter and foul, and he longed for a mug of tea; but there was no point in asking for it, if any had been made Anson would find it. He heard him come back and guessed by the way he climbed into the lorry that he was carrying a mug.

'I managed to get some tea, sir, the orderlies brewed it up on a spirit lamp.' He put his arm round Kent's shoulders and helped him to sit up. Their hands moved cautiously together in the dark and Kent took a few big sips before pushing the mug towards Anson.

'Fifty-fifty.'

'I've had mine, sir.'

'Shut up.' Together they finished the tea and Kent began to feel better, although he was still very tired and his body was heavy from morphia. He dressed slowly, pretending to himself that his arm was much more stiff and painful than was the case, trying to prolong the atmosphere of comfort and security of the canvas walls, reluctant to step outside and take up again the burden of decisions. He thought angrily that another inch either way would have been much better, either he would have had a wound that would have made it impossible for him to stay on duty, or he would have had nothing.

'How's your arm feel, sir, is it all right?'

'It's a bit funny and stiff but I think it will be O.K., don't worry about it.' In the dark he could hear Anson shaking out his equipment.

'I only hope it'll make you a bit more careful in future, sir. It's not your job doing things like you did yesterday.'

'Isn't it? I suppose not, but someone's got to do them, haven't they?'

'Yes, but not you, not all the time. You're too easy, sir, you ought to make other people do these things.'

'I don't like to,' Kent answered, smiling grimly to himself in the darkness. It was funny, playing the part of a hero when really he was too weak to tell anyone else to do it. 'Anyway, I'll remember what you say, and the next time something like that comes along I'll send you.'

'Right, sir.' And Kent was fiercely and bitterly jealous, knowing that Anson meant exactly what he said, that he was not afraid at all.

'Stop yammering like an old woman and give me my equipment. It's bad enough as it is without having you telling me how to run my own company.' He turned his back and held his arms behind him, deliberately putting the conversation out of his mind. As Anson helped him on, carefully keeping the straps away from his injured arm, their attitudes suddenly reminded him of Celia, helping him on with his overcoat as he left for the office. He smiled again, wishing she could see him now, unshaved and in a blood-stained shirt, strapping on his equipment and listening to the interrupted sounds of firing.

He finished buckling his belt, and struck a match to see if anything had been forgotten; while the flame was still burning they went to the end of the lorry and Anson held back the canvas flap for Kent to jump down. The day was just beginning to form in the east and he could see some yards ahead; it was cold, and he could hear the dew falling from the trees on to the ground. There was a *chagal* of water hanging on the back of one of the trucks and he filled his bottle from it.

The runner came up and saluted, and Kent was surprised and rather annoyed that he did not enquire about his arm. They made their way through the wet bushes, and when they reached the road turned towards the sound of the firing. A little further on they came to a group of people talking by the side of the road; they were almost level before Kent recognized the C.O. and he stopped.

'Hullo, Tony, nice to see you up. I was worried in case you weren't going to be fit enough; how is it?'

'It's all right, thank you, sir.'

'You don't sound very enthusiastic about it, are you quite sure?'

'Yes, really, sir, it's a bit stiff perhaps but that'll wear off.' The presence of the commanding officer acted, as always, like balm to Kent's mind, as though for a short time he was relieved of all worry and responsibility.

'Well, that's good; I was just coming along to find out. We're pulling out of here straight away, your company first. There's a battalion of Gurkhas behind us in position across the road, we're to withdraw through them as soon as we can. Have your scouts out, of course, but the road has been patrolled by armoured cars, and as far as we know it's still clear.' He peered at his watch. 'It's just about five-thirty now, and I've told Tarrant to start your company moving at 05.45. You're to go on until you reach our advance party nine miles away. Get everyone fed as soon as you arrive and Norton will show you where to go. We shall be right behind you, and I'll call a conference as soon as I possibly can after I get there.'

'Right, sir.' He glanced at the people standing with the C.O. and noticed one of them wearing the brigade headquarters' insignia. He stepped back and stood to attention. 'I'm afraid I can't salute, sir.' He smiled at the C.O.

'That doesn't matter, Tony, get along now and find Tarrant.'

Further up the road he met the first sections of his company straggling out of the bushes on the right of the road and falling in. As he walked by he noticed that one man held a lighted cigarette in his cupped hand. He went up to him.

'What the hell do you think you're doing, Viner. Put that

bloody cigarette out.' The man dropped it sullenly on the ground and put his foot on it. Kent glanced at some of the other faces he could see; they looked grey and tired. As always when someone in authority spoke sharply they looked anywhere but in his direction. He walked on down the road and heard Tarrant's voice, speaking as quietly as his exasperation would let him, urging everyone to hurry on to the road as quickly as possible. He was standing with his back to Kent, who walked up behind him and put his hand on his shoulder.

'I'm back.'

'Hullo, sir! I'm delighted to see you. Will you take over now?'

'In a minute. You carry on and get them moving and I'll march with you for a bit.'

Tarrant bustled up and down the line of men, pouring abuse on the late-comers and cursing the N.C.O.s for not, as he put it, getting a grip on these dozy bastards, and Kent knew that they were muttering obscenities at him under their breath. In spite of their tired looks there was an air of urgency about them as they fell in. Tarrant hurried to the head of the column, looking at his watch, and in the dim light Kent could see the first section move off, with two men hurrying in front to act as scouts. Each section left an interval of thirty yards and Kent joined Tarrant behind the leading platoon. They marched in silence down the road and past the group of officers, who still talked together, not looking at the men as they marched by, and a little further on Kent saw a section of Gurkhas lying by the side of the road with a Bren gun in position and a British officer standing behind them. He waited until he judged they were clear of the battalion and then he spoke.

'How was it last night, what time did the firing start?'

'About three o'clock, I think, but if you ask me I don't think there were any Japs there at all, not until much later, I think our firing brought them on to us. The C.O. was hopping mad about it. One of the forward sections had a bit of jungle in front of them and swore they had seen the Japs moving in it and started firing, and of course everybody saw Japs except us, all we could see were the backs of the company in front. Then about four-thirty the Japs did start firing tracer at us from two points. I went forward through the other company, but it was almost impossible to judge how far away they were.'

'In spite of the tracer?' Kent asked curiously. 'I should have thought it would have been easy.'

'Well, it wasn't,' Tarrant said quickly and then paused. 'It seems a funny idea, doesn't it, using tracer at night. As though they wanted us to come and find them.'

'I expect that's what it was,' Kent answered casually, but it struck a chill in his mind; it seemed unnatural, on a par with using a sword.

'Did you have a good night, sir? How's the arm?'

'I had a fine night, and my arm's all right until people start asking about it and then I think perhaps I ought to have it off.' They marched on in silence and then Kent spoke again: 'This pulling back the whole time seems odd to me. I know it's got nothing to do with the C.O., but we couldn't be going back faster if we had a hundred Jap divisions after us.'

'I expect the high-ups know something we don't,' Tarrant said confidently. 'I've heard a rumour that we're being sent right back to Mandalay and being joined by a new division that's marching in from India.'

'Do you mean we're going back straight away?' Kent asked, his voice a mixture of hope and disbelief.

'I'm not sure about that, but it would be a bit of all right, wouldn't it? Mandalay's a big place, plenty of good grub and women.'

Yes, it would be a bit of all right, Kent's mind echoed Tarrant's words. If one has to do something as unpleasant as fighting at least it ought to have a civilized background, one should be allowed every fourth night off and a half-day once a week, there should be luxurious hotels where one could bath and sleep and ring bells for servants to come and tie one's laces. As things were, the height of comfort was a stretcher in the back of a dirty lorry. He turned to Tarrant again.

'I never saw the M.O. this morning; what's happened to Goodwin, don't tell me he's dead?'

'I wouldn't be knowing for sure, but I'm fairly certain he was sent back last night by ambulance. I'm told they were trying to get him away with one or two others who were sick, but evidently he wasn't as badly wounded as we thought. You don't sound very upset about him, sir.' Tarrant glanced at Kent; he was smiling and at the same time there was an underlying suggestion of amused malice, and Kent knew he was thinking that his interest in the men's welfare was wearing thin now that the testing time had come.

'No, you're quite right,' he answered, 'I'm not upset at all. Have you any news of those two men missing from Bonar's patrol, they've not shown up yet, have they?'

'Not a word. I expect the Japs have got them by now.'

'You don't sound very upset either.'

'No, I'm not, but if you'll forgive my saying so I've never

pretended anything else. You forget that I'm one of them, and I understand the men in a way that you never could. You thought you could come along and by being kind and reasonable alter their whole outlook and characters; it was as big a slice of conceit as any I've seen, and I've seen plenty from young officers, and old ones, in the last twenty years. You think you can persuade men to be brave and uncomplaining by making yourself popular and setting a good example. Believe me you can't; the way this army's run you can only do it by discipline and punishment, proper punishment, not a couple of years' jail for desertion of which they'll only serve fifteen months. But you've been different with them lately, and I'm glad, for all our sakes.'

'That's ridiculous!' Kent interrupted quickly. He was surprised and annoyed that Tarrant should have been so outspoken, the fact that it was the truth only made it the more unpalatable. 'Of course I know they're not miracles of goodness and bravery, but I don't consider they're any worse or any better than other people. If you treat them in such a way that they can tell you've got a low opinion of them then naturally they're going to behave badly. The difference between you and me is that I try and treat them as I would like to be treated if I was a private soldier.'

'Well, it's no good arguing about it, you've got your opinion, and I've got mine. But I do know that you're different to these people, and what might apply to you doesn't apply to them. Look, supposing we were sent to Mandalay and the C.O. had you up and said that in order to set a good example to the men you weren't to stop out after ten o'clock. Even if you knew that you couldn't be found out you would do what the C.O. said. And then you passed that order on to the company; would you rely on just telling them or would you have patrols out in the city?'

'I'd have patrols out, of course, but then I'm an individual and a request or an order's always much stronger if it's made to one person than if it's made to a hundred. You know that.'

'Up to a point, yes, but you don't seem to realize that you're a civilian and most of these men have been regulars since they were eighteen. The majority of them have got into a habit of disobedience, it's looked on as smart, and it's the easiest way they know of asserting themselves as individuals. There's no conscience about them; if they can do something wrong and get away with it, that's being clever. I'll put it this way. If practically any man in the company had been nicked in the arm like you he would have been on his way back in the same ambulance as Goodwin. And if by some miracle one of them had said to the M.O.: "It's only a scratch, it'll be all right", the rest of the company either wouldn't believe it or else they'd think that he had been walking about in the sun with his hat off.'

'Do you blame them?' Kent asked with a faint smile, remembering his regrets that he too would not be jolted about in an ambulance, drowsy with morphia, his arm useless.

'I don't blame them, but it's our job to see they don't get away with things like that, and I'm glad that you're not feeling so soft towards them.' He smiled, trying to end the conversation flippantly.

Kent shrugged his shoulders in a vague way and said nothing. He knew that everything Tarrant had said about his feelings towards the men was true, and that the process had started from the moment he realized that he might be killed within the next few weeks or months. As the course of events had unfolded over the preceding weeks the thought of death had crept into his mind until subconsciously it dominated everything else, and he had thought more and more about himself and the miracle of living. The taste of a cigarette, the smell of a flower, or the sound of running water, everything that he did or saw took on a deep significance. With a shock he suddenly saw how far he had withdrawn into himself during the last weeks until nothing that happened to other people seemed real; the death of his men yesterday had left him completely unmoved except for a feeling of horror that what had happened to them might also happen to him. And yet if pity came to him as it still did sometimes, without warning because the cause would be so trivial, then it struck at him with a piercing intensity that he had learnt to fear.

He would have forgotten the ten-minute halt at the end of the hour's march if Tarrant had not reminded him. Unnoticed by him the character of the country had changed and the semi-metalled road had petered out into a wide dusty track with broad verges of baked earth and scorched grass, the paddy-fields had given way to country that had imperceptibly risen above irrigation level and was covered by a tangle of tall scrub and studded with bushy trees. It stretched away in front of him as far as he could see, a curiously untidy country; some of the scrub was leafless and some was covered with matted festoons of loofah creeper or was green with leaves.

He halted the company and sent the leading platoon to the other side of the track, ordering everyone to take cover in the scrub and face outwards while they rested. It was impossible for most of them to see more than a few yards through the undergrowth, but at least it was some protection against surprise. When everyone was lying down he walked past the end of the line and made his way into the scrub for some distance, then he squatted down and lit a cigarette. It was very quiet, the sky was fresh and of a deep blue, there was a film of gold in the upper air from the sun that was still below the ridge to the east. He stayed squatting longer than he need have done, wanting to prolong this moment of peace and privacy, but the back of his knees began to ache and he finished and stood up.

While he was making his way through the scrub again he heard a faint hum from the direction in which they had come. As he identified it as the noise of planes the rhythm of the engines was broken by a sound like a roll of drums and then came the rumble of explosions. He started to run through the scrub towards the company, and all at once the noise had become deafening and swept over his head to die away along the track. He reached the first section and called for the commander.

'Did you see those planes?' he asked.

'Yes, sir, three of them, they looked like ours to me.'

'So they might be, the Japs are probably using our planes captured in Singapore. Anyway if they come back take cover, and if they open fire on us fire back whether they're our markings or not.' Kent walked down the line of men repeating his instructions and Tarrant told the platoon on the other side of the track. The column started again, but now it was more widely spaced and the men kept as near the cover of the scrub as they could. Kent sent Tarrant back to the rear of the column to see that the sections kept their proper intervals, and told Anson to march next to him.

The track began to climb a shallow slope, and as they were about to reach the crest there was a sudden roar of engines and Anson had a vague impression of Kent pitching forward on his face and men hurling themselves into the scrub; then he found himself lying under a small bush burying his face in his arms, listening to the whip of bullets smacking towards him up the track with the speed of sound. He knew that only his head and shoulders were under the bush, and suddenly the rest of his body felt enormous, a target that it would be impossible to miss; then everything was wiped out of his mind as he realized that he had left Kent on the track. He lifted his head to see if Kent was hit. He saw him lying on the verge of the track in full view of the planes, his strained face turned towards the cover, his eyes shut. The plane had gone past, its bullets had lashed up a thin haze of dust from the track. A terrible pain filled Anson's chest and throat as he looked at Kent lying so still by the side of the track and then he saw him move, and he started to get up himself to go and help when the next

104

plane was on them without the slightest warning. Anson looked at it, lying on the ground with his head craned back and his mouth open. It seemed to come towards them very slowly and close to the ground, he noticed the tips of the wings swaying slightly up and down, and then its guns began to fire and he bowed his head down to the ground. Dust and earth sprang from the ground in front of them and raced over their bodies; a muscle in Anson's calf jerked when a small stone fell on it. When he opened his eyes he saw Kent walking quite slowly towards the scrub and stand against it so that he could watch the sky and he got up and joined him. He was confused by the violence of his emotion when he thought that Kent was dead and ashamed that he had left his side. He wanted to speak about it, but there were some men lying very close to them in the scrub and he said nothing. Further down the track they heard one of the planes fire a short burst and then there was silence.

'O.K., everyone,' Kent shouted, 'all clear. Fall in again as quick as you can.' The men scrambled to their feet, brushing their clothes with their hands, asking one another if they wanted to borrow a clean pair of drawers and whether they had remembered to wave to the nice pilot.

Towards the end of the third hour's march Kent began to feel traces of fatigue, sweat trickled down his forehead and the back of his neck, gathering at his chin and splashing on his dusty shirt. Dark patches spread from his armpits and showed beneath the thick stiff belt round his waist. The right side of his face burnt from the sun that had struck beneath the brim of his hat and he began to wonder if there was a slight soreness about his right heel. The thought worried him; it would be a serious thing if a blister began to form at this stage; if it did he would be crippled before the day was over.

He moved to one side of the column to avoid the dust and gazed up the track for any signs of the advance party, but it was lifeless except for a shimmer of heat and a drab white butterfly that could not make up its mind whether to fly on the right side or the left. About a mile away the scrub gave place to a solid square of dark green and Kent recognized it as a rubber plantation and guessed that it would be the rendezvous; when they came to within a few hundred yards he could see Norton standing by the edge of the plantation. Tarrant joined him, and they halted the men and went forward to where Norton was standing in front of a group of fresh-looking administrative N.C.O.s.

'Hullo, old man! Was that you having an argument with those planes? Have any casualties?' Norton asked breezily.

'No casualties, but they weren't firing blank. I think they must have had a crack at the rest of the battalion, I don't know if they had any casualties or not.'

'Oh well, we shall soon know. I'm glad you've arrived, we had a party of Indian troops here about half an hour ago with an old Burman in tow. Luckily one of them spoke fairly reasonable English and told us that the old man had seen what he took to be a party of Japs about two miles to the north of us, beyond the far corner of this plantation. As soon as you get your men fed I want you to take up a position along the edge of the plantation covering that corner. This is about half a mile square I reckon, you'll be responsible for a quarter of a mile each side of the north-west corner.'

'Right,' Kent answered, thinking that it was just his luck to be put furthest away from battalion headquarters, which would be here, nearest the road. But that was not the sort of thing one could mention, even jokingly. 'While the men are getting fed I want to go somewhere and have a look at my arm. I jolted it up badly when those planes came over. Where's the best place?'

'I should think behind those lorries over there, the drivers will have some water. Is there anything I can do to help?'

'No thanks, my orderly will look after me. Send Anson over to me, will you, Tarrant, and you carry on getting the men fed and in position.'

By the time he reached the small group of lorries Anson had caught up with him. 'Let's get cleaned up first and eat afterwards,' Kent said. 'I told them I wanted to look at my arm but I don't really, I'd rather not disturb the bandage, all I want to do is wash and shave and look at my feet. Is that all right with you, or do you want to go and eat?'

'No, sir, I can hang on for some time yet, I'd rather get you cleaned up first.' It was cool and pleasant under the thick shade of the rubber-trees, away from the glare of the sun on the light-coloured track and the rising dust. There were some kerosene tins of water standing near them, and Kent found a ground-sheet in one of the lorries and spread it on the ground. Then he took off his clothes and hung them over the low branch of a tree to dry them a little. His arm was rather more stiff and swollen than it had been, but he thought that it was only due to the three hours' march. He sat down and examined his feet minutely, but he could see nothing that warranted using any of his precious store of elastic tape.

'How are we off for razor blades?' he asked as he started to wash his face.

'Only about ten left, you had a new one in yesterday.'

'I don't care, I'm going to have a new one in today as well.' He washed himself quickly all over, glancing round now and again to see if the battalion had started to arrive. He knew that although nothing would be said his action in leaving the company to go and wash would be frowned on—what was not possible for the men was not possible for the officers; but in his own mind he made his arm sufficient excuse. By the time he was dressed again his cotton vest and drawers were still damp and cold with sweat, but even so he felt infinitely refreshed.

The men were finishing their meal when Kent returned. Tarrant was standing by the edge of the cooking area, and as Kent joined him he called to one of the cooks to bring him a mug of tea. Kent leant against a tree listening to the murmur of conversation and the scratching of spoons in mess-tins as the men scraped out the last shreds of stew. By the time he had finished his tea Anson brought his food and without saying anything took his mug and refilled it. They saw Norton hurrying from the direction of the track and Kent turned to Tarrant.

'Here he comes, I suppose he must have spotted the rest of the battalion. Get the men away from here and into position as soon as possible, I'll join you as soon as I've finished my food.' Tarrant saluted and walked away while Kent continued eating slowly. As soon as Norton came within speaking distance he looked up.

'Don't worry, Tarrant's moving the company to where you said straight away. How far off is the battalion, half a mile?'

'Yes, just about.' A three-ton lorry turned off the track and lumbered slowly into the plantation. 'They've had some casualties from that air attack, this is some of them now.' He stood watching the lorry, his face alive with curiosity. 'I'd better go over and see if they want anything.'

'Don't forget where I am,' Kent called after him as he moved away. 'I'm going over to the company straight away, so you'll know where to find me for the C.O.'s conference.' He suddenly had an unreasoning fear that Norton might forget all about him. He finished his food and as the sections of the battalion turned into the plantation he silently handed Anson his mess-tin and started after the company.

Now that he had eaten he felt lethargic, and dawdled through the plantation, stopping to examine the herring-bone pattern of cuts on the trunks of the trees, picking out little pieces of coagulated rubber and rolling them into a ball. In the centre of the area were some long corrugated iron sheds surrounded by smaller huts, but everything was deserted and silent and gave Kent the impression that it had been abandoned for a long time. When he reached the company's position Tarrant had already sited two platoons along the edge of the trees and had kept the third in reserve so that Kent could, if he wanted, add the finishing touches.

They walked to the extreme corner and stood in the shade while Kent looked at the country. He saw at once, with a feeling of relief, that the position was ideal for defence. He had expected scrub and tall thorn to come almost to the rubber itself and had resigned himself to the necessity of having to put at least one platoon well forward with its sections widely scattered; to have sited it properly and carefully would have taken him at least three-quarters of an hour. But at some time in recent years a large area had been cleared and burnt, and the jungle had not been allowed to rush back again. Moreover, the land sloped gently away to the north and west, and he could see once more the plain of paddy-fields vanishing into the haze that now hid the hills.

'We needn't bother to have anyone out in front,' he said, 'let the third platoon keep well back, at least a hundred and fifty yards, and tell them to rest. They're not to go wandering off under any circumstances. They can also dig a small latrine with their bayonets; warn the other two platoons that they're to use that one and no other. We might be here for the rest of the day for all I know, and I don't want a swarm of flies settling on their filth and then walking all over me. Besides, the C.O. will go mad if he comes here and finds the place confettied with latrine paper. We'll have company H.Q. thirty yards back from this corner and make sure everyone knows where it is. Warn them to watch out for runners coming here, the C.O.'s having a conference some time this morning. While you're seeing to the third platoon I'll have a look at the other two.'

'Right, sir. Do you think we ought to send back to the battalion and borrow some picks and shovels?'

'No, not yet, let's wait and see how long we shall be here, for all I know we might be off again in an hour's time. And if you're thinking of the latrine, by the time they've fiddled about borrowing shovels it'll probably be too late.'

He walked round the two platoons, making some of the men move into better fire positions and talking to the section commanders. The men were tired and dirty. He was constantly being asked what was going to happen next, and whether they were going to move on again that day. Each time he was asked he said that he did not know, and made the same reply to the questions whether it was true that they were going back to Mandalay. He understood their hunger for information, any information, but there was nothing he could do to appease it.

He walked back to the spot he had chosen for his own headquarters and took off his equipment and lay down against a tree. He heard Tarrant come back and he pretended to be asleep, wishing to be alone. He tried to sleep but the ground was too uncomfortable, and he had to shift his position and lie flat on his back. Eventually he managed to relax and his mind drifted towards the borders of sleep without crossing them.

An hour passed before a runner brought him a message to report to the C.O., and he stood up and put on his equipment quickly, excited by the thought that he was about to find out something definite. He noticed that some of the men in the forward platoons had turned round and were watching him hopefully as though they believed that he already knew the plans and they could find out merely by looking at him.

When he reached battalion headquarters he saw a group of officers talking together, and Anson left him and leant against the side of one of the trucks with the other orderlies. Kent joined the group and they talked about the air attack; one of the lorries had been wrecked by a bomb, and the driver killed, three men in Maguire's company wounded by the machine-gunning, someone had had their water-bottle smashed by a bullet without being touched himself and then, ten minutes after it was all over, had hysterics and fainted. Kent laughed with the others, it seemed so incongruous and ludicrous. He turned to Maguire.

'What's happened to him?'

'Oh, I think he's all right now. The last I saw of him he was sitting down under a tree having a nice strong cup of tea and a couple of aspirins. I couldn't see any burnt feathers lying around. A disgraceful carry-on, I've never been so ashamed in my life, and Stack was one of the last people I should ever have expected to have the vapours. He nearly became my batman a month ago, think of that for an escape! That's something one could never live down. If I die today I shall still feel I've had my share of good luck, avoiding that. Did you have any casualties?'

'No, we were lucky. Except that for the last two months I've been telling everyone that the moment they hear a plane they've got to dive for cover, and everyone did it perfectly except me, and I practically ruptured myself diving for the centre of the track. Still I think most people had their eyes quite tightly shut and weren't particularly interested in my whereabouts. That reminds me, where's our lord and master?'

'Brigade sent for him about a quarter of an hour ago. They said they only wanted him for five minutes so I suppose we can compose ourselves and sit in that jeep and be patient for the next hour.'

The four company commanders sat in the jeep and Rogers handed round a half-empty tin of cigarettes.

'Have you got enough?' Maguire asked before he took one.

'Well, I've got another tin that ought to last me three or four days, and the Q.M. thinks he'll have some more in by then, but only those stinking little issue ones made out of bark and bamboo.'

'By that time you'll be able to go shopping in Mandalay,' Brampton said as he lit the cigarette.

'Don't you believe it,' Maguire answered quickly, 'the mere fact that it's been suggested means that it'll never come off. Think of the most unpleasant thing you can and if your mind is nasty and imaginative enough you'll know exactly what we shall be doing this time tomorrow.'

'Then my guess is that we shall all be marching in thick dust with enormous blisters and raging thirsts.'

'You always were an optimist, Tony,' Maguire said, 'that would be child's play compared to what Brigade really have got up their sleeve for us, and what Division have got in store for Brigade would probably send my Mr Stack off again into convulsions.'

They talked on, made unusually amicable by their common difficulties, their laughter and voices pitched a little higher than usual. They had sat in the jeep for nearly three-quarters of an hour before the C.O. returned, and they joined him at the edge of the plantation nearest the track. Kent looked at his face intently and suddenly realized that he was looking at the C.O. in exactly the same way as his own men had looked at him when he left to come to the conference. The thought that his mind and theirs might work in the same way made him uncomfortable.

'I'm afraid I haven't any good news for you,' the C.O. began, 'quite frankly the situation seems to be getting very confused and out of hand. It's now definite that the Japanese force from the Toungoo valley did cross the hills into this one and got across the road some fifteen miles north of Paganle late last night. The force, which was reported two hundred strong south of Paganle, has been re-estimated at a battalion and there are additional reports, not yet verified, of further strong forces coming up this valley. It's clear that at the minute this brigade is number one target for the Japanese.

If they smash us they'll have the whole of this valley, and both divisions will be hopelessly outflanked, and their lines of communication from the north cut. Instead of withdrawing when they do, they're having to keep pace with us. Already Rangoon has been evacuated, and the other division has begun to swing north towards Prome.

'To counteract all this, army headquarters are going to reinforce us with a battalion of tanks from the brigade that arrived from the Middle East a week ago. This valley ends about forty-five miles to the north, and now it's the only place where tanks can get into the valley. There's a river that runs across the mouth of the valley and joins the Irrawaddy near Yenangyaung. There's no road bridge, but a branch line of the railway runs from Toungoo to Yenangyaung and crosses the river at that point. They've got engineers working on it so tanks and transport can cross. The whole brigade is going to fall back and hold that bridge until the tanks arrive, and then we're going to counter-attack with the object of at least retaking Paganle. Once we get the tanks it should be easy, the Japs haven't been able to get any into Burma, and the dry paddy-fields make ideal tank country.'

He looked gravely at the four men. 'Not one word is to be passed on to the battalion about the tanks, otherwise someone will get taken prisoner and might be fool enough or gutless enough to open his mouth. You understand that quite clearly, don't you, all of you. If the Japs get an inkling that they might meet tanks in this valley they'll immediately start rushing up every anti-tank weapon they can lay their hands on. It might wreck the whole of our plans.'

There was a murmur of agreement and he glanced at a piece of paper in his hand, but not because he wanted to refresh his memory. 'All the companies will patrol actively, but no patrol will be away for more than an hour. After the first patrols have come back you will find out from battalion H.Q. whether the next batch are to go out or not. Except you, Kent, your company will not patrol because you had a hard day yesterday. You'll still be responsible for your sector, but make the men rest as much as possible. I warn you all that the river is a long way off still, and that we might have to do it not only in one march but against opposition, and there's damn all water *en route*. Right now we're staying here until the Gurkha battalion has withdrawn past us and then Brigade will let us know when we're to start ourselves. Any questions?'

Maguire looked up. 'Yes, sir. Can you give us any idea when the Gurkhas are likely to be clear of us?'

'No, I'm afraid I can't. The most I can say is that it's about eleven o'clock now and they can't possibly be clear before one. It might be any time after that; they might run into a road block and we should have to go and help them out. I just can't say.'

As they walked away from the conference Maguire came over to Kent. 'Get a nice rest, Tony, you'll be on the road again shortly. Remember what you said about dust and thirst and blisters? They're going to be all yours, plus a road block in the opposite direction to that nice river.' And Kent answered him lightly, but the thought stayed in his mind.

As soon as he arrived back he sent for the platoon sergeants and passed on the gist of what he had been told. Then he settled down and tried to sleep away the time of waiting. But sleep refused to come, an ant would crawl over his bare legs, a fly settle on his face, he would open his eyes and peer up through the thick leaves, trying to catch the sparkle of the sun as they rustled in the wind. As the minutes dragged by he became more and more restless. He decided to go back to the battalion headquarters on some pretext or another. He could find out then if the Gurkhas had already passed. That at least would be a positive piece of information; once that particular uncertainty was out of his mind he thought he would be able to come back and sleep.

He got to his feet and as he did so he heard the faint hum of planes in the far distance, and he went to the edge of the plantation. The noise slowly grew louder but they were flying very high, it took him a long time to pick them out of the dazzling sky but at last he found them and counted five groups of six. Now they were heading away from him towards the north. It gave him a strange feeling to know that in a comparatively few minutes those men above him would be over some town and that people would die, a town that perhaps it would take him days to reach on foot. And of the tiny specks of silver now disappearing one by one, not all would necessarily come back, some might fall out of the blazing sun, smashed, full of fire and tearing icy wind, their goggled and parachuted crew already paralysed with death.

He stepped back under the trees. But the Japanese would not mind at all, he thought. Even if they jumped out of the plane they probably wouldn't bother to open their parachutes. A large hunting wasp flew past him and he watched it out of sight, then he went back again and leant against his tree. Anson was on the ground unpacking his haversack and he looked up at Kent.

'I'm just checking over exactly what you've got, I'm afraid it's not very much. About forty cigarettes, two tins of bully, all your small washing tackle, and a spare pair of socks. We lost everything else in the lorry, except I have got a vest of yours in my pack.'

'It doesn't matter,' Kent said indifferently, 'at least I can't lose anything else, and it's better than having to lug a mass of stuff around. You ought to be very pleased.'

'Well, I'm not, you had a lot of good stuff that you'll need sooner or later. Underclothing and shirts, and that sleeping-bag. It's still cold at night.'

'As soon as you can you had better get some more stuff off the Q.M.,' Kent said. The domestic details bored him, and he was moving away when he saw Tarrant and the C.O. coming towards him.

'I'm having a quick look round, Tony, also to tell you to let the men eat now and be ready to move off at one o'clock. I've just heard from Brigade that we are not to wait for the Gurkhas after all. You will be the last to leave the plantation, Maguire will be in front of you, and he leaves at twelve forty-five. Tarrant tells me that you're all right at the moment for bully beef, but I'll send a truck over here when I get back and you can issue some more out. There will also be a tank of water for the men to fill up their bottles, and make quite certain that they do. We shall march at least until it's dark, and then possibly form a battalion perimeter for the night. I shall be in the front of the battalion if you want me for anything.'

When he finished looking round the position and had moved on to the next company Kent turned to Tarrant: 'That's fine,' he said. 'I had a nasty feeling when I saw him that we were going to have to help those Gurkhas out of a road block or something, or else hang about here for most of the afternoon and then have to march all night. This is just what I wanted to have happen.'

But at two o'clock that afternoon Kent was still in the plantation. He had moved down to his starting point at the proper time only to find that the battalion was halted along the track in front of him. No one knew what was the cause of the delay, there were the usual crop of rumours, the most likely one being that brigade headquarters had started to withdraw and then halted some miles down the road while a company of Indian troops were sent on ahead to investigate a report that a party of Japanese had been seen crossing the road. By half-past two he began to despair of their leaving the plantation that day, and he looked back at the dark avenues of trees with resentment, but suddenly there was a stir in the company in front of them and Maguire shouted back that they were moving.

As he left the plantation he had an unreasoning sense of great relief.

Once on the track again the heat and glare of the sun seemed to strike to the back of his eyes. Although he marched at the head of the company in order to keep a proper interval between himself and Maguire he was soon powdered with dust. In front of him the long file of men disappeared in the haze of dust kicked up by their feet, and sometimes a lorry piled high with bedding and stores would go lurching past sending a thick cloud of choking dust rolling over them like a destroyer laying a smoke screen.

It took almost an hour for the column to spread itself out to its proper intervals, and until it did there were continuous halts ranging in time from a few seconds to several minutes. Although they had only covered a short distance in the hour and a half Kent felt as if he had been marching for a long time and already he would have liked a long drink of water. But once they started moving at a proper pace he settled down and forgot his thirst. At the end of the second hour he walked back down the line and once more warned the platoon sergeants to stop any men drinking water before he gave permission. The breeze was beginning to slacken, and although the day showed signs of wearing itself out it was still extremely hot. The scrub and trees seemed to absorb the fading wind like blotting-paper, and the sweat that had dried on their faces while it trickled towards their necks now dripped from their chins and glistened on their throats. Some of the men sat on the ground with their knees drawn up, smoking cigarettes, but the majority had slipped off their packs and lay on their backs with their eyes closed.

They started marching again, and had covered nearly a mile when Kent heard machine-guns firing and then the sound of planes. Before he could shout instructions the column of men, in front and behind, ran jumping into the scrub and threw themselves down. He looked back quickly and saw a single plane appear above the track and he too ran into the cover and lay on the ground. As the plane passed over him the guns started firing and then that sound was drowned by the crack and burst of bombs. Three more planes followed the first, firing indiscriminately into the cover on either side of the track. The noise of the planes died away and Kent lay on the ground for a few moments wondering if they would return. Then he got up and shouted to the men to re-form. In front of him he could see groups of men making their way awkwardly to the edge of the scrub, carrying casualties. He went quickly back asking if anyone had been wounded, but apart from one man who had cut his knee deeply on a stone they were untouched.

It took a long time for the column to move again, and when it did it was with the same exasperating halts every few minutes while messages were shouted down the line warning everyone to keep their proper intervals and avoid bunching. By the time Kent reached the first group of wounded men they were already being lifted on to stretchers; as two medical orderlies bent down to lift a man Kent looked quickly away, as though he could avoid hearing the gasp of protest. An ambulance came down the track, its well-sprung body swaying from side to side, and he heard someone say that if they weren't dead after a mile of that they must be shamming now.

Further on there was another little cluster of wounded, and just beyond them and out of their sight were two bodies with their hats laid over their faces. One was unmarked, but the other was soaked in a mess of darkening scarlet from his waist to his knees. As the column went by, the same question was asked of the silent stretcher-bearers time and time again: 'Who are they, who are they?' Once they were out of hearing some of the men laughed and said that they were lucky not to have to go on marching and wondered what their first request would be when they reached St Peter.

The sun was now low enough in the sky to shine under the brims of their hats, but still strong enough to sting the sweat- and dust-sore skin. Kent's thirst had slowly grown until now he could think of nothing else but how he would relieve it if he could. First he would skin a large cool peach—he could feel the wet soft flesh as he broke off one half and crammed it into his mouth, crushing it with his tongue, and feeling the juice pouring down his throat. Then he picked up a cut-glass tumbler and turned on the cold-water tap in the scullery at home. He turned it on to its fullest and stood there watching the water splashing furiously into the sink. It wetted his hands with spray and when he could bear it no longer he thrust the tumbler under the tap and drank, and again and again and again.

He put his hand behind him and felt his water-bottle; he wondered how much longer he could go on before he would have to drink. A long time yet, he told himself; I won't touch it until I know for sure that I can get some more. The jingle of the last words stuck in his mind, and he went on repeating them over and over, fitting them to the rhythm of his marching.

Just before the sun set the column halted, and he thought that they had stopped for the night, but no message reached him and they went on again, marching in rose-coloured dust on a pale coral track. He decided to speak to Maguire while it was still light enough to find him, and telling Anson to stay where he was he hurried on and found Maguire marching silently by the side of his company sergeant-major. As he came level with him he noticed that Maguire's face was drawn and tired, he would have looked haggard if the pink glow from the sunset had not lent a spurious air of health and colour to his face; when he saw Kent he smiled questioningly. Kent had had to walk quickly for some distance in order to catch up with him, and he was too tired to waste words, and the skin of his face felt too hot and tight for him to smile, he thought that the skin would split if he did.

'Have you had any message yet about tonight?'

'No, but Rogers just sent word back that the C.O. was sent for and has gone to Brigade in the jeep. Apart from that I know nothing, but if he has gone you can take it for sure that we shan't halt and settle in while it's still light.'

'Then I hope we go on a bit, the sooner we get to the river the better. Thanks, Tom.'

Kent stepped to one side and waited for the head of his company to reach him. It took him a little time to get back into the rhythm of marching, but once he did his mind wandered about as erratically as a child in a summer wood. He tried to concentrate on immediate problems, but it was impossible; in the middle of evolving a plan if the company was ambushed after dark he suddenly remembered a dinner in a Jermyn Street restaurant shortly before he was sent abroad, then he recalled the theatre they had gone to afterwards and the taxi that had broken down in Coventry Street. He tripped over a lump of earth and jerked his mind back; in another quarter of an hour it would be completely dark, if they were ambushed would it be better to form a circle of his own company or join up with Maguire? Or do neither, but bring the last platoon up and put it on the other side of the track with Tarrant in command? What tip had he given the driver? Something ridiculously extravagant considering they had had to walk the rest of the way and were late for the first act. Afterwards they had gone on to the Florida and sat there for hours, occasionally dancing to relieve his boredom, having little spurts of gaiety at longer and longer intervals, stupid with brandy and cigarette smoke. He was sure that, secretly, everyone had longed to go to bed, and when at five o'clock he and Celia had gone back to their hotel he had made himself sick in the bathroom.

He suddenly found himself blundering into the back of Maguire's company, which had halted. He passed word back for his own men to close up, and saw by his watch that they were not due to halt for another quarter of an hour. He went back and spoke to Tarrant, and as he made his way to the front again he asked one or two men about their feet and once more warned the platoon sergeants not to let the men drink or smoke without permission. He thought he heard the sound of a cork being furtively pulled, but he was not sure, and although he felt a quick stab of anger he said nothing.

The men sat or stood silently in the darkness; occasionally if they realized that he was near them they would ask each other in an audible aside when did they think they would sodding well get something to eat, or stop this bollocking march. It annoyed him that they should vent their exhausted irritability on him, they knew that it was not his fault, and that in fact he had more reason to be tired than they.

As he reached the head of the column Anson bumped into him. 'They're moving off, sir,' he said quickly, and Kent shouted to Sergeant Peters to lead on while he and Anson hurried past them until they were marching head to tail with the company in front. It was much more tiring marching in the dark; during the daytime one subconsciously watched the ground in front, it was as though there were eyes in the toes of one's boots that ceaselessly signalled to step an inch short to avoid that stone, a fraction higher to avoid that slight unevenness, and now those eyes could no longer see, and the pace too seemed much quicker than before. It was the reverse tendency of the morning, when the platoons and sections were stretching themselves out at long intervals; now everyone was closing up to keep contact. Kent tried to set a steady pace but he dared not risk falling too far behind, he was afraid that the track might suddenly fork or that the men in front might file off into a plantation or clearing in which to spend the night. In the darkness he might miss it and go blindly on. Behind him he could hear the men grumbling and swearing as they stumbled over the uneven ground, and at last he turned round and angrily told them to close up and keep quiet. There was silence for some time, and then a man tripped over a stone and almost fell, the man in front of him cursed, and the muttering started once more.

Now that it was dark the temperature fell rapidly, but the pace of the march more than offset any relief they might have gained from this. Kent and everyone else was streaming with sweat and his nostrils were so clogged with dust and dried mucus that he was forced to breathe through his mouth, which seemed to have lost all the qualities of a mouth, it was completely dry and he could hardly move his tongue. Wherever the straps of his equipment rested the skin was chafed and sore, and his drawers seemed to have worked themselves into a large wad of wet hard cloth in his crutch and the inside of his thighs were burning. He realized now that the previous halt must have been meant as a ten minutes' rest and that although he was feeling exhausted and wanted to lie down almost more than he wanted to drink, there was at least another forty minutes' marching to be endured.

He started repeating to himself: 'Everything *must* come to an end', over and over again, saying the words in his mind with tremendous emphasis; it helped to push his physical discomfort a little way into the background, it was a thread that guided him away from reality. Everything must come to an end, to an end; he wished that he had realized that his first term at his public school, when the years until he should be eighteen stretched away more solid and enduring than eternity itself. Next week's half-holiday was unimaginably remote, the end of the first term would happen in a hundred years' time, he would stop being a fag when the world was cold.

But on the other hand if he had known that everything must come to an end it would have spoilt the university for him, and once he had settled down time had stood still, and he could never imagine any other existence except to be at Cambridge. He used to lie in a punt with two or three friends, someone who enjoyed it doing the work and someone to play the gramophone. Time on my hands. Lying flat on the cushions trailing his fingers in the cool waters, watching the May sky above the willow-trees through the blue spirals of cigarette smoke, listening to the sentimental music, filled with the contentment of being nineteen and squandering one's days on nothing, with the thought of neglected work as an added pleasure. Going to afternoon cinemas, sitting in one's rooms in college arguing pointlessly with friends, tipsy on cheap claret. He remembered an inn outside Cambridge on the road to London, there was a garden set with tables and chairs where they used to sit in the late spring. The tulips would be full blown, bent over by the weight of their curled-back petals, and the apple blossom loose on the boughs above them. He remembered one evening sitting with his friends, the empty bottles of beer stacked in front of them as a public testimonial to their drinking prowess, and a light rain began to fall. Out of bravado they had stayed at the table while the rain dripped through the leaves and the apple blossom fell, and they forced the gassy beer down and racked their fuddled brains for another dirty story.

In the hot sweaty darkness he smiled to himself; it didn't sound

very romantic, rather worse than tiresome in fact, yet it was preferable to being a little older and staying up until five in the morning
in a night-club drinking brandy with one's wife, at least the garden
had been fresh and being drunk in public still a novelty. But however it appeared to other people there was a magic in that garden,
although what its essence was eluded him; a strange compound of
innocence and timelessness.

And it had come to an end, with a worse than mediocre degree,
debts that had seemed crushing, one or two highly undesirable
sports jackets and an assortment of beer tankards and ash-trays
given him on his twenty-first birthday. But he would always
remember the rain in the garden; if only it would rain now, he
thought, and lifted his face to the sky as though he expected the
cool drops to splash into his parched mouth. The stars shone and
there was a soft glow in the east spreading from the rising moon.
Already the darkness held a promise of light, and one could pick
out the verge on which they marched from the whiter track.
The pace too had slackened, and the men no longer cursed and
muttered, if only because they were too exhausted.

The column halted again for its ten minutes' rest, and Kent passed
back an order that everyone was to take off his equipment and lie
down. He and Anson went a little apart from the rest of the company,
and when Anson had lain down Kent lay on his back at right-
angles to him and rested his head on his chest. He could feel
Anson's shirt wet against the back of his neck, but he was past
caring, he lay with his eyes shut luxuriating in every moment of
the exquisite relief of not marching, feeling the sweat trickling down
his face. He picked his nose clear of the clogged dirt and kept
his mouth closed, the saliva spread again from beneath his tongue
and he let it collect until he had enough to swallow. His forearms
and hands rested in the dust by his side, the sweat was rolling off
them, and when he moved his fingers he knew that they were
coated in dust. Something small crawled on to his knee and then
stopped as if wondering which way to go. He told himself with
indifference that if it went up his shorts he would have to do something to stop it, otherwise it could please itself. He heard the men in
front begin to move, and thought angrily that they had not been
allowed their full ten minutes—when he looked at his watch he
saw that they had been resting for a quarter of an hour.

Starting to march again was so painful to his legs and back that
he thought it would have been better not to have stopped at all, but
gradually the extreme discomfort wore off, and as it did he began
again to think about his thirst. Now he no longer tried to control

his mind, letting it wander torturedly among the imagined fountains of water, climbing cool mountains by the side of waterfalls, clouds of mist swirling wetly in his face. He thought of clusters of grapes that he could crush with his hands, and of green-mottled watermelons split in half, the black pips standing out in lines against the rose wetness of the flesh. He decided that he must drink at the end of the next quarter of an hour, but time passed and he managed not to drink, and a part of his mind began to enjoy his physical wretchedness.

At the next stop he put his hand on Anson's shoulder. 'Rest here,' he said huskily, his whisper not under control. 'I'm speaking to Tarrant, I'll come back.' He longed to lie down but he remembered what it would be like when he stood up again, and there was a streak of bravado in his action, he wanted the men to think that he did not need to rest. He walked as briskly as he could down the line of silent men, lying inert in the soft moonlight like scattered matchsticks. When he was near the end he saw someone get unsteadily to his feet and recognized Tarrant, and then he was sorry he had come and needlessly disturbed him.

'I was just coming along to see how you were, sir.'

'Yes,' Kent answered, amused in spite of his wretchedness that Tarrant should still have the energy left to bluff, 'I saw you getting off your knees. I'm sorry I disturbed you.'

'You really didn't,' Tarrant protested, 'I was coming to tell you that two of the men have fallen out.'

Kent was silent for a minute. 'What's the matter with them?' he asked indifferently. 'Are they ill or just tired, or is one helping the other?'

'They've both got terrible blisters, so they say. I've told them to follow on as best they can and that if they fall too far behind the Japs will get them.'

'Who are they?'

'Banks and Crayshaw.'

'Tell their platoon sergeant to keep a good look-out for them when we stop for the night, if we ever do, and tell him to leave a sign or something by the side of the track. I expect what'll happen is that they'll hear the Gurkha battalion coming up behind them and they'll start firing at them.'

'I shouldn't worry about that, sir; if they do hear the Gurkhas and think they're the Japs those two are much more likely to forget their blisters and rejoin us at a smart double.'

'How are you feeling?'

'Oh, I'm all right, but I shan't be sorry when we stop.'

And an hour later they did stop, and a message was sent back telling him to wait until guides came to show him where to spend the night. They took so long to arrive that he began to feel cold and rolled down the thin khaki sleeves over his forearms. He remembered that he should have done so as soon as the sun went down as a protection against mosquitoes, but he saw no point in covering his arms and leaving his legs bare from above the knees almost to the ankles. He followed the guides stiffly, and soon they left the track and pushed through the scrub.

It took a long time to settle the men; in spite of the moonlight it was difficult establishing contact with the companies on his flanks and then he had to find battalion headquarters and enquire about the water supply, check on the password, and make sure that his platoon sergeants had prepared proper sentry rosters. He found that to most of his questions the answer was an optimistic no, there was no water tonight but perhaps tomorrow morning if the water truck arrived, there were no blankets here but Brigade said there might be some when they reached the river, there were no definite orders for the morning, except stand-to half an hour before first light. And when he thought he had finished he remembered the two men who had fallen out and his conscience nagged at him until he went to the track and warned the guard on duty to watch out for them.

On his return he found that Anson had smoothed a patch of ground under a tree clear of the worst of the rock-like lumps of earth. He sat down and took off his boots; his feet seemed to have become grafted to the leather. Then he struggled out of his equipment and undid the straps holding his water-bottle. He took one big mouthful of water and then strapped the bottle up again quickly, holding the water in his mouth, pushing it into the corners of his cheeks with his tongue and letting it dribble down his throat.

'You haven't drunk too much of your water, have you, Anson?' he asked severely, the thought uppermost in his mind being that he would find it impossible not to give him some of his own if he really needed it tomorrow, although he would be furiously resentful if he had to.

'No, sir, I've hardly touched it yet.' He prised a stone out of the ground with the point of his bayonet and threw it to one side, and then reached over and pulled Kent's equipment towards him, arranging it as best he could in the shape of a pillow, putting his own next to it. They lay on their backs, side by side, and Kent closed his eyes and waited for sleep. The small night wind seemed confused by the thick undergrowth and wandered about the ground in chill little draughts and Kent edged his body against Anson's for warmth. He lay quite still listening to Anson's breathing; he knew that his tiredness would eventually overcome the hardness of the ground and the cold wetness of his clothes wherever the wind touched him, the only question was how long it would take and how long he would be able to stay asleep.

Soon after midnight he woke up, passing from unconsciousness to consciousness in a flash, but still too late to catch the sound that woke him. He lay very still, staring up at the cold moon, but everything was silent. He was bitterly cold and his back and legs ached intolerably; he rolled painfully on his side towards Anson and saw that he too was awake.

'Did you hear anything just now?' he whispered.

'Yes, a machine-gun fired, but it was a long way off.' They lay still, listening, but there was no sound.

'I've never been so cold,' Kent muttered and without replying Anson turned his back and pushed himself against him. Warmth flowed slowly back into Kent's body, through his chest and stomach and along the length of his thighs and legs and almost at once sleep came rushing back. But the relief was only a temporary one; as soon as his body was at all rested the cold hardness woke him again, and the night was spent in an endless shifting of position trying to find comfort and warmth, drifting into dream-haunted snatches of sleep so vivid that he could hardly distinguish between dreams and reality. The night seemed interminable, he would look at the time and then lie still until he dozed. It would seem as though he slept for hours and when he woke he would look at his watch hopefully, only to see that a mere half-hour had passed.

He had given orders that everyone should be called at five o'clock and be ready to stand-to by five-past, and he prayed for that time to come quickly. But at ten minutes to five he felt sleep smothering him, and the minutes now seemed to flash by. When he sat up and pulled on his boots he was yawning continuously and felt more tired than he had the night before. His feet had swollen, and he had to unlace the boots as far as possible before he could cram them inside, his eyes were gummed with sleep and sore from the lack of it, his skin ingrained with dust and dried sweat, and his mouth tasted vilely. The thought of the day that stretched ahead weighed on him and would not be dismissed. He glanced at Anson and wondered what he was thinking about but he could only dimly see the outline of his face as he moved in the shadows lacing up his boots, and Kent envied him the comparative simplicity of his day.

He suddenly remembered the wound in his arm and was amazed that he had forgotten about it for so long.

'If we have another day like yesterday I don't think I can take it,' he whispered, not because he believed it but because he wanted sympathy. There was also a thought at the back of his mind that if he did by any chance fall out he would be able to say that he had felt ill as soon as he woke up. 'And what's more, my arm's hurting badly.' He pretended to raise it with difficulty.

'You'll be all right, sir,' Anson answered, 'as soon as we get a chance I'll dress it properly. Don't worry about today, if you can't take it no one else will, so we'll all be in the cart together. Let me know if there's anything I can possibly do to help you.'

'I shall be all right,' Kent answered quickly, ashamed that he should be taken so seriously.

They made their way to the middle of the centre platoon and for the next half-hour Kent watched the dying moonlight change imperceptibly into day. The only noise was an occasional muffled cough and the small sounds of the men moving their feet. When they stood down, Kent sent for Tarrant and the platoon sergeants and told them to have an inspection of the men's rifles, and to find out how many were complaining of bad blisters.

'While you're doing that I shall go and find out what's happening, and see if I can cadge some plaster from the M.O.; I'll do their feet when I come back. And while I'm away, Sergeant Peters, I'll also do what you forgot to do last night, and doubtless have forgotten to do again this morning, check up on Banks and Crayshaw.'

'I hadn't forgotten, sir,' Peters answered in an injured tone of voice, 'I was just going to speak about them.' Kent shrugged his shoulders and turned away.

He came back after three-quarters of an hour carrying a roll of cotton-wool and some sticking plaster. It was of cheap quality, but he thought it would be better than nothing at all, and he had also been given a small bottle of surgical spirit and some iodine. He sent Anson round to collect the men whose feet needed attention, and while he waited he talked to Tarrant.

'I'm afraid there's no definite news at all. We don't know when we're going to start marching again, and there's a rumour that we might have to take up a position across the road here. Don't ask me why because nobody seems to know, it's just an idea floating around. But guessing's useless, we might be doing anything. All I can tell you is that the men are to eat now and drink as little as possible, and then wait until we get orders. We're not to light any fires so there's no tea, there wouldn't have been in any case because the water truck hasn't arrived yet. In fact you had better tell the men that there won't be any water at all, and then if it does come so much the better.'

There was a group of six men standing a few yards away, and more were coming through the scrub. Kent told them to sit down in a line and take off their boots and socks, and Anson produced an old razor blade to cut the plaster. Their feet were in bad condition, the toes caked with tacky-looking filth and the soles white and wrinkled as though they had been soaked for too long in water. The weave of the sock was patterned on the top of the foot. He knew that the smell would be bad enough to make him retch, and before he started he lit a cigarette, which dried his mouth up even more than it was already and made him feel swimmy and depressed. Most of the blisters were on the back and sides of the heels, raw patches bigger than the top of his thumb, some of them with flaps of skin still hanging from the top edges. One or two of the men had patches rubbed off their toes, but Kent knew that these were not so crippling as the others. He cut away the flaps of skin and wiped round the sores with surgical spirit and then dabbed neat iodine on the raw flesh. When the men had stopped whistling and rocking to and fro from the burning sting of the iodine he covered the place as best he could with a strip of plaster. He touched their feet as little as possible with his hands, knowing that he would be unable to wash off the contaminating stench.

The ball of one man's foot seemed to be abnormally swollen, and when Kent pressed it with the tip of his finger the man groaned with pain and pus oozed out of a crack in the hard skin.

'Get your boots on and go to the M.O. straight away, tell him I sent you, and that I don't think you're fit to march.' The man looked at him with an expression of deep gratitude, and Kent smiled back at him, realizing what relief and pleasure the man must be feeling. The few remaining men looked at him enviously and then hopefully at their own feet.

The last two men in the line were Crayshaw and Banks, whom Kent had found sleeping soundly under a blanket borrowed from the guard; it had been the blanket that annoyed him most as he remembered his own miserable night. He was anxious to see their feet in case they were not bad enough to warrant falling out. Their blisters were large, but no worse than anyone else's, and while he attended to them he rehearsed in his mind what scathing words he should say. He finished and straightened up, drawing in his breath to speak; they sat on the ground silently pulling on their socks and he was swept by a feeling of futility. He turned away without speaking.

124

Anson and he shared a tin of bully beef and a packet of dry biscuits for their breakfast. He was so hungry that he had forgotten about his thirst, but the biscuits reminded him, and he took another mouthful of water. The sun was beginning to shine through the tangle of branches and withered leaves, and he was no longer cold. When he had finished eating he lay down and slept as easily as if he had been in his own bed at Sialpur.

He woke to find Tarrant by his side shaking his shoulder. He had slept deeply and dreamlessly, and when he opened his eyes they had the puzzled stare of someone waking in a strange room.

'We're off straight away, sir, the men are all ready.'

He stood up in one quick movement. 'You ought to have called me sooner,' he said reproachfully. 'What's the time?'

'Eight-thirty. I only got the message a few minutes ago, I thought I'd let you sleep as long as possible.'

Kent had scrambled into his equipment and he and Tarrant led the company towards the starting point. He waited until the company in front had gone some way up the track and then told Peters to lead on. He stood and watched the company and was relieved to see that none of them were limping too badly; to have men falling out was always a constant source of worry, and in the end usually meant sending back search parties to look for them.

As he marched at the head of the company he told himself that it was only twenty-five miles to the river, about eight hours' marching, it shouldn't be too difficult. But he knew that it was not the distance that mattered but the time it took and the heat of the day and above all whether they would be able to find any drinkable water.

The hours passed without incident or delays, and his spirits rose. His thirst had returned, and nagged at him incessantly, but it was bearable because he believed that the end of the march was in sight. There would be plenty of water once they reached the bridgehead.

When they started on the seventh hour's march he saw a jeep being driven rapidly towards them and stop at the head of the column. Before the cloud of dust rolled over it he recognized the C.O. standing up. It made him uneasy, he was sure that now there would be a change of plan, it was too much to expect that they would be told to do something and then allowed to do it. As the dust cleared he saw the jeep turn round and the C.O. marching behind the leading company, talking to Norton. As time passed his fears began to subside; perhaps the C.O. had only come back to march the last two hours with the battalion.

At the next halt he lay in the shade hoping that he would not be sent for, but soon he heard hurried footsteps coming towards him. When the runner was still a short distance away he sat up resignedly.

'All right; the C.O. wants me. I'll go quietly.' The runner smiled.

'Yes, sir. They're just off the track at the head of the column. The C.O.'s sending for all company commanders.'

Ten minutes later Kent returned and as they moved off he sent Anson to find Tarrant. He was so exasperated that he could scarcely wait for him to draw level before he began speaking.

'God knows when we shall get water now!' he said passionately. 'Those bleeding Japs are uncanny, they seem to know in advance every damn' thing we do, evidently they're much closer to the bridge than anyone believed possible.' His mind, burdened by his craving for water and prickling with the unexpected nearness of the enemy, sought a scapegoat. 'Stinking bastard fifth column! By Christ, I'd like to crucify them!' Unconsciously he had raised his voice and a man in front turned his head and looked at him. He spoke more quietly. 'Brigade's got one battalion in position round the bridge and they want to get the Gurkhas in as well. This track runs between a couple of ridges about two miles from the bridge and if the Japs get there first it means we shall lose a hell of a lot of transport that's being escorted by the Gurkhas, as well as having the bridge split in two. So we've got to hold the ridges while every-one slips in, and then follow on afterwards. I won't say what we're likely to slip in, your guess is as good as mine.'

'How far behind do you think the Gurkhas are, an hour's march or more than that?'

'They seem to think somewhere between an hour and two hours, but it's quite obvious to me that they simply don't know. And I didn't like to ask the C.O. why Brigade doesn't send an armoured car down the road to find out. He wouldn't tell me to mind my own business because he's not like that, but he'd be quite entitled to. Besides, between you and me I'm so anxious to get settled in a position we intend holding on to for a bit, and sit in a slit trench having pints of water brought to me every ten minutes, that I'm frightened to ask too many questions in case I give myself away. Just think, once we get there we might not have to do any more marching for another week!'

They went on in silence—it required too much effort to talk for very long, the dust seemed to penetrate right into the lungs and one's throat became so parched that it felt as though it would crack if it was needlessly strained by speech. When Kent next looked up he could see the tops of the ridges coming into view above the scrub and trees. It was difficult to see from this heat-laden distance, but the ridges did not appear to have very much cover on them, and he sighed as he visualized being pinned between the baking stones and the blazing sun.

He had hoped that this new change of plan would at least be carried out quickly and smoothly, but when they were still a mile away from the end of the ridges the pace of the column began to slow down and sometimes they stopped altogether. And now he could hear spasmodic and very faint rifle-fire from the general direction of the bridge. At last he could distinguish the C.O. standing with a little group of officers pointing towards the ridge that lay to his left, and he could see Rogers standing by his side and nodding his head. A few minutes later Rogers's company was filing off the track and disappearing into the scrub. He led his company to within a short distance of the C.O. and told them to halt and keep under cover while he went forward. When he reached the group he saw that the brigade major was standing next to the C.O. and his immediate reaction was that the situation must indeed be serious.

'Tony, I want you to take your company to the ridge over there on your left. Rogers is occupying one half from the southern tip and you're to take the rest. The whole ridge is less than a thousand yards so you won't be very stretched out. C Company and two platoons of D Company will occupy the ridge on the other side of the track, battalion headquarters will be here, and the last platoon of D Company will be further back along the track, from the direction in which we've come. Since I last spoke to you the Japanese have made contact with the Indians to the right of the bridge as you face it now, but we don't know yet in what strength. As soon as we can get the Gurkha battalion back safely they will go into the bridgehead and the Indians will counter-attack, and while that's going on we shall also go into the bridgehead and expand it to about a thousand yards on either side. Our job is at all costs to keep this track open for the Gurkhas and the transport; whatever happens you will stay on the ridge until I send for you. I don't think there should be any questions on that, Tony.'

'No, sir, no questions,' he replied. If the brigade major had not been there he would have said that water was essential within a very short time, but he was afraid that they might think he was only speaking for himself, that he couldn't stand a little hardship. As he went back he looked at the shallow valley between himself and the ridge, perhaps there might be a trickle of water running down the centre towards the river; if there was he would let the men drink as much as they could, and if anyone got dysentery or typhoid that would be their good luck.

He led his company towards the spot where Rogers had left the track and then started to zigzag his way through the scrub; when they reached the centre of the valley he suddenly saw the bed of a narrow little stream, but it was dry.

They came to the base of the ridge and he began to climb. It was very steep, and there was little vegetation to cling to, to counteract the loose shale-like rock. Behind him he could hear the men swearing venomously as their clumsy nailed boots slipped and slithered on the loose stones, and as they tried to save themselves from falling forwards their slung rifles would slip from their shoulders and clatter to the ground. He expected at any minute to hear a rifle explode, followed by a cry of pain.

By the time he had reached the top his shirt, which had almost dried during the last hour, was once more black with sweat, his heart was pounding and his eyes sore and bloodshot. He stood on the top of the ridge watching the men toil up, not caring whether he could be seen by the enemy or not; he was so exhausted that he thought he would scarcely have the strength to draw his revolver if the Japanese suddenly appeared. The ridge was broader than he had imagined, and on the opposite side to the track dipped gently down for two hundred feet and then flattened out. The ground was uneven and rocky but it was impossible for them to be surprised.

He positioned the men along the top of the ridge and they lay down, then he walked to the northern tip and looked at the country. From here he could see the narrow bridge and its high tracery of girders; although it crossed the river at its narrowest point he judged the length to be almost a hundred yards, and immediately below it the river increased in width. The railway line embankment ran diagonally across his front, keeping to the paddy-fields and avoiding the broken ground to his left. The only prominent feature between himself and the bridge was a long low ridge that ran out from the track at right-angles, and at the end of it was a dazzlingly white pagoda and a large square building that he guessed housed Buddhist monks. Near the bridge was a green carpet of dark palms and light tamarinds. He knew that the village would be beneath the palm-trees, and his first thought was that there would be wells in the village.

He sat down below the crest of the ridge to take in the scene, but
128

unconsciously his eyes were always wandering towards the distant plains to the north, hazy and remote.

The firing from the bridge appeared to be increasing in volume, and he moved his position so that he could only be seen by someone looking straight up at him from the paddy-fields. Above him on the top of the ridge he could hear the men nearest him talking and as he turned his head to tell them to be quiet he saw a long line of transport coming down the track towards the bridge. Behind them, through the clouds of dust, he had a glimpse of a long line of marching men and he felt a surge of relief. Now they would soon be recalled and follow the Gurkhas through the village towards the bridgehead. And that would mean he could drink. His hands were shaking as he unstrapped his water-bottle and eased out the cork with elaborate care in case any of the men should hear. Once he put the bottle to his mouth he found it almost impossible to take it away again, it was with great difficulty that he managed to leave a mouthful undrunk.

He made his way back along the ridge to the point where they had climbed up, then he sat down and waited for a runner to bring the order to rejoin the battalion. He did it as nonchalantly as possible, trying to make it appear that he had spent half an hour at one end of his sector and now was spending half an hour at the other. The afternoon was already far advanced, and he knew that they would have to reach their positions soon if they were going to be able to put them into a state of defence before dark. Time passed and no runner came, and as his impatience began to consume him so time crawled by the more slowly. To relieve the suspense of waiting he left his own sector to look for Rogers, and after he had talked to him he came slowly back, expecting at any minute to hear the clattering of loose shale as the runner crawled up the slope. But nothing happened except that slowly but surely the firing increased in volume.

He had waited for over an hour before the runner arrived, and by then he was so impatient that he almost left the top of the ridge and went down the slope to meet him. He read the message to withdraw on to the track, and he had difficulty keeping the jubilation out of his voice as he told Tarrant to go back along the ridge and bring up the rear while he started on down, venting his excitement by slipping and sliding down the steep side as quickly as he could.

When he reached the track he found that there was already one of the other companies in front of him and that battalion headquarters had moved, leaving Norton to bring the companies into the village. He found Norton at the head of C Company talking to Maguire, and only a hundred yards in front of them was the last platoon of the Gurkha battalion. Norton was looking tired and worried; he stood by the side of the road slashing occasionally at a bush with a piece of cane and repeatedly glancing at his watch and peering up the track. It was no use asking any more questions, Kent told himself, no one would know the answers and really it was rather undignified; he smiled at Maguire and went back to his own company, telling them to sit down in the undergrowth and keep quiet. He found Anson sitting by the side of the track and he stood near him in a position from which he could watch the Gurkha troops in front and see as soon as they moved off. He was very sorry now that he had almost finished his water; he felt even more thirsty than he had before, as though what he had drunk had merely revived his craving without giving him even a temporary relief.

Once more he began to despair of ever reaching their positions; all the time he was imagining a steady build-up of the enemy strength while they themselves seemed to remain in a state of paralysis; they would wait here, he thought, in unprepared positions until the Japanese were ready to deal with them. Now, mingling with the small-arms fire he could hear the vicious split of mortars. In an effort to occupy his mind he walked round the company to find out how much water the men had left in their bottles. They lay on the ground without smoking or talking, but as he moved among them one or two sat up and looked at him enquiringly or asked him when he thought they would move into their positions. Their faces were scruffy with beard and grey with dust and fatigue, they were exhausted, and many of them were bordering on heat exhaustion. Very few had any water left at all, and when he reminded them that they had been warned against finishing their bottles completely they replied that it had either been a case of that or having to fall out on the line of march. They grumbled bitterly that they had not been issued with water, that it was impossible to go on longer without. He tried to encourage them by saying that they would find water in the village, but he was anxious lest brigade headquarters should already be there, in which case drinking water from the wells might be impossible. He dreaded the idea of the brigadier finding them jostling each other to drink from some bucket of well-water; he would almost certainly tell them to leave it alone, and in their present extreme need they would equally certainly be grossly insubordinate.

As he finished talking to the men he heard Maguire shouting to him to get ready to move, and at last they started along the track.

It took a long time to move a very little way, but the village came slowly nearer, and now he could see that the road ahead was choked with a long line of vehicles—ambulances, jeeps, and supply lorries all packed bonnet to tail. A little group of anxious drivers had gathered by the side of the road, standing silently with their hands in their pockets looking up the track towards a bend where the line of vehicles disappeared from sight. Kent spoke to a man who stood a little apart from the rest, leaning against the side of an ambulance.

'Why don't they get this transport over the bridge, is it being fired on, or what?'

'Nobody seems to know, sir. I'm told Brigade are up there and we're not allowed anywhere near the place. There's a rumour that a three-tonner's got itself jammed on the bridge; they laid sleepers across the rails for the transport, and something slipped when the three-tonner was crossing and it's got itself wedged in the girders. They say it's difficult getting it clear because the Japs are sniping the bridge; they haven't done much damage because the girders are pretty thick, but even so they've killed a couple of men working on it. I think they're going to wait for night and then have another go at it.'

'Have you got any wounded with you?'

'No, they've been taken out and carried up towards the bridge, and I believe some have got across.' The column started to move again and Kent turned to the driver.

'I hope you get across tonight all right.'

The driver smiled: 'Oh, we shall get over all right, either driving or swimming.'

'Why swimming?'

'I've heard they've had sappers on it fixing explosives.'

Kent hurried after his men. He wondered whether the last piece of information was true, and if so what its significance was. It might mean that they didn't expect to hold the bridge and therefore the talk of counter-attacking to Paganle was only bluff, but on the other hand it might merely be a precaution against the bridge being rushed.

They rounded a bend in the track and Kent saw that they were now in the village itself. Although the sun would be above the horizon for at least another half-hour the palm fronds meeting overhead and the thick tamarind-trees already shadowed them with a faint touch of night. He could see Maguire talking to someone in front, and then he halted his company and came towards him.

'Tony, you and I have got to take our companies through the

village and take up a position on the other side. The rest of them are going to stay here for the time being. The C.O.'s having a conference with the brigadier right now; everything's gone wrong that possibly could as far as I can see, but I'll tell you about that when we get settled down. And Brigade say that under no circumstances whatsoever are we to touch the well-water here as it's the last word in badness. What are you going to do about the water question?'

'Let's get over to our side of the village and see what the wells look like there; if it's good enough for the Burmese it's going to be good enough for me, and Brigade can go and stuff itself. I expect their stomachs are so distended with tea they're feeling irritable. Let's go before they change their minds and send us back to the ridge.'

They led their companies off the track towards their left. The village extended further than Kent imagined, and by the time they reached the far side they were out of sight of the track. They quickly settled their respective sectors and then separated to look for water.

Kent found two shallow wells in his area; the brickwork of the well-heads was old and crumbling. They were more in the nature of tanks of water than wells, and when Kent looked into the first one he saw a large toad leap from a ledge in the wall and plop into the water. As far as he could judge the water was good, it was clear and tasted fresh, but before he let the men drink he warned them that they did so at their own risk. He let them come to the wells a platoon at a time; they crowded round the variety of containers that were quickly improvised and thrown into the water, and drank with a silent intensity that removed their snatching and pushing beyond mere greed. Some of them drank as much as they could hold and then poured the water over their heads and down the front of their shirts, rubbing it into their bodies.

At last Kent ordered the first platoon away from the well, some of them grumbling that they had not had enough to drink or been able to fill their bottles, but he rounded on them fiercely, calling them hogs, telling them they could come back again when the other platoons had been allowed a little time at the well. After everyone had drunk as much as they could and refilled their bottles Kent felt as relieved as though all his troubles were now over. He waited until everyone had finished and then drank three bottlefuls slowly, promising himself some more when his stomach was a little less distended.

He walked over to Maguire's sector and then went forward to

the edge of the trees and undergrowth and examined their position. Immediately to their front, towards the south, was a roughly triangular area of paddy-fields. The apex of the triangle, to Kent's left, was formed by a stretch of the track and beyond it the ground rose, covered with jungle. The ridge with the white building and pagoda that Kent had seen from his last position formed the opposite side of the triangle to the one from which they were looking, and at this point was about five hundred yards away. The end of the ridge fell away to level ground and then there was a wide gap until the railway line appeared, forming the third side.

They quickly made their way towards the right, the line of trees curving all the time until at last they found themselves facing north. From here there was a short gap of open uncultivated ground between themselves and the railway, which now began to make a wide sweep before it crossed the bridge. They could see the tops of the girders showing above the trees about half a mile away, and there was a column of black smoke billowing into the sky at the near end of the bridge.

As they watched the smoke they heard planes, followed almost at once by the swish of bombs and split of explosions. Before returning they ran to the railway; the line of trees they had come along continued to the edge of the river, and in front of the trees were open fields.

All the time they made their way back they could hear the planes machine-gunning the track and the bursting of bombs. They had hardly returned and organized a joint headquarters at the junction of the two companies when the C.O. arrived and told Kent to show him where his company area extended.

'You and Maguire will have to have separate headquarters, and you'll have to take on another two hundred yards to your left, up to but not including the track, and also quite a lot of Maguire's sector as well, I'm moving him down to the railway line. The other two companies will be on the far side of the railway along the line of trees down to the river. The Japs are here in strength already, and Brigade says their numbers are increasing the whole time. The essential thing is the pagoda ridge in front of you must be held at all costs. I'm told that a company of Gurkhas are going there now, but if for some reason they don't get there or are sent elsewhere then you'll have to move your company forward, or at least two platoons of it. And if they should want help during the night you must provide it. Keep me informed of everything that goes on; as soon as I'm settled down I'll let you know exactly where my H.Q. will be, I expect near the railway line. Get on and cover that two hundred yards to the track now, I must speak to Maguire.' He hesitated for a moment, wanting to wish Kent good luck, but he had a horror of sentimentality and turned away without saying anything more, and Kent saluted his back.

There were many questions that he had wanted to ask but he sensed that the time for questions was past. He called for Tarrant and Anson and told the former to site the platoon that was taking over part of Maguire's sector and he himself took Peters and showed him where he wanted the platoon placed that was to cover the two hundred yards to the track. When they reached the track he and Anson crossed over; there were Indian troops here and Kent found an English officer in charge of them. The sun had set, and it was almost dark under the trees as Kent hurriedly pointed out the line of his company, then he started towards the ridge to liaise with the Gurkha company commander. By the time he had gone half-way he realized that everything was dangerously confused; there were anxious-looking men digging slit trenches only a hundred yards in front of the Indian troops and none of them seemed to know why they were there or whether there were any troops on their left and right.

Kent decided it was useless to interfere, in any case he was in far too great a hurry to get back to his own men and have a last check on their positions before it was too dark. He made his way along the ridge and found the Gurkhas busily digging in around the pagoda and the square building, which he was surprised to find was hollow, and the roof only half completed. But the walls were built of thick concrete, and some of the troops were laboriously picking at it to form loop-holes. He spoke to the English captain in charge of the company and they arranged that if he needed help he would fire a red Very light followed by a green.

When Kent returned he was just able to visit all his sections before the last vestige of light drained out of the wood. His front was now so long that he decided to put Tarrant in charge of the platoon nearest Maguire, and for himself to sleep immediately behind the junction of the remaining two platoons. About thirty yards behind this junction was a thick clump of bushes and Anson cut away some of the low branches so that they would be able to crawl underneath; when he had finished he got up and without saying anything to Kent walked away in the direction of the track. Kent had kept one section in reserve and these he put round the clump of bushes in a circle of about twenty yards' radius, not only for protection but also to make it easier for any runners from battalion headquarters to find him in the darkness. As the night had fallen so the volume of firing from the direction of the bridge not only greatly increased but also seemed to be spreading towards him, and he was aware of a mounting tension.

He sat on the ground and took off his bush hat; his hair was wet with sweat and felt rough and lifeless. He stretched one of his legs and the muscles twitched as though they were about to knot themselves into an agony of cramp. He wondered where Anson had gone to, and just as he was beginning to feel impatience he heard him come back and drop something on the ground beside him. He put out his hand and felt blankets. He knew that he ought to be angry with him, but his only emotion was one of gratitude although he began to protest automatically:

'You shouldn't have done this, no one else has got them. Where did you manage to scrounge them?'

'Out of the empty ambulances. I took two. No one saw me bringing them back here,' he added, knowing that that would be the most important thing as far as Kent was concerned. 'I'll put them under the bushes and once the cut branches are in front of the entrance no one can see them or feel them, and they can wake you just as easily by calling if they want to.'

'All right. Let's eat some food now and then lie down, I shall be useless unless I get a few hours' sleep.' He was not feeling hungry but he thought that he ought to eat something while there was still time. His body suddenly jerked as a mortar bomb exploded behind him, and before he had time to turn his head three more exploded almost simultaneously. There was a pause in the firing, and from the direction of the pagoda he heard a shouted word of command, but it was too far off to be able to tell what had been said, and then he wondered if it had come from that direction or from the track. Unconsciously he lifted his head to hear better; high above him the leaves glimmered very faintly in a yellow light and he looked round. One of the village huts a hundred yards away had begun to burn, the flames spreading with astonishing speed through the thatched roof, and the yellow glare flooded between the gaps in the trees and bushes like an incoming tide. There was another explosion, nearer than the last one, and he twisted over and lay on his stomach, waiting for the rest of the salvo, but nothing happened. The thought came to him that the Japanese knew where his company was and he felt fear cold in his stomach. From behind the village and the railway line, almost, he judged, from the river itself, the brigade battery of twenty-five-pounders began to fire, and the salvo rushed sighing over his head; he heard them burst in the distance.

He sat up again reluctantly and found Anson was kneeling by his side with a mess-tin in his hands. Had it been anyone else he would have felt foolish at having rolled over on his face for mortar bombs that had not fallen. But with Anson nothing seemed to matter, and in any case he was so tired that he had no energy left to care. He picked up a lump of greasy meat in his fingers and began to chew. By the time he was ready to swallow the first mouthful he thought he would be sick.

'I'm sorry, I can't eat it for the minute; put it on one side and I'll have it later if the ants have left anything for me. Let's get some rest, we shall need it if this bloody noise is going on all night.' While he spoke there was an uneasy lull and he could hear his section post's whispering and the sound of bayonets being driven into the hard earth. He suddenly felt guilty because he had forgotten even to try to borrow any picks and shovels, but it was too late now, and he argued fiercely with his conscience that it was impossible to do everything himself.

He crawled into the bushes and lay back on the top blanket while Anson arranged the branches across the opening. He was thinking that even when the moon rose it would still be very dark under the trees, and before first light in the morning he would get Anson to uncover the entrance and hide the blankets away. If they were lucky enough to have an undisturbed night, he mentally reserved. Anson crawled back and sat next to him. Behind him and to his left there was another explosion, very near this time, fragments tore through the tops of the tree above him and someone in the village began to scream in a way that made Kent think he had been blinded. The scream ran down to the tips of his fingers and seemed to beat against the inside of his skin; without thinking he put out his hand and caught hold of Anson's. The battery by the river fired again and the shells rushed over them, were silent and then burst, much nearer this time. The man who had screamed started again, and Kent dragged his hand away from Anson's grasp. He wanted to block his ears, bury himself in the ground, anything not to have to listen to that sound.

'For God's sake let's get some sleep.' His voice was a thick whisper. He took off his equipment quickly and stuffed it carelessly under the lower blanket for his pillow. He found that he was shivering and laboriously took off his wet underclothes and put on his shirt and shorts again. In the darkness he could tell that Anson was doing the same. They pulled the top blanket over themselves and the guns fired again; as the shells burst, a Bren gun on the ridge in front broke in, its steady beat interrupted by a fresh outburst of rifle-fire. Kent fumbled with his equipment and laid his revolver on the blanket near his head. He rolled over on his side and lay facing Anson; they were very close together, their chests touched as they breathed, and he could feel Anson's breath warm on his cheek and chin. From the ridge and the far side of the track the firing was now almost continuous, interspersed with the explosions of mortars and shells. And suddenly the thought came to Kent that perhaps this was the last time he would ever lie down to sleep, and self-pity filled him. There was nothing he could do to help himself or anyone else but lie there in the darkness, waiting in the warm darkness until they were attacked or the jagged fragments of the mortars found them. There was a splitting explosion that seemed to come from the trees above him and left his ears stunned.

Moved by a compulsion that he did not understand, without considering the consequences, believing that what he was about to do was utterly disgraceful and criminal, he put his arms round Anson and pulled him closer. They lay still for a moment and then Kent lifted his shoulder from the ground and Anson put his arms round him. Kent was dimly aware that although his body might demand more, he himself did not: it was sufficient that they should rest in each other's arms, no longer hearing the firing or the man who had begun to scream again.

In the distance and from near at hand there was a macabre and badly rehearsed *feu de joie* punctuated by heavier explosions. But although Kent heard the noises they no longer meant anything to him, his own mind was chaotic with remorse and fear at what he had done, and with the pleasure and relief he felt at having done it. He was too exhausted and bemused to reason properly; all that he was certain of before he fell asleep was that he dreaded the morning, when sooner or later he would have to look at Anson and be looked at in return.

It was a measure of their exhaustion that they slept unbrokenly for nearly three hours, until a lorry near them on the track was hit by a mortar bomb and the petrol tank exploded. Anson opened his eyes and remembered everything and was glad. He lay still in the same position in which he had gone to sleep and wondered what had woken him, and why their screen of bushes was riddled with yellow light. He heard one of the reserve section tell the corporal in charge that a lorry was burning and should he call the company commander, and the corporal said something sleepily blasphemous. While the glare was at its fiercest he kept watch in case someone might come and find them, but the fire soon died down and he closed his eyes again.

He was afraid of their being found out because he knew that if they were they would be separated. He was also aware that whatever punishment was meted out would affect Kent infinitely more than it would him, and that offended against his sense of fairness. But for himself he was not afraid of being court-martialled and sent to a detention barracks for a few months; although it would be unpleasant he did not look on it as a disaster—during the last few days he had heard men talking about a six months' sentence at Lucknow with open nostalgia. Apart from how it might affect Kent his thoughts were quite uncomplicated; it was wrong, of course, and disapproved of by the vast majority of people, but then so were many other things; people, he thought, always disapproved most of what they didn't want to do themselves. It was surprising about Kent, being like that. At least, it would have been at Sialpur, but it wasn't surprising here. He felt very happy and fell asleep as though the firing and explosions were no more disturbing than the song of the nightingale heard from an orchard.

Kent lay awake much longer. His right arm had started aching but he did not move it, thinking that Anson was still asleep and that if he disturbed him he might move his position. For Kent nothing but misery and regret lay in wait if he started to think. He closed his eyes and excluded everything from his mind except the peace of lying in the darkness with someone for whom at that moment he could almost feel love.

'Sir! Captain Kent! Wake up, sir!' He and Anson opened their eyes at the same moment and drew apart as swiftly as though they had been awake. Before the sleep had left his mind Kent recognized the speaker as Tarrant and answered him in a voice that was perfectly under control. He threw the blanket to Anson, seized his equipment and revolver, and crawled through the camouflaged opening. There was a deafening volume of continuous fire coming from the ridge and the guns by the river; the shells seemed to scream just over his head and burst a little to the left of the ridge in front of him. As he got to his feet his first feeling was one of fear that Tarrant might have somehow managed to peer through the thick bushes and seen them lying so closely together.

'Have you got your torch?' he asked, peering at his wrist-watch. It was two o'clock.

'No, I haven't, sir, it's broken. One of the sentries has just told me he's seen the red and green flares go up from the ridge. The fool says he thinks it was twenty minutes ago, but I expect it was more. He said he didn't know where anyone was.'

'Christ Almighty! Remember the bastard, I'll deal with him

later, but everyone knew where I was,' he protested, afraid of the possible repercussions if the ridge was lost and the survivors said that the promised help had never come.

'Of course they did, sir,' Tarrant said quickly, understanding at once the workings of Kent's mind. Whether they knew or not he could always swear that they did.

It had been Kent's intention to send the centre platoon as a reinforcement under Tarrant if the signal was given, but now he was suffering from intense guilt on account of the time it had taken to report the signal and more particularly because of Anson, and he decided to take the centre platoon forward himself. Tarrant was brave, Kent knew, but no one could enjoy a task like this, and if he was not sent he would be bound to feel obligated; he might have need of Tarrant's loyalty. And also he wanted to prove something to himself and to Anson, but what it was he did not know.

'I shall take the centre platoon myself, Tarrant,' he said, fumbling into his equipment. 'Move a section from our right flank to help the gap a little. And get me a spare tommy-gunner in case I want an additional runner.'

Anson joined them and gave Kent his bush hat; he had also brought the mess-tin of bully beef and now Kent ate ravenously. They hurried to the centre platoon, and Kent quickly explained what they were going to do. By the edge of the trees it was much lighter; although the moon was no longer full and there were broad silvery streaks of high thin cloud in the sky it was still strong enough to throw an almost sharp shadow. He led the platoon on to the track and started towards the ridge.

The noise here was tremendous, all the isolated groups he had seen before were blazing away indiscriminately into the tangle of trees and bushes, using their ammunition very much as the Chinese use crackers to frighten away devils. Kent thought that it would only be a matter of seconds before a group caught sight of him and fired without thinking. They were like stabled horses who can smell fire, panicking without knowing whether there was cause or not. The shells came so low that Kent could not stop himself flinching at the noise, and were bursting on the slope in front of him and to the left of the ridge. He whispered to himself that the Japanese must be creeping down that slope, that the smell of smoke was more pronounced than he had thought. He looked back and saw that the track was marked at irregular intervals by burning vehicles and near the bridge an oil dump sent black clouds of smoke billowing towards the moon; the centre of the cloud glowed and sometimes tongues of flame licked through. When he had almost reached the ridge he decided to leave the track and cut across the last thirty yards of open paddy-field in single file; the risk of being seen by the Japanese, he thought, was not so great as attempting to slip through the undergrowth and penetrate the Gurkhas' lines.

He stopped to allow the platoon to close up, and while he waited glanced quickly at Anson, who had taken off his hat and stood where a patch of moonlight fell on his face. He was watching Kent and when their eyes met he smiled and Kent's blood stirred and he smiled back, surprised to find that it was so easy. He told the men to follow him in close single file and jumped down the small bank that separated the moon-white paddy-fields from the shadow-strewn track. He imagined that there would be a Gurkha section at this end of the ridge, and he took off his hat so that they could distinguish him more easily. He walked steadily across the open, his heart pounding with fear, expecting a stream of bullets to hit him at any moment, either from the front or from the left. There was a scream above his head and then immediately the explosion; he ducked his head, raging at himself for being afraid even as he did it. He felt a hand on his shoulder and then Anson was whispering:

'Let me go in front, sir, I'd much rather,' but Kent shook his head stubbornly and walked on; there were only a few more yards to go before he reached the start of the ridge and the cover of the undergrowth, his eyes were wide open and cold, his lips parted. He wondered what a single shot through the throat would feel like, or being hit in the testicles, having one's knee shattered by a burst of bullets. He reached the slope and the shadows of the small trees poured over him like a cloak of invisibility; his knees felt weak and his face was wet with an icy sweat. Then he realized that all the firing came from the top of the ridge fifty yards in front of him, and he began to climb the slope, keeping as often as he could to the open moonlight and making as much noise as possible, and just as he thought that another step must be his last he found that he was inside the perimeter with thirty men and no one seemed surprised that he was there.

He ordered the men to lie down behind the top of the ridge while Sergeant Peters and Anson crept forward with him to the command post near the pagoda; as he made his way along, doubled up, he caught glimpses of groups of men lying curled up in shallow hollows that they had scooped out of the rocky ground, protected in front by flimsy semicircles of rough stones as though they were children playing at damming a brook. They were firing over the tops of the parapets towards a long patch of jungle to the left of the ridge; the noise at these close quarters made Kent screw up his eyes and hammered in his ears. He found the company commander standing in a small weapon pit; there was only room for one other person and he jumped down and told Peters and Anson to take cover behind them. The pagoda was about thirty yards away, and beyond that he could see a corner of the square building.

The officer turned to Kent; in the moonlight his face looked drawn and savage. Before Kent could speak he leant towards him and rasped out: 'Taken you nearly an hour to do three hundred yards—hardly worth coming at all, was it?'

Kent's tongue almost foundered in a sea of resentment: 'Who the bloody hell do you think you're talking to?' he managed to choke out, 'you're not the only rat squeaking for help tonight.' He glared at the other man, who dropped his eyes, afraid that he had gone too far, and Kent quickly added: 'If we're too late I'll wish you the best of luck and good night.' He moved as if to leave, and he was not bluffing.

'No, you're not too late. I'm sorry, I'm a bit . . .' He looked away for a second and Kent was immediately sorry.

'So am I,' he said, trying to smile. There was a sharp explosion by the pagoda and something sang past his head as he ducked. 'What do you want me to do?'

The officer pointed back along the ridge. 'I've got a section the other side of the track about a hundred yards up on the rising ground. They keep sending back reports of Japs trying to filter down to the edge of this ridge. My men have killed a few but I'm afraid that some of them will get near the track and begin to snipe, or if they get established in any strength at the track end of this ridge I've had it, because I can't withdraw except across open ground. I can put in an attack across the track, of course, but it won't be much fun if they get a couple of machine-guns there. I've managed to get a message back to the gunners and they've been wonderful and got an O.P. in that building and are shelling the area in front of me. I think it's holding the Japs temporarily, but they can't go on using ammunition at the rate they are for very long, and in any case they'll probably have to switch to another target soon. If you can get a platoon near my section it should hold the Japs for quite a while, and I've been told by my C.O. to expect new orders at first light.'

Before Kent could answer, the bushes and ground around him were momentarily stained blue-white and then a tremendous explosion came from the direction of the bridge. They spun round, but there was nothing to see except the glow of scattered fires reflected on drifting smoke. There was a moment of silence as everyone in the whole area listened and then the firing broke out louder and more sustained than before, as though the firers wanted to push the sound out of their minds.

'What the hell was that?' Kent had to shout above the pandemonium of firing that broke out. He knew the answer to his question before he had finished asking.

'They've blown the bridge, we'd better stop fighting and indent for water wings!' the other man said, and there was a strained edge to his voice. I suppose that's my cue for a scarcely controlled outburst of hysterical laughter, Kent told himself. He felt nothing either way, his mind was too full already to allow room for any problem that was not of immediate concern, all he wanted to do was to get this present job finished as soon as he could and for a few hours forget everything in sleep.

'Give me a guide to your section and I will take my platoon there. I can't stay with them myself, there's the rest of my company that I'm responsible for, but I'll leave them under your command until I get any orders from my C.O. to the contrary. If you retire you must see that they come back with you and rejoin me. I couldn't agree to letting them do a rearguard action just to let you get clear —not that you'd do that of course, but you understand?'

'Yes, old chap, that's perfectly fair. If I'm ordered to abandon the ridge I'll see they're not left behind.'

Kent explained the position to Brewster, recrossed the track and began to climb the slope, ducking every few yards as the shells tore over his head at tree-top level, convinced that the gunners were using instantaneous fuses and that at any minute a shell would touch one of the topmost branches and explode above him. The face of the Gurkha that he had been given as a guide had been split from ear to ear by a smile when they had first started, and now, when Kent called softly to him that he was going too fast, he turned his head and Kent saw that he was still convulsed by some inner joke. It made him envious and he tried to smile back but it was a sickly effort.

They covered what Kent judged to be a hundred yards, and he caught hold of the guide's shoulder to stop him going any further. His Urdu was barely good enough to ask the guide if he really knew where the section was; he could not understand the man's confident whisper but he gathered that they still had to go forward, and at every step he expected to fall into an ambush or be shot down by some hidden sniper. He could hear the clatter of the men's boots above the firing, and each loose stone and snapping twig jangled like pain in his mind. They went on for another hundred and fifty yards, and he had almost decided not to go forward any more when he stumbled over the feet of one of the Gurkha section. The relief was so great that he started to heap the foulest blasphemies possible on the Gurkha officer who had judged two hundred and fifty yards to be one hundred. He and Brewster crept round with each section, spreading them out at short intervals. The men were silent and apathetic, some of them choosing firing positions from which it was impossible to watch their front, and Kent made them move until they could at least see a few yards ahead. He did so reluctantly, understanding how they felt. The noise of the bursting shells was terrifying, they seemed to be exploding among the trees only a few yards in front of them, and occasionally one would smash into the side of the hill and the debris of splintered stone came pattering through the trees like heavy rain.

When the men were in position Kent whispered to Brewster to make his headquarters with the Gurkha section commander. He looked round for the guide but he was nowhere to be seen; without waiting he and Anson started back down the hillside. Kent was counting the yards to himself, he had just reached fifty and was saying to himself that if he reached a hundred they would get back safely when a shell touched the top branch of a tree in front of him and exploded. Anson dropped to one knee and put his head in his arms; the pain in his ears made him feel sick. He shook his head and looked up. Kent had walked on five paces; as Anson got unsteadily to his feet he saw Kent pitch forward on his face and lie still.

13

When Kent regained consciousness for the first time it held the same reality for him as a vague nightmare, he thought that he dreamt that it was daylight and that he was lying on the ground. But as time went by his bodily pain pushed him gradually further away from sleep, and little by little, so slowly that he was hardly shocked at all, he realized that he was lying in a clearing bound hand and foot. On the far side of the clearing there was a group of Japanese soldiers clustered round a pot and cramming rice into their mouths. He watched them through half-closed eyes; his first coherent thought was how lucky they were to be free, then he became aware that his hands were throbbing with pain and that one side of his head seemed to be full of blood trying to burst through his skull. He twisted his wrists to ease the pain and noticed for the first time that he was resting against another body.

'Are you awake, sir?' He recognized Anson's voice and was overwhelmingly glad that he too had been captured.

'Am I badly wounded?' His voice was not under control, and someone in the group heard the noise and walked over towards them. Kent watched his legs come nearer without any fear and heard Anson breathe something that sounded like 'I'm officer', but it made no sense. The man reached Kent and kicked him as hard as he could in the solar plexus. All the pain in his head and arms drained away and regrouped itself in his throat as he frantically tried to draw breath. He was aware that the man was urinating in his face, and roaring with laughter, but although the warm jet sometimes splashed in his open mouth he neither cared nor shut his mouth, he was only concerned with getting breath back into his choking lungs. The rest of the group came running over, crowing with laughter and fumbling with their trousers, but just as they reached him someone shouted and they stood still. A short stocky man stepped into Kent's line of vision; he went up to the soldier who had urinated and struck him violently across the shoulders with a thick stick.

He shouted to the group and they picked up Kent and Anson and undid their cords. Kent was still gasping, lurching on his feet, and two men had to support him. He felt very sick, and the ground swayed up towards him. The short man came and peered up at him; he was impatient to begin the interrogation, and he was trying to decide whether brutality or kindness would produce the quicker results. He spoke to the two men holding Kent and they took him over to a tree and let him sit down while a third man brought hot water and bathed his head. The sting of the water and the pain of having the worst blood clots rubbed out of his hair cleared Kent's head. He could see Anson standing a few yards away with a guard by his side and he raised his head and looked at him miserably; as he did so Anson bent forward slightly as though he was looking at his boots and touched one of his shoulders. Kent saw the small square piece of cloth on his shoulder-strap but it took him a long time to understand that he was pretending to be an officer, and when he did understand he was sorry; he thought that no one could possibly be taken in by such a crude deception, and that when they found out they would shoot him out of hand.

They brought him a tin of strong bitter tea which he managed to force down because he thought it would do him good, and then sat quietly resting, trying to coax back his strength. He saw that the sun was beginning to strike into the clearing, and he glanced at his wrist but the watch was gone. He noticed that the circle of white skin left by the watch itself was not quite in the centre of his wrist and he told himself that when he bought another watch he must get a tighter strap. In the distance he could hear firing; it seemed a long way off, but even so it was a comforting sound, friendly and familiar. For the first time the idea of escape came to him and he glanced round the clearing; as he did so he saw the small man hurrying towards them, and the guards pulled him to his feet.

While the man was still some distance away he started shouting orders and Anson was brought over and stood next to Kent against the tree. They were pushed very close together, and ropes were bound round their chests and ankles and pulled as tightly as possible before being knotted behind. The small man stood in front of them. Kent had no idea what his rank was, he had some badges on his shoulders but they conveyed nothing to him. He thought that he must be an officer and decided to treat him as such. He tried to remember exactly how much information he was allowed to give as a prisoner, he knew that he could give his rank, name, and number, but he could not remember whether he was allowed to identify his regiment. In his jumbled aching head the question seemed to be of immense importance.

'I ask again, how many regiments by bridge?' The officer was glaring and Kent looked at him in surprise, the stresses of the words fell in the wrong places, and the whole of the speech seemed mutilated. He leant forward and struck Kent across the face with his stick, not very hard, but enough to hurt badly even if he had not already received a four-inch gash on the side of his head. The officer saw him flinch and fear come to his eyes.

'Filthy swine, answer when I speak!' he shouted in his face and Kent involuntarily turned his head away, sickened by the smell of fishy dental decay, and the wet splutter that showered into his face. The officer hoicked his throat and spat a gob of stinking slime and phlegm that coated Kent's nostrils and before he could control himself a mouthful of hot frothy vomit had shot on to the sleeve of the officer's uniform. He tried to apologize but before he could say a word the officer screamed shrilly and started lashing at the side of his face. The stick rose and fell with unendurable violence, and again Kent's mouth filled with a rush of vomit, but this time he managed to keep his mouth shut while his cheeks bulged and it oozed between his lips. The officer stopped hitting him, afraid of again being spattered; Kent opened his mouth weakly and the sick poured down his chin and dripped slimily from his uniform. He looked at the officer's furious face and thought that he had seldom seen such a repulsive-looking man, his foul breath and skull-like bone structure seemed to make the pain in his head infinitely worse. Hidden by their touching bodies he felt Anson's fingers fumbling for his hand and then gently press it, stroking it with his thumb; until that moment the tears in his eyes had been tears of pain.

'Don't treat me like this,' his voice was husky, almost unrecognizable, 'I'm an officer, I've done nothing wrong.' The officer smiled affably at Kent and nodded. He turned his head and shouted towards the other side of the clearing; the unintelligible language seemed to go on for a long time, and then Kent saw a group of men come into the clearing. There was a tree about fifteen yards in front of him, and he watched while ropes were thrown over a branch. The group opened and Kent saw Sergeant Brewster and two other men from his platoon; they were brought over to the tree and then strung up until they were hanging by their arms, their feet almost touching the ground. In silence their clothes were roughly ripped off them and they hung naked, their bodies swinging.

The officer turned back to Kent. He spoke in a loud voice so that everyone could hear. 'You are officer; I understand. These men are not. How many regiments by the bridge?'

'I don't know,' Kent answered, 'I'd tell you if I did, but I don't know.' The officer spoke quietly, and Kent saw a Japanese soldier fix a bayonet to his rifle. He ran across the clearing and everyone began shouting and jumping up and down. Someone screamed and the running soldier lunged at Brewster and then pulled back his arms. Kent could see the naked body twisting and jerking, blood running down the belly. Brewster began sobbing and screaming: 'Let me down, let me down, oh God, it's hurting, let me down.' The Japanese soldiers were laughing, and now they closed in on Brewster, digging at his stomach and genitals with their bayonets while he screamed and jerked, pulling his body almost up to the bough and kicking with his bound legs. Suddenly the noise and movement stopped. The officer shouted and the men drew away from the body, which hung limply, the intestines slipping redly and slowly down to the ground, streamers of gut sticking to the bare legs.

'How many regiments?' The officer was shouting again and some of the soldiers were grinning and cleaning their hands with dust and dried grass. Kent was gazing across at the two men still hanging from the tree. Their eyes were open, watching him intently but he was hardly conscious of them, desperately trying to decide

146

what was the best thing to do to save his own life, whether it would be better to tell the truth and rely on his position as an officer not to be killed, or to say that he did not know and hope to be sent back for further interrogation. If they thought that he had told them everything he could they might not think it worth while keeping him alive any longer. He felt Anson press his hand urgently, but whether to tell him to speak or be silent he did not know. Quite near at hand he heard a lorry start up and then move slowly off, heading towards the south.

'I don't know,' he muttered in a low voice so that the two men should not hear, and the officer nodded approvingly at Kent and drew his sword. He walked to the tree and stood in front of one of the men, his sword held out in both hands, the point of the blade just touching the skin of the man's stomach. Kent saw the sword flash and shut his eyes, he heard a soft thud and the officer speaking, the clearing was suddenly ringing brazenly again with screams and shouts, but as long as he kept his eyes closed the noises had no human quality about them. He felt Anson's fingers signalling urgently to him, and he opened his eyes too late to avoid another slash across the side of his torn and livid face.

'You, now.' The officer stood in front of him and Kent wondered whether he was smiling or snarling. He raised the stick again and Kent heard himself shouting: 'There are three regiments, don't hit me again, please, please . . . I'll tell you everything, three regiments, two of them Indian and mine and some gunners, and I'll tell you about the tanks.' He stopped shouting. 'But not here, send me back and I'll tell everything.' He made his voice sound weak and faint, dropping his head on to his chest as if he was at the limit of his endurance, hoping that the officer would think that he was too weak to tell all that he knew and that the information was important enough to send him back. He could hear more lorries moving on the road and he opened his eyes. The officer was standing in front of him, his head held stiffly on one side. He said something to the man standing next to him, who nodded his head in agreement. They're going to kill me, Kent thought, and he began to open his mouth to scream for mercy when the officer and soldiers started to hurry away across the clearing and Kent heard the sound of planes. The group of men started running towards the noise of the lorries and as they reached the far edge of the clearing the first bombs exploded a hundred yards away and the remainder of the stick tore up fountains of scrub and earth past the end of the clearing and beyond. The blast tore at Kent's body and a lump of debris smashed through the tree above him. By his side Anson was struggling wildly. Kent saw that he had got his arms free and was dragging his body down, wriggling his chest past the rope.

'For God's sake don't, Anson, they'll see you, they'll kill us, stay where you are!' He was almost shouting, his head felt as though it would burst with his panic and pounding blood as he glared at the far side of the clearing expecting to see the little figures rush shouting out of the bushes that seemed to turn into men as the dust swirled round them. Before Anson could free his feet one of the planes began machine-gunning indiscriminately along the track. Anson was free now and the rope hung loosely at Kent's waist. He held it in his hands and looked at Anson. He was pleading, saying over and over again: 'Don't leave me, help me out, they'll kill me.' Anson pulled the rope up with one hand and pushed Kent down with the other and he fell on the ground with his feet twisted in the bottom rope. He lay there helplessly, shaking in every limb, and suddenly there was a rush of gas and excreta as he voided his faeces into his shorts; Anson calmly untwisted the rope and helped him to his feet. Now a faint instinct of hope came back to Kent and enabled him to start stumbling towards the jungle away from the Japanese. There were about fifteen yards between them and cover, Anson had his arm round Kent's waist supporting him, but at almost every step he would turn his head and look back into the clearing, shambling like a drunken man. When they were still five yards away from cover he turned his head again and thought he saw the officer pointing towards them with his sword, and his legs buckled under him and he fell to the ground. Anson bent down and exerting all his strength picked him up in his arms and staggered with him a short distance into the jungle and laid him on the ground.

Behind him he could hear the planes fading into the distance and people shouting. He shook Kent's chin and when he opened his eyes he smiled at him. 'Try and walk, sir, or they'll find us and you don't want that.' He spoke very gently, for some reason that he did not try to understand he felt deeply sorry for Kent, with a sorrow that hurt his throat. He helped Kent to his feet and half supporting him they pushed their way deeper and deeper into the jungle, choosing the easy ways as long as it increased the distance between themselves and the clearing.

They walked for what seemed to Kent to be a very long time, but in fact was half an hour and by then they were only a mile away from the clearing. They would have gone on walking towards the east but Anson realized that Kent would collapse at any minute with exhaustion and pain and when they reached a tiny stream that ran glittering towards the north he decided to halt and let Kent rest.

He changed direction and walked downstream until they came to a steep bank of rock overgrown with bushes and shadowed with tall trees. Near the water's edge there was a small hollow full of coarse sand and completely hidden from view. They drank as much water as possible before they crept inside and Kent wanted to lie down at once and close his eyes but Anson made him sit against a rock and took off his shirt and soiled shorts. He rinsed off the sick and the blood that had dripped from the side of his face and head and left the shorts to soak in the running water weighted down by a stone, and then he came back and swabbed his face with the shirt. The wound on the left side of his head was almost to the bone, and Anson used his own field dressing to cover it. He had no idea whether there was any other damage to the skull; the area round the cut was swollen and hard. The whole of the left side of Kent's face seemed by far the worse, broad welts ran from the ear down to the chin, the skin was split open and already turning black. He knew that he must be hurting him a great deal and expected him to start moaning and turning his head away, but he made no sound or movement. As soon as he finished Kent lay down on his right side and put the wet cold shirt on his face. He was crushed by shame and physical exhaustion, he wanted to find out if Anson despised him for his behaviour, but he was too wretched and weak to ask and almost at once he fell asleep.

He slept for a long time dreamlessly while Anson lay on his back and listened to the liquid tinkle of the water. A light breeze rustled the leaves above him and a bird sang sadly near at hand, but with a sadness that was unbearably beautiful, and the sun pierced their screen of leaves staining everything the palest green. Sometimes he went to the stream and drank the cool water and then he would come back and sit again, watching Kent and brushing away the flies that settled on his bare legs and body. Far away he could hear the continuous mutter of rifle-fire and sometimes the dull thump of an explosion. He was completely unafraid or worried, the problems confronting him would not exist until he had to deal with them. They had no weapons and no food; the thought scarcely touched his mind, and although he was unable to swim it had not occurred to him to wonder how he would cross the river. He felt that as long as Kent was alive all problems would be solved for him one way or the other, which particular way was of no importance.

Kent moved slightly in his sleep, and the wet shirt began to slip off his face. Very carefully Anson took it away and folded it more neatly before he put it back. The side of his face was swollen so badly that even the unbroken skin seemed as though it must burst and the lymph had trickled down his throat and across the top of his chest. There was nothing Anson could do to help except to let him sleep as long as possible and to comfort him when he woke up. He knew that people would say Kent had behaved like a coward and a traitor in the clearing, he told himself that maybe he had, but it did not alter his own feelings of love and respect for Kent in any way. He had known intuitively that Kent would let the three men die and give in when he thought that his own turn had come; he also knew that in the last resort Kent would have let him die, and horribly, if it would have saved his own life. He could see nothing to grumble about in that, nothing to condemn; people were like that, at least most of them were. They would say that they weren't, of course, and believe it, but they would learn the truth about themselves when the stick was raised a second time and with the thought present in their minds that this was only the beginning of repeated pain. There were heroes of course, he thought, leaning on his elbow and watching a handful of sand trickle through his rough fingers, that woman Joan of Arc, for instance, she must have been one. But there always seemed to be something odd about heroes, either they got religion or believed in something else or just wanted to show off. It wouldn't be easy for most people to be heroes, most people didn't believe in anything very much, at least nothing important, nothing except themselves. A lot said that they believed in God, but of course they didn't really, that was just like saying 'pleased to meet you' to someone you hated on sight.

But he still wished that Kent had not mentioned the tanks. That was the sort of thing he would remember first when he woke up and reproach himself with because as things turned out it hadn't been necessary. But perhaps it would be all right, there were several ways in which Kent could still excuse himself. He could pretend that he didn't remember anything that happened in the clearing because of the wound in his head, or that he had only been trying to save Anson. He might even pretend that he didn't believe there were any tanks at all, and only said it to confuse the Japanese. Anson could not make up his mind which one would be used, nor did he care, but there was a disquieting thought in his mind that Kent might grow to hate him because he had been a witness. There was also what had happened between them the other night, last night of course. The two added together might be quite sufficient for Kent to wish him dead; he remembered the bleak look on Kent's face when they had stopped on the track and that he had turned into a smile when he saw that Anson was watching him, and from that look he had correctly interpreted Kent's feelings. He sighed

150

deeply, here was yet another reason why he should pity Kent, it must be terrible to have to twist and complicate everything in your mind so as to exclude any chances of happiness. It seemed to him that the only satisfactory thing about the whole business was his knowledge that at least Kent had wanted him.

He caught sight of the crudely patched square on his shoulder strap and smiled sadly. He would leave it on until they got back, it was nice to pretend that he was an officer and didn't have to call Kent 'sir'. It had been a good idea, cutting a chunk off his puttees and sewing them on. He could remember reaching Kent after the bang and dragging him behind a tree, and then he must have passed out himself because the next thing he could recall were people shouting and crashing past where they were lying, people screaming further up the hill and the tremendous noise of firing and grenades. After a little while the noise died down and then he had heard furtive sounds and peering out had seen the Japanese slipping through the jungle all round him. It had been difficult in the extreme getting his shirt off, finding his hold-all, cutting the patches with a razor blade and then the long fumble in the dark to thread the needle. And he had been scared too, he told himself complacently, he could have threaded the needle blindfolded if his fingers hadn't been shaking, and he'd have still been trying to thread the thing if he hadn't suddenly thought how bloody funny it was trying to do a bit of sewing lying next to someone who might be dying and with the Japs all round.

Not that it was so very funny about Kent, it would have been terrible if he had died, but there was nothing he could do except stay with him until he came to. And then there had been that nasty moment just as it began to get light and a Jap had stumbled over them, an officer by the way he was ordering people about, and he had pointed to his sewn-on pips and then Kent's and watched the struggle going on in the man's face whether to press the trigger of his revolver and not to be bothered with them, or whether as officers they might be worth sending back for interrogation. Luckily he had been conscientious and had made Anson and another man and a guard carry Kent back over the hill and down into that clearing. When he did have to take those cloth pips off he would keep them in his breast pocket for luck.

Kent muttered something in his sleep and Anson touched the back of his head with his finger-tips. Then he lay down close to Kent and slept. When he awoke it was very hot and Kent was sitting up touching his swollen face gingerly. He had found his shorts and put them on, but his shirt had fallen in the sand and

Anson got up and rinsed it out in the stream. He came back and knelt in front of Kent, smiling at him, but Kent glanced away, his eyes dull.

'There's no need to look away, sir,' he said quietly, laying in a slight emphasis on the word 'sir'. 'I must clean your face up a bit.' He put his hand under Kent's chin and determined to force whatever issues might be between them straight away. 'You can't go around the place looking quite so much of a wounded hero, your head and arm are enough without a bashed-in face.'

'Wounded hero indeed.' Kent's voice was flat. 'Not much of a hero, I'm afraid.'

'Why not? You didn't do anything wrong, you didn't know what you were saying, you were raving half the time.' Anson was speaking quickly, insistently: 'Why, you were so vague and dazed you even wanted to stay tied up to that tree, that'll show you.'

'Well, I suppose I wasn't what you might call exactly in my right mind. It's a pretty nasty crack on my head, isn't it?'

'Yes, sir, it's a bad crack.' Anson spoke gravely. 'You're damn' lucky to be alive.' Kent put his hand to his head and felt along the bandage and round the dressing.

'I . . . I can't remember a lot about it, you know. Did the Japs kill all those three men?'

'Yes, sir, all of them.'

'Are you quite sure?'

'Yes, sir, positive, there couldn't be any possible doubt. And what's more I wouldn't be surprised if the Japs weren't killed themselves by the bombs.'

'That doesn't matter so much, I mean of course it does matter, but it's not like having one's own men killed. Oh well, I suppose one must try and remember there's a war on.' He knew now that Anson did not condemn him but he wanted to hear it said. 'So you don't think I screamed and hollered and opened my mouth too wide?'

Anson put his hand on Kent's knee and leant forward, pretending to wipe some more blood from Kent's throat. 'No, sir, I don't think you did; it was bloody awful there, and you were wounded and beaten up. Anyone's entitled to babble a bit and yell under those circumstances, I know I should.'

Kent did not answer. He had wanted, more than anything else, to hear Anson say those words, and now that they were said, perversely they brought him little comfort, and he was still oppressed by a sense of guilt. It seemed to him that in a matter of hours the whole façade that unconsciously he must have built up over the years to hide his true nature had crumbled away. Or perhaps the façade had been the true character, perhaps his whole nature was undergoing a terrifying change and he saw himself as a contemptible pervert, terrified of dying, prepared to sacrifice everything except his own life. But that was too harsh a picture for him to live with, and as his mind recoiled from it he told himself that in any case it was not the truth. As for being a pervert (and the word conjured up, for him, repelling images of furtive old men peering over the tops of public urinals, clergymen volunteering to undergo 'treatment' for six months to avoid prison, and effeminate shop assistants talking like a music-hall comedian), last night was the first time that anything of that nature had happened to him. And that of course he could stop, that was only due to being away from Celia for so long, as soon as he could he would find that nice nurse he had had on the boat and who was always writing to him. Helen, that was the name. He looked at Anson and knew that he ought to get rid of him and take another batman. But that was impossible, he knew far too much. He was honest enough to admit that he still felt attracted towards Anson, but he was certain that it would disappear once he started sleeping with women again. As for being a coward, that was true. He knew now that he was terrified of the possible physical agonies of death or mutilation, but he must in future steel himself to do his job and try not to think too much about its horrors. Cowardice was something that could be absolved at once by an act of bravery. What he had done could never be undone, but at least it could be counter-balanced.

He took his shirt from Anson and struggled into it, leaving the tails flapping to dry more quickly. As he got up he automatically looked for his equipment; it was a shock to find both himself and Anson were now weaponless, and he felt fear move again in his blood like a sickness, but he pushed it away.

'We've got to get back to the battalion as soon as we can,' he said. 'It won't be very nice getting through the Jap lines without any weapons but I can't help that. Of course we could avoid them by heading upstream and getting across and then coming down and crossing again below the bridge, but that would take so long and quite honestly I don't think I'm strong enough to tackle two crossings. We must take a chance, that's all.' He spoke as though what he proposed was just a boring piece of routine, but he heard the firing in the distance and his body felt heavy with reluctance to go towards the sound.

Before they started Kent stood by the stream listening to the faint noise of firing. As he faced north towards the river the sounds

F   153 came from his left and he judged about two miles away. Once away from the stream the trees were neither very thick nor very high, but even so the undergrowth would make it impossible to see more than ten yards ahead. Apart from the fact that he knew there was a jungle-covered ridge between himself and the battalion he had no idea what other obstacles he might meet, but that was the least of his worries.

By the sun's position and the heat of the day he judged the time to be between two and three o'clock. They knelt down and drank as much as they could hold and then left the stream and began to walk towards the firing. Anson asked if he should go in front but Kent shook his head, he had learnt that his own flair for finding the easiest and most direct route in this type of country was not shared by many other people.

He soon realized that the task was much more formidable than he had imagined; after the first few hundred yards his head began to ache and at the end of what he thought was an hour he felt that his skull would burst with pain and that Anson must be able to hear the blood pounding in his ears. The ground was scored by a succession of small ravines running from north to south that they had to cross. The dry undergrowth and dead leaves hid the loose stones and going down they were constantly slipping, falling backwards to save themselves; climbing up was even more laborious, the sweat dripping from their chins, their hands becoming more and more lacerated as they clutched at the coarse tufts of reed-like grass and thorny bushes to stop themselves from toppling backwards.

Kent began to rest more frequently and for longer periods, the water that he had drunk seemed to have poured out of his body again and his mouth was parched. Every time he lay down he swore that it was impossible for him to go on any longer, but a little strength would creep back, the flies would settle on his broken face with intolerable persistence, and without saying a word he would get shakily to his feet and start pushing clumsily on. The firing gradually grew louder and he began to try to evolve a plan, although he knew that at this stage it was useless to do so, but his mind persisted in weighing the advantages of getting through the lines by daylight or waiting for darkness.

They clambered down the side of one ravine that seemed less steep than the others, and when the ground began to rise again Kent guessed that he was on the last slope between himself and the fighting. He went some way off his course until he found a clearing and looking up he could see the top of the ridge about half a mile away. He remembered that the other side was much steeper and that the jungle covered it down to the track; he thought it unlikely that the crest would be occupied by the enemy, who would have no field of fire because of the trees, and the firing that he could hear did not sound clear enough to be coming from the top of the ridge. He turned to Anson.

'I'm going to make for the top of the ridge to a point I think is half-way between where the company was and the river. By the time we get there the sun will almost be gone, and I'll have to decide quickly whether to have a crack at it while it's still light. The Japs were this side of the ridge first, so for God's sake be careful or we might bump into one of their casualty dumps, if they bother about such things, or maybe a mortar section. Anyway let's get it over, this last bit'll finish me.'

They skirted the clearing, and once more the trees pressed round them. They moved as silently as they could, but it was impossible not to make sounds which seemed to Kent to be audible for hundreds of yards. Once he thought he could hear movement on the slope above him and they made a long and exhausting detour, and once a quail started up from under his feet and his whole body jerked with fear. And then, when he thought that the top was still some way off, he found himself on flat ground that started to fall away sharply only a few yards in front of him. There was some thin cover near the far edge and Kent walked unsteadily towards it, too exhausted, his head and face hurting too much, to care whether the ridge was held or not. He lay down on his face, put his head in his arms, and lost consciousness.

When he awoke it was dark, the moon was some distance above the horizon, but it was still honey-coloured. Anson was sitting beside him, but Kent was feeling too ill to wonder at his patience, even with his help it was as much as he could do to sit upright. Now that it was night he was convinced that they ought to have made the attempt by day; he wanted to grumble at Anson for not waking him earlier, but it was too much effort. He sat still, leaning heavily against Anson's shoulder, sleep lapping at his mind, and only kept at bay by something that puzzled him. Suddenly he knew and was wide awake.

'There's no firing!' he whispered. 'When did it stop, why didn't you wake me, you fool?'

'It didn't stop suddenly, it gradually got less and less soon after dark, but there're still occasional shots. I was going to give it another quarter of an hour and then call you.'

Kent sat for a few minutes trying to understand what the silence might mean. The only explanation he could think of was that the

Japanese must have put in a last assault and swamped the opposition. If that was so, they must try to slip through and rejoin the battalion as quickly as possible, before the Japanese could reorganize themselves. The moon was not yet high enough to light the western side of the ridge, and the thought of the cavernous darkness into which they would have to descend, and what might be in wait for them at the bottom, made Kent close his eyes. Leaning on Anson he got to his feet and moved cautiously to the edge of the ridge; there was a smell of burning drifting up the warm side of the slope, and while he stood irresolutely there was a long burst of firing from the darkness below him.

'Take my hand, let's go,' he whispered. They clasped hands and Kent started down the slope with one arm held out in front to protect his face from thorny scrub and branches, the other holding on to Anson, who followed closely behind, pulling back on Kent's arm. Stones spurted from their feet and clattered down the hill, his hands were so slippery with fear that Anson was forced to shift his grip and hold him by the wrist. They reached the bottom of the slope and again firing broke out on Kent's left. There was thick undergrowth in front of them and Kent crawled slowly and carefully through, to find himself looking down a ten-foot bank on to the track below. To his left, away from the river, he could dimly see the outskirts of the village and the railway embankment curving round at the point where he thought that he and Maguire had stood and where the C.O. had said that he would possibly set up battalion headquarters. If no one was there he would consider himself at liberty to cross the river.

They slid down the bank and walked across the track. Kent wanted to run but physically it was not possible. His mind was paralysed by the thought of blundering into the Japanese or being fired at from the thick blackness under the palms and trees. His knees felt so weak that it was an effort to walk, his heart pounded slowly and irregularly, and the pupils of his eyes were enormously distended. He skirted the edge of the village expecting at any minute that the smouldering ruins would burst into flames and betray him; now the moon showed over the ridge, he glanced up and saw the charred fronds of palm-trees. Dribbles of drifting smoke caught at him like cobwebs. He passed a well and identified it as such; although a few hours before he had wanted water desperately, now it was blotted from his mind, he was utterly alone walking through a dead world by the light of a dead world.

By the time he reached the end of the trees he knew that the battalion was not there; without pausing he left the shadows and began to cross the railway line. There were strands of wire forming a fence through which he blundered carelessly, letting the wires squeak and jangle back into place before Anson could reach them. He crossed the line and then he found himself through the further wire, the embankment receded jerkily behind him and he was in the shadows again. As the river came nearer and nearer the mingling of hope and fear made it difficult for him to breathe and sweat poured from his body like an acid. Clumps of bamboo now started to take the place of the stunted trees, and then he was standing on the edge of a strip of open ground, and twenty yards away the river glittered past him.

He stood quite still with Anson next to him and let the scene soak into his body, washing away tiredness and leaving a fierce excitement and desire to wade at once into the water and begin to swim. In the darkness he could dimly make out the far bank and on the ground in front of him were heaps of discarded clothing and equipment that stretched to his left and right until the clumps of bamboo grew to the river's edge and shut off his view. As well as equipment and clothing the ground was littered with rifles and bayonets, Bren guns lying on their sides with magazines still clipped in position, lengths of bamboo that had been hacked down to build rafts and then for some reason or another discarded. He sat down and began to unlace his boots. Anson stood next to him, looking at the far bank.

'Come on, be quick,' he whispered, 'the Japs will be here any minute now, God knows why they aren't already.'

'There's not much point taking my boots off, sir, I can't swim a yard, let alone this lot.'

Kent looked up, shocked into anger. 'This is a fine time to start talking about not being able to swim, of course you can swim, any bloody fool can. You can dog-paddle, can't you, and float?'

'No, sir, I've never been able to at all.'

'You'd better go down on your knees for a few minutes and then try walking,' Kent said savagely. First he thought he would leave Anson to be killed by the Japanese, but that was too uncertain, he might only be taken prisoner, and after the war . . . Then he thought that it would be better to help him into deep water and let him drown, with Anson dead no one could ever know about the clearing and the night before. Anson sat next to him on the ground and touched his hand timidly, like a servant saying good-bye to a devoted master, wondering if he is taking a liberty by offering to shake hands. In the darkness Kent's eyes filled with tears, pity and gratitude wrung his heart, remorse was like a pain.

He was appalled and humbled that such thoughts could come to him and he caught hold of Anson's hand in both of his.

'Forgive me, I'm sorry. I don't know what I'm saying. I'll get you across somehow, don't worry, it's quite simple.'

'I'm not exactly worried, I think I could make my way up-stream all right and get across somehow. But I would like to come with you if I'm not going to be a burden.'

'You're not a burden, I couldn't get on without you. And it's quite simple. Get a piece of bamboo about four feet long and we'll use the water-bottles from all this equipment. We can tie them on to the bamboo with our puttees, and our boots as well. Then we can lie on it with our chests and dog-paddle over.'

Anson found a piece of bamboo and a few minutes later they had scrambled down the deep bank and were squatting in the water lashing on the empty bottles with their puttees, both of them drinking from the few bottles that held any water. When they had finished there was a useless length of bamboo sticking out and Kent whispered to Anson to fetch a bayonet and hack it off. It only took a few strong blows, but the noise the hollow bamboo made seemed tremendous to Kent and increased still more his feverish anxiety to get away from the bank. As Anson chopped through the last tough fibres there was an unearthly cry close behind them. They fell back against the high bank and their feet started slipping in the thick clayey mud until they were sitting in the water and could feel its gentle swirl tug at them. The puttee-swathed bamboo lay across their knees. The cry died away in a low moan of pain and then a voice spoke in English.

'Where are you? Come back, you bastards, and help me. Don't leave me, for Our Lord's sake, don't leave me!' Anson moved as though to get up but Kent caught hold of his arm and held him down. Then they could hear the man begin to cry, with the abandonment of great pain and the bitterness of fear and loneliness. Kent got to his feet and dragged off his shirt, throwing it into the stream. He signed to Anson to do the same and waded into the river until he was waist deep. He looked round and saw Anson standing irresolutely with his shirt in his hands. Kent spoke quietly and calmly, his voice pitched low but above a whisper.

'Come here, Anson, there's nothing you can do except shoot him. I'm giving you an order now.' He waded out to Kent with a dazed look of entreaty on his face, but Kent turned away and knelt in the water. 'Kneel down and get the bamboo across your lower ribs. Push off. Don't get frightened and don't panic, I shan't let anything happen to you.' Now they were floating very slowly

158

downstream and Kent could tell that the water-bottles were buoyant enough to support their weight. They started paddling with their hands and feet, and the gap between themselves and the bank began to widen. The wounded man had stopped sobbing and started to call out again.

'Where are you, chums? You swore you'd come back for me, don't leave me, please.' The moonlight glittered and silvered the muddy waters most beautifully; in the distance to his right Kent could see the bridge that rose from the river, black against the moon-washed horizon, the centre span dropped at a sharp angle into the water. He paddled on strongly, afraid that the man's shouts would bring the Japanese to the bank and that they would be shot. Although he knew that it was wrong he felt a vicious anger against the wounded man that he should endanger their lives.

They had gone another thirty yards when the man spoke again. He was obviously trying to keep his voice under control, to keep it within a certain radius, and now it was free from entreaty, but laboured and slow.

'I won't shout any more, I'm sorry I've made a noise. When you're ready, please don't forget me.' Kent paddled on, holding his chin high to avoid the tiny waves. He thought to himself how ghastly it must be to be left like that, wounded and alone, but he told himself that there was nothing he could do about it, absolutely nothing. He tried to make himself feel sorrow for the man, but all he could feel was the joy and relief slowly filling his whole being as each moment made it more certain that he, Anthony Kent, would continue to go on living.

PART
THREE

I

KENT lay on his back with his eyes half closed watching Helen move efficiently round his bed pulling out the mosquito net. She gathered it in her arms and threw it over the iron frames above his head so that he was lying under a narrow white panoply. Through the door of the private ward he could see the daylight, but there were still traces of night in the room, pools of shadow lingered in the corners, a half-empty glass of water with bubbles of air clinging to the inside surface had not been replaced by the morning cup of tea, and the ash-tray held a few stiff V-shaped stubs of cigarettes.

They had long since stopped giving him sleeping draughts, and then he had begun to dream of the fighting; night after night he would wake sweating and whimpering, weak with relief that he was safely back from that dreadful world where people shouted, making no sound, where he ran through ghostly trees and over the soft rocks, ran until he fell exhausted to the ground only to find himself still crouching at the man's feet, listening to the noiseless swish of the sword as it started its downward arc. If when he awoke the dawn was not too far away he would stay awake, propped high on his pillows, watching the light growing and colour creeping back to the tired grass and the hibiscus bushes he could see beyond the veranda. As the light grew so the remembrance of his night-mare would dwindle back into the furthest recess of his mind, like a tree by the side of the road seen in a driving-mirror. The white walls of the mosquito net, only guessed at in the darkness, would take on a comforting solidity as the light grew, lending an air of security, shutting out the shadows that crowded just behind the head of the bed.

Helen stood by the bedside and he could hear the flip of her cuff against her wrist as she shook the thermometer. It would be the last time his day would start with that noise and he was sorry.

'How are you this morning, Tony?' she asked as usual, waiting for his reply before she took his temperature.

'Fine, thank you. Surely you're not going to take my tempera-ture this morning, are you?' He sat up in bed and brushed his hair back with his hands, smiling at her.

'Of course I must.'

'And my pulse, and all those awful questions about how many times?' She nodded. 'You can take my pulse but I shan't tell you the other, you'll have to guess.' She put the thermometer into his

163

mouth and held his wrist; her touch was cold and light. When she had finished she picked up his chart and Kent lay back on his pillows.

'If you really want to know, it's ten times.'

'In that case you'll have to stay in hospital a few more days while we take some specimens, you must have dysentery.' An Anglo-Indian orderly came into the room and put a mug of tea on the bedside table. As soon as he had left the room Kent sat up and started to drink.

'Where's the boy friend this morning, not chaperoning you as usual?' He held out his hand and she came slowly back to the bed and held it between her own.

'You're not to say things like that about Sergeant Johns. He's not my boy friend, and he doesn't have to chaperone me.'

'Not in the hospital maybe. But once I move into my bungalow he'll have to start, won't he?' He shook his hand in hers and watched her face. 'Come on, say it, won't he?'

'Really, Tony!' she protested, half shocked and half pleased, 'you're dreadful. You're being allowed out of hospital because we're short of beds and you will need a few weeks' convalescence. You've got to be quiet, not start . . . start . . . having parties,' she finished lamely, and they laughed. 'I'll come back after breakfast and help you pack.'

She spent the next hour efficiently touring her wards, but all the time she was thinking about Kent and wondering whether (as she phrased it in her mind) to become his mistress or not. To begin with, she had been horrified that she could consider it so cold-bloodedly; until she met Kent such an idea would have been un-thinkable, and now she was not only thinking about it but also with a man whom she knew was married. But the last months had changed her outlook; she had mixed with large numbers of Europeans who were not steeped in the tradition of irrational bitter contempt in which Eurasians were held, and the resulting familiarity had brought, if not a contempt for, at least a relaxation in her former strict code of behaviour.

Her hospital had been sent back from Meiktila to Maymyo, now crowded with sick and wounded, European evacuees, Government and Army headquarters. To begin with, the alien atmosphere of the town had depressed her. Outwardly she said how preferable it was, but the cool climate and blue hills fretted at her mind, more used to the flat burning plains or the wet stifle of Calcutta.

But finding Kent delirious in the reception ward had altered everything. She and Rowland had gone to the ward just as it was

164

light to sort out a trainload of sick and wounded that had arrived in the early hours of the morning. She had started to undo the bandages that swathed his head and face and that were half suffocating him in their disarray. She had recognized him almost at once, and the surge of love and pity that she felt had blurred the bed and his blood-clotted and swollen face.

On her own initiative she had had him moved into a room so small that it could only hold the one bed, and she had gone to him as soon as possible and cleaned his wounds in a passion of tenderness. Rowland had said that there was no need to worry about his arm and head, but his face was in a dangerously inflamed condition, wherever the skin was unbroken blood and pus had collected in pockets and had had to be lanced. All the time during the examination he had babbled incoherently, twisting his head on the pillow, and finally Rowland had given him an injection of morphia and he had slept until the early evening.

But it was not only finding Kent that had made her remember that day so vividly. She had gone to his room whenever possible, looking at him, feeling his pulse, touching his hot forehead, and as she was leaving after one such visit a private soldier had appeared in the doorway and asked her politely if Captain Kent was there. She had stood by the door filled with an unaccountable animosity and said that Kent was there but on no account could he be disturbed. Oh, had been the reply, that's awkward. I'm his batman, and he told me as soon as we got to Maymyo he would write a telegram for me to send to his wife.

It had been a strange moment. She had stepped back into the room without thinking, instinctively trying to shield her face from the strong light of the veranda, and Anson had misunderstood and come into the room. He had tiptoed across the red-tiled floor, the metal studs on his new boots scratching and clicking on the stone, and stood looking down at Kent, who was breathing deeply and slowly in his drugged sleep, his freshly bandaged head and face turned towards him. She watched him squat down on his heels by the side of the bed and look closely at Kent's face as though to make sure that the hospital had done its work properly, and then he straightened up and had had the impertinence to fold back the sheet that just touched Kent's chin and tuck it firmly in again. He had seemed quite oblivious of her presence and had gathered up Kent's soiled clothing that she had folded and left on a chair to be taken away, and as he tiptoed on to the veranda again he had beckoned her to follow.

The whole incident had hardly taken more than a minute, and

she could remember nothing of what she had thought except her anger that he should have touched the bed-clothes. But she had answered sensibly and calmly when he asked how long Kent would stay asleep, and had raised no objection when he said that he would come back in four hours' time. She even forgot to ask him what he was going to do with Kent's clothes. Anson had smiled and thanked her and then left, making no effort to walk with her as far as the veranda steps. She had intended to snub him if he had.

And she had walked along the veranda repeating to herself: 'He's married, he's married'. She had gone to her room and tried to cry, but after a few sniffs in front of the cheap hospital mirror she had noticed that her hair was untidy and as she slowly moved the comb through her hair she gave up the attempt to cry. He was married, so that was that. She had tried to feel bitter against him but with no more success than with her tears. Nor had she felt bitter as the days went by and he rapidly began to recover, treating her with a familiarity and making allusions to the boat which she knew were not meant to hurt but which she resented, and resented the more because he never mentioned his wife.

She had determined that she would not be the first to speak of it, but after a time her curiosity became too strong to master, and one day when she came into his room and found him writing a letter she had asked if it was to his wife before she could stop herself. He had looked up at her and smiled, completely unembarrassed or surprised, and said yes, it was. And she knew then that he had never loved her at all, and she thought that his present behaviour was designed solely to persuade her to sleep with him as soon as he was well.

'Oh,' she had said, 'I didn't know that, not when we were on board. It would have been quite different if I had known.' At that moment she could have cried, because he had never loved her, even for a matter of hours, and the knowledge was bitter and deeply humiliating. She glanced at him quickly and then turned away, pretending to arrange his shaving brush and razor on the rickety wooden wash-stand, afraid that she might betray herself. He was looking at her and no longer smiling, his eyes hurt and concerned.

'I never made any mystery about it, Helen,' he answered quietly, 'Rowland knew. If you want the truth, it didn't occur to me either way whether to tell you or not; I'm sorry if I've hurt you. Besides, if you had told me something about *your*self I certainly wouldn't have done what I did. Don't be upset, after all you're not in love with me.'

'It doesn't matter, Tony, I can't explain properly, and even if

166

I could I don't think you would understand. I'm beginning not to understand myself any longer.' And she had gone out of the room and to her own quarters.

There had been no need to try to cry, she had lain on her bed and the tears of deep unhappiness had welled out of her eyes. She thought that she cried for Kent, but it had been for her childhood, for her mother and family, for the years of humiliation because she was a Eurasian; she cried because she felt that she had betrayed them, those people who bound themselves together by acts of love and charity to help them bear the cold contempt of the world they knew.

When she next saw him she was surprised that he mentioned the matter again, she had thought that it was a subject that he would prefer to forget as being too embarrassing to discuss. But he had apologized again and caught hold of her hand, rubbing her finger-tips gently against his bandaged face, looking steadily at her with an appeal that she found disturbing and did not understand. But after that the subject of his wife had not been mentioned and now she found it difficult to think of him as being married unless she made a deliberate effort to recall the fact.

She finished her round and went to the mess-room for break-fast, forcing herself to eat although she wanted nothing except the strong tea. She could not decide in her own mind whether she was still in love with Kent or not; she was sure that before Kent left the hospital he would in some way demand an answer from her as to whether she would agree to sleep with him again. Not only did she not know what her answer would be, she was also hurt and puzzled by her knowledge. She felt that it was an unusual thing for a man to do, the behaviour of someone who was either too lazy or too indifferent to make her want to sleep with him whether she thought it right to do so or not. If he had taken her for granted she would have been far more deeply insulted and would certainly have refused, but that was not the case; apart from his familiarity he was almost humble, as though he was asking a great favour and begging not to be refused.

When the time came for her to help him pack his few belongings she was still confused. As she walked to his room she made up her mind that whatever the outcome might be she would try to do whatever was best for Kent, and as soon as she had made that decision she was at peace with herself. But when she entered the room she knew at once that her intuition had been wrong. Kent and Anson were kneeling on the floor strapping up his new valise, and the room had a vacant atmosphere as though he had already left.

2

As they drove through the town in an open gharry Anson wondered whether Kent's attitude towards him would change now that he had left the hospital. He felt that Kent had become a stranger to him, and that they were further apart than when he had first started working for him. At that time a feeling of strangeness was to be expected, but now Kent behaved as though he wished to forget everything that had happened between them. For a little time Anson had put it down to the effects of his wounds, but it had soon become apparent that this was not the cause. Then he thought that Kent was ashamed of himself and despised him; for a few days he had been very unhappy and finally he had gone to Kent and suggested that he should return to the battalion, hinting at the same time that when Kent came back he might prefer to take another batman. Kent was sitting up in bed reading, and as soon as the suggestion had been half made he had put down his book and lit a cigarette. There had been a long silence while he tapped at his cigarette with his forefinger. Without looking up he had asked if he wanted to go back, and when Anson said no he had picked up his book again and replied coldly that in that case the question seemed rather pointless.

But since then he had improved a little. He had been polite and very generous, giving him sums of money that to Anson were very large and telling him to go out and enjoy himself and if he felt ill the next day not to bother to come to the hospital. Anson had tried to refuse the money, but Kent had insisted and in order not to give him any cause for annoyance Anson had accepted but not spent it. When he had first heard that Kent had been lent a small bungalow on the far side of the town from the hospital and barracks, he had been secretly delighted, thinking that he would want him to live there in order to look after him. He had never expected to live in the house with Kent; there were the usual tiny brick-built servants' quarters at the far end of the garden, and he had already spent a whole afternoon scrubbing out one of the hovels and throwing buckets of disinfectant over the walls and corrugated iron ceiling, only to be told the next morning that Kent had arranged for an Indian bearer to look after him and that he would continue to live in the barracks.

As they passed through the centre of the town Kent told the driver to stop and he went into a liquor store and bought some

168

bottles of gin and brandy. When he came back to the gharry he made no comment about it, and Anson felt an emotion that was almost jealousy.

'It looks as though you're going to have a good time, sir.' He was smiling as he touched the box of drink on the seat in front of them.

'Oh, I don't know,' Kent answered, 'but I expect I know a few of the officers in Maymyo just now and I shall have to ask people back to the bungalow for drinks sometimes.'

'If you're going to have a lot of parties won't your bearer need a bit of extra help?' He tried to speak casually but his voice was anxious. 'Don't you think it would be much better if I stayed with you? I could easily doss down at the end of the garden.' Now that he had started to speak he could think of an enormous number of advantages in his staying with Kent, but before he could go on he was interrupted.

'No, I'm afraid it's impossible. I want you to come out every day of course, but you must stay in the barracks. And don't forget that if you're asked at the depot why you're still with me it's because you're doing my dressings and stuff like that.'

They drove on in silence, and the gharry turned into a gateway and stopped in front of a small bungalow half covered with purple bougainvillæa. Anson started to carry Kent's valise up the veranda steps, ignoring the Indian bearer who had appeared, but before he reached the open door Kent called out sharply to him:

'Leave all that, Anson, the bearer will see to it. You push off now and be back at six tonight. Take the gharry and tell the driver to come here at twelve o'clock, I want to go to the club.' Anson put the valise down and walked slowly back to the gharry. He paused before he put his foot on the step and then suddenly turned and looked at Kent, who was telling the bearer to be careful of the drinks.

'Don't do too much today, sir, and don't drink too much.' He tried to smile, angry with himself for having spoken, and Kent looked coldly back at him.

'Don't start worrying about me, I'm perfectly capable of looking after myself.' And Anson saluted with an expressionless face and drove away.

3

When the gharry turned out of the short drive Kent crossed the veranda into the narrow hall. The lounge was on his right; he went in and threw his hat and belt into an arm-chair. He sighed with relief; in spite of having had a ward to himself he had never been conscious of privacy, people were coming into his room at all hours of the day until he had almost forgotten what it was like to be alone. He knew that his problems still remained to be solved, Helen and Anson and his cowardice, but he had decided to enjoy the luxury of not thinking about them for two days, and then he would deal first with the question of Helen. Now he would relax and pretend that his life was uncomplicated again, he would let the two days drift by, eating and sleeping and getting drunk.

He was pleased to see that the bearer had filled a few vases with hibiscus flowers and although they were crammed together in the usual breathless fashion he decided to leave them alone until tomorrow. It was a large room, running the full length of one side of the house with windows and double doors giving on to the garden. He opened all the windows and wedged back the doors to let the sun stream into the room.

He spent the morning wandering aimlessly about the bungalow and garden, examining the bedroom and bathroom on the other side of the passage from the lounge, deciding to use one corner of the veranda for his meals, making the bearer stagger across the lawn with a large arm-chair in which he intended to sit and sunbathe, picking a few scarlet and yellow canna lilies to put on his dressing-table. There was a stack of old records and a gramophone in the lounge; occasionally he would put on some sentimental tune and then go into the garden and walk away, listening to the gentle sadness of the faint music.

When the gharry came back at twelve o'clock he had almost decided to stay at home and let the bearer cook him some eggs for lunch. Now he felt diffident about going to the club and mixing once more with officers, but he put the idea sternly out of his mind and went into the bedroom to get ready. The sight of his face in the mirror seemed to give him confidence; the left side was still streaked with long red scars and his head was neatly bandaged. He hoped that people would realize that he had been wounded and not merely involved in a truck accident.

He had expected to find the club almost deserted, but it was surprisingly full, and judging by the noisy laughter at the bar a few of them had already been there some time. He noticed that most of the officers had either been wounded or injured, their arms in slings or they stood leaning on heavy sticks. There were also a number of middle-aged civilians who had been forced to leave their jobs or properties; now they did nothing except sit about the club, waiting to see whether they would be forced to leave for India.

Kent had only been at the bar a short time when the man next to him asked if he had heard the nine o'clock news; at once another man leant across and happily volunteered the information. They introduced themselves and began to argue as to who should pay for the first round of drinks; by half-past one Kent realized that he was nearly drunk and that his head was aching. He pretended to go to the toilet and left the club without saying good-bye or waiting to have lunch. As soon as he had paid off the gharry he walked stiffly and awkwardly into the bathroom and was sick in the chipped enamel commode, then he went into the bedroom and flopped down on the bed without bothering to take off his boots. He propped himself up on the pillows and lay there with his hands folded in his lap, gazing out into the sun-flecked garden, listening to the sounds that drifted in through the open windows, waiting for sleep. He heard his bearer moving about in the corridor and then some whispered instructions in Urdu followed by the sound of the commode being taken out of its wooden container; the thought came to him that the sweeper was beginning to earn his pay and he smiled. Then he shouted to the bearer to come into the room.

'What's your name?' he asked. 'Why didn't you tell me this morning? I can't guess these things, you know.'

'Sammy, Sahib.'

'Sammy. That's an English name.'

'Yes, Sahib. I'm Christian boy from Madras.' Kent looked at him. His skin had the colour and curious bloom of a black plum and when he spoke he showed large pinky yellow teeth stained beyond cleaning by chewing betel nut. The whites of his eyes were muddy.

Kent looked away and suddenly thought of Anson. 'Go into the lounge and put on the first gramophone record on the pile. The first one,' he said, speaking to the window and slurring his words. The sentimental tune began and Kent closed his eyes. Before the music stopped he was asleep and when he awoke it was nearly six o'clock and Tarrant was sitting on the end of his bed, drinking a cup of tea.

4

Kent sat up slowly, rubbing his hand over his face; he was pleased that Tarrant should find him resting and almost certainly, he thought, looking ill.

'Well, well! What a pleasant surprise. Have you been here long?' There was a tray of tea by the side of the bed, and while he spoke he poured himself out a cup. It was very pale, with leaves floating on the surface.

'Just this minute, sir. I went to the hospital to find you and that nice nurse told me where you were. A nice place this, a bit better than Monbyeik. How are you feeling? Your bearer told me you had been to the club this morning and when you came back you were sick. I thought to myself that's Captain Kent all right, back in his old form, he'll be with us again any day now.' He laughed shortly and looked hard at the cup of pale watery tea.

'Have some gin,' Kent said. 'Sammy! Actually you're quite wrong, I did go to the club and I did have a couple of gins and I was sick, but like a fool I sat in the sun too long while I was there and I think that must have done it. Damn it all, I've only been pushed here because the hospital is so full, you don't expect me back the day I come out, do you?' He tried to strike a medium between banter and seriousness, but Tarrant's joke had revived his feelings of guilt. The bearer came into the room and Kent told him icily to take drinks on to the lawn and another chair, promising himself a few words in private on the subject of bearers who talk too much. He got off the bed and from long habit Tarrant stood up as well.

'I'm just going to the lav,' Kent said, 'wait for me on the lawn, will you, it's through the lounge, and help yourself to a drink.' His stomach was uncomfortable, and he guessed that he was about to start an attack of diarrhoea. He walked with Tarrant through the lounge and as soon as he had gone on to the lawn Kent picked up a paper and pencil and went to the lavatory. While he sat on the commode he scribbled a note to Anson. 'Sergeant-Major Tarrant is here. There's nothing I want. Come back at nine tomorrow, and don't forget to pick up the bandages from Sister Dean.' He did not sign it, and when he came out of the bathroom he gave the note to Sammy and told him to wait by the gate and give it to the soldier sahib who would be arriving in a few minutes.

'And don't come up and tell me when you've done it, you

stupid black bastard. And remind me I've got a bone to pick with you in the morning.' Sammy looked hurt, not because Kent had sworn at him but because he judged that it was expected of him.

Kent sat next to Tarrant and wondered what size gin he should drink. He could still feel the effects of the morning and knew that he ought to have some food, but he had not seen Tarrant since the night he had left the company to go to the ridge, and he wanted to be able to talk easily about it straight away. He poured himself out a large measure and splashed a little water into his glass.

'Good luck, here's to our joint survival,' he said, drinking half the contents of his glass. 'What's new?'

'I don't really know, sir. I suppose you heard all about the river fiasco?' He uncrossed his legs and leant forward eagerly.

'Yes, indeed I have,' he answered quickly, unwilling to hear yet another version of what had happened. He had already listened to five or six accounts from different men who had visited him in hospital, and now he knew that all the versions he might hear would differ fundamentally from the others, that they were, and could only be, accounts of what had happened to individual people. 'The man I'm most sorry about is the C.O. Terrible luck that, getting almost across and then being killed. It was mortar fire, wasn't it? Someone told me he had been hit in the head by a stray bullet, but I thought that sounded a bit funny, I don't see how you tell a stray bullet from any other.'

'Definitely mortar. Norton was killed at the same time. They say the C.O. would have got a good decoration if he had lived.'

'Can't you get a posthumous one?'

'No, sir, only a V.C.' There was a pause while they looked at the glasses in their hands.

'What's the new C.O. like?'

'Bloody good. He's the second we've had since you left. But what about you, sir? Of course I've heard roughly what happened from Captain Maguire; he saw you in hospital, didn't he? And while I remember I want to confirm about Sergeant Brewster and the other two men, Caffery and Bullock, wasn't it? You're quite sure they're dead? I've been sent back to the depot for a few days to give them a hand getting out a list of casualties.'

'Yes, I'm sure they're dead. I'm rather vague about the whole thing, I had only half come to from the crack on my head and being beaten up didn't help me to think any more clearly. But the Japs practically disembowelled all three, at least so Anson tells me.' He finished his drink and poured out two more; he was beginning to feel better and more confident, awaiting the next question almost with interest.

'Is Anson coming back to the battalion, sir?' Kent watched Tarrant's face carefully while he spoke; the question took him by surprise and without thinking he reached for his drink.

'Good God! yes, why shouldn't he? You seem to think I'm up here on leave. I didn't suggest coming to this bungalow or Anson staying, it was Rowland's suggestion.' What he said was very nearly the truth, and he looked Tarrant straight in the face, unsmiling. He knew that from one point of view it would be better if Anson did go back, but he told himself that it was not really necessary, and always at the back of his mind was the fear that away from him Anson might talk.

'Oh, it doesn't matter, nobody's worried about him. I just wondered if he had got extra-regimental employment. Apart from helping with the casualty lists I'm also having a comb through of different people while I'm here; we're only about quarter strength, you know, it's incredible where they've all got to. But to go on about yourself, tell me how you got across.'

Kent shifted more easily in his chair. The rest of the story came with the ease of truth, except for the embellishment that he had tried to find the company where he had left them and omitting any mention of the wounded man calling for help. But by the time he had finished his hands were sweating with remembered fear; every time he had to tell the story it was the same, the incidents would come crowding back with a vividness that he could not express in words. When he listened to other people's stories he would watch their faces, wondering if they too were feeling as he felt. He poured out more gin and lit a cigarette.

'Where is the battalion now? The last news I had was just after Probyin.'

'We're a long way back from there. The rumour just before I left was that we were going to be flown into China and re-form there, but there's a new rumour every five minutes. When do you think you'll be fit enough to come back? We've had a lot of new officers; they're all right, but I'll be glad when you take over the company again.'

'I'll be back soon,' Kent answered, 'probably in a fortnight. I suppose it's pretty hot now?'

'Hot? That's not my word for it, and there's damn all water where we are now. Every time we do a march back about ten people fall out with heat exhaustion, and what water there is comes out of stinking wells.'

'It sounds attractive.' He wanted to stop talking about the battalion and the fighting and abruptly he stood up. 'Let's go and get some food in the town, shall we? I'm hungry.'

The next morning when Kent woke up he could remember very little about the previous evening, except that they had gone to a Chinese restaurant and drunk quantities of cheap brandy and eaten a large meal of sweet sour pork. He could remember being ill over the side of the gharry afterwards, and Tarrant holding on to him drunkenly to stop him falling out, encouraging him to go on and bring it all up. He got out of bed and walked unsteadily into the living-room, expecting to see Tarrant sleeping on the sofa, but the room was empty. There were two half-full glasses on the table, and a few cigarette-ends that had been stubbed out long before they were finished. He picked up the glasses and smelt them; they were almost neat gin, and he threw the contents out of the window with a shudder of disgust. He felt cold standing in his cotton pants and vest, and went back to bed. He lay for a time trying to summon up enough energy to go to the lavatory and then someone walked past his window from the drive, and he heard Anson speaking to Sammy. He called out to him, lying on the bed half hidden by the mosquito net, listening to the heavy boots clumping along the wooden passage into his room.

'Tell Sammy to get my bath ready, will you, and tell him I want a proper bath; he's to boil at least four cans of water; I don't care if it takes him two hours. And you make some really strong coffee and change my bandage. I feel ghastly this morning. Tarrant was here last night; had you seen him?'

'No, sir, but I got your note all right. The nurse said she didn't know what you meant about the bandages, you've got plenty.'

'Have I? I didn't know. Listen, Anson. If Tarrant asks you anything about how we got back over the river I want you to say that we went to the old company position before we went to the river, and I don't want you to mention anything about that wounded man. You and I understand the position perfectly, there was nothing we could possibly do except get ourselves caught again. But you know what people are: if it gets out, then before you can turn round I shall have been rowed across by twenty loyal Burmese in a completely empty barge leaving loads of scarcely wounded men shouting for help on the far side. It's much better to forget the whole thing.' Through the mosquito net he could see Anson's face quite clearly. 'You agree, don't you?'

'Yes,' Anson said slowly, 'I don't suppose there was anything we could do, but I would have liked just to——'

175

'Yes, I know,' Kent broke in roughly, 'you would have liked to go and have a look at him. But that was just your bloody awful morbid curiosity, looking at him would only have made it fifty times worse for the poor devil, making him think you were going to help him when you weren't. You don't imagine I enjoyed leaving him, do you, or that I haven't . . .' He stopped himself from using the word 'regretted'. 'It just happens to be my bad luck that I'm the one who has to make decisions, and I decided, quite rightly I'm certain, that there was nothing we could do about it. We should have been a nice little trio getting across, two wounded men and a non-swimmer, don't forget that!' The compulsion to go on piling up arguments to prove himself right was almost overwhelming, but he managed to stop speaking and watched Anson anxiously.

'If you think it best not to say anything, then I won't,' but there was no servility in his voice; it had happened, it was finished, he accepted it. He looked steadily at Kent, who glanced away. 'I'll get the coffee.'

Kent followed him out of the room and went to the lavatory. His diarrhoea was much worse and he knew that unless he started to take large doses of chlorodyne it would go on like that for days. He thought wearily that the two days of peace he had promised himself had been a signal failure, he had not been allowed to forget anything that had happened, and suddenly he longed to be back again with his battalion so that he could try to make peace with his conscience. Then he remembered that first he must make his peace with Celia. He shifted uncomfortably on the wooden seat, propping his head in his hands and groaning in spirit. All the time he had been in hospital he had tried to feel desire for Helen; whenever she came into the ward to spend her few moments of freedom with him he would hold her hand and watch her face, trying to relive the drunken moments on the bed, trying to graft the desire he had then felt on to the present moment. His cold behaviour towards Anson had all been part of the pattern he was trying to weave, but nothing seemed to go right, he could not understand what was happening, he only knew that he was deeply frustrated and un- happy. He got off the seat and shut the lid viciously; he would ask Helen to come to the bungalow tonight.

He went back to the bedroom and threw the net untidily over the frame. Anson brought a large jug of bitter coffee and before Kent had finished the first cup came back with a basin of hot water and the clean dressings. Kent reluctantly moved his position so that Anson could sit close to him and then bent his head forward.

He could feel Anson's fingers fumble once with the safety-pin and unwind the bandage. The line came away easily; Anson's breath stirred his hair as he peered at the long scar.

'What's it look like?'

'It's fine, sir. It's healed completely since I last saw it, except for a small bit in the centre. I shan't bathe it at all, just a dry dressing.'

'Good. Be as quick as you can, this is vilely uncomfortable leaning forward like this.' Suddenly he was conscious of every movement of Anson's body, the tiny alteration in the folds of his shirt as he moved his arms preparing the dressing, a crease that appeared in his shorts as he turned towards Kent to rewind the bandage. He closed his eyes and moved his head further away.

'We're going back to the battalion very soon, Anson. Are you sorry?'

'No, I'm not, I'll be glad to get back. There's nothing for me to do here.'

'What do you call this, for God's sake?'

'It's only half an hour a day. The rest of the time I just spend kicking around barracks listening to a lot of lousy bastards telling each other what a terrible time they've had and what brave chaps they were, and isn't it a bloody shame about their fallen arches.' Kent was not listening, he could feel Anson's strong fingers winding the bandage tightly round his head. He was afraid that his fingers would brush against his forehead and Anson would notice that he was sweating.

'I want you to take a note to Sister Dean for me as soon as you've finished. I'm asking her to come here tonight for drinks, and do you know what I'm going to do?'

'I can guess.'

'You're dead right. When I've had her a few times we'll go back. What do you think of that?' His voice was unsteady and held a suggestion of a sneer.

'I don't think anything. It's your business.' He pushed the safety-pin into position and Kent leant back and opened his eyes. He ran his hand across his forehead as though he was feeling the bandage; his fingers were quite wet when he took his hand away. He went into the lounge and sat down at the desk.

'My dear Helen,' he wrote, 'I wonder if you would come and have a drink with me at six o'clock this evening. I'm not sure if this is one of your evenings off but in any case you could probably manage a couple of hours. If Rowland says anything tell him I'm not feeling very well and you want to have a look at me—the first part is perfectly true and I hope the second part is as well.' He signed the note 'With love, Tony', and handed it to Anson. He left the desk and started to walk slowly out of the room.

'I've asked her for six o'clock,' he said without looking back, 'you had better pick her up in a gharry and bring her out here yourself.'

5

Soon after six o'clock Kent heard a gharry grating and rumbling along the road and then the sound of hooves slowing down to a walk. He got up from his chair on the lawn and went back through the lounge, pausing long enough so that he could appear on the veranda as Helen and Anson drew up. The sun was about to set behind the low bank of cloud that gathered every evening, but at this moment the golden light was flooding through the tall feathery trees and lay in broken pools across the garden. For Anson and Helen it had been a surprisingly pleasant drive; it was the first time that they had been quite alone together, and after a few moments of awkwardness they had started talking about Kent. Very soon Helen had forgotten all her vague feelings of resentment against Anson; it had been a relief for both of them to talk about him, and although there was only time to touch on the merest superficialities it had served as a link between them. As the gharry pulled up Kent saw them smile at each other, and then Helen got down and Kent kissed her awkwardly on the forehead as he put his arm round her.

'What time shall I tell the driver to come back? You don't have to go too early, I hope?'

'I promised I would be back by ten o'clock, is that all right?' She looked at him enquiringly and noticed that he smiled and glanced at Anson.

'Yes, that's fine. I thought we would have a few drinks on the lawn and there's some cold food in the lounge we can have when we're hungry. I won't pay him now, I'll tell him to be here at a quarter to ten.' There was the usual argument ending in the usual defeat for the driver, and as they walked through the lounge Kent turned to Anson, who was following hesitantly behind.

'Did you get the chlorodyne for me?'

'Yes, sir.' He fumbled in his breast pocket and pulled out a small bottle.

'Mix me two teaspoonfuls in a little water, I'll take a dose straight away.' Anson walked away glad to have something to do. He did not want Helen to think that he had come all this way from the barracks merely to bring her out and then go back.

'You're looking very smart tonight,' Kent said from behind her chair as she sat down, although he had only just noticed that she was not in uniform. It was a remark that he often made to Celia, thinking it was an abracadabra that automatically produced pleasure. He pulled his chair as close as possible to hers and put his hand on her knee.

'What would you like to drink, gin or brandy? I'm on brandy myself, I think it's better for my tummy.'

'A very little gin, please, Tony. Don't give me too much, it only makes me feel ill and I really don't like it.' Kent poured out the drinks and waited until Anson had brought him the medicine; he drank it down quickly and handed him back the glass.

'Don't bother about doing my head tonight. You'll find a few dirty clothes in my room I want you to take away and get washed, and Sammy's got some dinner for you at the back and some beer. I'll see you in the morning at nine o'clock.'

Anson thanked him in a low voice and said good night; just as he was turning away Helen looked round and said good night to him, and Kent saw them smile at each other again as though they shared a secret. It made him feel uneasy and he started talking quickly about how well his head was healing, and asked Helen if she thought he would be fit enough to go back to the battalion soon.

But it was not until he had drunk two large brandies that he was able to talk easily to her. They sat holding hands watching the shadows slowly blot out the garden and he began to feel a sense of peace and security stealing over him that he had not experienced for so long that he had forgotten what it was like. Sometimes when he turned his head towards her he could smell faint traces of her perfume and it made him sad; he would touch her cheek with the back of his fingers, so lightly that all he could feel were the hairs on his fingers moving. They heard Anson walk through the house and the crunch of his boots fading away down the road, and he was conscious that they were both listening to the footsteps. He started to speak again, asking if she had heard from her parents.

'I had a letter a week ago from Daddy, they seem very worried about me. Evidently they met some people in Calcutta who had just walked out of Burma, and these people told them what a ghastly trek it was. I can understand people who've lost their homes in

179

Rangoon going to India, but surely it can't be so serious that we'll have to go?'

'I don't know, there seem to be so many different rumours flying around. Some people say that we're going to hold Northern Burma, or that everyone is going to withdraw towards China, or that troops are already coming in from India, and the Japs are going to be pushed back before the monsoon starts. They'll have to be quick to do that. I don't know what to think.' They began to talk about the war, and the same uneasy feeling that had come to him the night before as he talked to Tarrant returned. He poured out another drink and looked at his watch. 'Don't let's talk about the war, it couldn't be more depressing, let's go in and have some food, shall we?' He stood up before she could answer and drained his glass.

They sat together on the sofa balancing plates of cold chicken and tinned ham on their laps. The room was softly lit by one standard lamp, and he had spent a long time arranging bowls of flowers. Their moods had changed from the easy talkativeness of the garden and the silences that now fell seemed to Kent to be almost unbreakable. The small noises of their knives and forks seemed to fill the room, and every time he swallowed his food he expected his stomach to give a long uncontrollable rumble.

He had managed to find some wine in the town, and he kept pressing her to drink, but she would shake her head and only touch the wine with her lips. He was wondering what she was thinking about, and whether she would resent what was going to happen taking place on the sofa, next to the litter of their meal. He told himself that he couldn't help it if she did. He had rehearsed everything in his mind, drinks on the lawn, flowers, dinner, and a lot of wine, and then they could lie together on the sofa. Like that it could all happen easily and naturally; he was afraid of having to interrupt their love-making just at the moment of intimacy and go into the bedroom; once there he would have to start all over again.

When they had finished eating he insisted vehemently that she should drink a glass of brandy, and suddenly, made miserable on his account by the nervous strain that emanated from him and filled the room, Helen turned towards him. She put her thin arms round his neck and kissed him on the mouth, pushing back a long wavy strand of hair that had fallen over his white bandage and touched his forehead. It was impossible for her to know what was in his mind, all she knew was that he was unhappy. The thought came to her that he was thinking about his wife.

'Don't worry so much, Tony, darling, you don't have to make me drunk, you know. I understand how you must feel about everything, don't worry, I shan't be troublesome, or ... or expect too much.' They looked at each other in the lamplight, their young faces set and stern. She saw him open his mouth as though to speak and then to her horror his eyes filled with tears that spilled over before he could hide his face.

'Darling! What's the matter? Don't cry!' She moved quickly so that he could lie beside her with his face buried in a cushion, and he lay still, trying desperately to control his tears. She kissed his hair, stroking it with fingers that shook with pity, whispering words of endearment as though he was her child. And Kent gave up the unequal struggle and cried, because he had had too much to drink, because she had said that she understood, and he knew that that was impossible, mourning for himself and his cowardice, for the man who had called by the side of the river, for his dead love and the unknown terrors of the new. And Helen's gentleness and the scent that came from her like flowers in a warm room acted as a catalysis to his tears.

After a time he felt the pain in his throat and behind his eyes relax and he sat up with his back to Helen and blew his nose.

'I'm terribly sorry,' he said huskily, 'I must be drunk, behaving like a schoolgirl. Excuse me a minute.' He got up and went to the bathroom, bathing his face in cold water and combing his hair. It was difficult walking back across the room towards Helen with the light in his face but he managed to avoid her eyes and when he sat down again he poured himself out a very large brandy and lit a cigarette. In the silence that followed she wondered what she ought to do next, whether to stay a little while with him and then leave or whether to offer herself to him. Because she would have preferred the former course she decided on the latter. And while Kent smoked his cigarette he also wanted her to leave, his feelings towards her now made the thought of sex seem almost incestuous, but his new love for her and his feeling of gratitude made it impossible for him to suggest that she should go.

Helen had made her decision but found it was too difficult to put into words. She stood up and held out her hand and he took it in his with a questioning look. She smiled at him reassuringly, nodding her head slightly and he stood up. Still holding his hand she led him through the lounge and into the bedroom. For a moment he had imagined that she was taking him on to the veranda to say good night, but once they were in the room and she had shut the door he realized what she intended. In silence and against both their wishes they took off their clothes and crept under the mosquito net, then they clung to each other in the darkness like children.

Later on, after Helen had gone, Kent went moodily back into the lounge. He took a blanket with him and sat wrapped up by the open doors looking into the dark garden, drinking brandy until he was sure that he could go to sleep without having to lie awake in the dark, thinking.

6

For the next week Kent spent nearly all his time either at the club or else lying about the bungalow. He would be called at nine o'clock and have breakfast on the veranda; however ill he felt he would eat something and drink cup after cup of strong coffee. Then he would wander into the garden and sit in an arm-chair in the sun, reading until the glare of light from the page hurt his bloodshot eyes and he would drop the book on the grass and lean back, dozing in the warmth, listening to the birds and the small domestic noises as Sammy and Anson went about their work.

There were a pair of golden orioles that often came into the garden, and Kent would watch them through half-closed eyes, listening to their infrequent liquid notes that fell like bright golden coins from the trees in which they searched for food. There were hoopoes that strutted near his feet, the crests on their heads rising and falling as though they possessed an independent life of their own, and thrush-like mynahs chattered from the wooden tiles of the roof or energetically quivered in their dust-baths in the dry flower-beds. It was warm enough for him to sit in a pair of white drawers, and he would let the sun draw out some of the previous night's debauch, sometimes watching the sweat trickling through the hairs on his chest, sometimes with his face turned so that the sun could camouflage the red weals that still showed.

The hour and a half that he spent in the garden were the only happy hours of the day. At the end of that time he would begin to feel restless and the sun would be too hot for comfort. He would go into the house and take a large dose of chlorodyne and wash it down with bismuth powder. He would shave sitting in the small tin bath with a piece of mirror propped on his knee, then dress slowly and by half-past eleven go to the lounge and drink a weak brandy and water. He would send Sammy out to fetch a gharry, and then wander casually to the back of the bungalow, glass in hand, and lean against the wall watching Anson busy himself with some voluntary job, carving a crude boat for one of Sammy's children or stripping his tommy-gun and soaking the parts in oil. They did not talk very much to each other after the night of Helen's visit, but Anson was aware that there was no longer any feeling of strain between them, and he was happy; he now spent his whole day at the bungalow, going back to barracks after his supper in the evening.

The gharry would come and sometimes Kent would drink another brandy before he left for the club. Once there he would soon be joined by other officers with whom he had spent the previous evening. They would sit round a large table on the veranda, telling each other how they had managed to get home the night before, whether they had been sick or not and how ill they had felt when they woke up. After a few rounds of drinks they would talk about the news bulletins, and then the latest crop of rumours would be gathered, endless rumours and each one partly believed in, if only for a short time, until the mind jumbled them together and then produced new variations. Every day there was a mounting atmosphere of crisis and break-up, not from the larger incidents of the Japanese advance, but the little stories of silver being buried by night in flower-beds, servants suddenly vanishing without waiting to be paid, women leaving by car for Lashio or Kunming, their husbands' civilian revolvers ostentatiously slung round their waists and wearing gaily coloured corduroy trousers. And others headed for the Chindwin and India, taking their servants with them, their cars piled high with tinned food that later they were to share with anyone who asked.

Their happiness and excitement once their decision to leave was made had a profoundly disturbing effect not only on Kent but on all those who had to remain. Their attitude was either quite unconscious or else assumed with the good intention of not wishing to add to the worries of their already harassed husbands and friends. People who had lived for years in Burma nonchalantly left their houses for ever, taking with them only their most precious and smallest belongings; their furniture and linen, wardrobes and china that had slowly been acquired were abandoned apparently without a qualm of regret, and their talk was all of Delhi and Calcutta and the new homes that they would try to start once they arrived. Married or single the men listened and caught the infection as well, the impossibility of their leaving only acting as a further irritant.

By one o'clock the club would be crowded and women would

come to the group of officers on the veranda and wish them good luck and tell them to be sure and visit them as soon as they too arrived in India. Then they would have a farewell drink and the men would joke about the Naga head-hunters and the thin shoes that the women were wearing. By two o'clock they would be tipsily hungry and eat a rowdy meal in the dining-room, always ending in an argument as to who should pay for the wine and liqueurs. Kent would drive back to his bungalow through the hot afternoon sun, the swaying gharry making his head ache and swim, and then tumble on to his bed and sleep heavily until six o'clock. He would wake up as the sun was beginning to set and lie for a little while dazed on his bed, watching the golden light change to blue, his tongue furred with cigarette smoke and his face puffy from sleep and drink. He would bathe and shave again to freshen himself, take more medicine and sip brandy until he felt better, and then go to the club, sitting at the bar playing poker dice, talking all the time about the war and what was likely to happen in the next few weeks, drinking brandy and water as though he was thirsty, and smoking incessantly.

There were four or five other officers with whom he spent most of his time, and who were heavier drinkers than the rest. By ten o'clock the others had gone into the dining-room or joined various parties around the dance floor, and then Kent and his friends would buy a few bottles of spirits and sit in deck-chairs on the lawn in front of the club. By this time they would be drunk, but still with some hours to go before satiation forced them to find their sleepy drivers and sprawl in their gharries to their various quarters. It was on the lawn that their moods changed from being flippantly gay to the morbid and macabre, once more in a low voice telling the man next to them how they had seen their best friend die in battle, how they had been wounded, how low morale was, and which officers had disgraced themselves by showing fear. Most of this circle had in fact been wounded and they behaved as though this gave them the right to criticize every aspect of the campaign; drunkenly they damned their general and the whole organization, and when those subjects were exhausted they discussed in detail what they themselves would do if they had the good fortune to capture alive any Japanese.

At midnight the club would begin to close, and the sound of music stop; they would sit on for some time yet, more out of bravado than enjoyment, and when the first person yawned and stretched and got unsteadily out of his chair the others would follow suit. They would linger in a little group by the side of the club

184

where the gharries waited, leaning heavily on each other and trying to make up their minds whether to go to a brothel or not. When the time finally came for them to leave they would fortify themselves against being alone by arranging the inevitable meeting on the following day, and with a last swig of raw spirit out of the bottle they would climb into their gharries and be driven away.

Kent would sleep heavily until thirst forced him awake. He would blearily gulp down two or three glasses of water and then sleep uneasily for the rest of the night, haunted by dreams until the day showed palely through the net. Then he would sleep again for a few hours and awake feeling ill and depressed.

He did not see very much of Helen, although occasionally he would ask her to come to the club during her supper hour. They would sit in the dining-room and he would watch her eat a hurried meal while he drank, and immediately after supper she would leave to go back to the hospital. He never drove back with her, and if when he returned to the bar anyone showed surprise that he was back so soon he would hint mysteriously that there were reasons why they did not want to be seen together too often near the hospital. To his friends he pretended that if it were possible he would see her every night, and by evasive answers to direct questions let it be understood that she was in fact his mistress. But he knew that he would never sleep with her again, and when he kissed her good night it was merely an affectionate formality. He only asked her to the club because he was fond of her, and because he wanted to be seen in her company.

Tarrant had gone back after only two days in Maymyo, taking with him a draft of men recruited from the debris of various battalions. They had met once more and Kent had told him to expect him back in a few days. But once he had left Kent scarcely thought about him at all, it was as though all the long time that they had been together had never happened. At the end of his first week away from the hospital he had gone to be examined by Rowland, who was exhausted with work. He had glanced at the scar on his head, noticed vaguely that Kent was looking tired and unhealthy, and told him to report back at the end of the next seven days. Kent had gone back to the club and complained bitterly about the fussiness of doctors, ashamed of the inward jubilation that made him want to laugh hysterically at the feeblest of dirty stories.

7

A few days later he was sitting in the garden when the sirens started in the town. There had already been several false alarms, and he took no notice until he heard the first faint sounds of planes. He was not afraid, the bungalow was on the outskirts of the town, and there were only a few scattered houses near him, half hidden by trees. He judged that the planes were flying very high and were unusually numerous. He lay on the grass when he heard the bombs whistling down and exploding in the town, and then the planes passed over him in the direction of Mandalay.

He went to the club earlier than usual that morning and found the bar already crowded with people talking excitedly about the bombing. By one o'clock there was a rumour that Mandalay had been bombed, and that the city was on fire, but nobody was very interested. By the time Kent went home for his afternoon sleep he was more drunk than usual and slept later. He went back to the club again but he felt too ill to do more than eat a little chicken and drink two glasses of wine. He sat at the bar afterwards and tried to drink some brandy, but every time he took a sip it seared his stomach and without saying good night he left the club.

Outside the air smelt faintly of carnations and a young moon was setting. After the club it seemed so fresh and peaceful that he decided to go a long way round and then cut back through the town towards home. As they drove slowly up the main street he looked for signs of damage but there was very little to see; only fragmentation bombs had been dropped, and apart from one or two smouldering ruins there was nothing. When they reached the end of the line of shops he saw Anson standing by himself outside a small restaurant; without thinking he called to him and told the driver to stop, and Anson came quickly towards the gharry.

'Have you had food here or at the bungalow, or what are you doing?' Kent asked. He suddenly felt much better and wide awake.

'I had food at the bungalow, I was just going back to barracks. You're going home early tonight, aren't you, sir?' His voice was frankly curious.

'I got bored and thought I'd have an early night for a change, and now I'm sorry. Why don't you come back and have a drink with me, it's only ten o'clock, you needn't be back until twelve.' There was a moment's silence and then Anson got into the gharry and the driver flicked his whip along the horse's emaciated flank.

Kent made some remark about the bombing but Anson did not reply, and they drove in silence along the dark roads, with the stars moving slowly through the trees above them.

All the way back to the bungalow Kent wondered what to do when they arrived, whether to keep the gharry and send Anson back to barracks in an hour's time or whether to pay the man off and let him go. He now knew quite clearly what he wanted to do but he was still struggling against himself, bitterly resenting the truth and terrified of the consequences, all his upbringing and fundamental ignorance shouting at him that what he was considering was unthinkable, beyond words dreadful. As they turned into the drive the thought came to him that some of his friends at the club might miss him and decide to look for him at the bungalow; the mere idea of being found treating a private soldier as an equal, sitting in the lounge drinking together, was enough to panic him, and he decided to tell the driver to wait.

They drew up at the veranda steps and Kent turned to Anson. He could see his face in the starlight. 'I think we had better keep the gharry, don't you?' He whispered as though someone might be eavesdropping. 'I don't want to make you late getting back to the barracks and catching seven days' C.B.' He tried to smile but his face was stiff. Anson answered in the same low tone of voice.

'Don't worry about that, sir, it's dead easy getting into barracks without being seen, and the bloke in charge of my room won't say anything.' Kent didn't reply for a moment, and then he nodded his head and got out. He was telling himself that he had done nothing wrong so far, and that drinking to a time-table spoilt an evening. He gave the driver the full amount he was asked, suddenly anxious for him to go.

They walked quietly into the lounge and Kent felt for the light switch. Before he turned it on he whispered in the dark towards Anson.

'I left the club this evening without saying good night to the officers I was with. If we hear anyone coming up the drive slip out through the french windows and go back to barracks. Whatever you do, don't be seen.'

'Right, sir.' He turned on the ceiling light and they stood with their eyes narrowed, smiling at each other, then Kent pulled the cheap curtains and opened the doors into the garden. There was a tray of drinks by the sofa and as they sat down Kent asked him what he would like.

'Beer if there's any handy, sir, I'm not very used to spirits.' He smiled almost apologetically at Kent, who passed him a bottle of beer and a glass, helping himself to brandy. His feeling of illness and repulsion at the thought of alcohol had completely gone, he was happy and excited as though about to start a long planned journey.

As he drank and talked at random he was aware of a mounting physical sensation that was not unpleasant but made him feel that he had no control over his stomach and at any minute might be sick, not with a sweaty nausea, but as though one had drunk champagne too quickly and threw it up easily before the wine was corrupted by the stomach. As they talked they looked each other straight in the face; it became difficult to disengage their eyes even when a silence fell, and the silences began to fall more frequently and last longer.

Kent looked at his watch and saw to his amazement that it was nearly one o'clock. Then he felt relief, no one would come to the bungalow now.

'Good God above! It's nearly one o'clock,' he said, at the same time reaching for the bottle. He poured himself out a drink and looked at Anson over the rim of the glass.

'Do you want me to go, sir?' Anson spoke quietly, sitting back against the cushions in the corner of the sofa.

'Do you want to go?' Kent swallowed some neat brandy. He was afraid he would be sick where he sat, his eyes felt enormous, immovable, the words were said almost, it seemed, without any volition on his part, and the word 'want' balanced all the other words. Far away they could hear a dog barking and the curtains across the garden doors stirred.

'No, sir.' He shook his head slightly without moving his eyes. Kent drained his glass and got up, knocking the low table with his leg. A long-stemmed glass fell over and splintered, but he did not notice, he was suffocating, the palms of his hands slippery and cold with sweat; without thinking he wiped them on his trousers and held out his hand to Anson.

They crossed the room like dreamers, the blood in Kent's ears pounded and the shadowed doorway swayed. 'Oh, God, I'm drunk,' he thought, 'I must send him home. Oh, God, I'm drunk!' They reached the doorway and he saw the light switch, and then the room was in darkness and they moved together.

In the darkness of the bedroom they stripped off their clothes swiftly, laying them on the floor at their feet, noiselessly taking off their boots as though the faintly showing mosquito net held a sleeper who must not awake. Lying down side by side on the bed they encircled each other with their arms, until Kent was aware

188

that he was cold and pulled up a sheet and one thin blanket. In the darkness Anson turned to Kent.

'Do you think I ought to go now?' He still spoke as though there was someone asleep in the room and Kent was pleased, although he could not have told why. He peered at his watch and for the second time could hardly believe the swiftness with which time had passed.

'What's the latest you can be back with safety?'

'Six-thirty would be all right.'

'Why don't you stay here until six then, there's no point in going back now, unless you want to. Let's have a cigarette and then sleep for a while, as long as we don't oversleep.' He fumbled for the cigarettes and matches on the table by the side of the bed and lit two together. He knew that the end of the one he handed Anson was wet but it didn't matter. Nothing mattered now, he thought, as he lay back and slid his arm between the pillow and Anson's shoulders, watching the inside of the net glow faintly as he drew deeply on his cigarette, nothing at all. He had committed the unforgivable sin and now there was nothing to be done except not to be found out.

They lay in the dark security of the net, and Kent felt sadness stealing over him, a sadness of regret and emptiness. He wanted Anson to leave and yet he wanted him to stay, his mere presence was a comfort, a shield against the darkness of the night and the remorse that would come with the day. He finished his cigarette and reaching down the side of the bed crushed it out on the bare floor. Silently Anson handed him his own cigarette and as Kent stubbed it out he noticed that it was only half smoked. As though they were going to sleep Anson put his head on Kent's shoulder and they closed their eyes, listening to each other's soft breathing, wide awake in the darkness. And now Anson's closeness gave Kent a feeling of great tenderness for him and he fought against sleep, trying to prolong the few hours before he must leave. But at last it overcame him and when he awoke the open windows were grey.

He looked at his watch and saw that it was five-thirty. Anson's head was still on his shoulder and he was asleep; Kent rubbed his eyes and wished that he could reach the glass of water on the table without disturbing him. He lay quietly for a few minutes until he was wide awake and then noticed that the arm Anson was lying on was completely numbed. As he tried to move it away Anson stirred and lifted his head quickly.

'Sorry,' Kent whispered, 'I must move my arm.' Anson smiled at him sleepily and half sat up in bed.

'Is it time to go yet?' he asked, yawning.

'Not for half an hour.' It would be quite light by then but he still wanted to postpone the moment when he would hear Anson tiptoe across the veranda and he would be alone. 'Are you quite sure you can get back without being caught?'

'Yes, I'm sure. But even if I was I'd simply say that I had spent the night with some bibby.'

'Yes, of course,' Kent answered quickly, 'I wasn't thinking of *that*, but if you were caught they might send you straight back to the battalion.'

'No, you needn't worry, I promise you.'

Kent drank a glass of water and without bothering to put on any clothes walked to the bathroom. When he came back Anson did the same. While he waited Kent propped the crumpled pillows against the wooden head of the bed and lit two cigarettes. The smoke made him dizzy and his body felt light from lack of sleep.

They sat up in bed leaning against each other and smoking, watching the light grow steadily outside and come seeping through the net. Now Kent could see the two untidy piles of uniform on the floor and even as he wondered why the sight of them filled him with nostalgia he realized that he had already made up his mind that this must never happen again. He lit another cigarette and turned to Anson.

'Are you sorry?' He spoke sadly, not looking at him.

'No of course not, I'm not sorry at all, why should I be? If I was going to be sorry I wouldn't have let it happen.' He was quite ready to discuss the matter but not from the point of view of regrets, and he did not want Kent to begin feeling remorse.

'I'll be back at nine but I won't wake you.'

'Yes, do that,' Kent answered listlessly.

'Good-bye,' Kent said, 'be careful about getting back.'

'Good-bye, sir, I'll see you later on.' Kent watched him leave the room and the door closed carefully behind him. He knew it was despicable but he was glad that Anson had called him 'sir.'

8

Kent slept for two hours, and when he awoke he lay in bed listening to one of Sammy's children crying outside his window. Then he heard the swift pad of bare feet as Sammy rushed in terror from the kitchen to snatch up the child and carry him back to his mother, who, against his repeated warnings, had let the child stray near the bungalow and disturb the Sahib. There was silence until Sammy considered that he was safely out of hearing and then the child started crying louder than before. With reason this time, Kent thought. Normally he would have shouted for Sammy but this morning he had no stomach for anger, feigned or otherwise.

He put on his pyjamas and dressing-gown and went to the kitchen; Sammy was busying himself fanning the charcoal fire and looked at him warily, but Kent only told him to get his bath ready as soon as possible and to bring him some coffee. He wandered round the garden trying to bring some order to the jumbled chaos of his mind, but it was impossible, and instead he would find himself absorbed in watching a butterfly opening and shutting its wings in the faintly warm early sunlight, or he would pick up crumbs of gravel and try to drop them on a large beetle scurrying across the drive.

When Anson arrived he had already dressed in clean shirt and shorts and was reading on the lawn. His back was to the french windows, and as he heard Anson's footsteps almost reach his chair he had to make a tremendous effort to turn his head and look at him. He tried to smile but his eyes were anxious.

'You got back all right?'

'Oh yes, no trouble at all,' Anson answered casually.

'Did anyone ask any questions where you had been?'

'Yes, Goodwin did.' He bent down to pick a stem of grass and began to chew.

'Goodwin!' A rush of panic reddened Kent's face. 'But he's in hospital!'

'No, he's not, he came out two days ago and he's in my barrack-room.'

'Why on earth didn't you tell me?'

'I didn't think to. I don't have anything to do with him now, not since we had that row in Sialpur.'

'Does Goodwin know anything about you?'

Anson looked up in surprise. 'No! Nothing at all!' Even though Kent was wholly preoccupied with the question of how this might affect him personally the fierceness of Anson's reply reached him and he spoke more calmly.

'All I'm trying to get at is whether Goodwin might have any reason to suspect me because you're my batman. Don't you understand my position?' He nearly added the words 'it doesn't matter to you', but he stopped himself. They looked at each other. Anson had meant to tell the truth but he knew by the fear and anxiety in Kent's face that he would be far happier not to know.

'No, sir, there's no reason at all, I promise you that.'

Kent lit a cigarette and noticed that his fingers were trembling. 'All right, forget it,' he said, not sure himself exactly what he meant. Now that he was dressed and it was broad daylight, the strain of having to talk about the subject was so great that he felt he must get away from the bungalow. 'I'm going out now, I'll see you after lunch some time.'

It was too early to go to the club, and he left the town and walked quickly along the rides cut through the surrounding woods and jungle, and all the time remorse at what he had done mounted in him until he was nearly distracted. Once he started to think, he saw how easily he could be found out, and writhed at his criminal carelessness. Anyone could have seen them drive back to the bungalow, Sammy might have heard them talking during the night and crept to the window and listened, or even more likely he might have been awake and seen Anson leave; even the crying child could be woven into the menacing pattern. How had Sammy behaved this morning, had he been more familiar than usual, as though he had some hold over him? Goodwin might come to the bungalow, he might even be there now, talking to Sammy, who would tell him everything, thinking it very funny. Perhaps Anson himself was not to be trusted. He vowed never again to put himself in such an appalling position, and as he made the resolve he decided that the best thing he could do was to go back to the battalion as soon as possible. He was due to see Rowland the day after tomorrow and he would insist that he was fit and must return.

He reached the club shortly before one and stayed until three. He tried to behave as though nothing had happened to him and no one made any comments on his unusual quietness, but he felt very strange, and the familiar faces seemed to have become alien to him as though he and they lived in different worlds, theirs wonderfully carefree, peopled by brave men who did not beg for mercy from the Japanese at the slightest pain, and sleep with their batmen. He envied them with his whole heart, wondering sadly why he should be so different, trying to think back over his life for some cause, but he could think of nothing. Once again he told himself that he must make amends, and the first thing to do was to go back to the battalion.

Before he left again for the club in the evening Anson came into the lounge where he was drinking and Kent asked him if he would like a bottle of beer. Anson thanked him and stood sipping at the beer in silence. They heard the gharry turn into the drive and he put the glass down carefully on the table and turned to Kent.

'Do you want me to wait for you tonight, sir?' His voice was hesitant.

Kent walked over to the desk, he picked up a pen and pretended to examine the nib. 'No, Anson, I don't. I'm sorry about last night. I'm not blaming you at all, it was my fault because I ought to know better; the only explanation I can give is that I must have been drunk. I like you very much, too much, and I want you to stay on as my batman, but last night has got to be completely forgotten as far as you and I are concerned.'

'I'll do whatever you want.' Anson spoke very quietly; he was hurt and unhappy, but at the same time he had been prepared for some such reaction and he was not surprised. There was no censure in his mind against Kent, he did not understand why other people's behaviour was so completely unpredictable, he only knew that it was so.

Kent came back at eleven o'clock that night; he had had a large amount of brandy but he was not drunk, although the alcohol had slowly blotted out his fears and resolutions. He told himself that he was leaving early because he was tired from his long walk, but in reality having to listen to other people talking interfered with the fantasies of his mind and he wanted to be alone. When his fingers touched the light switch in the lounge the remembrance of the previous night flooded back and he leant against the wall and closed his eyes. Then he poured out half a tumbler of brandy and while he undressed he forced it down sip by sip. He threw his clothes about the room and turned off the light, and then lay on his back and felt the bed twisting and swaying before the brandy swamped him.

The next day he felt much calmer and told Anson to be prepared for them to move very soon, that when he saw Rowland he would tell him that he was fit again. Before he left for the club he called for Anson to come into the lounge and started to discuss his plans for their return.

'There's no point in hanging around now I've made up my mind. I shall see Rowland first thing tomorrow morning, and when he's O.K.'d me, which he will do, I shall go straight to the area commandant and make arrangements to leave here as soon as possible.'

'Is there any chance we might leave here tomorrow?' Anson asked.

'I shouldn't think so, but I suppose it's just possible. Why?'

'Well, if you don't mind I think I would like to hang on here this evening and go through your kit. Some of the new shirts want pips sewing on, and those new socks could do with another wash through. Will it be all right if I stay till ten?'

'Yes, I suppose so,' Kent answered unwillingly, 'but no later. I shan't be back until long after you've gone.' He went out of the bungalow without saying good night and waited by the gate for the gharry to arrive. As soon as he reached the club he began to drink steadily, trying not to think, but he looked at his watch at eight-thirty and again at nine and then at nine-fifteen. All around him people were talking loudly and laughing, their faces flushed with drink and crumpled with the fixed smiles with which they listened to one another. The sound of dance music came fitfully through the hubbub of voices, it made him feel sentimental and unhappy. It was nearly five-and-twenty-past nine, he would have to decide soon or Anson would have left, he might very easily have left already. As he lifted his glass there was a sudden roar of laughter from a group of officers at the end of the bar. The noise grated on his nerves and he made up his mind; he finished his drink and got down from his stool.

'You're not off early again tonight, Kent, are you?' Someone standing behind him clapped him on the shoulder and he turned round sheepishly, not sure what to say. 'I suppose your girl friend's sitting at home doing a bit of sewing and waiting for you, eh?' and Kent felt the blood flush in his face.

'Nothing like that, I'm afraid, but I've got to be fit in the morning for my medical. I'm trying to persuade the M.O.s to let me get the hell out of here and back to my battalion. I don't want a stinking hang-over tomorrow.'

'When do you think you'll leave?'

'Can't say yet, but I'll see you tomorrow, anyway.' He pushed through the crowd and almost ran to his gharry, now the decision was made he was feverishly anxious to get back to the bungalow as soon as possible. As they approached he tried to peer through the screen of trees to see if there was a light on, leaning forward in his seat. For a moment his heart sank and then they turned into the drive and he saw a light shining from his bedroom window.

He paid the man and waited until he was almost out of the drive before he mounted the veranda steps. He went straight into the bedroom and threw his bush hat and stick on to the dressing-table. Anson was kneeling on the floor laying shirts and shorts in the valise, but as Kent walked in he stood up. Kent opened his mouth to make some excuse for coming back so early but no sound came, and then he shut the door very quietly and turned out the light.

9

The area commandant looked at Kent and held out his cigarette case; this was the first thing that had gone right all morning and his mounting irritability vanished. He had about him the air of sang-froid and authority that comes to senior officers attached to an army headquarters, and although he repeatedly stated in public that the most junior officer at the front was worth ten of himself, neither he nor anyone else believed it.

'I've got a mixed bag of forty British other ranks standing by to go to Mandalay. The whole place is a shambles, most of it burnt down and what isn't burnt is being looted. I was looking for an officer to command them and now I've found him.' He smiled hopefully, almost as though he was asking Kent not to raise any objections and spoil the pleasantness of his visit, with a hint behind the smile that in any case objections would be useless.

'But, sir!' Kent expostulated, 'my colonel's waiting for me to come back. I've got my own company to take over again as soon as I arrive!' He was dismayed by the sudden turn of events, hating the idea of such unfamiliar and probably responsible work.

'If you're worried about the *size* of your command I assure you your own company won't be very much larger.' He almost spoke with a sneer, but remembered in time the maxim that officers in higher formations may condescend to, but not bully, those in lower commands. 'I'm afraid there's no use arguing, Captain Kent. I understand exactly how you feel, and if I was in your shoes I'd be standing there and calling me every old B F I could lay my tongue to. Of course you want to get back to your own lads, and I promise faithfully that as soon as I get hold of another suitable officer in a day or so I'll have you relieved and you can go. In the meantime be here at four o'clock this afternoon to pick up your instructions and take over the draft. And just to show you how grateful I am to you for turning up out of the blue I shall give you a jeep so that you can get around Mandalay easily.' Before he could be answered he smiled and nodded towards the door, and Kent decided to put as good a face on it as possible and smiled back at him ruefully when he saluted.

At four o'clock he was cursorily inspecting the two lines of men drawn up outside the office. Only five of them possessed rifles, the remainder were armed with revolvers. Before he started on the second row he glanced down the line and saw Goodwin. He was glad to see him; if he was a potential danger to him it was far better that he should have him under his eye, and now there was no chance that he might be able to contact Sammy, who Kent still thought might have some suspicion concerning himself and Anson. And Kent also remembered that he had saved Goodwin's life; that was a piece of information almost bound to reach the rest of the detachment, and Kent found that a very satisfactory thing. When he reached Goodwin he stopped in front of him.

'How are you, Goodwin, your leg all right now?' He spoke affably; out of the corner of his eye he could see one or two men lean forward and glance at them.

'No, sir, it's not properly healed up yet, sir.' His rigid bearing and the way he spoke was a parody of the parade-ground manner, suitable if being addressed by a visiting field-marshal but bordering on the insolent to a junior officer taking an informal parade. Kent glanced back at the line of men and saw some of them smiling.

'Too bad,' he said coldly, loud enough for everyone to hear, 'you probably haven't had enough exercise on it, I'll see what I can do to help when we get to Mandalay.' He moved on to the next man.

There was a flabby-looking sergeant with the detachment, and while Kent went to the office for his instructions and movement order he told him to get the men into the two lorries that were taking them down to Mandalay.

'All set, Kent?' The area commander handed him an envelope of papers. 'You'll be stationed inside the Fort, there are any number of large empty bungalows in there that you can take over to billet yourself and the men. There's a supply officer in the Fort who's in direct contact with me by phone when it's working, which isn't very often these days. He'll look after your rations and petrol and pass on any messages for you from me. First thing tomorrow find the police superintendent and work in with him. You're not under his command in any way, but if you'll take a tip from an old hand you had better do exactly what he says and then if something goes wrong you'll have a scapegoat!' He laughed heartily, remembering himself as a pale second lieutenant in Central India listening indignantly to exactly the same advice. 'You'll probably only be called on to find a few guards for places like the bank or the railway station, and one or two roving patrols, but I can leave all that stuff for you to sort out.'

And an hour later Kent, driving the jeep himself with the driver sitting next to him and Anson and the luggage piled in the back, reached the edge of the hilly jungle-covered plateau on which

Maymyo stood and started the main descent. As the road twisted and turned he caught occasional glimpses of the plain below, and tried to pick out the dark patch of Mandalay or the strip of flickering silver beyond that would be the Irrawaddy. But everything was merged into a flat brown haze of dust and heat, already he could feel hot gusts of air that rose against the baking sides of the hills. By the time they reached the plain, and the last giant handfuls of bare towering rocks were behind them, his body was dry and burning wherever the air could circulate and soaked in sweat where it could not.

'Hot, isn't it, sir?' the driver shouted to Kent. Three months ago he had shivered in Scotland waiting to embark, as he thought, for North Africa, and this furnace appalled and fascinated him.

'What do you expect for the middle of April?' Kent answered. 'Wait till three o'clock tomorrow afternoon before you start talking about heat; this is cool.' He took one hand off the steering-wheel and watched the sweat marks contract and disappear in a matter of seconds leaving only tiny ridges of caked dust. He had had to drive slowly to let the lorries keep him in sight, it was nearly six o'clock and the sun was dipping towards the horizon, biting fiercely through the orange haze. Now they were travelling across the flat plain, the road raised above the general level, shaded against the midday sun by thick-trunked leafy trees, the metalled part of the road wide enough to allow two lorries to pass, and on either side were deep-rutted tracks along which the carts squeaked and crawled, dust spurting from the feet of the bullocks and coating the lower leaves of the trees with a grey film.

There was nothing but bare paddy-fields stretching away as far as one could see on either side of the road; occasionally the monotony would be broken by a distant patch of palms and mango-trees hiding a village, or they would cross a narrow bridge over an irrigation canal, the muddy slow-moving surface dotted with little green blobs of floating water-hyacinths bearing stems of papery blue flowers. As they approached Mandalay they began to pass orchards of mangoes and mangosteens, and sometimes they saw huge crumbling bell-shaped pagodas, their white plaster long since gone, leaving the dull red bricks to burn themselves away.

They reached the outskirts of Mandalay and Kent smelt the city for the first time. It was a smell that he was to remember for the rest of his life, the smell of smoke with an underlying tang of decay, sometimes unbearably strong, sometimes as faint and sweet as a withered gardenia. Garbage had already piled up in the streets, and as he drove slowly towards the Fort flies were continuously settling in clusters on his hands and face. The streets should have been packed with people at this hour, loitering in the comparative coolness of the evening after the long baking afternoon in shuttered rooms, but now there were few people to be seen and no one loitered.

It was difficult finding his way to the Fort. Whole streets were blocked, not by piles of masonry and deep craters but by festoons of telephone wires, abandoned carts, palm-trees and dead bullocks. And everywhere were the marks of fire: huge peepul-trees that had shaded the wooden houses stood with their leaves a blackened ruin, tall palms grew blue tendrils of smoke from their crowns in place of green fronds, charred furniture stood in front of the heaps of ash that represented homes, and the stench-laden smoke drifted everywhere. At last he managed to pick his way through the town and reach the long straight road that borders the moat on the east side of the Fort, and he saw the rose-red machicolated walls mirrored in the water. He crossed the moat by a low white bridge, through the gates, and into the Fort itself.

Only the club and a few scattered buildings, all hidden by trees, had been destroyed. As he drove into the Fort he suddenly remembered Sialpur, and he felt as though he had stepped back into a life that he could only recall with dim enchantment. All the boredom and dissatisfaction that he might have felt in those far-away days was forgotten and nothing remained except the memory of peace and his own illusions, an oasis of peace where he had once rested, forgetting the past and too happy to think about the future. Now everything lay in ruins about him, as destroyed as the city beyond the walls. A fly settled on the corner of his mouth and he spat it away with disgust, wondering from what filth it had just come. But perhaps it would be a good thing if he did die, he told himself; if already cholera was on his lips. He shuddered; at the thought of death his mind grew hard again, as long as he was alive nothing was irremediably lost, nothing else really mattered.

He stopped outside a bungalow signed up as the supply officer's and switched off the engine. The leaves of a tree moved as the hot dust floated past him, he heard a kite-hawk whistle and the two lorries pulling up. He was tired and depressed, dreading the next two hours of arrangements for food and sleeping accommodation, and the multitudinous details that always seemed to follow in the train of even the simplest problems. He badly wanted a drink, but that would be worse than useless until he could settle down and drink at leisure. He climbed out of the jeep and walked slowly into the bungalow, calling over his shoulder for Sergeant Gately to follow.

IO

On the eighth afternoon since the detachment had arrived in Mandalay Goodwin was given a few hours off duty and set out once more in search of loot. It was the hottest part of the day but it was impossible for him to rest. Ever since he had first arrived in Mandalay he had been seized by a fever of greed, and the ruined shops and houses of the almost deserted city still fanned his imagination although his frantic searches had so far produced nothing of any real value. Today he had decided to investigate the north-east corner of the city. He had not been there before because it was one of the more badly damaged areas, without, as far as he could see, any European houses at all.

His way lay past one of the larger Buddhist temples of the city. The first time he had come upon it he had been shocked by its similarity to the Aranyaka Temple, and for a moment the fear of what he had done and the fear of leprosy had flared again in his mind. But only for a moment, only because the similarity had been so unexpected. Now when he passed it he told himself yet again what a fool he had been to have worried about catching leprosy. While he had been in hospital he had casually discussed the disease with one of the nurses in his ward and her remarks had convinced him that he had nothing to fear. He could never think of the fear and worry he had gone through without resentment seething in his mind against the girl who had caused it all.

He spent a fruitless and exhausting afternoon and started to make his way slowly back. He wandered down a side street and turned into the garden of what had once been a large house, now a pile of blackened debris. The only sign of life were the occasional eddies of ash spiralling up in the breathless blaze of the afternoon. Behind the house was a garden of fruit trees, and he sauntered through them looking for mangoes; as he was reaching up to pick one of the green fruits he was sickened by an unbearable stench of decay. There was a clump of jasmine bushes some yards away; he walked cautiously round it and saw the bodies of three Chinese lying on the ground, bloated and discoloured. Pushed into the bushes was a clumsy handcart and on it, half hidden by some sacking, was a heavy old-fashioned safe. The bodies were alive with large blue-bottles, and maggots that crawled slowly as if they were dazed by the stench: the sight and the smell made him vomit with such violence that he had to stagger away, afraid that he would choke.

But the safe drew him back like a magnet, and by going to the far side and holding a filthy handkerchief over his nose and mouth he examined it and found that it was still locked.

He thought at first that the three men were looters who had been caught trying to escape with the safe and had been murdered, and for some reason the murderers in turn prevented from making away with the safe, but then he noticed that the trunks of the trees around him had been spattered with bomb splinters and after a little search he found a shallow crater fifteen yards away. While he recovered from his vomiting his mind slowly reconstructed the events: the house set on fire by incendiaries, the owner and two servants dragging the safe out of the burning house, loading it on to the gardener's handcart, and pulling it into the depths of the orchard as a temporary refuge. And then the fragmentation bombs falling along the twinkling line of fires.

He went back to the cart and put his hand on the safe, wondering how he could open it. If it was of such importance as to be the first thing to be saved it must be valuable, and if it was so valuable the owner most probably carried the keys with him. He looked more closely at the three bodies, and now he could see other crawling horrors moving about the torn clothes and lines of big ants marching to and fro across the ground. He stamped his feet and glanced down to see if any were on his boots. One of the Chinese wore a long robe buttoning in a collar round his neck; the quality of the material was infinitely better than the other two. He stepped gingerly over to the body and looked down at what had been a plump smiling face. He half bent his knees as though to kneel, but it was impossible; the buzz of the dazed bluebottles, the blazing heat, the stench that seemed to be breathed from the open black mouth—suddenly his handkerchief was full of slimy vomit and his stomach was heaving so violently against his chest that everything swayed redly. Only by a tremendous effort did he manage to avoid pitching forward across the bloated mass of corruption.

He went away and lay down in the garden until his stomach returned to normal. He told himself that what he really wanted was a can of petrol to pour over the body and then burn it, at least it would remove the surface filth and burn away the collar so that he would not have to fumble with the buttons; he was certain that the key was round the neck. But petrol would be too difficult to get; while he was away someone might stumble across the safe even as he had done. He lay there and let his imagination play with the possible contents of the safe; curiosity and greed mounted in him until his mind was resolved.

He got to his feet, and without hesitation went to the corpse and knelt beside it. For the next three minutes the only sign of distress that he showed was the sweat streaming down his green face, and when he stood up the key, tacky with putrescence, was in his hand.

And now, almost a week later, he sat on his bed with his back turned to the only other occupant of the room, once more fingering the contents of his pack, the leather pouch that held twenty-five medium-sized rubies, and the thick wads of ten-rupee notes that more than half filled his pack. He had never imagined that it was possible to feel so rich, or that its possession could fill him with such absorbing satisfaction—merely to hold one of the jewels in his hand was enough to make his heart beat thickly. He was determined that at any cost he would escape to India so that he could enjoy what he had gained; the whole of his waking day was spent scheming as to how this could best be done. He had come to the conclusion that it ought to be done by legal means, he would only desert as a last resort, if the Japanese came to within striking distance of the city, or if he was ordered to report back to the battalion. The difficulties of leaving Mandalay as a deserter and finding his own way into India were immense in themselves, without the further hazards of, once having arrived, making his way to some big city like Calcutta where he could dispose of the rubies and set about the difficult task of trying to find a completely safe hiding-place for the money before he was picked up as a deserter. Each plan as it had come to him had been examined carefully and rejected as too unsure. He had considered the possibilities of reporting sick, but he knew from experience that although he could malinger long enough to be sent from Mandalay up to Northern Burma it would be most unlikely that he could maintain the pretence sufficiently long to be evacuated into India. In any case, until that very morning, he had not been certain that all hospital patients were in fact being evacuated.

He had been on duty at the railway station, and a trainload of patients had arrived at Mandalay from Maymyo. He had talked with some of the patients and from them he learnt that they were all going north to Myitkyina and from there would be flown direct to Calcutta. At once he had seen the overwhelming advantages to himself if only he could bluff his way on to a plane, somehow convince the doctors that he was unable to walk. He could use his wounded leg as a basis for his plans, but it would need something stronger than his own assertions that his leg had never recovered properly and had in fact become much worse since he had left the hospital in Maymyo. Slowly but inevitably the idea came to him that what he wanted was a written statement by Kent that in his opinion he was not fit to undertake the march into India. He knew that Kent would not give him such a statement unless pressure was brought to bear on him; there was only one chance he had of doing this, and he decided that he must make the attempt. There was no time to be lost, he must do it now, this evening. Reluctantly he strapped up his pack and hid it carefully behind the head of his bed and then got up and left the bungalow.

I I

The fortnight Kent spent in Mandalay seemed to stretch on in time until he could hardly remember ever having done anything else except live in the Fort and drive round the filthy blackened streets visiting patrols and pickets, or being called on at all hours of the day and night to investigate reports of looters or suspected fifth column seen prowling around the marshalling yards or the power station. After the first few days had passed he began to worry about his promised relief; mentally he was exhausted by the strain of the past months and craved to return to the battalion at whatever cost, if only to be able to shed some of the burden of his responsibility and once more be under someone's direct command. He constantly made excuses to visit the supply office in the hope that a message might have come through to say that his relief was due to arrive from Maymyo, and on the fifth day he phoned the area commandant himself, only to be told that no suitable officer was available, and that he was not to phone again about a matter of no importance.

The heat was almost unbearable, much worse than he had visualized. He had been in the plains before, during the hot season, but then he had lived in comfort with fans and cold drinks, and during the hottest part of the day everyone had retired to their beds and slept beneath the soft whirr of an electric fan; he had eaten light meals and changed his clothes at least twice a day. Now there were no fans or ice, he was constantly out in the swimming blaze of the middle afternoon, and it was impossible to change his clothes more often than once every two days. Within an hour of getting up each morning his clothes were dark with patches of sweat, and the heat rashes spread until the whole of the trunk of his body and his arms were covered with inflamed skin that either pricked like needles or itched so intolerably that in a frenzy he would scratch at one selected spot until the skin was raw.

All day long he would keep Anson with him, using him unmercifully for any and every job he wanted done, longing for the sun to drop behind the curtain of dust that stretched mistily to the horizon. Then he would sit in a tin bath and Anson would pour cans of what passed for cold water over him. Without drying, a small towel round his waist, he would sit on the veranda drinking and watching the blue hills deepen in colour until they disappeared. The veranda faced away from the road and was hidden from anyone approaching the bungalow; he and Anson formed the habit of sitting there together, not talking very much until a few drinks had loosened Kent's tongue and then they spoke of the incidents of the day or speculated on what was likely to happen to them in the immediate future. Sometimes Kent would go on drinking until his fear was pushed into the back of his mind, fear of the future and fear of being found with Anson, and when fear had almost gone desire came. Without saying anything he would signal to Anson and they would leave the veranda and lie together on his bed, but even then Kent would raise his head and listen intently to the slightest sound, the scuttle of a rat in the roof or the creak of a board as the bungalow breathed again in the slightly cooler evening air.

But it was too hot and too dangerous for them to sleep together all night. When they were finished Anson would reluctantly go to his own room and Kent would drag the hard mattress on to the veranda and sleep there, naked except for a pair of thin drawers and a sheet folded across his stomach. Almost every night, sometimes twice, the guard would call him, and he and Anson would dress and take the jeep with a few soldiers to investigate some unusual occurrence in the city. And when they came back Kent would find it impossible to sleep again, twisting and turning in the heat, trying to resist the temptation to scratch and rub his inflamed skin. Towards dawn a little breeze wandered across the Irrawaddy and he would fall heavily asleep, waking when the sun was striking the tops of the trees and the freshness of the day already gone.

After the first week a new worry took the place of his desire to go back to the battalion. The first echelons of administrative troops began to pass through Mandalay, beginning to make their way towards India, and he began to think that he and the detachment would be left behind as a rearguard in Mandalay, a token gesture to hold the Fort for purposes of propaganda. Sometimes the transport of these first echelons would drive into the Fort to load up with cans of petrol, and he would ask casually how many troops were still in Maymyo and whether headquarters had left yet, and again he started to haunt the supply office hoping for some news to end the uncertainty.

Towards the end of this second week one of the soldiers who had been on duty at the station brought a letter and told him that a nurse had asked him to deliver it to Kent. He looked at the handwriting blankly, wondering if the man had made a mistake, and it was not until he had opened it that he realized it was from Helen. The letter was very brief, written while she was on the train, saying that she was leaving with the last group of patients and giving him an address in Calcutta where he could write to her. The note itself meant nothing to him except that if this was the last trainload of wounded they could now expect an increase in the tempo of the withdrawal.

For the next two days troops were pouring through Mandalay and then the flood suddenly stopped. In the afternoon he went down to the supply office and found the clerks busily packing, and at once asked if orders had come for everyone's withdrawal from Mandalay.

'Nothing about you,' the supply officer answered cheerfully, 'but we're off first thing tomorrow morning.'

'But what about our rations and things like that?' Kent asked. He was suddenly conscious of the stifling heat and wiped his finger across his forehead, feeling the sweat running down the side of his face and the back of his hand.

'I'm afraid I know nothing about it at all, old boy. This was a written message and when I tried to get through about you the phone was dead. Try it.' He picked up the receiver and held it out to Kent. It was lifeless.

'Just what I expected,' Kent said savagely, 'pull up the ladder, Joe, I'm all right. Those stinking bastards are going to leave me here!'

'Holding the fort and the baby, eh?' The supply officer laughed heartily and Kent turned away, afraid that his fear and rage might show in his face. He thought that the Japanese could not possibly be more than three or four days away from Mandalay and unless he received a message very soon it would be certain that he was going to be left in the Fort.

He went back to the bungalow and lay down on the veranda, but the flies found him at once and every time he moved the heat rashes itched or pricked. He got up and wandered through the bungalow, his head was aching and he felt tired and sick. Just as he was going into the bathroom for a glass of water he heard a motorcycle coming along the road and stop outside, and he felt an intense excitement as he hurried out. The despatch rider was already halfway up the steps when Kent met him and took the message, trying to tell himself not to show his disappointment when he found that his instructions were to stay in Mandalay.

He read the message and looked calmly at the man when he handed him a scribbled acknowledgment, then he went into the bungalow and called for Anson.

'Find Gately for me as quickly as possible. We're off first thing in the morning, north to Shwebo.' He tried to appear calm but his voice was jubilant, his face lit by excitement and relief, and then without any warning he suddenly leant against the wooden wall of the hall and was sick.

He had his bath as usual that evening and sat on the veranda. His head was aching violently, and for the last two hours he had been repeatedly sick. He poured himself a weak brandy and water and tried it but the taste was nauseous. He knew that he was ill but he was too relieved by his orders to worry, if he was going to be seriously ill he could go to Shwebo by jeep and leave Gately in charge of the detachment. Anson came and sat next to him.

'You're looking pretty sick, sir, do you feel very ill?' He leant forward and peered at Kent's face.

'Yes, lousy, but I shall be all right tomorrow, I must have eaten something.'

'But nothing that I haven't,' Anson answered, his voice made anxious by the remembrance of the hundreds of cases of cholera in the city.

'For heaven's sake stop worrying, I shall be all right once we get away from this stinking hole. The smell's enough to give one cholera without all the filth and flies.' He shifted uneasily, thinking to himself that if it was cholera he would very soon know and would probably be dead by the morning. If the message had told him to remain in Mandalay he thought that he would not have minded so much, but now the idea terrified him.

They heard footsteps coming towards the bungalow and Anson got up quickly and went to the front door. Kent could hear a low murmur of voices and then Anson came back.

'It's Goodwin, sir, he says he wants to see you.' They looked at each other anxiously for a moment, afraid to say anything in case they could be overheard.

'Did he say what he wanted?' Kent asked. His voice was husky with a sudden premonition of danger.

'He wouldn't say, sir, he told me to mind my own something business.'

'Tell him to come in and don't go away once he's here.' He took another sip from his glass and thought that he was going to be sick again. He listened to Goodwin's boot clumping across the floor and turned quickly to face him; he suddenly felt bare and defenceless with only the small towel round his waist.

'What's the trouble, Goodwin, why come here at this hour instead of seeing Sergeant Gately?'

'I wanted to see you, sir,' he answered stiffly, 'I want to report sick.'

'Your bloody leg again, I suppose. What's the idea, trying to get out of having to march to Shwebo? I want to report sick as well, but I'm waiting for the morning and so can you.'

'It'll be too late in the morning, sir, I happen to know that the last hospital ship goes from Sagaing to Myitkyina first thing tomorrow. If I can get to Myitkyina I can get flown to Calcutta. My leg's really bad.'

'I don't believe a word of what you're saying. Get back to your own quarters and report sick in the morning, and heaven help you if you're malingering.' There was a pause and Kent heard Goodwin swallow noisily.

'I'd like to speak to you privately, sir.' He glanced at Anson and Kent hesitated. Now he was certain Goodwin was planning something and his anxiety returned. He spoke carelessly.

'All right, go to your room, Anson, I'll call you in a minute.' They listened until they heard his door shut, looking at each other in hostile silence until at last Goodwin spoke.

'That might be his own room but he sleeps on the veranda here, doesn't he?' His voice was venomous and sneering. This is it, Kent said to himself; for God's sake keep your head and bluff it out, he can't know anything for certain. He stood up.

'What the hell do you mean?' He kept his voice as low and steady as he could.

'Anson and me were muckers for a long time, I know all about Anson, thank you very much. I don't like brown-hatters, that's why we split up, once I found out.' He stopped and Kent felt his brain falling to pieces inside his head, but he still managed to speak calmly.

'I understand what you're getting at, you filthy-minded swine. Apart from the fact that such a thing has never entered my head concerning Anson what's it got to do with your going sick?' He felt as though there was a bottomless gulf of disgrace yawning at

206

his feet into which he would fall unless he kept his head and found out exactly how much Goodwin knew.

'I want you to write a note I can show the M.O.s saying you've noticed my leg getting worse and worse ever since I've been in Mandalay and you're convinced that I can't make the march into India. If you give me this I swear I shan't say a word to a living soul; if you don't I'll tell everyone I can about you and Anson. And when I get back to the battalion I'll tell the C.O. and the whole lot of them. I'll say I went to your bungalow one night when I was drunk to see you and found you and Anson in bed together. I'll tell them what you are, nothing but a bloody nancy boy!'

'But it's a lie, you bastard, no one's going to believe you!'

'It's a lie that I've seen you together, but you know as well as me that the rest of it's true. I knew in Maymyo when Anson didn't come in till six-thirty one morning and told me he had spent the night in a knocking shop, but I know him much too well to swallow a thing like that. I wasn't born yesterday, I'm bloody certain it was you, you're just the sort of person he'd like. And if I'd needed any proof the way you've behaved down here would've been enough, even the other blokes have been making jokes about the way he follows you around. Maybe I can't prove anything but you know it's the truth. How will you like having me telling everyone, and supposing someone else knows a thing or two about Anson and backs me up? It wouldn't be difficult for me to find someone, you know.'

Kent's equipment was lying on his bed, the revolver in the holster. The idea of giving Goodwin permission to leave never entered his head; he would rather be suspected of murder than homosexuality; his only fear was that at the last moment he would not have the courage to shoot him. He walked casually past Goodwin and picked up the equipment, his hands icily cold and shaking, then he walked back with it and put it on the table. He splashed brandy into his glass and gulped it down while Goodwin smiled, certain that he had won.

Kent took out his revolver and cocked it: 'You'd be very surprised indeed if I shot you, wouldn't you?' He smiled grimly and turned the revolver over in his sweating hands, a plan forming in his mind. 'But you needn't worry, I don't want to swing for a lying bastard like you.' He moved nearer to Goodwin until there was only a yard between them. 'Or do I?'

'You haven't got the guts.'

'I had the guts to save your life for you.' Kent looked at him

207

steadily, he felt his resolve weakening, his head was bursting with pain and the brandy seared his stomach.

'You draw your pay, don't you?' Hatred suddenly glowed in Goodwin's eyes. 'Do I get that note or do I blab?'

Kent fought to keep the fear and loathing out of his face. He raised the revolver slowly until the muzzle was level with Goodwin's mouth and pointing slightly upwards. He was smiling apologetically and slightly nodding his head, trying to make the gesture appear as theatrical as possible, mere face-saving. He was still not certain.

Goodwin started to speak: 'Put that thing down, you gutless nancy.' Still smiling Kent fired. He heard Anson's door open and as Goodwin fell to the ground he dropped the revolver. It was almost dark, a bat swooped under the veranda eave and out again, and they stood side by side looking down at Goodwin, who lay on his back while a pool of blood quickly formed beneath his head and then began to run towards their feet. One of the veranda posts behind Goodwin was spattered with lumpy red clots.

Kent knelt and looked at the hole by the side of Goodwin's thick nose. Blood was running out swiftly but even in the half light he could see the powder burns quite clearly. He knelt there watching the blood dripping on to the floor from the side of Goodwin's face; as he stood up he turned to Anson to tell him exactly what had happened. He looked at Anson's set face. Because he had done it only to save himself, only he should have the burden.

'Tell Gately to come here at once and bring two men with him. Tell him Goodwin wanted permission to go on the hospital boat and when I refused he grabbed my four-five and shot himself.' He felt quite calm but very tired. 'Be as quick as you can, when you come back you'll find me in the garden.'

In a very short time Gately and two men reached the bungalow, bringing with them the indefinable air that is a combination of respect for the dead and an intense curiosity to look at the body. Kent took them on to the veranda and showed them the powder burns on Goodwin's face, then he picked up the revolver and demonstrated how Goodwin had held it.

'It was all so quick,' he said, 'he simply grabbed the gun and it was all over. I don't think I could have done anything even if I had been standing up. Has he been peculiar lately, Sergeant? Has he said anything to anyone sort of out of the ordinary?'

'He's hardly spoken to anyone since he's been down here, sir, he seemed sort of doped if you know what I mean, and the last few days he seemed to be more funny than usual. As far as I know he hasn't a single friend in the detachment.' He turned to the two men. 'That's right, isn't it?'

'Yes, Sergeant,' they said together.

Kent felt the tension begin to relax and he turned to Anson. 'Go and get all his kit and bring it up here, take the jeep.' He stood in silence until Anson had gone, pretending to think. 'He had better be buried tonight,' he said slowly, 'seeing that we're off first thing in the morning. I'll write a note to the police superintendent telling him what's happened, and I'll make a report about it to the area commandant as soon as I contact him again. I want you three to remember the position of the body and the wound because you'll have to give evidence. There's some waste ground just across the road, mark the grave with a cross, and put his name and number on it; and Gately, I'd be grateful if you got the body out of here as soon as possible, I was feeling bloody ill before this happened and I want to get to bed. I'll write the note now and you can send it down with the next patrol.'

As he wrote the note he was certain that he had nothing to fear, that the police were far too busy to worry about something that under the present circumstances was really no concern of theirs. The note was a formality in case any questions were asked about the newly dug grave, if in fact it was noticed before the Japanese arrived, and it would also help to make everything appear correct and official as far as his witnesses were concerned.

By the time Anson came back Kent had dragged his mattress into the living-room and was lying on it. He was feeling much worse than a few hours ago, his head and eyes ached intolerably, and his stomach was sore and bloated as though it was full of acid. He watched Anson put the kit by the head of his bed.

'Do you want to go through it now, sir? The pack weighs a ton.'

'No, not now, I can't be bothered.' He shut his eyes and wondered if he should go to the lavatory again to be sick. Four men came in carrying a door and took the body away. After they had gone Anson sluiced the veranda down with cans of water and then sat on the floor by the side of Kent's mattress.

'What did Goodwin really want to see you about?' He took one of Kent's hands and stroked it gently with his strong fingers, his voice coaxing, full of sympathy; Kent kept his eyes shut in case the tears he could feel beginning to prick his eyelids showed. He longed again to tell Anson exactly what had happened.

'I've told you already, there was nothing else. It happened just like I said, don't go on about it. In any case I expect you had your ear to the keyhole, so why ask when you know?'

209

'I did try to listen,' Anson admitted, 'but I couldn't hear a thing at all, that's why I thought he must have come about something else. You know I don't care whether you killed him or not, he was a rotten swine.'

'Well, I didn't, so shut up. Push off to bed now, I must get some sleep, I'm feeling absolutely ghastly.' Anson got up and walked towards the door. In the distance they could hear faint voices and as Kent strained his ears he imagined he heard the thud of a pick being driven into the earth. 'Look, you can do one thing for me, Anson.'

He stopped and turned round : 'Yes, of course, what do you want ?'

Kent hesitated. 'Just . . . just leave your door open.'

12

When Kent woke the next morning he knew at once that he was no better, he was a little less weak than the night before, but that was all. It was light, but the sun had not yet risen; he could hear Anson moving about in the kitchen at the back of the bungalow. He began to dress, his head swimming as he bent down to lace his boots. He glanced round the room and saw Goodwin's pack by the head of his bed. He felt too ill to go to the trouble of looking through his belongings, but at the same time he had an impulse to get rid of it. He remembered that there was a pit at the end of the garden, planked over and with a hole cut in the floor for the servants to use as a latrine. He picked up the pack and left the bungalow, avoiding the kitchen. When he reached the latrine he peered down the hole, but it was pitch-dark. The pack seemed extremely heavy and he hesitated, wondering whether he ought to examine the contents quickly, but the smell of the latrine was making him feel sick and he dropped it through the hole. From the blackness came a soft thud, and as he walked back he congratulated himself on having chosen the safest possible hiding-place.

He went into the bathroom and peered into the mirror, putting out his tongue. He was shocked by what he saw : the whole of the tongue except the tip was coated with a thick white film and he was so surprised that it was some time before he noticed the skin of his face and the whites of his eyes were stained a sickly yellow. He went slowly into the kitchen.

'I've got jaundice.' He spoke casually, picking up a mug of tea. Anson came close and peered at his face.

'What can you do about it?' he asked.

'Drive into Sagaing straight away and see if I can get some dope for it. I don't know anything about the disease except that I feel bloody awful, I could no more march than fly. If I manage to catch one of the doctors on the boat I'll see what he says, maybe it goes in a few days. We've got to go through Sagaing, anyway; if they keep me on board we can leave a message for Gately with the driver. I've already been over the route with him and he can report to the commandant at Shwebo; the commandant can do what he likes with them after that, although I don't suppose he'll do what I'd like him to. You'd better get Gately up here and I'll tell him.'

While he waited for Gately he thought that in many ways his sickness was providential. He was almost certain that the doctors would keep him on board and without him there could be no court of inquiry into Goodwin's death. By the time he was fit enough to attend anything might have happened, now that their role in Mandalay was finished the detachment might be disbanded and the men returned to their units. It could be weeks or even months before the inquiry was held, if indeed it ever was held, and he might even be the only surviving witness. In any event he felt that the longer it was delayed the less chance there would be of the truth coming to light.

When he heard Gately arrive he went on to the veranda; it was gloomy inside the bungalow and he wanted him to see the colour of his face and his sick appearance.

Before he started to tell him his plans he asked what the police superintendent had said about Goodwin. 'I took the note down myself, sir,' Gately answered virtuously; 'when the super read it he asked me if you wanted him to come and look at the body. I said I didn't think you did particularly, and he just grunted and put the note in his pocket. I told him it was suicide, but he didn't seem very interested; they were all busy packing up and burning a lot of stuff, I think they're leaving for Myitkyina today.'

'Right. Now I've got some more news for you,' and he told him what he had decided to do. It was obvious to Kent that Gately disliked the idea of being left in sole charge intensely, but he was not in a position to argue and he could see quite clearly that Kent was sick.

An hour later Kent was crossing the Ava Bridge over the Irrawaddy and he could see the little paddle steamer moored against the bank and the red crosses painted on its side and on the wooden awning covering the deck. They pulled up under some toddy palms near the boat and he and Anson got out.

'See you in twenty minutes, sir,' the driver said cheerfully. He liked Kent, and felt sorry for him; he thought it was bad luck that he should go sick just as they were starting the first stage of the journey to India.

Kent smiled weakly at him: 'I hope so,' he said, turning away. But they never saw each other again. Two days later, as Kent walked unsteadily down the gang-plank some hundreds of miles to the north, the driver was lying dead by the side of his wrecked jeep a few miles south of Shwebo. Some crows were hopping anxiously round the body, wondering if it was too soon.

13

On the evening of the second day they reached Tisaw. From here it was still two hundred miles to Myitkyina, but the captain decided that the river was too low to go further and arrangements were made for all those too ill to walk to go on north by rail.

By now everything was in utter confusion, no one seemed to know whether there was still any organized resistance to the Japanese nor how far away they were, the only positive information was that planes from India were trying to evacuate the worst casualties from Myitkyina and that two trains were available to take the wounded from Tisaw.

There was a large map of India and Burma pinned on the wall of one of the cabins and Kent had studied it carefully. If he went on to Myitkyina and was not flown out he would then be faced with a much longer and more difficult journey into India than would be the case if he started from Tisaw. On the other hand he felt so ill and weak that he doubted whether he was capable of walking any distance, let alone the three hundred or more miles across the plains and mountains into India. And until he reached those mountains, two hundred miles away, he would be travelling straight across the path of the Japanese advance.

To begin with he had decided to go on to Myitkyina, but then he began to imagine what that might entail, possibly having to wait day after day in the hospital until his turn came to be evacuated, not knowing from one day to the next when the Japanese might arrive or the rains break and turn the airstrip into a useless sea of mud. The thought of further uncertainty was unbearable and he decided to leave from Tisaw.

A few hours after they had moored against the bank one of the doctors told him that he was too ill to walk into India and that he would go on by train the next day. Kent nodded his head, but said nothing, and soon afterwards Anson came to see him and he got up and leant against the rail so that they could talk with their backs to the rest of the crowd of officers.

'Have you heard anything definite yet?' Anson asked.

'Yes, they want me to go north and be flown out.'

'That's good,' Anson replied, 'I thought they might have dumped you here. There seems to be a lot of people who can't walk at all; I was worried that there wouldn't be room for you.'

'I don't particularly want to do it,' Kent answered slowly, 'I've got a feeling that the arrangements won't work properly, and it means we shall be separated.'

'Don't worry about that, sir, I shall be O.K.'

'Do you want to be shot of me?'

'No, of course I don't, the only thing I want to be sure of is that you get out safely.'

Kent said nothing; he leant against the rail listening to the gurgle of the water as it ran past the boat and watching a fire-fly zigzag against the dark form of a tree on the bank.

'I don't want to leave you,' he said at last; 'once I'm gone you'll be at everyone's beck and call, you'll probably be grabbed up to help form a rearguard or something equally bloody. I've had a look at the map and I might be able to do ten miles a day, maybe more, I can't say. The Chindwin is about two hundred miles from here, once we get across it into the hills we need never be caught. On the other hand if you'd rather not be saddled with me I'll go to Myitkyina.'

They looked at each other and Anson smiled. 'If you're sure you can walk, that's what we'll do, that's what I'd like to do.'

In the morning Kent woke as soon as it was light enough to see the far bank. He lay on his back and tried to decide if he had chosen the safest way out; provided Anson was there to help him he thought that he had. He knew that it was unfair to keep Anson with him, he ought to insist that when they started Anson should concentrate on saving himself. But he knew that he had not the courage to suggest such a thing; although he was as certain as he could be that Anson would not desert him under any circumstances he shrank from putting it to the test. He promised himself vaguely that if he could not march he would let Anson go.

He dressed and found one of the medical officers, who looked at him warily as he came up, thinking that it was someone who had not been included on the list of those to go north and who was now trying to talk his way on to the train. When he heard that Kent was volunteering to walk he was so surprised that he tried to make him change his mind, thinking that he must be too ill to know what he was doing.

'But my dear chap,' he said, 'you can't possibly do it, not with an attack of jaundice like yours. You might not realize it but it's a very serious illness, needs complete rest. I couldn't hear of you walking!' But his opposition only made Kent the more determined and he spoke with intense conviction.

'I don't care what you say, Doc, I'm perfectly fit to walk, and walk I shall. If I get on the plane I shall only be taking the place of someone much worse than I am, or doing some woman out of a seat. I've got an orderly to look after me and nothing will induce me to get on that train.' The doctor looked at him, puzzled by such vehemence; he was sure that there was some ulterior motive, but he was too busy and too worried to care. He shrugged his shoulders by way of agreement and Kent went aft and found Anson.

'O.K.,' he said, 'I've fixed that, let's get clear of here before they change their minds or someone grabs you. I'll get my equipment and meet you here in a minute, just bring your equipment and tommy-gun, nothing else.' He went back to his bed and put on his webbing. He was only carrying a haversack, water-bottle and revolver, but it seemed impossibly heavy. The doctor he had spoken to saw him getting ready and began to thread his way through the stretchers on the deck towards him. For a moment Kent thought he had changed his mind and was going to be officious.

'Aren't you a friend of Helen Dean's?' he asked, smiling suggestively.

'That's right.'

'I've heard she's only a few days' march ahead of you with a party of walking wounded and one or two medical orderlies. I should try and catch her up if I were you.'

'Thanks, I will. Don't worry about me, I shall be all right.' He clipped his belt into position and walked towards the passage leading aft.

Anson was waiting by the head of the gang-plank and without saying anything followed Kent. The main street of the tiny town ran in a straight line from the bank where the boat was moored and when they reached the end and looked back all they could see of the boat was the top of the funnel. A few hundred yards further on was a red-roofed bungalow; they made their way to it and found an open space all round crowded with parties of soldiers and

214

civilians sitting on the ground, Indian, British, and Chinese, and a large number of Eurasians, old women and young girls who sat as close together and as far away from the soldiers as possible. Near the gate was a group of English civilians; there was a large map on a table next to them and behind were four bullock-carts loaded with rice. Kent asked how far away the next village was, and whether there was water along the track.

'It's a damn' sight too far for you to walk looking like that,' one of the men answered, 'it's about fifteen miles from here, and there's only one stream. If you drink out of that you won't get very far, a party of people camped there a few days ago and the whole lot got cholera and died. Why don't you wait here a few days and get rid of some of that jaundice?'

Kent was feeling too wretched to argue. Although the few hundred yards from the boat had made him feel sick and dizzy it had also increased his compulsion to start the journey in earnest. He shook his head and moved to the table where the map was pinned down; someone had traced a wandering red line from the Irrawaddy to the Chindwin and then on over the hills to Imphal. He beckoned to Anson and they studied it together, memorizing the names of some of the larger villages and the general direction of the track. The man who had spoken to Kent joined them.

'Don't worry about losing your way; as long as you don't try travelling by night you can't miss it. Hundreds of people have already started from here, you'll find it well signposted,' he added grimly.

'What about water?' Kent asked. He had eaten practically nothing for three days, but the thought of food made his head swim with nausea.

'It's bad. There are plenty of streams near the villages but by now they must all be contaminated, you ought to boil everything you drink. Or else buy green coconuts, they're just about ready now. If you're determined to start I'll fill your haversacks with rice, and you had better have a good drink of water from the well at the back and fill your bottles. I think you're mad to go in that condition.'

But Kent only shook his head. They went to the well and drank as much as possible, and when they came back their haversacks were filled with rice.

'Thanks,' said Kent, 'we'll get cracking while it's still not too hot.'

By the time they had covered a mile Kent was exhausted. There was a low thorny tree by the side of the track and he leant against

215

it, then he bent over and began to retch and he fell on his knees pressing his hands to his stomach. Anson came quickly over and knelt beside him, holding his sweaty hand, and when the attack was passed helped him to his feet. He stood leaning against the tree, gasping, his mouth bitter and foul with the yellow froth he had sicked up; he could feel the sun, not yet high, resting like a hot hand on the back of his neck. Sweat ran down his face and glistened on his fingers as he fumbled with his shoulder straps.

'What do you want, sir?' Anson asked.

'I'm dumping everything,' Kent answered, 'everything except my water-bottle.' He let his equipment fall to the ground. 'Fix my belt so it just takes my water-bottle.' The heat of his body burned yellowly in his face, he took off all his clothes and threw away the thin vest and drawers that were already limp with sweat. The whole of his body showed bright yellow through the dulled patches of heat rash, even the dark brown tan of his bare forearms and legs was stained the same sickly colour. When he had put on his shirt and shorts again he let Anson fasten the belt around his waist.

'What about your revolver and the rice?' Anson asked, and Kent cursed foully and weakly:

'If you want to carry the bloody things you can, what the hell's it got to do with you, scared I'll eat your bloody rice? You needn't worry, I'd sooner die!' He knew that what he said was vicious and untrue, but he was almost ready to cry with weakness and irritability, and he lashed himself into a rage like a sick child. And then it was over and he was bitterly sorry. 'Don't take any notice of me, Anson, I'm sorry, I just feel desperately irritable. Leave the stuff by the side of the road; if we want rice we can buy it in the villages, I expect, and I don't intend getting near enough to any Japs to use long-range artillery, let alone a revolver.'

For the next three hours they scarcely spoke at all; occasionally Anson would make a remark, but Kent was too weak to reply. He had already finished his own water and most of Anson's, he could hear the last few mouthfuls slapping wetly inside Anson's bottle and the sound tortured him.

On each side of the track were high thick bushes tangled with flowering creepers and the sun blazed down on them without a breath of air to cool their bodies. Kent's shirt and shorts were black with sweat, it dripped from his chin and he tried to wipe it into his mouth with his fingers. He was so desperate for water that once he stopped and turning his back on Anson tried to urinate into his hand, but nothing came and he was frightened. They had walked very slowly, and he reckoned that the river was still two hours away. Whenever they came to a break in the hedge he would stop and look through it, hoping that possibly there might be a shallow pool of muddy water used as a wallow by the water buffaloes, but there was nothing to see except the endless shimmering paddy-fields and sometimes, dancing in the distance like a mirage, a dark clump of palms. When Anson asked him if he wanted to rest he shook his head impatiently; he was afraid to stop in case it was impossible for him to go on again, and he was obsessed by the thought of the water only a few miles away. He would fix his gaze on a point some distance ahead and watch it waver and creep towards him, hardly conscious of the movement of his legs, and when the point was passed he would look again and select another. The minutes crawled as slowly as lava and his heart was pounding; suddenly the sky and track swirled slowly round and he pitched forward into the powdery dust.

When he opened his eyes he found that Anson had dragged him into the side of the track where there was a strip of shade. Anson was putting back his bottle and Kent's mouth felt wet; he knew at once that Anson had given him the last of his water, and at the same moment he felt the terrible mingling pain of gratitude and remorse and love. He rolled over and laid his face in Anson's lap, rubbing his cheek against the sweat-soaked khaki shorts, his eyes tightly shut to hold back the tears that seemed to come so easily to him now. He could feel Anson stroking back the wet hair from his forehead. He lay in peace and happiness until he felt a little stronger and then he sat up.

'I shan't do anything like that again, I'm all right now. We'll go on to the stream they told us about and follow it up a little way in case it's contaminated near the track; we've got to drink before we get to the village or I'm afraid I shan't make it, and you must want water terribly badly as well.'

Some time later they passed a group of four Indian soldiers sitting by the side of the track. There was a little pile of sticks smouldering to one side of them and a blackened cooking-pot half full of a milky brew of tea. Kent glanced away quickly; the tea looked as delicious as anything he could ever remember, but out of an obscure desire to pretend to Anson that the water he had given him had satisfied him he could not ask for any of the tea. The soldiers watched them go by and one of them quickly filled a small mug and ran after them.

'Sahib! Sahib! Chai munktha?' They stopped and the Indian held out the cup to Kent, a smiling man whose proud face was softened by his gesture. Kent took the mug and thanked him, he could have drunk that and four more and still have been thirsty within a quarter of an hour. He turned and handed the mug to Anson.

'This is yours, Anson, drink it up quickly. If I had any tea I should be sick.' He smiled at the Indian and walked slowly on, afraid that if Anson tried to make him drink he would not be strong enough to refuse.

By the time they reached the stream Kent's last reserves of strength had gone and he was slightly delirious. Anson had been worried that he might become crazed with thirst at the sight of the water and flounder into it without caring about the possibility of cholera. The track crossed the stream by a bridge just wide enough for a bullock-cart to pass, there were tall trees, and the undergrowth had been trampled down by a succession of parties that had camped near the water. There were swarms of flies and many large emerald-green butterflies of exquisite beauty that settled with quivering wings on the little piles of drying human ordure. Anson could not see any bodies but there was a large clump of rushes by the edge of the stream on which the flies were settled so thickly that the strong reeds were bent. Kent's eyes were half closed and he was swaying on his feet, the sweat had dried from his body and his skin was burning. Anson took him by the hand and skirted the whole area until he was several hundred yards upstream. There was a tall cottonwood tree whose roots had straddled the stream and Anson helped Kent to lie down beneath it and then he filled his bottle. When he came back Kent was unconscious, scarcely breathing, and Anson had to prop him up and pour water over his face and head before he opened his eyes. He helped him to drink a cup of water, afraid that more might make him sick, and then he watched life creep slowly back.

He kept on giving him small quantities of water, and suddenly Kent's whole body was once more soaked in sweat. Anson made him as comfortable as possible, he took off his boots, stuffed his puttees into them and then put them inside his bush hat and let Kent use it as a pillow. Within a few minutes he was sleeping and Anson made a fire of twigs on the other side of the tree and cooked some rice in his mess-tin, leaving half for Kent.

When Kent awoke it was four o'clock, and the first thing he did was to go to the stream and drink as much as he could. He crawled back to the tree again and closed his eyes.

'I've cooked some rice if you'd like it,' Anson said, picking up his mess-tin and showing Kent a grey-white stodgy mass.

Kent sat up and took the tin, looking at the contents glassily.

'I've never seen anything more revolting,' he said, trying to smile. He took a lump of the stuff on his forefinger and put it into his mouth. It was like cold porridge strongly flavoured with wood-smoke and he spat it out and handed back the tin.

'It's no good, I couldn't eat that to save my life. Maybe we can get some fruit in the next village; take my money and look after it.' He undid his breast-pocket and took out some sweat-soaked rupee notes.

'We'd better get on, see the bottles are full.' They drank again and climbed across the roots of the tree to the other bank, cutting across the paddy-fields and rejoining the track. For a short time Kent walked quite strongly, but he could feel his energy draining away, and by the time they reached the village five miles on he was too weak to pass through it as he had intended, and lay down in a corner of a paddy-field on the outskirts while Anson went on to see if he could buy some fruit.

He was away a long time, and Kent had watched the golden light thicken and the shadows of the village stream across the paddy-fields in front of him. Somewhere, hidden from sight, little strips of glass and metal tinkled together from the spire of a pagoda and blue smoke began to mingle with the dust and drift across the fields. Kent was hidden from the track by a thick line of bushes, and he listened idly to the sounds of other refugees who intended to spend the night in the village; he heard an Englishwoman wonder whether the rest-house beds would be infested with bugs and a party of laughing soldiers discussing the chances of being offered the headman's daughter for the night. Soon afterwards a bullock-cart creaked past and a woman groaned in pain. By the time Anson came back it was almost dark and Kent had begun to fret. He dropped two large coconuts in their husks by Kent's side and sat down.

'The village has been cleaned out of everything except rice. I had a job to get these, and then I had to pay ten rupees for a knife to open them with.' He started to hack away inexpertly with a large knife and eventually cut a hole through the husk. The liquid was delicious, cool and with an underlying sharpness and when Kent had drunk it they split the coconut in half, and he scraped out some of the jelly-like flesh and ate it. They lay down side by side and Kent at once drifted off into the jumbled world of sickness and sleep, unconscious of the mosquitoes that hummed by their ears and settled on their bare flesh, the clammy chill as their sweat-soaked clothes slowly dried, the iron hardness of the paddy-fields.

He only woke once in the night and lay listening to a woman

screaming in terror in the village, and then a confused shouting. Anson was sitting up with the tommy-gun across his knee, and then Kent slept again until colour slowly crept back across the paddy-fields and into the village. His clothes were still damp and he felt wretchedly cold and stiff; he twisted round so that he could rest his head on Anson's stomach and almost fell asleep again as the warmth spread from his neck and shoulders. He found Anson's hand and held it against his chest.

'Did you have a good night?' he whispered.

'Pretty bad, I didn't sleep very much, nothing but yells and screams from the village all night, or dogs barking, or mosquitoes. And up to two o'clock it was too hot to sleep and suddenly it seemed too cold. And all the time you lay there like a log, not moving hardly. I could certainly do with some tea,' he added wistfully.

Kent glanced across the paddy-fields and saw that in a few moments the last vestiges of night would be gone. 'Let's get on, shall we, before the sun's up? We can sleep at midday.' They ate the second coconut, and as they were going through the village another group of Indian soldiers saw Kent's haggard yellow face and gave them tea. It was a brew in which everything had been boiled at the same time, it was delicious, but by the time Kent had finished a small cup he was feeling sick again. They filled Anson's mess-tin with cooked rice, not the stodgy mass that he had made the day before, but a snowy mound of fluffy grains, dry and tasting faintly of curry.

After they left the village Kent was sick, first the tea came frothing back and then the greeny yellow bile thickened this time by the coconut pulp.

For the next ten days he existed on gallons of water, and occasionally Anson managed to buy a coconut or a withered-looking tangerine. Once he was given a lump of bully beef, and he tried to eat it because he felt that he could not continue drawing on his reserves of strength for very much longer, but he had only been able to swallow a minute quantity before his stomach heaved and the all too familiar taste of bile was in his mouth again. He soon realized that the only thing his body craved for was water and still more water. He learnt that it was useless for him to reach a stream, drink his fill and then continue; he had to rest by the stream and drink for a long time, mouthful by mouthful until his body was once more saturated. But even by doing this he could not avoid spending long hours every day in an agony of thirst. Once the sun was above the level of the plains the temperature rose rapidly until it was over a hundred degrees in the shade and unless he drank every two hours the sweat would stop pouring from his body and his burning skin would feel as though it was about to split. Then he would begin to fantasy himself with gushing taps and glittering fountains, muttering to himself and swaying as he walked.

Each morning they started at first light and made good time for a few hours, and then the pace would slacken and the halts lengthened until they reached a stream or a village well. If the morning was far enough advanced they would stay by the water and Kent would sleep heavily while Anson cooked his rice or searched for fruit. They would start again when the sun was past its zenith and the pattern of the morning would be repeated except that everything seemed intensified, the heat a heavier burden, his thirst a dull fire, and irritability walked by his side like a screaming child. It was always the last hour of the march that was the worst, and it was only the compelling spur of water that drove Kent on; his mind would wander and occasionally he thought that it was still the morning. It happened sometimes that they would see a well-head in a grove of palm-trees and Kent would lie down only to have Anson come back and tell him that the well was dry. Although he tried to control himself it was not always possible and in his rage and necessity he would curse Anson, croaking out the vilest blasphemies mingled with recriminations that Anson had persuaded him against his better judgment to choose this route instead of going north and being flown to India.

But Anson took no notice. He would sit next to him with his back slightly turned in order to avoid giving Kent the embarrassment of knowing, once his fit of rage was over, that Anson had watched his twisted face, and the tears of anger and exhaustion that he hardly knew were trickling down his cheeks and through the stubble of his beard. He knew that Kent's sufferings were terrible, and he was amazed that they had managed to cover the distance that they had; time and again he thought that Kent could go no further, and he had still managed to carry on for another two hours. The storm of rage would pass, he would get unsteadily to his feet and they would go on until water was reached. Then Kent would apologize quietly and Anson would laugh and make his excuses for him.

Once the sun had set there was nothing to do but go to sleep; they were in less cultivated country now, and the track would have been dangerous to follow on the moonless nights even if Kent had been able to continue.

Anson always lay awake for a long time and then drifted in and out of sleep, but Kent would only open his eyes a few times if the ground was particularly rough, and, comforted by Anson's nearness, fall asleep again at once. Towards the end of the night his deep sleep would give way to dreams, a timeless horror when each smash of the stick across his broken face stretched to eternity, or a smoking grenade lay against his stomach about to disrupt in steel and flame and gut while his hands crept down his paralysed body to push death away. Desperately he used to fight his way back to consciousness, moaning with relief as the reality of his dreams faded into the unreality of the awakening. His face would be wet with sweat and he would cling to Anson like a child, staying awake until the light came, afraid to sleep.

At the end of the first ten days they were walking by the side of a broad stream when Kent lifted his heavy head and looked towards the horizon; for a moment he was unable to interpret what he saw and then suddenly he gripped Anson's arm.

'My God! Look, the Hills!' Unconsciously he walked a little faster: 'Look at them!' He was babbling excitedly, pointing eagerly at the pale violet ranges that rose like the ghost of clouds and seemed less substantial. The achievement of getting at least within sight of the foot-hills acted as an immediate tonic, and when they halted in the middle of the day he felt the first faint stirrings of hunger and he ate a minute quantity of rice. They were sitting by a well and just as he was about to fall asleep an Englishman came along the track and sat next to them. He started to eat handfuls of cooked rice ravenously.

'You've seen the hills, I suppose?' he asked, looking at Kent, and without waiting for an answer added: 'You look pretty rough, what's the matter, jaundice?' Kent nodded without speaking. The rice he had eaten rested uneasily on his stomach, he wanted to sleep before he had a chance to be sick. There were grains of rice sticking to the man's lips, which made him feel even more queasy, and he looked away quickly.

'I've got just the thing for you,' the man went on, 'I don't suppose you've been to the lavatory for days, have you?'

'No, I haven't, but I've eaten nothing for days so I don't suppose it matters. Besides it's quite a change for me, usually I spend half the day sitting on a bucket.' The man was fumbling in his haversack and at last produced two large grey pills.

'Calomel!' He spoke with immense satisfaction. 'Enough to clean out a bull elephant.' He uncorked his water-bottle and handed the pills to Kent, who looked at their size with something approaching horror. 'Swallow them while I watch you.' Kent chokingly forced them down, afraid that he would vomit, but after a few minutes his stomach returned to normal.

'How long will they take to work?' he asked.

'About an hour, maybe longer. Have a nice rest, you'll soon know all about it.' He laughed shortly and got to his feet. 'I must push on now, my wife's waiting for me on the other side of the Chindwin. That's two days from here, and there's a rumour that the Japs aren't too far away, I should get on as fast as you can if I were you.' Kent thanked him, and they watched him disappear round a bend in the track.

Two hours later Kent came wearily back to the well. The pains in his stomach had been so violent that at one time he thought something must have burst inside, but relief had come at last, and he was appalled at the quantity of foetid matter he had voided. They went on, but for several hours he was continuously having to leave the track and squat down until the spasms were relieved. It made him feel very weak and they finished the day earlier than usual; the hills seemed just as faint and unsubstantial as in the morning, but he was too tired to care and he fell asleep at once and slept deeply and dreamlessly for nearly fourteen hours.

For him it was the turning point of his sickness. He was far from cured, but he no longer vomited at all hours of the day, and the leaden headaches that he had almost become accustomed to only struck at him when he was very tired. They began to make better time and the hills yielded, their colour changing from palest violet to a deep blue and then quite suddenly the lower foot-hills were green.

On the afternoon of the thirteenth day they were sitting in a dug-out canoe trailing their fingers in the cold jade-green water of the Chindwin, watching the little village on the other side glide towards them until Kent could see the scarlet trumpets of hibiscus flowers.

14

There were many refugees here, and a few bamboo shelters had been erected where the sick and exhausted could rest or die. Kent and Anson wandered through the village looking for somewhere to spend the night, and a hut where they were told that bully beef was being issued for people to take on the next stage of the journey. As they passed one of the shelters Kent heard his name called; he looked round in surprise and saw Helen. She was kneeling by the side of a man who lay under a grey blanket and as he turned towards her she stood up and stepped down from the raised bamboo floor. Apart from her nurse's uniform being torn and dirty Kent could see no change in her.

'You look terribly thin and ill, Tony, you've got jaundice, I see.' She looked at him with concern.

'Yes, I have, but I think I'm getting over it. I don't know which was the great healer, time or a depth charge of calomel. Why aren't you half-way across the hills by now?' She looked down at her shoes and Kent saw that the leather of one of them had come away from the welt. 'Can't you walk in those shoes, or what?' he asked, and she laughed.

'Oh no, it's nothing to do with these stupid shoes, I could walk in bare feet if necessary.' Her face became grave. 'No, it's Robert, I'm afraid, he's got typhoid and I said I would stay behind and look after him. Besides, there's lots of sick people here and I'm making myself useful.'

'Robert?' Kent asked, puzzled. 'Robert who?'

'Johns. You know who I mean, he's been a hospital orderly with me for a long time. At least, he's a warrant officer now,' she added proudly. 'You used to tease me about him.'

'No, I can't seem to place him, Helen. Did I meet him with you?' She looked at him sadly, suddenly realizing that it was for this man, who did not even know of his existence, that Robert had suffered so much during the last months.

'No, you wouldn't know him, he's a Eurasian.' There was no trace of bitterness in her voice, and when she said 'Eurasian' she lifted her chin slightly. Kent wanted to say something to take away the implication, but he fumbled for words and the moment passed. Behind him he could hear Anson shuffle his feet in the dust and suddenly he wanted to be alone with this woman to whom he brought nothing but humiliation and unhappiness.

'Anson, see if you can find that store and come back here and pick me up afterwards.' He sat down on the springy bamboo and moved a little for Helen to sit next to him.

'Is that Robert there?' He jerked his head backwards and Helen nodded. 'Will he be all right or is he very ill?'

'I can't say,' she answered; 'it only started a few days ago, he must have caught it from some typhoid patients we had with us at Tisaw. One just doesn't know with typhoid for about fourteen days whether they are going to get better or not.'

'Fourteen days! But the Japs will be here by then!' He looked at her in amazement as though she had taken leave of her senses.

224

'Yes, probably. But that's not Robert's fault, is it?' She looked at him steadily, and he read accusation in her glance, although none was there.

'Why look at me, Helen, it's not my fault either,' he protested.

'I never suggested such a thing, Tony, I know it's not your fault, everyone I've met from your regiment says how brave you were, escaping from the Japanese and getting across the river when you were wounded. I'm not blaming anyone, but it's still not Robert's fault, is it? I can't leave him now.'

'Are you in love with him?' It was the only possible explanation he could think of.

'I can't really say,' she answered hesitantly, 'it's so difficult to tell. So much has happened recently that I've given up trying to think. But certainly I like him sufficiently not to be able to leave him for the Japanese to get. He's very much in love with me, and that seems to put me under an obligation to him.'

Kent peeled a long sliver of bamboo from the floor and began to chew it before he remembered that there was a typhoid patient within a few feet of them, and he spat as though he had put filth in his mouth.

'Does he know about us?' He whispered the question; he was curious.

'No, at least not everything. He knows that I was . . . very fond of you. At one time.'

'And you aren't any longer.' It was a statement.

'There wouldn't be very much point in it if I was,' she answered with spirit. 'Quite apart from the fact that you're married you've never been the slightest bit in love with me, you only wanted to . . . to . . . use me.' She moved her shoulders with embarrassment. It was quite true, Kent told himself, and for a moment he was tempted to try to vindicate himself, to say that in reality he had been driven by a compulsion that had sprung from almost the opposite root of physical desire. But that was something he could never speak about to another living soul, least of all to those people that he loved; unforgivable, unforgettable, unshareable.

'You don't understand, Helen. It wasn't really like that. I can't explain, but I didn't . . .' He could not go on, and they looked at each other sadly. In the silence that fell they could hear voices in the village and then they saw Anson coming slowly back.

'Don't worry, Tony. I understand how you felt, I don't blame you a bit. We'll meet in Calcutta or somewhere soon and be good friends. Are you going on tonight?' She looked at her hands and Kent felt a lump in his throat; she spoke so casually and yet she must be suffering deeply, waiting every day for the last scurry of panic-driven refugees and soldiers before the Japanese arrived, chained to someone Kent was sure she did not even love, yet. And then to have to face the arrogant bestial Japanese troops, who even if they did not rape her one after the other, pressing their foul syphilitic mouths to hers, or torture her with outlandish horror, would at least put her in some concentration camp which she would probably never leave. He could not bear to leave her, and he could not bear to stay a moment longer.

'Yes, Helen, we're going on now. There's nothing I can say except to wish you the very best of luck, and that Robert's fit enough to get a little way into the hills in the next few days, even a few miles in would give you a better chance. But you're not completely alone, are you?' He suddenly began to feel trapped, in another moment he would have to offer to stay with her and help to get Robert into India. He could not do it, he was sick himself, it wasn't fair to Anson, expecting him to stay and help someone neither of them had known existed. He stood up, sweating.

She looked up at him and saw the sweat beading his face, and in a flash she understood what he was thinking. 'No,' she said, 'I'm not alone, there will be people to help me as soon as Robert can stand. You wouldn't be any good, Tony, you're too weak yourself. Go now.' Her eyes filled with tears as they held hands for a moment, and Kent saw them and turned on his heel. She could not watch him out of sight because her eyes were blurred, instead she went and knelt beside Robert and put her hand on his burning face. She dried her eyes. When Robert was fit to stand, if he didn't die, perhaps with a little luck there might be someone still in the village who would help her get him into India.

15

Kent took Anson to the end of the village before he could trust himself to speak, and Anson kept silent, knowing that Kent was upset, but understanding nothing except that it was to do with Helen.

'Did you manage to get any bully beef?' he asked at last.

'Yes, four tins. I told the bloke in charge I was getting it for you as well, but all he said was that he heard that story twenty times a day, and if you wanted it you could get it yourself.'

'Four tins will do, it's only six or seven days from here, I think.

Look, there's still an hour to go before it gets dark, let's get out of this place while we can. It's full of sickness, and if we stay we might be grabbed for something. Anything might happen. What do you say?' He felt a compulsion to get away from Helen and leave the village as soon as possible.

'It's all the same to me, if you think it's a good idea let's do it.'

They slept that night in a small valley overgrown with tall rushes. It was only a few hundred feet above the level of the village and the mosquitoes and heat were so bad that even Kent found it difficult to sleep, and in the morning their faces were puffy with mosquito bites. It took them an hour to climb the first ridge and when they reached the top Kent was appalled at the weakness of his legs and the amount of sweat that rolled off his body. Below them was another broad valley covered with the same sort of rushes and elephant grass as the previous one; looking down, Kent was hardly able to pick out the thin black line that wavered across the valley and marked the trail; he followed it with his eye until it was lost in the blue early morning haze that covered everything. Beyond the valley rose the next ridge of hills, much higher than the one on which they stood, its steep sides covered with jungle.

They started the descent, slipping and sliding on the loose stones, and by the time Kent reached the bottom he was again pouring with sweat and breathing laboriously. For a long while they had to walk in single file with the reeds and plumes of grass almost reaching over their heads – some of the reeds by the edge of the trail were bent over and had to be brushed aside; in a short time their arms were criss-crossed with little cuts from the sharp edges of the reeds and as the sweat washed away the beads of blood the cuts smarted. The track itself was a mixture of sand and dust; for the first few hundred yards Kent enjoyed its softness after the jarring descent from the ridge, but his legs soon began to ache as he plodded along in the loose surface.

He had expected to find water in the centre of the valley, but there was nothing except the broad bed of sand where the stream ran during the monsoon, and he stared avidly at it as though by doing so he might make the water flow. As they stood for a moment before crossing the bed a long yellow and black snake slid from the rushes on the far side and undulated effortlessly across the sand. The instinct to kill all snakes on sight swept over Anson; he stepped in front of Kent and fired a long burst from his tommy-gun, the sand shooting up in fountains round the krait, hiding it, and a flock of white egrets rose swiftly from the rushes in front of them. By the time the sound of the firing had rolled back to them from the hills the dusty sand had settled and the snake was rolling and twisting its broken body.

'Cruel bastard!' Kent said indignantly, 'it wasn't doing any harm. I hope I step on one and it gets you. Go on, kill it properly.' Anson looked at him, surprised and faintly ashamed of what he had done. He started towards the snake.

'Don't go near it, for God's sake!' Kent caught him roughly by the arm. 'They're deadly. Kill it from here,' and another long burst of fire died away and rolled back. The snake's body was smashed into the sand. Kent walked on, the firing still jerking in his ears; he could hear Anson clipping on another magazine and hurrying to catch him up. The egrets were flying in a white line against the hills, the sun that had not yet reached the rushes glowing on their wings.

The belt of reeds ended suddenly and the ground began to rise. Soon Kent felt the sun on his back and looking up he could see that what had appeared as one long unbroken slope was in fact two. Wearily he began to climb, his legs felt as though they were lapped in lead and his fingers were trembling with fatigue.

When he reached the top of the true crest four hours later he lay down in the dirt of the track and let the leaves and sky swim above him while the blood beat in his ears. There was a light breeze that seemed deliciously cool and fresh after the burning breath of the plains, and half an hour later he felt strong enough to get to his feet and lean against a tree on the edge of the ridge. From this point he could look back into Burma, and he gloated over the scene, filled with a sense of triumph. 'You've made it,' he whispered to himself. 'Take a long last look, with any luck you'll never set eyes on it again.'

He let his gaze wander across the valley below him, hazily golden in the sun; the ridge that he had first climbed with such difficulty seemed puny, and he marvelled now to think of the effort it had been to reach the top. He tried to pick out the village where he had left Helen but it was invisible, although he could catch glimpses of the river through the low foot-hills, and further south it reappeared as an unbroken silver riband. Beyond the river the plains stretched as far as he could see, hazy and featureless, seemingly a different world from the one across which he had just crawled, with its flowering trees set in slender palms, streams and wells, green husks of coconuts littering the dusty white track, butterflies swerving in the twists of burning air. And he hated and feared it, every grain of rice, every creaking bullock-cart, every brick of every sun-rotted tinkling pagoda. 'God, I hate it!' he muttered, but against his will it held him by its beauty. The cool breeze fanned his damp neck; on the furthermost edge of the horizon, just showing above the haze of the plain, bulged the topmost tower of a cumulus cloud. It seemed to him that under the haze was death, walking brokenly out of the land along every track, walking into India with them, scattering his gifts as he went as though they were too heavy for him to carry, cholera and exhaustion, typhoid and smallpox, suppurating wounds and malaria, the double stroke of women big with child who lay down and died while they looked towards the violet hills for help, dark-eyed in agony. And behind death came death with a scourge in his hand, the split of small bombs and the over-wrought stammering of machine-guns, blazing towns and villages, the unanswered inhuman sounds of men and women who died alone, asking only a small gift, a cup of water. He shuddered, death had been left to sleep the night in the village, they must hurry, and as he turned away he saw again the black and gold snake twisting and coiling while its pall of dust drifted away.

From now on he began to lose all count of time, it seemed to him that he wandered for years in a maze of mountains that melted the flesh of his bones by day, and held him twisting and turning in their icy fingers by night. Ridge after ridge ran monotonously across their path from north to south. They would labour up five thousand feet and then be forced to squander all their gain on the other side, dipping down and down into steaming valleys shrill with invisible cicadas, the insane noise held to a steady note as though there was just one swarm of insects keeping level with them, hidden by the fringe of the jungle.

Kent could remember certain incidents, but the hills confused the sequence of events. He could remember the swarm of tiny bees, smaller than flies, that had covered his legs, and arms, and face, while he dozed exhaustedly on the top of a ridge. He had woken up shouting for Anson, who had wandered a little way, desperately brushing them off as they clung to the hairs of his legs and arms, their tongues avid for the salt of his sweat. They had crawled up his shorts and inside his shirt; he could feel his scalp moving with them, and he tore off his clothes and left them on the track while he walked away naked, combing them off his body with his fingers, trying to join in Anson's hysterical laughter as he followed him with his shirt and shorts brushing the insects off his back. When he looked up he saw that he was being watched in amazed horror by a group of English civilians and their wives who were resting just below the crest of the ridge.

But he was no longer sure whether that had happened before the storm that burst on them early one night as they lay huddled together in the biting cold, the rain lashing through the thick leaves above them with a violence that could scarcely have been excelled even if they had been lying in the open, and the ear-splitting crash and blue blaze of light as a tree within fifty yards burst into unnatural fire before the torrent of rain blanketed the flames. They had crawled on their hands and knees to the track and lay holding each other while the water gushed past them and the thunder seemed to split their heads. The hours of darkness that followed as they dozed against each other, soaked and frozen, while the forest dripped and the cicadas screamed, alone seemed to have occupied an immeasurable span of time.

But all the nights were infinitely long. They had tried sleeping in a valley to avoid the worst extremes of cold, but they decided it was preferable to freeze than to be eaten alive by leeches and mosquitoes, and then to have the cold air seep down from the hills above and form a thick dead mist that dripped from the trees like a heavy summer shower falling through the leaves of an English wood. And when they crept miserably back on to the track with the first light of day they found gorged leeches hanging on to their arms and legs. Their matches were too damp to strike so they could not burn them off, and without saying a word they had jerked them away from their flesh, feeling the bodies squidgy with blood, and the little red wounds had oozed blood for hours.

After this they had slept every night on the top of some ridge, enduring the cold and sleeplessness as best they could. They lay curled together with their arms around each other; but Anson knew that Kent wanted nothing more, the whole of his will-power and the last reserves of his strength were concentrated on fighting his way through the mountains and reaching India alive. Although his illness had run its course, and the yellow stain was slowly fading from his skin, each day's march was still a major undertaking, and at the end of it he was left utterly spent, without either the strength or wish to brush away the flies that settled on his face and mouth. And whatever advantage his body gained by throwing off the jaundice was more than offset by the merciless burden of the hills. The journey across the plains had melted the soft flesh that his time in Maymyo and Mandalay had let accumulate, and now the hills, helped by his inability to eat more than the bare minimum of food, were stripping off the rest.

His mind was so engrossed by the daily struggle to survive that he had almost forgotten what had passed between them. Sometimes as they lay awake waiting for the twilight of dawn Kent would feel his blood stir, and he would draw closer to Anson and touch his face with his fingers. But it was done subconsciously, his mind already walking away down the track, wondering if the coming day would mean long waterless stretches, or whether they might perhaps reach the last ridge looking down on the plains and swamps surrounding Imphal. But he was well aware of the pleasure that came from Anson's company and he refused all the suggestions made to him by other groups of refugees that passed them, civilians and soldiers, that he should join their parties and share their blankets. Their hardships and the months they had spent together, hardly out of each other's sight, had bound them by ties far stronger than either of them understood, and they had reached a stage of intimacy when the presence of other people made them feel strange and awkward.

One morning a solitary officer had caught up with them and insisted on joining them, talking feverishly about his own hardships and the route by which he had come. A numbing sense of strangeness had fastened on to Kent as he listened and noticed how in a hundred different ways the other man treated Kent as an equal and Anson as a private soldier, until he himself found it difficult not to do the same. He knew that the officer was right and that he was wrong, but he remembered everything that Anson had done for him, and was ashamed that this garrulous fool could make him ashamed. When they stopped at midday he managed to signal to Anson not to produce any food, and as soon as the officer started to eat, which he did almost before he sat down, Kent said that he was not hungry and wanted to walk on further. Before the man could protest they had left, hurrying on until they were hidden from sight and then they left the track and ate in peace, waiting until he had walked quickly by them. They could see him craning his neck as he hurried to catch them up.

And so it had gone with similar attempts by individuals to attach themselves to Kent. He understood their need for company but he shook them off ruthlessly, sometimes not even bothering to make any excuses. As the days passed and Imphal drew nearer Kent's desire for privacy became more and more marked, as though he was trying to amass a horde of hours spent alone with Anson to last him through the time ahead when they would never be properly alone again. Whether they drank at a stream or rested, ate or slept, they would do it as far away from other human beings as possible, and if they had chosen some comfortable place for their night's rest and other people came within earshot they would get up and move further away.

And then, soon after they had set out on the morning of the tenth day after crossing the Chindwin they came to the top of a curving ridge and saw a white-haired and emaciated Indian sitting against a tree, staring into the distance. As they came up to him Kent saw that the old man was looking down on the plains of Imphal and that he was dead.

16

There was still a full day's march in front of them; it took several hours for the track to wind down to the plain and even then Imphal was some fifteen miles away. They did not speak very much all day, and the nearer they came to the town the less they spoke. Kent had expected to feel pleasure and excitement when the journey was finished, but instead he became more and more depressed, the hills and paddy-fields seemed lifeless and heavy and suddenly he was shocked by the realization that he missed the white pagodas and the gaily dressed Burmese. The few dung-coloured villages that they passed through, watched by sombre groups of Manipuris, did nothing to lighten his mood.

When they reached the outskirts of Imphal Kent saw a British military policeman standing by the gateway of a bungalow, and behind him a large sign saying 'All Military Personnel Proceeding from Burma Report Here'. The policeman seemed almost insultingly smart and clean, his khaki shirt and shorts rigid with starch, his belt dazzlingly white, his boots glittering and repellent as jet. The sign and the policeman gave Kent a feeling of inferiority and resentment: compared to the latter he felt indescribably filthy, the stubble on his chin had become a beard, and his clothes were torn and foul with muck and sweat; and the wording of the notice irritated him, although he could think of no alternative. As they walked up to him Kent hoped that he would not notice the flat cloth badges of rank on his shoulder straps, the dirt of the journey had blended them to the same colour as his shirt. It would have given him the opportunity to disgorge some of his feelings of resentment, but he was disappointed, the salute came with the precision and indifference of an automaton.

As they reached the bungalow a group of private soldiers, obviously refugees, came out. They were talking and laughing excitedly, and Kent's spirits fell even lower. He did not try to understand the reason, but he knew that everything would give him cause for anger, whether he was treated as a hero returned from the dead or with indifference.

They went into a comfortless room where an officer sat behind a desk with a mug of tea in front of him and two N.C.O.s occupied smaller tables covered with files and bound cardboard folders of Army Instructions. He went up to the desk and saluted grudgingly, signalling Anson to stand next to him.

'Ah, hullo,' said the captain cheerfully, 'enjoyed your walk?'

'Yes, it was delightful, thank you.' Something in Kent's voice changed the cheerfulness of the captain's face. He looked up warily.

'You're sick, aren't you? I'll just take your particulars and then you'd better report to the hospital. I'm afraid you'll find it all pretty chaotic, we were bombed yesterday, and every sweeper and servant in Imphal has disappeared temporarily. We're very short of nurses as well.' He jotted down Kent's name and regiment and then nodded towards Anson. 'Is this man with you?'

'Yes, he's my batman.'

'Is he sick too?'

'No, I wouldn't say that. He's in perfect health except for any trifling physical inconvenience he might feel after helping me for three weeks and living on a bit of rice. Perhaps you'd like to speak to him, he's only a private soldier, but you'll find him quite intelligent.' The two N.C.O.s stopped writing and the silence was broken by the captain.

'Give your particulars to the sergeant over there, will you?' He nodded to Anson, speaking quietly and determined to keep his temper.

'I'm sorry I haven't any transport for you but the hospital's quite close. Turn left when you get to the road and it's about half a mile down, on the left.'

'Thanks,' said Kent; he was already ashamed of his childish outburst and tried to show his regret in his voice. 'I suppose there's no post office here where I could send a wire home? I expect they're a bit worried.'

'I'm afraid the bombing put it out of order, but you'll be evacuated tomorrow, and you can send one from Dimapur. That's rail-head,' he explained.

'Right.' He walked to the door and then turned and waited for Anson.

'I'm afraid you won't be able to take your batman on any further, as he's not sick he'll have to report to the rest camp for

233

a few days. But you won't need him anyway once you get into hospital.'

Kent said nothing; to gain time he bent down and picked a piece of mud off the toe of his boot. He wondered whether it would be possible to bluff this man into letting Anson go on with him into India, but he knew at once that it was impossible, and might cause dangerous comment.

'Yes, I quite see that,' he said as he straightened up, 'but I'd like him just to come to the hospital with me. I want to get settled in and give him a letter for my C.O. and messages to one or two other officers. I take it that he'll be sent back to the battalion as soon as they arrive, or are they already here?'

The captain tapped the desk with his pencil. 'All right, but he must go to the rest camp as soon as possible, it's just past the hospital.'

'And when do you think he'll go back to the battalion?'

'I can't say. I believe they'll be arriving in a day or so. He'll go as soon as they arrive here.'

They reached the hospital as the sun dropped below the saucer-like ridge of hills that ringed the plain. Kent had expected to find it full of sick and wounded, but the wards that he went through were not more than a third full. It was very quiet, the patients lay still in their beds, occasionally someone would mutter or a spring creaked. At last he found one of the nurses, who showed him into a small ward; only one bed in a corner was occupied, and she went hurriedly over and screened it. She came back and looked at Kent with the blank eyes of exhaustion, trying to remember what he had said to her.

'Is he dead?' Kent whispered. She gave a little start and picked up a blanket.

'Well, yes, I'm afraid he is. We haven't been able to arrange a burial party for him yet, he only died this afternoon,' she said apologetically. 'We're desperately short-staffed and no servants. I think there's another hospital group on the way, but it's difficult.'

'Don't worry about me,' Kent said, 'as long as I don't hear the screen fall down in the night I shan't mind. Why's the hospital half empty?'

'We only keep the people here we dare not move or who have something very infectious. That's why I put you in here, he had ... a wound. Everyone else goes down each morning at eight o'clock by lorry to rail-head. You'll leave tomorrow.'

She started to make the bed and Anson stepped forward: 'I'll do that, Nurse,' he said, taking the blanket from her. She looked at him curiously, brushing a strand of hair back from her forehead.

234

'Are you a patient too?'

'No, I'm Captain Kent's batman. I'm just going to fix him up for the night and then I'm going to the rest camp.'

'It's all right, Sister,' Kent said, 'you run along, we'll be O.K.'

'But you must wash and put on pyjamas, and medicine and your temperature and . . . and food,' she trailed off, trying to remember the routine of admission; sleep drifted across her eyes and made her sway a little. She rested her hand on the bed-rail and looked at them blankly, realizing that the strange pungent smell in the room came from the two men in front of her. She could think of no reason why they should smell so strongly, and then she remembered the young boy of twenty in the next ward who would be dead in a few hours.

'Please, Sister,' Kent was saying, 'I shall be all right till the morning. I couldn't do anything except get into bed and sleep. You must be desperately busy, don't bother until the morning.'

'All right,' she answered reluctantly, 'I'll try and look in later.' She walked out of the ward carefully, like a woman in high heels who knows that she has drunk too much.

The room was full of shadows now and a mosquito hummed by Kent's ear. He sat on a chair, taking off his boots, watching Anson make the bed with the heavy deliberateness of men, and he wondered whether mosquitoes would bite the dead man. He peeled off his socks, which were in shreds, his feet were puffy and white and his fingers stank from touching the sticky socks. He was afraid that Anson might notice; he stuffed the socks into the boots and walked bare-footed out of the ward. There was a fire bucket outside full of water with a grey film of dust on the surface and he washed his feet with his hands. When he came back Anson had finished and Kent took off the rest of his clothes and got into bed. He moved his body over and Anson sat close to him.

'How does a bed feel?' he asked wistfully, smiling at Kent.

'Not bad.' Kent answered his smile and they slid their hands together.

'Do you want to write to the C.O. or anyone?' Anson asked.

'I shan't bother. When you get back you had better find Tarrant or someone and tell them I'm in hospital.' As he spoke of Tarrant the memory of Goodwin struck at him. 'And tell them about Goodwin, that's most important!'

'What shall I tell them?' he asked.

Kent was silent. He had almost forgotten Goodwin, it had been so easy, so natural to kill him that he found it was difficult to remember exactly what had happened or what he said had happened. For the first time he realized that he was a murderer and what the penalty would be if he was found out. He drew his hand away from Anson's in case he should notice that the palm was wet.

'Say as little as possible. Just that he came to see me and you brought him on to the veranda and then went to your own room. And the next thing you heard was the shot. If they ask any questions about my revolver say you're not sure if it was on the table, but my equipment was and that the revolver would almost certainly have been there too. But don't be too definite, I'll do all that, I've got nothing to hide.'

'Shall I say that he seemed odd when he arrived?'

'Yes, if you like. Say you got the impression that he had been drinking, but that wasn't unusual. And whatever you do, tell them that I reported it to the civil police.' He moved his hand back and let it rest under Anson's.

'You did kill him, didn't you, sir?' He had dropped his voice to an almost inaudible whisper as though he was afraid that the sound might reach the pleated screen.

'No!' Kent answered firmly, 'and the sooner you put that bloody silly idea out of your head the better.' There was a long silence and Anson moved his forefinger in the palm of Kent's hand, and then Kent spoke again, his voice low and sad.

'Be careful when you get back to the battalion, won't you? I'm pretty certain no one suspects anything, but it would be dreadful if they did. I still don't understand what made me . . . do what I did, with you, I mean. I suppose it's the war or something. But we can't go on like that, not when I come back to the battalion. If we were found out we should both be court-martialled.' His hand was sweating again, but he did not take it away. 'Think of that. It would be ghastly enough if it was with another officer, but infinitely worse with a private soldier. You understand what I mean, don't you?' He shook his hand slightly and anxiously watched his face. Anson moved a little and stared miserably at the blanket.

'Yes, I understand how you feel about it, at least I think I do. But nobody knows about it, and there's no reason why they ever should.'

'Yes, but it's not only that, Anson. Look, I've never done anything like this before in my life. I never even thought about it except as a filthy joke. I couldn't bear to become like that, or even have people suspect me in any way. And there's no excuse for me, I'm married.'

236

'But you must have known something about it,' Anson protested, 'when you were a kid at school . . .'

'Yes, but that was different, utterly different. You must know what little beasts boys are. It was just dirty-mindedness, it didn't mean anything. Once, maybe twice, fooling around in the lavatories. It was being nastily clever, like seeing who could fart loudest.' He shook his head. 'It wasn't anything like this.' He turned away and swallowed, remembering the mosquito net that trembled in the grey light at Maymyo; brushing away the tiny flakes of ash that fell on his chest as they smoked in silence propped up against the flattened pillows. He could remember the feel of his neck as he had rested against Anson's arm. It was finished, it must finish.

'Does that mean you don't want me as a batman when you come back?' Anson looked at him intently.

'I hadn't thought as far ahead as that. You know I like you immensely, I always will. If it hadn't been for you I should be considerably deader than that.' He nodded towards the screen. 'Of course I want you to go on being my batman, but we can't always have what we want, sometimes it's bad for us. Actually I think it would be stupid of either of us to ask for a change when I come back, too many people have heard me say what a wonderful batman you are, it would look funny if I said I wanted someone else now. All I'm trying to say is that for my sake I want you to forget. Will you do that?'

'Yes,' Anson answered quickly, 'if that's what you want me to do. I don't really understand why you think like this, but I suppose we're different. The only thing I ask is that after a time you don't get someone else as your batman. You know I've liked working for you and I promise faithfully I won't . . . won't . . .' He was unable to finish, but Kent understood what he wanted to say.

'All right, that's a bargain.' The room was almost dark now, and they sat in sad silence. Occasionally their eyes met, but they would look away again quickly, afraid that the other one might start to say good-bye.

'How long do you think you'll be away?' Anson asked at last.

'I hadn't thought about it. Why?'

'I just wondered. I expect I shall be getting leave soon. But that's not why I asked,' he added quickly, 'in fact I might not take it, unless I can get it in before you come back. I only wanted to know.' He smiled bleakly.

'I'll probably go to Delhi first,' Kent answered, 'or Bombay, somewhere a long way away.' They heard footsteps coming along

237

the stone-flagged corridor and Anson stood up and moved away from the bed, pretending to fold Kent's clothes. The nurse entered the ward, carrying a hurricane lamp.

'Haven't you gone yet?' she asked. 'You've been here a long time.'

'We've been chatting,' Kent said. 'I think you had better get along now.' He turned his head to Anson and the nurse stood between them by the side of the bed. He sat up and held out his hand and she caught hold of his wrist. 'Not you, Sister,' he laughed, feeling embarrassed, 'I'm just saying good-bye.'

'Oh, I'm sorry.' She moved back uncertainly and stood watching them.

'Good-bye, Anson. I shall be back soon. Thank you for everything you've done.' The hurricane lamp was on the chair by the head of the bed, the soft yellow light shone on Anson's face. He was looking straight at Kent and moved forward awkwardly and took his hand.

'That's all right, sir,' he mumbled thickly, desperately trying to think of something to say. 'Hope you have a good leave.'

'I'll probably drop you a line as soon as I know where I am,' Kent said. They pressed their hands tightly together, and Kent thought of many things he had forgotten to say, but the nurse was standing there, watching. It seemed a long time to Kent before he reluctantly let his grip relax. Anson bent down slowly and picked up his tommy-gun from the floor, and touched Kent's folded clothes as though he had forgotten something. Then he turned away and his boots clattered on the stone floor; the nurse moved forward and put a thermometer in Kent's mouth. He listened to the sound of Anson's footsteps going slowly away, and then he remembered that the rest camp was very close, and he took the thermometer out of his mouth.

'An——!' He started to shout, to tell him to come in the morning before eight o'clock and see him again, but he stopped, suddenly racked with misery. 'It's no good,' he whispered, forgetting the nurse, 'I can't.'

'Have you forgotten to tell him something?' She spoke without interest, automatically.

'Yes,' he said, 'I have forgotten to tell him something, but it's too late now.' He put the thermometer back in his mouth and closed his wet eyes, waiting for the nurse to leave the room and take the lamp with her. When she had gone he lay on his face and cried silently; he had forgotten that the man was dead, and he thought that he was not alone.

17

It took Kent a week to reach a hospital in Central India, sleeping in makeshift medical centres already sinking into the mud from the rains that were just starting, being fed on bully beef and tea, loaded on to filthy trains crammed to suffocation with sick and wounded, the latrines clogged with every kind of filth, old dressings and vomit and excreta, but he was too tired to grumble at the conditions. He sat in the slow-moving train, either sleeping or looking apathetically out of the window, letting the wet heat and the flat monotony of the plains hypnotize him.

Once he reached his destination matters improved, but even so his strength only came back slowly. Often during the day he would ask the sister on duty for permission to use his mosquito net, and because his pulse and temperature were apt to be erratic they humoured him. As soon as the filmy walls shut him in he would relax and sleep for hours.

The doctor who first examined him had said that probably he would be fit to leave at the end of ten days, but it was a month before he was discharged, and when he went to the registrar's office to collect his leave pass and rail warrant he was still thin and weak.

'Where are you going?' the registrar asked him affably.

'Delhi, sir.'

'Delhi! At this time of year? But it's impossible, much too hot. Why don't you go to Kashmir?'

'Oh, I don't know, I'm sick of hills. I shall go to Delhi for a bit and if it's too hot then I might go to Kashmir.'

Delhi was some hours distant by rail, and he went early to the station and searched the train until he found a first-class compartment that was empty. He spread his belongings over the two lower berths and then stood in the doorway pretending that he was waiting for friends to join him. When the train started he lay down on the imitation leather couch and wondered how he could fill in a month's leave wandering around Delhi by himself. It had been different in Maymyo with a bungalow of his own, and the club almost next door. And Anson. No, not Anson, just the club and the bungalow. And then his mind began again, trying to recall the details of his face and body, the sound of his voice and the smell of his hair; he sat up with a groan and took a book out of his haversack. By the time he reached Delhi he had not turned more than a few pages.

He chose a dilapidated gharry to drive to his hotel instead of a taxi, not caring which way the driver went nor how slowly. His hotel stood back from the road and as the gharry drew up beneath the portico barefooted turbaned servants came sedately down the broad steps and took his luggage. He leant against the reception desk and let a kindly fat Hindu take change of him, raising no objection when he was given a room on the fifth floor, nodding his head when he was told that he would have to report to the station staff officer in the Red Fort on the following day, nodding again when he was asked if he would like a private bathroom and an Indian servant to look after him personally.

When he reached his room the porter had already turned on the ceiling fan and opened the faded green shutters. The room was on the top floor and was stiflingly hot. As he leant against the window-sill and looked over the flat low city, he could see veils of rain trailing across the outskirts, hiding the brown plains beyond. Beneath him was a sea of green palms and trees broken by flat white roofs.

'Salaam, Sahib.'

He turned round and saw a middle-aged Pathan standing in the doorway, dressed in baggy white trousers and shirt. His white flowing turban had a twist of gold braid which was repeated in the broad cummerbund round his waist. His eyes were creased at the corners as though from too much sun, his fine aquiline features blurred with fat. Kent liked him at once.

'Are you my bearer?'

'Yes, Sahib.'

'Do you speak good English?'

'Yes, Sahib, I have very good chits.' His hand disappeared into the folds of his shirt and a tattered greasy packet of letters was produced. He stepped out of his sandals and came into the room.

'No, I don't want to see them, thanks. What's your name?'

'Sher Ali, Sahib.'

Kent looked at his watch, it was almost six o'clock; he went to the writing-table. The hotel notepaper was limp with the humidity, the thick ink blurred as he wrote an order for some bottles of brandy and gave it to the bearer.

'Get these as soon as you can and then unpack. And try and get some ice as well, please.' Sher Ali looked at him gravely. He saw a tall young man with a thin face and sad eyes, and he thought him very beautiful. He went away, feeling sorry for him, one should not be young and a soldier and look sad; he decided to be a good servant, and only steal the minimum to preserve his self-respect. He was glad that Kent had ordered brandy, it was a good drink and for some reason the sahibs who ordered brandy seldom bothered to mark their bottles.

That evening Kent spent a long time in his room drinking brandy and talking to Sher Ali, who sat cross-legged on the floor sewing a shirt for his youngest child. He had no particular wish to sew, but he knew that when men sat alone in their rooms drinking they were often glad of his company, but unless he pretended to be occupied, they became embarrassed because they were talking to a servant. In reality he knew that they were talking to themselves. And Sher Ali listened because, not only would it mean a larger present at the end of his engagement, but also he considered that it was part of his duties.

As soon as Kent had asked him if he was married, and whether he had any children, he had sat on the floor with a resigned mind, and darned the only pair of socks that needed attention, and when that was finished he produced the shirt. He judged by the size of Kent's drink that he would not have long to wait before he knew why his eyes were sad, and when at last Kent went down for dinner, the only uncertainty in Sher Ali's mind was whether he was sad about something he had done during the fighting or because he loved his servant and was lonely.

He listened to Kent walking down the corridor, and he sighed as he folded the shirt and began to tidy the room. When he had finished he helped himself to some brandy and drank it down quickly. It was in the nature of a small punishment for the Sahib; he was very sorry for him, but by disclosing his innermost secrets so easily he had been guilty of great disrespect.

Late next morning Kent took a gharry to the Red Fort; it was raining, and everything he touched was damp and clammy. When he had shown his leave pass and was about to go, the S.S.O. called him back.

'Do you have a revolver, Captain Kent?'

'No, I'm afraid I don't, I handed mine in on the hospital boat I was on in Burma and I never got it back.' The lie came easily; what had seemed a perfectly reasonable action in Burma here took on the aspect of a major crime.

'You should have one, there's a lot of political unrest, and although it's all right in Delhi if you go into the country you ought to be armed. I'll give you a chit to our Q.M. and he'll fix you up. If you lose it, remember it'll mean at least a court of inquiry.'

It took him a long time to draw the revolver and when he returned to the hotel it was nearly one o'clock. The rest of the day stretched emptily away, and a warm rain fell from the low clouds that seemed to reflect the yellow mud of the city. He went to the bar and drank a few pink gins to give himself an appetite and make him sleep after lunch, and at five o'clock Sher Ali brought his tea. When he had finished he lay in a cold bath for a long time and then sat drinking brandy and talking.

For the next few days he did nothing, but at last time began to weigh so heavily on his hands that in desperation, and because he could think of nothing else to do, he went to the club in New Delhi and was enrolled as a temporary member. He was taken by one of the assistant secretaries into the bar and introduced to some other young officers; as he shook hands with them he was filled with a sense of futility that his own world was about to close round him once more.

As the days of his leave crawled by and the circle of his acquaintances widened he became more and more depressed and withdrawn. Every few days he sat down resolutely at his desk and wrote long letters to Celia and his parents, but the loving phrases that he wrote to Celia flaked off his pen like cold ashes and when he had finished he could not bear to read over what he had forced himself to say. Sometimes his mind, burdened with depression and alcohol, wandered while he was writing, and he would sit gazing vacantly over the city while the ink dried on his pen and he would have to glance back at the first page to find out if he was writing to Celia or his mother. The letters that he now began to receive from them he would leave unopened on his dressing-table all day, and then read them when he had drunk a few glasses of brandy and was talking to Sher Ali; endless talk about Burma and the fighting, his trek out and the progress of his sickness, and always it was 'if it hadn't been for Anson' or 'I can't think why he stuck to me like he did'. And Sher Ali came to understand everything, and one evening, moved with pity, he said quietly:

'Why doesn't the Sahib write to his servant and tell him to come to Delhi?'

Kent looked at him morosely. If any European had said such a thing to him he would have been instantly suspicious, but although he was fond of Sher Ali it never occurred to him that an Indian, of the servant class, could have the faintest suspicion as to the reason why he talked so much about Anson.

'I couldn't possibly do that, he's a private soldier, it would be unheard of for me to be seen going about with him, quite apart from the fact that it isn't allowed.' And Sher Ali sighed at what he considered to be Kent's stupidity and wisely held his tongue.

But his remark stayed with Kent, and that evening as he danced mechanically with a woman who was determined that he should sleep with her, his mind went over endless schemes wondering if somehow it could be arranged, but all the time in the back of his mind he knew that tomorrow morning he would never be able to write the letter.

'Why are you so quiet?' she asked quickly, hoping to slip past the guard he kept on his tongue. She knew that he was married, and she knew also that before young men committed adultery it was often necessary to listen to long and maudlin stories about their wives, but this man never talked about his wife at all.

'Nothing.'

'England or India?' She looked up and smiled, hoping that the heat of the room had not spoiled her make-up.

'Neither.'

'You shouldn't think about Burma while you're on leave, it's morbid and rather . . . young.' She smiled to soothe the sting that the words carried.

'I wasn't.' He shook his head and looked at her blankly, knowing what her intentions were and trying to pass on his own burden of frustration. She shrugged her shoulders, and when they sat down she began to talk and laugh with the man next to her in the hope of goading Kent into some show of jealousy, but he sat drinking steadily, not noticing anything that happened at the table. Her talk faded away and she turned back to Kent.

'How naughty you are, drinking away without me.' She took his glass and drank, looking at him over the rim, asking herself bitterly just how arch she could get if she really tried. Perhaps if he got drunk; and when the dance finished he was drunk. She glanced at him quickly as he helped her on with her cloak, trying to judge his mood: provided she could get him back to her house, on the outskirts of New Delhi, and dismiss the chauffeur, his present mood did not really matter.

She waited until they were standing on the steps of the club. 'Come back and have a nightcap with me, Tony, and then my chauffeur can run you back to your hotel.' She spoke casually, but loud enough for a group of young officers to hear. They looked at Kent, smiling enviously, and there was nothing he could do but accept so reasonable an offer. In the back of the car she kissed him with her tongue.

243

They went into the lounge, and when he had finished his brandy she came and sat on the arm of his chair, leaning over so that she could kiss him, and pushing her hand inside his shirt, and running her fingers over his chest and the top of his stomach. He tried to respond, afraid of what she might say about him if he was completely impotent, and all the time they kissed he wondered dully how he could escape.

But there was no escape. She took him into the bedroom, and he undressed with leaden fingers on the far side of the mosquito net that enclosed the double bed. He folded his clothes carefully on a chair, laying everything in readiness so that he could dress again in the darkness while she slept. He heard her get into bed, and he knew that she was watching him through the net. He was still wearing a pair of white drawers as he came slowly towards the net, and he told her roughly to turn out the light. Only when the room was in darkness did he undress completely.

After she had gone to sleep he lay awake for a long time in the hot wet blackness, his head aching and his mouth foul with kissing and drink and cigarettes, too tired to get up and find a glass of water. Occasionally he rubbed his lips with the back of his hand, trying to wipe away the taste of lipstick. As he lay there he thought of Helen, wondering and hoping if perhaps tomorrow he might receive a letter from her saying that at last she had arrived safely.

When he awoke the room was light. She lay facing him, her hair tousled on the pillow; her face was greasy, and he could hear her breath whistle faintly in her nostrils. He thought how angry she would be if she knew that he was watching her, and then very carefully he left the bed and started to dress. He felt ill and depressed, and longed to be back in his own room and hear the water gush into the bath. He tiptoed out of the room carrying his shoes, and sighed with relief when he reached the veranda and she was still asleep. He put on his shoes and hurried down the drive to the road.

He walked for a long way until he found a gharry, and by the time he reached the hotel it was almost eight o'clock. He went to his room and lay down on the bed for a moment before turning on the bath. He suddenly remembered that he had left his revolver in the top drawer of his dressing-table, and he got up quickly to make sure that it was still there. It lay as he had left it, beneath a jumble of grey socks, and he took it out and broke it, peering down the barrel absent-mindedly to see if the humidity was beginning to rust the steel. He closed it with a snap and turned it over in his hands, wondering if he would ever kill anyone with it, and then he remembered Goodwin, and the scarlet blood spreading and running over the veranda floor. As he put it back in the drawer he wondered whether having one's brains blown out would hurt very much; he lay down again on the bed, but he was no longer quite so depressed, for the first time he suddenly realized that he was not completely defenceless, that he could always commit suicide. When Sher Ali came into the room an hour later he found him lying fast asleep fully dressed on the bed, and he was surprised, not by that, but by the look of peace on the tired face.

Once the idea of suicide had come to him it quickly began to take shape. It seemed by far the easiest way out of the troubles that tormented him, with one stroke he could escape from them all, from Celia and the Japanese and Anson. Above all he would escape from himself, and the misery, and remorse, that seemed to have become a part of his existence, as commonplace as hunger or thirst but more persistent.

He stopped going to the club, and spent more and more time in his room, sitting in the arm-chair by the window, reading or gazing over the city's roofs, watching the kite-hawks wheeling, and the grey clouds moving steadily towards the east. He no longer wandered through the crowded seething streets, their vitality jarred on him, and instead he ordered a car every evening at five o'clock, and would let himself be driven aimlessly around Delhi or along the straight roads that led away from the city, dawdling along until he wanted to drink, and then he would tell the driver to return. He used to take Sher Ali with him, he was company without, Kent thought, the disadvantages of company, there was no need to pretend an interest in what Sher Ali had to say if in fact it did not interest him. He would loll in the back smoking cigarette after cigarette, and Sher Ali would talk or keep silent according to Kent's moods. When he came back he would go upstairs and sit once more in the chair by the window, drinking steadily and prodding the misery in his mind.

Sometimes when he was drunk he would get angrily out of the chair, heaping whispered abuse on himself, determined to go back to the battalion; no sooner was the decision made than he would remember the clearing in the jungle, the smell of burnt flesh, the man who called from the river bank, and his stomach would shrink with fear. He would go to the dressing-table and take out the revolver, pressing the cold ring of steel against his temple while he stood looking at himself in the mirror, imagining the split second of horror when one knew that the hammer was flashing down, remembering stories of men whose hands had shaken at the last moment and who had lived, blinded and broken, with the added disgrace of having failed even in that. And the more he thought about the revolver the more certain he became that he could never choose that way, he was sure that at the last minute his hand too would shake. It must be something that once started could not be stopped, like dropping from his window to the drive below.

And then he thought of another great advantage if he chose the window. No one could be certain whether it was suicide or not, provided he left enough evidence to show that he must have been almost unconscious with drink. The windows were wide, and the ledge was not very high, a drunken man leaning out for fresh air could easily fall. He told himself that even an open verdict would save practically all unpleasantness for Celia and his family; and Anson . . . well, he might be upset for a little while, but he would forget.

He made up his mind to kill himself that way on the last night of his leave.

18

On the last day he reported to Army Headquarters and was given a movement order to return to the battalion at Imphal. He smiled and thanked the man who gave him the slip of paper, pretending that he was pleased to be going so far forward and wondering what the man would do if he casually said that he was going to throw himself out of his hotel window that evening. As he went back to the hotel he was at peace and almost happy. Now that he was about to die the city that he had thought squalid and banal flared into beauty, and he looked at it wonderingly, noticing every tiny detail of form and structure, the infinite gradation of colour in the leaden sky. He drank more than usual at lunch and slept heavily during the afternoon, but when Sher Ali called him he woke easily, feeling fresh and excited.

As he crossed the hotel foyer to go for his evening drive one of the Anglo-Indian reception clerks hurried across to him.

'I do not think it would be advisable to drive out of the city tonight, sir,' his hands were fluttering with excitement and an unusual sense of importance, 'there are reports of a lot of rioting going on all over India. Gandhi has been arrested, and Congress are making trouble.' But Kent only smiled politely and thanked him; it was a matter of no importance.

When he came back he went to his room and gave Sher Ali double his agreed money. He told him to make quite certain that he should come early in the morning as his train left at nine o'clock. He wanted to shake his hand and thank him for making his leave bearable, but Sher Ali was certain to be called at the inquest, and the mere fact of paying him the night before he left was quite unusual enough.

When he had gone Kent sat down in the chair by the open window and began to drink slowly, watching the night rising from the city and the lights begin to appear. He tried to think about Anson but his mind was frozen to everything except the knowledge of his own death. He had expected the brandy to thaw out his mind and swamp the fear of dying, but the more he drank the more his mind concentrated on those last dreaded seconds when he would be kneeling on the window-sill looking down on to the gravelled drive.

At the end of two hours he had managed to finish one bottle of brandy, and he opened another, swaying on his feet, and feeling the room move slowly round. He went to the lavatory and poured half the bottle into the wash-basin, carefully rinsing it down, then he came back into the room, knocking a glass over by his chair and splashing brandy on the floor. He tried to drink another mouthful from the bottle but he felt his stomach heave and he spat it back again. He went unsteadily to the window and leant cautiously out; now the drop seemed abysmal, and there was a car parked almost under his window that he was afraid he would hit. Through the clouds of brandy that were rapidly fogging his mind he could feel his body being stroked by the cold wet hands of fear, his mouth hung loosely open, sweat gleamed on his face, and his hands were slippery. He knew that if he delayed another moment he would begin to be sick, and if he left the windows now he would never come back.

He threw them open as wide as he could and knelt on the sill, holding the sides of the windows with outstretched arms. The narrow wooden ledge on which he knelt cut into his knees, he shut his eyes and inclined his body slowly outwards, terrified of slipping unexpectedly, waiting to feel the pull of his body on his arms. The blood roared in his ears, his stomach began to heave, and without further warning vomit shot out of his mouth, he opened his eyes and saw it falling into the night, spreading as it fell. His face was running with sweat and his arms shook; as he straightened his body to get back into the room the ledge of wood broke and he fell forward across the window-sill.

His hands clawed at the woodwork behind him, but he could only touch it with the tips of his slippery fingers, and then he knew that he would fall. As his body began to plunge towards the drive he held his arms in a grotesque attitude as though to break his fall and he cried out; but not for mercy.